T0037544

"An escapist and empowering read . . . *From the Jump* is the perfect book for anyone who's struggled to step outside their comfort zone."

—Rachel Lynn Solomon, author of *Weather Girl*

"Funny, romantic, and exquisitely written, *From the Jump* will fill your heart with joy. I absolutely loved it."

—Katy Birchall, author of *The Secret Bridesmaid*

"*From the Jump* captivates with its true-to-life friendships, empowering journey of self-discovery, and a swoon-worthy romance that left me grinning for days. Lacie Waldon delivers yet another heart-tingling delight!"

—Angie Hockman, author of *Shipped*

"A compelling story about how friendships, family, love, and dreams evolve with this adventure we call life, and how all it takes is one brave step to change our lives for the better. With gorgeous, transportive prose, witty banter, and swoon-worthy chemistry, *From the Jump* is a perfect vacation must-read!"

—Samantha Young, author of *Fight or Flight*

"Filled with heart, evolving friendships, and the most delicious slow-burn, sexual-tension-filled, friends-to-lovers story, *From the Jump* will captivate readers. . . . You'll want to both devour this book in a night and slow down to savor it and keep it from ending."

—Sara Goodman Confino, author of
For the Love of Friends

The

Only Game in Town

A NOVEL

Lacie Waldon

G. P. Putnam's Sons
New York

PUTNAM
— EST. 1838 —

G. P. PUTNAM'S SONS
Publishers Since 1838
An imprint of Penguin Random House LLC
penguinrandomhouse.com

Library of Congress Cataloging-in-Publication Data

Names: Waldon, Lacie, author.
Title: The only game in town: a novel / Lacie Waldon.
Description: New York: G. P. Putnam's Sons, [2023] |
Summary: "The Westing Game meets Sweet Home Alabama in
The Only Game in Town, in which an eccentric millionaire's fortune could
change one woman's life forever . . . if only she can win it!"
—Provided by publisher.
Identifiers: LCCN 2022051036 (print) | LCCN 2022051037 (ebook) |
ISBN 9780593540800 (trade paperback) | ISBN 9780593540817 (ebook)
Classification: LCC PS3623.A35688 O65 2023 (print) |
LCC PS3623.A35688 (ebook) | DDC 813/.6—dc23
LC record available at https://lccn.loc.gov/2022051036
LC ebook record available at https://lccn.loc.gov/2022051037

Printed in the United States of America
1st Printing

Book design by Ashley Tucker

For Jane and Bob Anastario,
who are the best parents
a girl could ever ask for

The

Only
Game
in
Town

Chapter 1

· · · · · · · · · · ·

JESS

The problem with working remotely: There was nobody around to enforce some kind of schedule. Jess should be at home figuring out what, exactly, it was that was bogging down the novel she was supposed to be editing. The characters had been solidly fleshed out. The plot was strong. This was the author's fourth book, so it certainly wasn't the quality of the writing. It was . . . the romance itself?

Maybe the meet-cute was too cheesy. Or the chemistry could be steamier? Jess just couldn't put her finger on it. With a sigh, she pushed the Staple's scarred wooden door open and stepped through. Getting a drink in the middle of the day didn't feel like the most responsible way to approach the problem, but sitting at home, spinning in slow circles on the wheeled chair in front of her ridiculously cluttered desk, certainly wasn't working. And, hey, she'd brought her laptop with her. That had to count for something, right? Proof of intent? A token of professionalism?

Per usual, country music drifted from the speakers. She

recognized the song as "What Was I Thinkin'" by Dierks Bentley—not because she was a fan of the genre but because the Staple hadn't bothered to update their playlist. The exact same playlist had been looping for more than 365 days in a row, and Jess was pretty sure if she had to hear a roomful of out-of-tune Georgia boys howl the lyrics to "Friends in Low Places" one more time, she was going to be forced to embrace a life of sobriety. She should be safe today, though. Friends didn't usually sink into low places until they were at least three pitchers deep.

The Staple wasn't as empty as it should have been in the middle of a workday. It also looked messier than usual, probably due to the sunlight streaming through the windows. The mismatched tables and chairs, clusters of photos tacked haphazardly to the wall, and neon beer signs mounted inside were better suited to nighttime, seen through the hazy gaze of one too many. It smelled amazing, though, like everything doctors warned their patients against eating.

The fryers had clearly been working overtime.

Jess let the door swing closed on the chilly day, her mouth watering at the thought of the whole basket of fried pickles she was going to get for herself. She couldn't make the mistake of sitting next to Sammy Olson, though. He was a constant presence at the bar, and Jess had figured out years ago that he was never more talkative than when conversation could be used as a distraction while helping himself to other people's food. As far as strategies went, his was flawless. Polite conversation was the lifeblood of small-town living. There was no greater sin in Redford than being too busy to chat—except for being too high on oneself to chat, of course.

"Well, if it isn't Jessica Reid." The bartender, Bryce Howard, grinned at her truancy. While Jess could be counted on to pop in occasionally for line dancing on a Saturday night or a spontaneous happy hour with friends, she wasn't a regular. Not like the handful of people who were currently resting on their elbows, nursing pints and retelling the same old stories for the thousandth time. "Have you finished all the books? All the stories been told?"

"It's done." Jess met his grin with one of her own. "There's no shelf space left in the world."

Like the Staple's music, its staff never changed. Bryce had been working shifts behind the bar since the day he turned twenty-one, when Jess was still a senior trying to sneak in with a fake I.D. that claimed she was from Texas (as if she and Bryce hadn't attended pep rallies in the same gym her freshman year).

In his nine years of service in keeping the town's thirst at bay, his cheerfulness and easy laughter had remained unflagging. It was easy to resent only having one bar in town, but you couldn't argue that a friendly face like Bryce's made it a pretty great place to end up.

Jess waved hello to the people who looked up at the exchange and called out greetings. They weren't a closed-off crowd. Such a thing couldn't exist in Redford. Not when everyone knew everyone.

"Why don't you set up down here?" Bryce said, gesturing toward the far end of the bar. "Then, if you decide to get a late lunch, you won't have to worry about Sammy eating all of it."

"I wouldn't do that," Sammy sputtered. He grabbed a couple of his neighbor's fries and outrage-ate them.

"You know you can order food of your own, right?" Bryce said to him.

"I would if I were hungry. I'd order a whole basket of onion rings and share them with everyone. Because that," Sammy said, nodding approvingly at the fries' owner, "is what neighbors do."

Jess tried to focus on this exchange, but her eyes snagged on the far end of the bar where Bryce had directed them. A man was sitting there. A man she'd never seen before. She blinked, trying to determine if he was an illusion.

Sure, Redford, Georgia, got its share of visitors. Hikers came to do the Billy Goat Trail. People liked to spend a few days on the lake. Every now and then, someone even drove all the way from Atlanta to get one of Luanne's mixed-berry pies. Not one of those people, however, had looked like this man.

He was too put together, for starters. His crisp white button-up didn't have a speck of grease on it, no dinginess from age, and his gray slacks had a crease ironed into them like they'd been delivered on a hanger from the dry cleaners. His dark hair was styled neatly, and he sat a little too straight on his barstool. Tense muscles pressed through the material of his shirt, creating sharp ridges. Maybe, in another town, the presence of a man like this wouldn't be so shocking. Here, it was the equivalent of spotting the Virgin Mary on a piece of toast.

Jess took a step toward him, as Bryce had instructed, then faltered. The man didn't *look* like he wanted company. There were five empty stools between him and the rest of the bar patrons, and Jess would bet her basket of fried pickles plus a daiquiri that he'd created that buffer on purpose.

As if she'd already crossed the room, Bryce headed down and slapped a cocktail napkin on the bar in front of the stool next to the stranger. He looked at her expectantly and she shifted the messenger bag on her shoulder, rolling her eyes at herself. It wasn't as if she was going to pull a Sammy and start eating off the man's plate. She'd be respectful, not engaging unless he spoke first. She was here to work, after all. She definitely hadn't stuffed her laptop in a bag and dragged it along just so she'd feel less guilty about playing hooky.

Hurrying forward, she slid onto the stool next to the man and pulled out her laptop, setting it on the bar. To fully sell the illusion of intended productivity, she even opened it. The romantic comedy filled the screen, a massive block of text that stared at her reproachfully.

"Let me guess," Bryce said. "A whiskey. Neat."

Jess laughed. "Perfect."

The man glanced over in approval, and Jess noticed that he had a glass filled with amber liquid in front of him. *Of course.* It was exactly the kind of drink she would've given his character in a novel. Simple, no-nonsense, classic.

"Are you in town visiting someone?" The moment the words were out, Jess realized she'd not only failed in her determination not to engage but she'd also skipped a couple of steps. She was supposed to start with a "hello." Introduce herself. *Then* she could begin the interrogation.

"Kind of." The man glanced over at her without shifting his body. His dark eyes were shot with red. The stubble covering his jaw surprised her. Jess had pegged him as the type who would shave daily.

"How do you kind of visit somebody?" Jess grinned. "Are you like a bookie or something? 'Paying someone a visit' to collect your money?" She did that ridiculous thing where she curled her fingers to indicate quotation marks, then regretted it immediately.

Bryce looked up from the ingredients he was collecting for her drink. "He's in town for the funeral."

"Oh." The grin froze on Jess's face for a moment before shifting into a grimace. "Crap. I'm sorry. I should've realized that."

She *should* have. The fact that it hadn't been the first thing that occurred to her felt wildly disrespectful to Jasper Wilhelm. It made it seem like she hadn't even been thinking about him, which wasn't true at all. She'd thought about Jasper constantly since she heard the news. Obviously because she was sad and would miss him, but also because it was hard to believe he was really gone.

Jasper had always been such a massive presence in Redford. Larger than life, truly. And *fun*. It seemed like a silly way to describe such a powerful man, but Jasper truly had been. There was no event he couldn't turn into a party. No holiday he hadn't been ready to celebrate to the utmost.

"We're all reeling from the loss," she added before the man could speak. "Everyone in town loved him."

"I'm not surprised," the man said, turning back toward his drink. "He was very lovable."

He didn't want to talk about it. Jess could see that, and she wasn't inclined to judge him for the withdrawal. People coped with loss differently, after all. Some wanted to discuss every detail, like they could cling to what was gone if they only focused hard enough on it. Others held on by burying it deep.

"Are you hungry?" Jess wanted to change the subject, but since she didn't know the man, no obvious topics sprang to mind. Food was the one thing all people had in common; everyone had to eat.

"Me?" He squinted at her, and she wondered if he was drunk. That would explain the bloodshot eyes. She didn't think so, though. There was a sharpness to him, and it wasn't just due to the cut of his jawline.

"You're the only one here," she said. Bryce had walked to the other side of the bar after bringing up the funeral. She could see him dumping frozen fruit into the blender.

"I'm not hungry."

"Are you sure? Because I'm ordering a basket of fried pickles, and I was going to offer you five of them."

A smile tugged at the corner of his mouth. It wasn't big enough to show his teeth, but it was something. "Five?"

"It's a generous offer. If I was just letting you taste them, you'd only get one."

"Five is five times as many as one," he admitted.

"I'm a generous person."

"Clearly." For the first time, the man did more than glance over at her. His whole top half turned, shoulders shifting in her direction. "But let me ask you this: How many come in a basket?"

Lawyer, she guessed. Or maybe he worked with numbers. If he was a lawyer, there would probably be a suit jacket on the stool next to him.

"I don't know," she said noncommittally.

"Your best estimate."

Yep. Numbers. He was definitely a numbers guy.

"Probably thirty," she admitted with a laugh. "Maybe even forty."

"So, it wasn't really that generous of an offer." He grinned, this time showing a flash of white teeth. The sight made her want to lift at least one arm in victory.

"Better than a single pickle, though. I stand by that." Big talk for someone who could feel her cheeks flushing beneath the fullness of his attention. She shouldn't have broken out her sweaters this week. It was too early in the season. She was melting beneath the wool blend.

"I think this might be my masterpiece," Bryce said, breaking the charged moment by placing a daiquiri glass in front of her.

Jess pulled her eyes away from the man and blinked at the vibrant concoction in front of her. Bryce had managed to layer the colors. Bright blue on the bottom, red in the middle, and a sunshine yellow on the top. A chunk of pineapple and an entire strawberry balanced on the rim, and a paper umbrella was the cherry on top. It was the kind of drink that would look mildly ridiculous on sandy shores beside turquoise water. Here, where fall had shown up early, flaunting red and gold leaves through the windows of the bar, it looked downright absurd.

"I love it." Jess exhaled, her eyes going wide as she took it in. "Seriously, Bryce. It's spectacular."

The stranger grimaced at the sight of it. "What happened to whiskey?"

"It was never going to happen," Bryce said, sliding a straw into the center of the glass. "Trust me, I've tried. The woman won't touch anything that doesn't taste like liquefied Jolly Ranchers. She's got the palate of a toddler."

"That's unfair." Jess pulled the drink toward her, too excited to successfully feign offense. "If a toddler tried to drink this, they'd only make it halfway through before crashing into a sugar coma. I, on the other hand, have the experience and mature constitution that will enable me to order a second."

"I'm not making another one," Bryce said firmly. "It's too much work. The most you're getting out of me is a bottle of beer. And you'll have to twist the top off yourself."

Jess took a sip of the syrupy-sweet daiquiri, not bothering to argue with him. They both knew he'd be the one trying to talk her into a second when she was ready to leave. Bryce couldn't help himself. Life was a party, and he considered it his personal calling to keep it going. She hummed a little sigh of pleasure as the sugar hit her taste buds, her contentment flagging only slightly when the man covered his glass with his hand as Bryce attempted to top it off.

"I'm good, thanks," the man said, pulling out his wallet.

Jess guessed that was a no to her offer to share her fried pickles. Maybe she should've offered him ten. Five was really just a tease.

"You sure I can't talk you into a burger?" Bryce said, seeming to read her mind. "We have the best ones in town."

Jess laughed, and the man glanced over at her.

"Aside from the diner, the Staple has the only burgers in town," she said, answering his unspoken question—or what she chose to interpret as a question. If she was being entirely honest, the man gave the impression of already having left. His eyes had gone all distant, and the furrow in his brow was back. There wasn't even a hint of the smile she'd coaxed out of him a moment ago.

"Hmm." The man made the sound like it was a valid response, then dropped two twenties on the bar and lifted his glass to his lips, polishing off the last of his drink.

Jess felt more disappointed than was warranted. Sure, it would've been nice to talk to someone new, but there were plenty of people in the bar. She'd just drink her gorgeous drink, eat a mound of artery-cloggers, and start up a conversation with the nearest friendly face.

As if the world could hear her thoughts and took great joy in mocking them, the door to the bar swung open, and Jess twisted around on her stool to discover the unfriendliest face in all of Redford strutting in. Her stomach sank at the sight of Nikki Loughton, the one person in town who openly hated her. Behind Nikki, like snarling bulldogs flanking their owner, were Cara Tinley and Lexi Farley. They didn't hate Jess like Nikki did, but they were happy to pretend to for loyalty's sake.

"Why?" The word slipped out of Jess's mouth. Why did Nikki have to show up here, the one day Jess had actually left the safety of her own desk? Why now, when there

were so few people in the bar to distract Nikki from her favorite target?

Jess looked to Bryce and found him backing slowly away,
the sympathy in his eyes clearly not enough to override his
self-preservation. She couldn't blame him. Nikki didn't re-
serve all of her hostility for Jess; she had aggression to spare,
and standing too close to her greatest enemy would only put
Bryce in the line of fire.

"What?" The man looked at her, responding either to
Jess's *why* or the way she'd gone rigid, like a possum preparing to fall over and play dead.

"Nothing," Jess whispered, shifting slowly toward him
until she ended up facing him completely. Maybe, if Nikki
could only see her back, she wouldn't realize whose back it
was. Then again, maybe Nikki would stab her in it.

Jess could hear Nikki greeting other people in the bar,
her voice getting closer.

"Nothing?" The man said the word too loud, and Jess
wanted to pinch him in warning.

Through the speakers "Before He Cheats" was playing.
Until that particular moment, Jess had never truly related to
a man who was about to get his tires slashed.

"I just had something in my eye," she said, forcing herself not to whisper. The man didn't need to know that she
was scared of a woman holding a high school grudge. And
really, Jess *shouldn't* be scared of a woman holding a high
school grudge. They'd graduated eight years ago. If Nikki
was going to rip her hair out or break her fingers, she
would've done it by now.

Then again, the day Nikki had said, "Have you ever

considered how awful you must be for your mom to be willing to leave someone as great as your dad just to get away from you?" the words had hurt so badly that Jess wished Nikki had gone ahead and broken her fingers. At least they would've had a decent chance of healing.

The man leaned forward and peered into her eyes like he might spot some phantom lint. She should've told him she was lying. Instead, she leaned in, too, letting him search for something that didn't exist. He smelled expensive, like she imagined a private library might smell. Mahogany and leather-bound books. Up close, Jess could see little gold flecks in his deep brown eyes. All sounds faded for a moment, muted by the intensity of his attention.

"'Blaire spotted him through the car window. He looked distracted, and she wondered if she'd ever know what he was thinking about or if she'd always feel shut out.'" The words, read in an overly dramatic tone, pulled at Jess's consciousness, slowly registering as belonging to the novel she was meant to be editing.

Her head jerked back from the man, and she turned to see Lexi standing beside her, leaning against the bar as she read from Jess's laptop. Jess slammed it shut before twisting slowly around on the stool. Cara was beside Lexi. Then, like the intruder in a horror movie, Jess discovered Nikki standing directly behind Jess herself.

"Hello, Nikki." Impressing even herself, she managed to sound calm. "Cara. Lexi. Good to see you."

"Oh, it's *so* good to see you, Jess." Nikki flashed a beautyqueen smile. Her cashmere sweater clung to her curves, and skin-tight jeans skimmed to a stop just above her leather booties. Her look was an enviable blend of elegant and provocative.

"And your friend," Cara said, eyeing the stranger appreciatively. She lifted her hand at him and wiggled her fingers, hot pink nails flashing. "I'm Cara."

"Carter," the man said, leaning back on his stool.

As Lexi and Nikki introduced themselves to him, Jess reached for her drink. Lexi, pretending to help her, managed to knock it over instead. The glass arced toward her laptop, dumping blue, red, and yellow liquid all over it. Jess shrieked like a mother whose child had just run into the street. She grabbed at the soaked machinery, but Bryce was faster, picking it up and dumping the thick drink right onto the floor on his side of the bar.

"Thank you," Jess cried as he seemed to make a hand towel appear out of nowhere and swiped it across the laptop's protective shell. She wanted to leap over the bar and whisk it away to safety, despite the fact that she couldn't do anything more than he was already doing. She watched nervously as he opened it up, double-checking that no liquid had made it inside, before using a damp paper towel to rid it of stickiness and wiping it dry again. "Thank you, thank you, thank you."

"You're such a gentleman, Bryce," Cara cooed appreciatively.

"Jess, you should really be more careful with your laptop," Lexi said with feigned concern. "It's your livelihood."

"Thanks." Jess was usually careful not to engage, but the

attack on her most beloved possession caused her filter to slip, and a heavy dose of sarcasm slipped through. "I'll try to keep that in mind."

"My brother gets clumsy when he drinks, too," Lexi said as if it weren't obvious that she, herself, had spilled the drink. "Some people are just messy drunks."

"So, is this how you edit people's books? Wasted on daiquiris like a retiree on a Caribbean cruise?" Nikki shook her head, and her big blond curls bounced cheerfully. The angelic appearance was part of her power. It was as if her big blue eyes and rosy pink lips tricked the brain into perceiving a beautiful, sweet doll, lowering all natural defenses so her barbs could cut right through to soft, vulnerable flesh. "I guess now we know why none of the real publishing houses would hire you."

Jess froze, trying to absorb the blow without giving any indication of how hard it had landed. If she let Nikki see that it had affected her, Jess's job would quickly replace her wardrobe as Nikki's go-to ammunition. Clothes were fine; Jess was under no illusion that the mixed patterns and colorful combinations she gravitated toward were considered traditionally fashionable. Her job, on the other hand . . .

Giving up the opportunity to work for a major publishing house so she could return to Redford was a choice she'd begun to question lately. When Jess had decided to return home, she'd been confident that relationships meant more to her than a fancy office in a city full of strangers. Then her best friend, Liz, moved away, and Jess started edits on yet another book that would likely never find its audience, and she'd begun to doubt herself. What if it had been naïve of her to believe life was about the people you surrounded yourself with? Had she gotten her priorities wrong?

"Well," Jess said, "showing up for the interview drunk wasn't great, obviously. But I also don't think they were impressed by my rainbow tutu and hot pink tube top."

She fully intended to say it breezily, but her voice failed her; the quiver in it was far too noticeable.

"OMG!" Lexi squealed, her eyes brightening as she took the bait. "Do you remember when she used to wear that tutu to school all the time? It was so weird."

Lexi looked to Nikki for some sign of approval, but Nikki had caught the quiver in Jess's voice and recognized it for what it was: weakness.

"It must be so difficult," Nikki cooed, "spending day after day working on books no one is ever going to read. You must wish you could walk into a bookstore and see just one of them on display."

"Not really." *Yes.* Of course she did. But at what cost? She would spend a mere moment in front of a bookshelf, celebrating a book's success. But she spent countless hours on the editing process. Wasn't it better to do that here, where the smell of fresh pine and mountain air drifted through her windows, and Luanne was likely to pop by at any given moment with freshly baked blondies? "I mean, that's not the goal. I'm just happy to be helping authors hone their craft."

"Sure you are. But—"

"I don't want to be rude," Carter said, speaking over Nikki in a way that could only be interpreted as rude, "but Jess and I were in the middle of a conversation. So, Bryce, could you please make her another drink? And if the rest of you wouldn't mind giving us some privacy, that would be greatly appreciated."

Jess froze, too surprised to even laugh, although she was certain later she'd remember the expression on Nikki's face and absolutely cackle. If possible, Nikki looked even more shocked than she felt. With great effort, Jess pulled herself together, attempting to appear as if it were perfectly normal that this stranger had not only figured out her name but was actually willing to stick around after he'd clearly wanted to leave, just so he could spare her from a minor ambush by a pack of mean girls.

"Actually"—Jess looked at Carter meaningfully—"I'm done anyway. We should go."

It was Carter's turn to look surprised, but he covered it quickly, standing up and asking Bryce how much he owed him for Jess's drink.

"It's on me," Bryce said before Jess could protest. He looked down at the spatters on his shoes and added, "Literally."

Jess laughed in spite of herself and took her laptop from him, making a mental note to drop off a piece of Luanne's fudge pie in the next couple of days. Bryce had never been big on the fruit flavors, but give him something chocolate and he was guaranteed to forget all about his shoes.

"It was so good running into you girls," Jess said sweetly as she grabbed her bag and swept past the women, who were still standing there trying to determine how, exactly, the tide had turned so quickly.

"You, too," they parroted instinctively, the rules of Southern charm too ingrained to be bypassed.

Jess swanned out of the bar, calling out goodbyes with Carter in tow. When they got outside, she lifted her hand to shield her eyes from the afternoon sun. Redford's Main Street stretched out before them, picture perfect with its little wooden buildings tucked against the backdrop of rolling mountains, turned red and gold with the changing season. Brightly colored flowers adorned each storefront, so cheery they made her teary response to Nikki's needling feel melodramatic. Jess got to work on books for a living, a job she would've killed for as a child. Who cared if they never hit it big? All that mattered was that she did her part to make them shine.

"So," Carter said dryly, "they seemed nice."

"Yep," Jess said with a laugh. "Georgia peaches at their sweetest."

"Are they that friendly to everyone, or are you just special?"

It was a prompt for a story, and Jess did love to tell a good story, but the one with Nikki didn't qualify as such. Jess hadn't ratted out Nikki for skipping school, or dumped pig's blood on her at the prom, or even spit in her Cheerios. She'd done nothing but stupidly manage to end up in the wrong place at the wrong time.

"I'm just special," she said. "Seriously, though. Thanks for helping me out in there. It was really nice that you were willing to stay when you were clearly about to leave."

"Don't give me too much credit." He looked at his watch,

a sleek silver thing with Roman numerals to indicate the hours. "I still have fourteen minutes until I can check into my B&B."

"Fourteen minutes, huh?" Jess considered explaining to him that time wasn't that precise here. He could've arrived two hours early, and Mrs. Loveling would've pretended that was the check-in hour and ushered him right to a room. Southern hospitality was a recognized concept across the country for a reason.

If Jess told him that, though, she'd have no choice but to go back to her house and give the manuscript the attention it deserved. The thought was depressing. This day was too gorgeous to let it go to waste.

"Well, we can cover the entire town in fourteen minutes," she said brightly. "Care for a tour?"

Chapter 2

· · · · · · · · · ·

CARTER

Carter's instinct was to say no. It had been a rough day. A rough few days, really, despite the fact that he was a Barclay, and Barclays didn't do grief. He just wanted to be done with all of this.

Except that he also didn't.

Once he left this town and returned to Atlanta, his grandfather would really be gone. Nothing more than a memory.

"Lead the way." Carter swept his arm forward. There was something to be said for civility, after all. And who could argue with fourteen minutes?

If Jess was offended by his less than effusive show of gratitude for her offer of a tour, she didn't give any indication. He wasn't surprised. There was a brightness to the woman that seemed incapable of being dimmed. Her eyes shone with it, even when they also gleamed with unshed tears like they had when that terrifying blonde in the bar had been taunting her.

Bouncing a little on her heels, Jess looked around like

there was so much to show him that she didn't know where
to start.

The notion was ridiculous; there was nothing to this
place. But it was also kind of cute. *She* was cute, in that ridiculous sweater with at least seven different colors of polka
dots. She had a contagious smile, all bright teeth and pink
lips. The little dimple on one side reminded him of the bottom of an exclamation point.

"Let's see," she said, her hands going to her hips. "You're
staying at the Lakehouse?"

Carter took a step back in spite of his effort to be polite.
"How do you know that?"

"The bag boy at the market told me. You're all anyone's
talking about."

"Really?" His jaw tensed.

"No, Carter." Jess laughed. "Not really. The Lakehouse
is the only B&B in Redford."

"Ah." He cringed, aware of his overreaction but unwilling to explain himself. What could he say? *Usually, when
people talk about me, it's to call me shortsighted and ungrateful
for abandoning my family and an exceedingly generous trust
fund.* An admission like that was guaranteed to prompt a
conversation Carter had no interest in having.

Fortunately, an explanation didn't appear to be expected.
Jess was already starting down the sidewalk, flicking a hand
over her shoulder in a gesture for him to follow. She looked
so carefree that he found his shoulders easing, like she was a
breeze that had drifted through, jostling loose something
heavy.

"It's that way," she called back to him, "so we'll start this way and loop back."

Carter hurried after her, falling into step at her side. He could smell the scent of apricots that drifted from her long auburn hair. Sunlight glinted off the strands of it, causing the lighter parts to spark like fire. It matched the trees that peppered the sidewalks.

Main Street was peacefully empty, but the chirping of birds and the rustle of leaves in the breeze kept it from feeling abandoned. For a moment, Carter almost forgot how badly he didn't want to be here.

"This is the bakery," Jess said, pointing at the upcoming yellow-and-white-striped awning. "Luanne makes the best cupcakes you've ever tasted. Weirdly, though, her muffins leave a lot to be desired."

For such a simple description, Carter had questions. He'd always assumed cupcakes and muffins were the same thing, one just topped with sugary fluff. He didn't have time for a pastry debate, though, so he opted for the most obvious question.

"Luanne?" He gestured to the cursive script on the sign above the awning that read "Evangeline's."

Jess grinned. "Luanne owns the place, but she decided to name it Evangeline's. She says it's because of her French ancestry—she's supposedly got a great-grandmother named Evangeline—but everyone knows Luanne's roots don't spread beyond Georgia. She probably heard the name in a movie and liked the idea of making the bakery sound fancier than it is. She even tried shipping in croissants from Atlanta for a few years, but they were always stale by the time they arrived."

"I guess that means I'm out of luck for breakfast this weekend then. Nothing other than a warm, flaky croissant will do for me."

"Really?" Jess's nose wrinkled with obvious judgment.

"No, Tutu," Carter said, perfectly mimicking the way she'd caught him out with the bag-boy gossip.

Jess laughed, and Carter felt a flash of satisfaction, even though he'd already realized she was the type who laughed easily.

"Lexi was wrong, for the record," she said. "It was a very pretty tutu. There was absolutely nothing weird about it."

"I'm sure there wasn't. Nothing says normal like wearing a recital costume while dissecting frogs." Carter tilted his chin toward the bakery window, because the mental image of Jess's legs stretching out from beneath a tutu proved more appealing than it should be. "So we've covered the bakery then. What comes after breakfast? Is the next tour stop a diner?"

"Actually, we haven't fully covered the bakery yet." Jess widened her eyes, grinning impishly. "There's a secret side to Redford, and it involves"—she leaned forward to whisper in his ear—"the distribution of muffins."

The feel of her breath on his ear sent a shot of desire down his spine. "Illicit muffin trading? Was I not paying attention the day blueberries were banned?" Carter pulled away to look her in the eye.

"It's a rival business, run by Sally Parker. But here's what you need to understand, Carter. Sally and Luanne used to be best friends."

Carter nodded, mainly because Jess seemed to expect some kind of response to this . . . news.

"Until a huge fight," she continued. "Now, half the town says the fight was over *The Bachelor*. Sally was apparently convinced he should pick the blonde with the cello, but Luanne insisted there was no way that relationship could work out. The other school of thought is that their fight isn't really even about the two women, that they just ended up on different sides when Gloria Berner and Samuel Wallace went head-to-head over the last bag of gummy bears in the checkout line at Joe's. Either way, it should've just been a normal argument between friends, until Sally went nuclear by claiming she could make better muffins in her sleep and then *actually started selling muffins out of her house.*"

"Below the belt!" Carter was aiming for sarcasm, but the words came out more earnest than intended, because it did actually sound like a bit of a dirty hit.

His grandfather used to tell him these stories about Redford and its residents, too. At first, they seemed like nothing more than silly anecdotes that might as well be fiction. But after a while, the stories became so real they could've been about his own neighbors—if, of course, his neighbors in Atlanta had been the kind of people who actually talked to one another.

"Right?" Jess looked delighted by his inadvertent ruling. "And the biggest problem is that Sally's muffins are really good. Like, *really* good. And I've already told you about

Luanne's muffins, as well as her failure to provide the town with fresh croissants. So as much as the town might want to stand by Luanne, we're having a hard time boycotting Sally's new business. Especially since Sally is more than willing to secretly deliver anything we want to order, which saves us all from publicly revealing our betrayal to Luanne."

"And who can blame you, really? Especially given the fact that everyone knows Sally was right and the Bachelor clearly should've picked the blonde with the cello."

Jess's eyes sparkled with amusement. "You watch *The Bachelor*?"

Watch probably wasn't the most accurate term. But Carter worked at a large investment firm and spent his days managing asset allocation and diversification for a variety of clients. He often ended the day so mentally exhausted that he'd settle for anything that appeared on his TV once he'd crashed onto his couch and fumbled for the remote. It just so happened that, between *The Bachelor*, *The Bachelorette*, and *Bachelor in Paradise*, some version of that show always seemed to be on.

"Only when they're there for the right reasons," he said, using a phrase quoted so often by both Bachelors and Bachelorettes that it must surely have spawned its own drinking game.

Jess laughed and directed her attention toward the bait shop across the street. "Speaking of bachelors . . ." she said, before spilling more of the town's gossip.

According to her, Marty Beauford, the owner of the Bait & Tackle, had developed a crippling crush on the town librarian. Sadly, the librarian was either too shy or too disinterested to have given any sign of returned affection. Then there was the owner of the grocery store, Joe, who hated Tommy, the twenty-three-year-old mechanic (who worked with Jess's dad), because Tommy had broken his daughter's heart. As Jess told their stories, she painted them with just the right amount of detail to bring them into Technicolor, leaving Carter feeling like he'd met each of the townspeople personally.

"You work on books, right?" As soon as the words exited Carter's mouth, it occurred to him that this might be a sensitive subject, given what the woman in the bar had been saying about Jess's job.

To his relief, Jess merely smiled. "I'm an editor for romance novels. I work for an independent press, but I also take freelance projects when I have the time."

"You have a way with words. It's impressive."

"Thanks." She glowed beneath the compliment. "I've always loved writing. What about you? What do you do?"

"Watch *The Bachelor*, mostly. And read the occasional book."

She grinned. "And what do you do for a living?"

"Financial management at a firm in Atlanta."

"Hmm. That sounds . . ."

"Boring?" He nodded. "Accurate. But it pays the bills."

"And enables others to successfully pay theirs?"

"I suppose you could say that."

Carter liked the way she made it sound like he was helping people when, really, it was just a job. He had used his skills to help people before, though. He'd assisted his grandfather in anonymously paying hospital bills. Investing anonymously in local businesses. Investing in *her*, although he was certain Jess had never been made privy to his grandfather's—not to mention his own—involvement. Carter had recognized her name the moment Bryce called it out across the bar. She'd been a recipient of one of the scholarships he'd helped his grandfather set up for bright Redford kids who wouldn't have otherwise been able to afford to go away to college.

Jasper had managed to get his hands on a school assignment of Jess's and had insisted Carter read it. For proof, Jasper had explained, that Jess's talent deserved to be cultivated through further education. As if Carter ever had any actual sway over the people Jasper chose to invest in.

Still, Carter had done as his grandfather asked and read it, despite the failing grade the paper had received. Surprisingly, Carter had found himself rereading it more than once. It had been charming. Inspiring, even. Clearly, given the dark red F scrawled across the paper, Jess's teacher hadn't appreciated the story she'd written about penguins instead of the factual report she'd been assigned. You couldn't argue that it wasn't well-written, though.

Jess had taken a huddle of penguins and brought them to life, creating a community of conflicting personalities who relied on one another to survive the arctic conditions in which they'd found themselves. Carter had genuinely laughed at how much humor she'd brought to the project. Then the end had nearly moved him to tears. Those penguins had just been so close. Like a family. Not the kind that Carter had grown up with, obviously. But the kind you heard about, the kind that you wanted to believe was really out there.

Jess hadn't been the first person Carter had helped his grandfather invest in, but she'd been the first Carter felt inspired by. Things had begun to change after he read her story. Instead of being the impartial financial arranger, Carter shifted into more a member of the team. While he never got to pick the people they would help, he was given enough details about them to understand the choice Jasper had made. It felt less like Jasper's mission and more like a shared one. Jasper would always be Batman, but Carter had become his Robin.

Foolishly, Carter had even begun to believe he would be expected to carry on their work after Jasper was gone. He'd imagined Jasper would leave him the remainder of his fortune, trusting Carter to continue to dole it out to the people of Redford. Granted, Carter didn't live in his grandfather's little fairy-tale town. He didn't know Jasper's neighbors personally. But it had felt like Jasper was preparing to work around that. Why else would he give Carter so many details about complete strangers? Why quiz Carter on their backgrounds, their relationships with one another, like he was preparing his grandson for some upcoming test?

Carter had been wrong, though. He'd gotten enough of a heads-up from his grandfather's lawyer that morning to convince him of that. Ever the eccentric, Jasper had opted to provide his town with something flashier than his continued help. A week or so of fun. One final hurrah.

Carter smiled ruefully. It might not have been what he

hoped for, but he couldn't deny that he admired the way his grandfather managed to make the most of life, even after his own death.

"Is something wrong?" Jess peered up at him, searching his expression. "You look like you just went somewhere sad."

"I'm fine," he said, glancing at his watch so she wouldn't see that he hadn't merely gone somewhere sad but seemed to be stuck there. "It's after four, though. I should go."

"Perfect timing," she said easily. "We're almost to the Lakehouse."

Carter considered telling her that his car was parked at the bar, but he had a feeling she'd insist on walking him back to it, and he didn't want to take up her whole afternoon. Instead, he slid his hands into his pockets and lengthened his stride. But his steps immediately faltered in response to the intense interest from someone on the corner.

The man looked like a snowman perched on the stool he'd dragged out to the sidewalk, his round cheeks pushed up so far by his smile that they made his eyes squint. He had an unopened book clutched to his belly and wore a top hat.

"Beautiful day, isn't it?" the man called out as they drew closer.

"Couldn't get any better, Oscar," Jess sang in response.

"No." His head bobbed cheerfully. "It certainly could not."

"Did he get kicked out of the bar?" Carter asked in a low voice once they were far enough down the street to avoid being overheard.

"Who? Oscar?" Jess glanced back over her shoulder as if

there might be someone else who had decided to preside over a public sidewalk. "No, that's his spot."

When Carter looked at her askance, she shrugged.

"That's where he sits," she said, "and that's what he says."

Carter had questions. *Why*, for starters. Why wouldn't Oscar leave the stool where he'd found it and just sit there? Or, if he wanted to sit outside, why not walk his stool over to the grassy courtyard a few yards away? Carter didn't ask, though.

It had been almost ten years since Carter walked away from his family, freeing himself to reach out to his long-estranged grandfather. Ten years of hearing stories about Redford, of finding himself caring about people he'd never met. But Jasper was gone now, and Carter's connection to this town had been severed. Unless Oscar decided to move his stool into Carter's room at the Lakehouse, where he sat shouldn't matter to Carter.

And it didn't matter how pleasant a tour guide or talented a storyteller Jess might be. She didn't matter to Carter, either.

Chapter 3

· · · · · · · · · · ·

JESS

After yesterday's run-in at the bar, Jess had found herself a little nervous to see Nikki at the funeral. It wasn't often she came out of one of their encounters feeling like the victor, and she suspected her unintentional triumph might leave Nikki feeling like she had something to prove. Now, though, surrounded by mourners, Jess felt ridiculous for giving a petty feud any airtime in her mind. Today wasn't about them. Even Nikki Loughton knew that; she hadn't looked over from her side of the church once since the funeral had begun.

The aisle between the pews was a dividing line between the two of them, between many of the town's residents, actually—everyone from Mr. Walters, who was convinced the man with the big teeth who lived one door over had been stealing his newspapers for the better part of ten years, to the couple whose arguments had escalated into impressively creative death threats before self-preservation had finally caused them to divorce, splitting their homes between the two far ends of Redford. It wasn't as though there had been arrows guiding people to sit on one side or the other; it had just been obvious. This was not a day to squeeze in next to someone known to push your buttons.

Today was about Jasper Wilhelm. The man who had been the mayor of Redford in every sense but formally. He'd been the man behind the curtain. The Wizard to their Oz. Everyone had loved him, in their own ways and for their own reasons. And now he was gone.

Jess swiped at her eyes and was surprised when her fingers came away streaked with black. Was there no end to her mascara? Had she applied three extra layers without noticing? The silent trickle of tears slipping down her cheeks would not cease. It was just so sweet, all these stories people were sharing about the way Jasper had changed lives. Or maybe it was the anecdotes that made her laugh out loud, the reminders of his eccentricity that had actually brought her to tears. She'd known Jasper would like those stories the best; he'd never taken himself too seriously.

Her father shifted in the pew beside her, tugging at a button on his collared shirt. There was a pastiness to his complexion that she didn't like. She'd noticed it lately, here and there, and had tried to convince herself it was just him getting older, despite the fact that he was only forty-three and was still, to her discomfort, considered one of the town's most eligible bachelors. But now, in contrast with the sunlight streaming through the church windows, his pallor was harder to explain away. He was working too many hours at the auto shop, not eating enough, and the dinners she kept making so she could take him the "leftovers" didn't seem to be doing the trick.

Jess wondered if he was staying up too late at night. Before she'd moved into her own house down the street from him, he'd always crashed right after they'd watched Jimmy Fallon's monologue together, leaving her to watch the rest of the show alone. But maybe, without anyone there to remind him how early he had to get up the next morning, he'd started staying up for the whole thing. She could ask, but it would only offend him. "I took care of you, didn't I?" he'd say in his gruffest voice. "What makes you think I can't take care of myself?"

"Thank you all for coming today," Pastor Dave said from the pulpit. "In lieu of a burial, we'll be having a celebration of Jasper's life in the town square."

At the indication things were wrapping up, Jess finally allowed herself a little peek at Carter. She'd noticed him as soon as she entered the church—not that she'd shown up at a funeral intending to feed yesterday's ridiculous little crush, but she could hardly be expected to miss him. With his height and ramrod-straight posture, his head sat inches above everyone else's, showing off his dark, professionally cut hair. Surely, she wasn't the only person in the room who'd found her gaze pulled toward him more than once. He was sitting in the front row, after all.

And he was alone.

Not *alone*, of course. The church was too packed for that. But there was a noticeable gap beside him, and the woman rumored to be Jasper's estranged daughter—so she must be Carter's mother—was also in the front row, but on the other side of the aisle from him. She was wearing a black-veiled hat that looked borrowed from Wardrobe on a soap opera set, which she kept tilted toward Carter like a wall she'd erected between them. Clearly, there was a story there, but Jess was sad that Jasper's death hadn't given them enough of a reason to sweep their issues under the rug. Nobody should be alone at a funeral.

"One last thing," a prim male voice called out, seeming to come out of nowhere. The church rustled with noise as the entire crowd shifted in their seats to see a man scurrying up the aisle.

"If I could just have your attention for a moment." The bespectacled man climbed the stairs to the stage and edged into the spot behind the pulpit where the pastor had been speaking, causing the crowd to murmur with disapproval.

"No respect," Dad's neighbor Agnes muttered beside Jess.

Agnes undoubtedly intended this to be heard as a defense of the pastor or even Jasper Wilhelm himself, but the way she dug into her purse for a butterscotch made Jess suspect the real breach of respect she was reacting to was the delay in the potluck that was about to take place outside.

"I'd like to thank you all for being here today," the man said breathlessly from the front. "My name is Eli Novak, and I am the executor of Jasper Wilhelm's will. As you know, Mr. Wilhelm was a very wealthy man."

The murmur grew louder, causing Eli Novak to pull the handkerchief from his jacket pocket and dab gently at his brow. People in Redford didn't talk about money. If you had too much of it, any reference would be perceived as bragging. Too little implied begging. Either was guaranteed to be off-putting.

"He made his money in Texas," Mr. Novak continued

squeakily, either failing or refusing to read his audience's cues, "but he chose to invest it in Redford. This was his home. For that reason, he decided to leave the remainder of his fortune—ten million dollars—to you."

For the briefest of moments, the church went silent, as if the man had spoken in a different language and it was taking everyone a few seconds to translate his words. Then the crowd erupted into cheers and chatter.

Ten *million* dollars. Enough to stock the school library with books written more recently than the nineties. Or fix the potholes on Cherrywood Lane that people had been complaining about for years. Jasper Wilhelm was a hero. That kind of money would transform Redford.

But even as the audience rejoiced in all that could be fixed with such a gift, Jess heard a few of the people around her begin to expand on the theme. Sure, it would be nice to have smooth roads, but what about the small-business owners who'd been fighting to stay afloat? The people who were struggling to put food in their kids' mouths? With ten million dollars, wasn't it possible to help both the town as a whole and a few individuals like themselves?

The man held up a slender hand, quelling the noise.

"Before his death," he said loudly, "Mr. Wilhelm devised a game, of sorts. It will be an event lasting an unspecified amount of time and will be comprised of various challenges, in which you will be invited to compete against each other for the ten million dollars. In each challenge, those who succeed will make it to the next round and will be awarded an unspecified amount of points for their performances. When the competition is over, I alone will be responsible for determining who has accumulated the most points, using a rubric designed by Mr. Wilhelm. That team will win Mr. Wilhelm's fortune."

Jess gasped at both the lawyer's words and the roar that filled the room in response to them. Questions rang out, some people in the audience waving their hands like children, others simply shouting toward the stage. It was madness, and rightfully so. Surely, Jasper wouldn't be the first millionaire to donate money to the greater good. But this? A *game*? It was an absurd way to distribute such a vast amount of money.

It must be one of Jasper's jokes. He was messing with them. Playing a game by making them pretend they were going to play a game. Jess laughed aloud at the realization, but it was drowned out by the wild reaction of the crowd. Excitement and incredulity had all but replaced the grief that had weighed down the room. Jasper would've loved it. He had, after all, been the brains behind Thanksgiving in May the year the town market was at risk of closing its doors. It had been his idea to cover the courtyard in slip-and-slides that summer the high hit 103 degrees. Why wouldn't he have found a way to make his own funeral the most exciting event the church had ever held?

A few pews ahead of her, a big, burly man—Bobby Randall, the owner of the garage where her dad worked—jerked to his feet. He had the bearing of a gorilla, though he lacked the emotional intellect of one.

"I assure you," Novak said, gesturing for Bobby to sit back down, "all will be revealed in due time."

"Understood," Bobby said in his deep, gravelly voice,

making no move to sit. He prided himself on his refusal to take instructions from anyone, and a man half his size who carried around a reusable tissue with initials embroidered on it wasn't going to be the exception. "But just so I understand, you're telling us that Jasper Wilhelm left his money to the people of Redford, but we're going to be separated into teams. So, if you divide the town into two different teams, half of us will get to split all the money and the other half will end up with *nothing*?"

"No, no." Mr. Novak shook his head and smiled reassuringly, stuffing his handkerchief back into his jacket pocket. "Mr. Wilhelm has taken the liberty of pairing each of you up. Only *two* of you will win any money."

A collective gasp met his words, and then the audience erupted again. Surprisingly, this time the room filled with cheers. Jess heard a few complaints about fairness and sharing and not wanting to compete against their friends and family. But most of the people around her seemed to be thrilled at the thought that they might win five million dollars. As they should be.

It would be like playing the lottery, only everyone's odds of winning were a whole lot better than one in fifteen million. Two of the people in this room were about to become ridiculously, fantastically wealthy. *She* might even be one of them. Tilting her head back, Jess joined in with her neighbors, letting loose a loud, boisterous whoop of her own.

Chapter 4

ROSS

The tables of food beneath the gazebo were teeming with untouched platters of deviled eggs, pulled pork, potato salad, and all the other dishes one typically found at a Southern potluck. Normally, the line would be stretched down the stairs and into the grass, filled with people chatting distractedly as they side-eyed the heaping plates of those lucky enough to be ahead of them. Not today, though. Today, Ross and his daughter, Jess, were two of only five adults in the gazebo, although the dessert table was thoroughly surrounded by children who'd been forgotten in their parents' desperation to see who they'd been paired with.

The *board* had trumped hunger. It had been set up on the far end of the grass, on the other side of the folding chairs that had been brought out for the meal, and it was at least six feet across and almost as tall, with notecards tacked over every inch of it. Each had a pair of names written on it. At least, that's what Ross assumed the words were. He'd caught sight of them as he passed but hadn't bothered to stop and take a closer look. The crowd around it had already grown too thick, and it weren't as if it was going anywhere. Novak had said from the stage that the game would start tomorrow. Ross and Jess would have plenty of time to see who they'd been paired with.

At least, that's what Ross had said to Jess. The far smarter strategy, he'd explained, was to hit the buffet while all the best dishes were still mostly untouched. It had been a bluff, an effort to avoid the frenzied reaction to Jasper's game—a bluff Ross was now regretting. A waft of sweet barbecue sauce hit his nose, and his stomach turned.

"Should we get two?" he asked, doubling down.

"Two what?" Jess grinned gamely.

"Plates." Ross tilted his chin up like a conqueror relishing his spoils. "We can take all the food we want, for once, without some busybody behind us tutting about leaving enough for everyone else."

Jess laughed, but her head was already shaking in a silent no, just as Ross had expected it to. She was no doubt thinking about all the other people this food was supposed to feed. For an only child, his daughter had always been surprisingly good at sharing. Perhaps because of Liz, a sister to her in every way but by blood from such an early age.

Jess opened her mouth to chastise him, but then something in her expression shifted. She looked him over again in that way she'd been doing lately, like she was paying too close attention. Sometimes Ross wished she could be more like other kids, seeing their parents as nothing more than the sun—that big ball that hovered over their world, there to provide light and warmth and a schedule, without ever needing anything for itself.

Ross's stomach turned again as he realized, whether she understood it or not, she was about to call his bluff.

"Three," Jess said, her mouth stretching into a daring grin. She grabbed one plate with her right hand and two with her left. "We'll need one for desserts."

"If there are any left." He stalled, making a show of shaking his head at the little girl who was stuffing cookies into her tiny pants pockets. But then he played the hand he'd dealt and followed Jess's lead. Reluctantly, he grabbed three plates and dug into the fragrant vat of pulled pork.

In a routine perfected by years of experience, Jess started down the other side of the table, keeping pace with him. The seven-layer dip was on her side, so she scooped a heaping serving of it and reached across to dump it on his plate. He did the same for her with the watermelon chunks. They knew each other's favorites like only two people who'd grown up together could. They'd always been a team, ever since Jess was six months old and her mom had come to the realization that teenagers weren't meant to be parents. At the time, Ross had understood that she was right. Teenagers *weren't* meant to be parents. Luckily, no one else seemed to realize how wildly unqualified he was, and he'd been allowed to remain one anyway.

Rather than heading down to the chairs in the grass, where they'd have to balance their plates on their knees, he and Jess settled against the railing that wrapped around the gazebo. As soon as they'd balanced their plates, though, a group of people broke away from the board and headed up to get food. Ross shifted to get out of their way.

The chilly breeze cut through the dress shirt he'd excavated from his closet for the funeral. He sank a tortilla chip into the pile of seven-layer dip, creating a valley between the refried beans and shredded cheese. Would it be disrespectful to Jasper if he cut out of here early to get back to the garage? It was the perfect time of year to be outside working on a car. Summer was still fighting for dominance, but the world was shifting its face toward the holidays. Ross couldn't think of anything better than an open hood under colorful leaves, the heat of the sun cut by crisp air.

"I can't believe Jasper paired me with Louisa Cunningham," Retta Moore said to Rosa Sternard, her arm nearly brushing against Ross's as she stomped past where he and Jess were perched. Retta grabbed a plate and slapped pulled pork on a bun so hard the plate almost bent in half. "Jasper *knew* Louisa stole Ryan Jenkins from me in high school. Didn't he? How could he put the two of us together? There's no way he didn't know."

Ross made no effort to hide his eavesdropping. He lifted an amused eyebrow at Jess.

"Everyone knows," Rosa said lightly, taking the tongs from Retta's hand and setting them gently back on the pork. "You do tend to talk about it."

"How could I not?" Retta said. "I'd be married now if she hadn't lured him away with her tiny shorts and sparkly backpack."

"Ah, yes." Rosa caught Jess and Ross looking and winked

mischievously. "Bedazzled backpacks *are* often considered the push-up bras of high school sophomores."

Ross stifled a laugh and turned back toward the railing, nudging his plate away as his gaze drifted beyond the gazebo. The grass had survived the summer, remaining thick and green, and it stretched the entire length of the square. Beneath him, a couple tromped across it, coming to a stop next to a riot of colorful flowers.

"I just don't understand why you have to be on his team," the man whined loudly.

"Because we were paired together." The woman's voice was sharp, like she'd lost patience with the argument, or perhaps with the man himself. "Did you not see the board? It was right there, written in ink."

Ross leaned closer toward the rail, even though he could hear them perfectly from where he was. He didn't take joy in the couple's argument, but he couldn't pretend not to be interested in it. He'd begun to notice a peculiar theme emerging from the pairings: No one appeared to be happy with them.

"But I hate him," the man said.

"If it helps, I suspect he hates you more."

"Does that seem like it would help?"

It was surprising to Ross that Jasper could've made so many mistakes. Feuds, or fights, even small disagreements were as much a part of small-town life as the sense of extended family. Ross attributed it to the unchanging population; just like you couldn't forget who had shown up with a casserole when you broke a leg, you also couldn't forget the ones who'd done you wrong. They were always there, sitting next to you in the diner or standing behind you in line at the grocery store. And maybe, somewhere else, somewhere every day didn't feel identical to the last, people could just move on, forgiving and forgetting. But in a place as small as Redford, there was no such thing as moving on. There was simply nowhere to go.

Jasper had known that.

Ross was certain of it. That clever old coot had known everything. So Ross couldn't, for the life of him, figure out how Jasper had managed to form so many unfortunate pairings. If Jasper were anyone else, Ross would suspect he'd done it as some kind of prank, a little joke he could chuckle at from the grave. Jasper Wilhelm wasn't like that, though. He might have been eccentric, but Ross had never known him to be anything but kind.

"Do you think we got paired together?" Jess asked, her question likely prompted by the same conversation he'd been listening in on.

Ross shrugged. They'd find out as soon as they looked at the board. And then he'd have to decide if he could play. He needed the money, obviously, but he wasn't feeling particularly athletic lately. And it didn't seem like the smartest plan in the world to give up guaranteed hours of work for an unlikely shot at the jackpot. Not right now.

"I hope not," she continued. "Being on different teams doubles our chances of winning the money."

"You say that like I'd share my winnings with you," Ross said, unable to resist teasing her.

"Well, I'd share with you," Jess said. "But I'd obviously

do so with the stipulation that some of the money goes toward a couch that doesn't smell like old chili."

A laugh rumbled from his throat. "You've been snobby about that couch ever since I let Norman Reitfield sleep there for a week when his wife kicked him out."

"Norman Reitfield oozed gas like a toxic waste facility left unmanned. The entire house should've been fumigated after he left."

"He was sad."

"And I'm sorry about that." Jess bowed her head in an exhibit of shared mourning. "I'm just equally sorry his sadness carried the odor of expired yogurt and congealed vomit."

"Appetizing," a man behind her said.

Ross tilted his head with interest at both the interruption from a sharply dressed man he'd never seen before and his daughter's reaction to that man's voice. Jess's eyes brightened and her cheeks flushed a shade of red Ross hadn't seen on her since the time he'd caught her and Liz stuffing tissues into the tops of their dresses before their first middle school dance.

"What a perfect conversation," the man continued as she spun toward him, "to have over tables full of food."

Ross's eyes narrowed at the insinuation Jess had done something wrong, but the instinct to defend his daughter sputtered out when he saw how the man looked at Jess. Granted, the man was trying hard to disguise his amusement—his expression was intentionally blank, and he was leaning back so far Ross could almost see the invisible wall he'd erected between the two of them—but the smile that tugged at the corner of his mouth was one Ross himself had tried to hide a million times over the years. It reassured him the man *saw* Jess, that he'd discovered her quirks and been unable to resist being charmed by them. Ross's shoulders loosened.

"Yes, well, I am renowned in Redford for my sparkling dinner conversation." Jess was clearly attempting to match his dry tone, but her goofy smile spoiled the effort.

"Clearly," the man replied.

Ross wondered if this was what it felt like to disappear. The man and his daughter had barely begun a conversation, so it wasn't as if he felt ignored, but their focus on each other was so intent, he was absolutely certain he'd faded to mist in their peripheral vision.

"I'm Jess's dad," he said, inserting himself into their force field. "Ross."

"Carter," the man said, reaching for his hand. "Carter Barclay."

The man's handshake was quick and firm, coolly polite rather than warm or friendly.

"How do you know my daughter, Carter?"

Jess cringed at the question, and Ross wondered if it had come out more interrogatory than intended. Then he realized she'd probably met the man at the bar yesterday. News of Jess's run-in with Nikki had made its way to the garage through a series of whispers that led to Bobby, who had then bellowed it out to Ross.

Ross assumed Jess hadn't brought it up because she hadn't wanted him to know that she'd been ambushed. He hadn't brought it up to her because he didn't want her to feel judged for drinking when she was supposed to be working. When two people were equally determined to protect each other, it didn't matter how often they spoke; some things went undiscussed.

"I ran into her yesterday when I arrived in town," Carter said smoothly. "She was kind enough to give me the lay of the land."

Ross caught the way Jess's eyes widened in gratitude. Carter had probably massaged the truth, but he'd clearly done so because he'd noticed her grimace as well. Ross decided he didn't mind that the man wasn't overly friendly. He didn't even mind being misled, not about this.

"And will you be staying for a while?" Ross asked.

"I hadn't planned on it." Carter's face lost its impassivity for a moment. A hint of uncertainty flashed across it. "But apparently I will be. My name is on the board?"

His voice lifted, making his statement sound like a question, and he gave a short shake of his head as if displeased with himself. When he continued, his words were decisive. "I'll be playing the game."

"Will you?" Jess looked as surprised as Ross felt.

That lawyer had said Jasper was giving the money to the town. The whole point was that a Redfordonian would win it. While Ross was confident this man was the grandson everyone had been whispering about, being Jasper's family didn't make him a local.

"Looks like it." Carter turned toward her. "What about you?"

"Am I playing the game? I haven't looked at the board yet, but I'm assuming I'll be on it." Jess's brow furrowed as if she was only now realizing that her inclusion wasn't necessarily a given. "At least, I hope I will be."

Carter seemed to wince.

"What?" Jess asked.

"Nothing," Carter said. "Just . . . You know that phrase, 'Be careful what you wish for'?"

"Yeah?"

"Let's just say it isn't the worst advice."

"Meaning?"

Ross heard the dread in his daughter's voice and knew she was trying not to acknowledge the worst possible scenario. Jess had heard the same conversations he had, though. She must have noticed that the pairings all seemed to be people who had a history of not getting along. And, unfortunately for Jess, she got along with everyone . . . with one notable exception.

"I saw your card," Carter said. "That woman from yesterday . . . wasn't her name Nikki?"

"No," Jess groaned. But it was too late. As if the mention of her name had been a summoning spell, Ross spotted Nikki stomping up the gazebo steps, heading directly toward them.

"Hey there, partner," Nikki sang out and slung her arm around Jess's shoulders, her nails angling noticeably into Jess's arm.

"Hi, Nikki," Jess said, pulling at Nikki's fingers in an unsuccessful attempt to dig them out of her skin. "I'm so sorry, but I can't be your partner. I was planning to team up with my dad."

"The pairings are nonnegotiable." Nikki spat out the

words as if they were distasteful to her. Ross wondered if it would be considered an overreaction if he picked his grown daughter up and slung her over his shoulder, running her from the gazebo like he was rescuing her from a tiger rather than a department store mannequin come to life.

Jess flinched and broke free. "We'll just explain it to Novak. My dad is . . ."

"Weak," Ross said quickly, jumping at the opportunity to assist. "And senile."

Carter scoffed but had enough sense to cover it with a cough, despite the fact that even Ross knew he was more likely to be mistaken for Jess's brother than pegged as her father.

"Yes," Jess said gratefully. "Without my help, he won't even be able to read the instructions to the game."

"That's blindness, not senility." Nikki's eyes narrowed as she turned toward him. "Are you blind, Ross? More important, were you blind last week when you were working on my car?"

"No," Ross said, backpedaling quickly. "I, uh . . . I'm—"

"I just spent ten minutes arguing with that lawyer," Nikki said, cutting him off and returning her attention to her preferred target of prey. "Jasper's rules are ironclad. Nobody can play the game unless they play with the person he paired them with. If one person is unable or unwilling to participate, the person they've been paired with is ineligible to compete. According to Novak, Jasper's pairings are in writing and notarized. And as we all know, Jasper's dead, which makes him extremely unlikely to change his mind. Now, Jessica, I know you're not the smartest person in town, so let me make this very simple for you to understand: You can either play the game with me or you can write a five-million-dollar check to me for the prize money I would've won. Either choice is fine by me, but those are the only two you're going to get."

"Right." Jess visibly gulped.

Ross wanted to step in, but there was nothing he could do. Even if he could come up with an excuse to get his daughter out of her pairing with Nikki, that would only prevent Jess from getting her own shot at the prize. With money like that, she could stop editing whatever book came her way and focus on the ones she truly loved instead. She could even start her own publishing company. Ross had always suspected half the reason she'd come home after college instead of taking the job in New York had been because she'd been so determined not to be like her mother, to become another person willing to leave their family behind. If Jess won Jasper's prize money, maybe she could have both the stability of home and the excitement of new opportunities.

"And you really think we can survive playing together?" Jess asked.

"Since we can only win as a team, I guarantee we will," Nikki said. When Jess smiled, she added, "Of course, I have no idea what will happen afterward. Ten million dollars would more than cover a top-notch hit man."

"You'd only have five million," Jess said, chin raised. "The other five would be mine."

Nikki smiled enigmatically.

"Well," Carter said, interrupting the uneasy moment, "it looks like I'll be seeing you on the battlefield."

He said the words to Jess, as if she were the only person he'd be playing against, and Ross felt her chest tighten in response like it was his own. His poor daughter. As if it weren't bad enough that she'd been paired with someone who despised her, the first guy she'd had a crush on in ages had just become her competition.

Ross made a note to pick up some ice cream on the way to the house. He'd stopped buying it since she moved out, but Jess always came back home when things got rough, and there was no easier way to comfort her than with a gallon of mint chocolate chip.

If this game of Jasper's was going to go like he thought it might, Ross figured he should grab an extra gallon of cookies and cream while he was at it. If he'd learned anything from being a single father, it was that you could never underestimate the amount of ice cream that might be needed.

Chapter 5

· · · · · · · · · ·

CARTER

I n Atlanta, Carter woke up early. He was out of the house by five thirty for his morning run past parked cars and slowly filling streets. When he got back home, he chugged a bottle of water. Then he had breakfast: black coffee.

His apartment in the city was sparsely but expensively furnished. Its clean lines and muted grays gave it an ordered feel, like he lived in an office that just happened to have an OLED TV and a bed covered in seven-hundred-thread-count sheets. Even when he was in a relationship, he rarely invited anyone to spend the night. He preferred to start the day alone.

Here, at the Lakehouse, Carter had continued to wake up early. He still ran, only he did so on a footpath around the lake instead of uneven city sidewalks. Instead of being surrounded by cars and buildings, he was treated to lapping water and colorful trees.

He loved it.

What he didn't love were the other differences. The B&B he was staying in was clean but cluttered, filled with

clashing colors, busy wallpaper, and yard-sale trinkets lining every available surface. More important, it contained
Mrs. Loveling. She was a tiny woman with a button nose
and deep-set wrinkles whose footsteps were so light Carter
might've felt like he was living in the Lakehouse alone. Instead, she was constantly popping up with no warning. Less
than thirty minutes into his stay, she'd knocked on his door
with a plate of freshly baked cookies, looking for all the
world like one of Santa's elves. An hour later, she'd caught
him heading out to his car and insisted he join her in front
of the fireplace for "happy hour," at which Carter was the
only guest. As if being in town for his grandfather's funeral
weren't a clear indication that he wasn't feeling particularly
happy.

Then yesterday, before Jasper's funeral, she'd spotted
Carter after his run and guilted him into eating a breakfast
not only of poached eggs and bacon but blueberry-and-
cream-cheese-stuffed French toast, too. Afterward, despite
the afternoon potluck, she'd ambushed him with chicken
potpie. "Comfort food," she'd called it, insisting he take at
least three bites, like he was a toddler in a high chair. Carter
had felt lucky she didn't hold a fork to his face, making
airplane noises and announcing that it was coming in for
landing.

He couldn't decide if she was simply nurturing or if she
was terrified he'd wither and die in her home, despite all
evidence that he'd managed to stay alive for thirty-two long
years before he'd rented a room under her roof. He'd been
raised by hired help, a series of people who had tolerated
him in exchange for a paycheck, so he had no reference from

which to draw a conclusion. He just knew that this morning's scrambled eggs, served with sausage gravy and biscuits, had made him later than he wanted to be for the kickoff of Jasper's game. He could not risk being disqualified. Not when his grandfather had given him a chance to continue their work.

Carter glanced distrustfully at the sky as he made his way down Main Street. It was dark with the threat of rain, and the moisture in the air made it feel colder against his face. Without the sunlight, the town didn't look quite as idyllic as it had when he'd arrived. The buildings looked worn out. Weathered.

That man was sitting on the corner again, the one Jess had called Oscar. He looked over at the sound of Carter's footsteps.

"Beautiful day, isn't it?" he called out when Carter got closer.

Carter squinted at him. "Not particularly."

Oscar looked so confused by his response that Carter felt obligated to add, "It looks like it's going to rain."

This didn't seem to help. Oscar opened his book and peered inside, like it might explain how the conversation had gone so awry. Carter grimaced and settled for nodding at him as he passed, an unspoken goodbye.

It bothered him that the interaction left him feeling like he'd failed in some way. What had Jess said to the man? *Couldn't get any better, Oscar?* There was no way Carter was going to say something so blatantly ripped from a *Sesame Street* script. He'd answered honestly. There shouldn't be anything wrong with that.

Still, Carter was in Redford now. The standards of politeness were clearly different here. Standards he probably would've learned if he'd visited his grandfather even once instead of always allowing Jasper to come to him. But Carter had been unwilling to take time off work. Ironic, given he'd finally put in for a whole week of vacation when he'd received news of Jasper's death. He'd told himself he'd need the time off to deal with his grandfather's estate, rather than facing his suspicion that grief was affecting his ability to concentrate. His mother had been Jasper's only child, and she certainly wouldn't be offering to help out. She and Jasper had been estranged since Carter was a child. To Carter's mother, Jasper had died years ago.

He'd been shocked to see her at the funeral. He'd been less shocked that both she and his dad had ignored him completely. Later that night, Carter had gone to Jasper's expecting to find his parents there pilfering valuables, but the mansion had been empty and showed no signs of visitors. He supposed he shouldn't have been surprised by that, either; his mother had all the money she needed, and she'd never been one for sentimentality. Carter doubted she'd stuck around long enough to discover her name wasn't on Jasper's board. She wouldn't have wanted to risk giving the impression she'd ever consider stooping so low as to compete for pocket change.

Like yesterday, today the town square was teeming with people. There was a different feel to the crowd, though, an underlying current of anger that didn't seem appropriate for a day that was meant to be fun. Carter spotted Bryce near the front of a line and threaded his way through the mass of bodies to join him. The bartender was slated to be his team-mate. Fortuitous, given that Bryce was one of the only people in town Carter had already met. Or maybe attributing it to good fortune didn't give Jasper the credit he deserved for the pairing. Jasper had to have known how hard his death would hit his grandson. Carter wouldn't be surprised if Jasper had put them together in hopes that spending some time with someone as cheerful and uncomplicated as Bryce might take the edge off his mourning.

"Cheater," someone behind him muttered as he fell into line beside Bryce.

Carter turned in surprise, but no one was looking at him. On the contrary, everyone's eyes seemed to be deliberately trained elsewhere.

"Morning." Bryce looked over and slapped him on the shoulder enthusiastically. "You missed Novak's announcement. Apparently, this thing is going to go on for at least a week, maybe more. And it will be taking place whenever he says it will, mostly during working hours."

"Really?" Anything more than a week would be almost impossible to swing. In his job, vacation time was more like permission to be out of the physical office than license to actually stop working. He'd still have to keep a close eye on his accounts and send nightly emails to his assistants detailing what trades they should make the next day.

That could be done through next weekend—it would have to be—but anything longer would cause problems. Not to mention, he wasn't sure he could survive Mrs. Loveling's kindness for another seven days.

"That sounds excessive," he said. "And, frankly, more than a little chaotic."

"You're not the only one who thinks so. Everyone is freaking out. They can't just close their businesses indefinitely. They wouldn't be able to pay next month's bills. Half the town is going to have to miss out on the game."

Carter scanned the crowd, finally understanding the change in mood.

"I don't get it," he said. "Did Novak provide any other details? I don't understand how he doesn't know how long it will last."

"You and me both, brother." Bryce shrugged, taking a step forward as the people in front of them moved to the table. "He talks a lot, but he says very little. The details were sketchy, and I don't think they're going to get any clearer. All we got from him is that there will be tasks and points, and he'll let us know when he feels like sharing what those are."

"Helpful."

"Yep."

Carter glanced back, searching for Jess, and spotted her at the back of the crowd. She was wearing an orange sweater and plaid pants too garish to miss, laughing at something her dad was saying. He hoped that partner of hers wouldn't find a way to wipe the smile off her face.

"We're up," Bryce said, dragging his attention back to the table.

Novak was sitting in a folding chair behind it, with two iPads and a rose-patterned china teacup in front of him. He shifted his spectacles and directed them toward the screens, where a digital form was waiting to be filled out. The many questions on it explained why the line was taking so long. Carter filled it out as quickly as he could, putting in his Atlanta address because he couldn't remember the B&B's, but when he got to the Dickensian-length block of fine print, he paused.

"Sign below the box," Novak prompted him as if he was too dim to figure out how to fill out a form.

Carter squinted at him in response. Granted, Carter worked with numbers, not legal documents, but he knew enough about them to understand that you didn't put your name to something without understanding exactly what you were agreeing to.

"I'll read it first, thanks," he said coolly.

There was a collective groan from the line behind him. Strangely, he could've sworn he'd heard someone yell the word *plant*.

Bryce turned and waved them down before bending over to sign his name.

"Come on, man," he said to Carter as Novak reset the page. "Is there really anything in there that would keep you from competing?"

It was a fair point. Even if Carter were willing to walk away from the game, which he definitely wasn't, he couldn't do so without ending Bryce's chance to play as well. With a sigh, he signed his name to the slick screen and stepped to the side to allow the woman at the end of the table to affix a neon pink band to his wrist.

....

"YOU'RE JASPER'S GRANDSON, right?" Luanne peered at Carter curiously. She leaned toward him, her long, slender frame bowing slightly, like a reed in the wind.

She'd just kissed him on both cheeks, an affectation befitting the name of her bakery. If Jess hadn't informed him otherwise, Carter would have believed Luanne was French and that Evangeline really was the name of one of her close relatives. She'd nailed the look, with her monochrome dress and sleek bob of dark hair. He wouldn't have been surprised at all to see her pop a beret on her head and take off on a Vespa.

"I am," he said, grateful for the lack of suspicion accompanying her question. Bryce had been introducing him to people while they waited for Novak to collect the last of the signatures, but the reception had been noticeably icy. It clearly bothered people that he was related to the man whose fortune was at stake. And that he wasn't a Redfordonian but was being allowed to compete for a Redfordonian prize.

"Well, welcome to Redford, darling," Luanne said, waving her hand elegantly. "Jasper was as proud as could be of you. You must be devastated to lose him."

Carter's chest tightened in response to her words. It was just a thing people said. An effort at politeness. Still, it meant something to him, hearing that Jasper had been proud of him. Having someone recognize that his death was a terrible loss. Jasper had been the only family Carter had still been able to claim, and their strategy sessions on the phone had been the highlight of Carter's week. They'd laughed and talked and worked together to add something to the world. Without that, Carter felt untethered. Alone.

"Thank you," he said, taking a step back. "That means more than you know."

Luanne patted his arm but kindly moved on from the subject. "So what do you think your grandfather has in store for us today? Some mud wrestling? Pistol duels?"

"If there are guns," Bryce said, "I hope they have paint-balls in them."

"My guess goes to a water-balloon fight," Carter said. "I think Jasper would like the idea of people finding little strips of colorful rubber on the ground for the next couple of years."

Their laughter was cut short when an enormous man turned around. His face was tanned and weathered, and his nose looked like it had been broken more than once. "Water balloons, huh? Well, you would know."

"It was a joke, Bobby," Bryce said.

"Sure it was," Bobby said. "City boy there has probably been filling balloons up all week, throwing them at walls to practice his aim."

"Yes," Carter said. "Thank goodness my company provides a wet room for those of us who need to beef up our water-balloon skills during work breaks."

"Watch it, smart-mouth." Bobby pointed a warning finger at him. He probably would've looked silly if he hadn't been so intimidatingly large. "You shouldn't be part of this, and everyone knows it. The only way you could've ended up on the board is if you took advantage of your relationship to Jasper and snuck your name on his list."

"I can assure you that's not true," Carter said.

"Oh, can you?" Bobby sneered. "Can you *assure* me of that? Then tell us, smooth talker. How did you get on there? How did you become the only person playing the game who's not from Redford? Because I'll tell you what I think. I'll tell you what all of us think. We think Novak is your *family's* lawyer. We think you two are in on it together. Isn't that why Novak can't tell us how long the game will last or how the points will be awarded? Because he can't take the chance that you'll lose? Admit it. You have a deal. You're going to give him a cut of the money once he declares you the winner."

Too many people were paying attention now, the suspicion on their faces clear.

"No." Carter's denial sounded weak, even to his own ears. He wasn't guilty of pulling strings, obviously, but it wasn't like his thoughts hadn't gone in the same direction. He *wasn't* from Redford.

He was Jasper's family.

His partner.

Carter had been so confident that Jasper would leave his fortune to him. He'd fully believed that Jasper would want him to carry on their work. And then he'd heard about the game. It was one thing for Jasper to come up with such a bizarre idea—Carter had no problem picturing the way Jasper would've snickered with delight as he put it all together. What Carter couldn't believe was that Jasper would give up helping his neighbors, the town he loved, for nothing more than a silly spectacle.

And then Carter had found out he'd been included.

He'd heard Novak talk, noting the way he said so much yet revealed so little. And Carter had *known*.

He was being set up to win.

It was the only thing that made sense. *This* was how Jasper could get everything he wanted. He'd have his spectacle, cement his legacy as Redford's Master of Merriment, and he'd take care of everyone, too. With Carter's help, of course.

It was so obvious. The funny thing was, it wasn't even the first time Jasper had pulled a trick like this. He'd done it to Carter. More than once. Most notably was the time he'd called Carter in a panic, claiming to be on Tybee Island, desperate for a ride home. So Carter had gone. He'd jumped in his car and taken off like Sir Sucker Lancelot, driving for four hours only to discover that nobody had checked in to the room Jasper claimed to be staying in.

"You needed a break," Jasper had said when Carter called from the hotel lobby. "Go to the beach. Enjoy yourself. I promise that your office will survive a day without you."

That was it. No apology. No consideration for the fact that Carter had been in the middle of something before he'd jumped in his car. Jasper hadn't even pretended to be sorry, because he wasn't. He'd gotten what he'd wanted. And Jasper would get what he wanted this time, too. It probably hadn't even occurred to him that a lot of people would be disappointed when they didn't win. His grandfather would've been too focused on the idea that they would enjoy the game.

"I hope you don't play poker," Bobby said, "because you're a piss-poor liar."

"He's just here to play, Bobby," Jess said, pushing through the circle that had formed around them, "same as the rest of us."

"But that's my point. He shouldn't be."

Luanne shook her head and gave an audible tut. "I'm surprised at you, Bobby Randall. I remember when you were the best defensive lineman this town had ever seen, and now look at you. Scared of a little competition."

Bobby's head jerked back at the accusation. "I'm not scared."

"It kind of seems like you might be," Bryce admitted good-naturedly.

There was a noticeable shift in the crowd, not a unanimous pardon by any means, but a concession that the jump to judgment might've been too quick. A few people stepped away, clearly distancing themselves from the metaphorical pitchforks. Others remained, though, unconvinced.

"Watch your back," Bobby said, pointing at Carter again.

"See?" Luanne frowned with feigned concern. "That's your problem, right there. You shouldn't envision yourself being behind him in the race. You should have confidence that you'll be ahead."

"Oh, I will be." But Bobby sounded uncertain now, like the conversation had gotten away from him. He backed up, shouting, "I'll win this thing," before turning around and stomping away.

Jess giggled adorably, and it seemed to be contagious, because the next thing Carter knew, they were all laughing. Even him, despite the fact that it wasn't exactly great to discover that half the town considered him a cheater, especially knowing they weren't entirely wrong.

"I got the scavenger hunt list!" Nikki cried, appearing out of nowhere, waving a sheet of paper. She flapped it at Jess, who jerked back in surprise.

"Scavenger hunt?" Bryce asked.

Nikki rolled her eyes and swung the paper from Jess's face toward the table, where Novak was speaking.

"He's over there droning on about the rules in excruciating detail, like we've never heard of a scavenger hunt. Anyway, it's the first challenge, and we've got the list." She swung it again, this time waving it in Bryce's face.

Nikki seemed to be the kind of woman who could turn anything—even a flimsy sheet of paper—into a weapon. Bryce didn't flinch like Jess had. Instead, he smiled genially, then tilted his head and attempted to read the paper.

"Back off, beer peddler," Nikki commanded, shoving the paper behind her back. Her eyes narrowed as she grabbed Jess's arm and backed away. "Head starts are for winners."

"Sharing is caring," Bryce said, but Nikki merely flipped him off, somehow managing to make the gesture look elegant.

"You can't possibly believe I care about you." She turned on her heel.

As Nikki hauled her away, Jess turned and mouthed, "I care about you, Bryce," before waving goodbye to Carter.

"You've got to give it to her," Bryce said admiringly. "Nikki Loughton brings energy."

Carter watched her stomp toward the street, the spikes

on her shoes stabbing the grass. "Is that what we're call-ing it?"

A middle-aged man in front of them turned and started to pass Carter a small stack of papers but stopped, shifting to Bryce and handing them to him instead.

"Thanks, Charlie," Bryce said, giving one to Carter be-fore passing them on. Around them, people began to dis-perse, their heads bent over the printed scavenger hunt lists as teams tried to emulate Nikki's plan and get the teeniest lead on everyone else. The rest of the crowd grabbed at the stack, eager to catch up.

It was such a long list, though. Carter couldn't imagine a couple of minutes could make any difference at all. He scanned the numbers, flipping the page over to discover that they went all the way to twenty items. Not just cut-and-dried items, either; many were clues that would have to be solved. Once they'd figured out the item and found it, they weren't supposed to collect it. They were supposed to take a pic-ture with it.

"How are you at riddles?" Bryce asked, looking up from the list.

"For five million dollars?" Carter shrugged. "I'd better be amazing at it."

Chapter 6

· · · · · · · · · ·

NIKKI

We should sit down somewhere and work through the clues," Jess said excitedly as if this were some inspired idea Nikki hadn't already had herself. They were reading Novak's list as they walked down Main Street. "That way, we won't waste time backtracking."

"No." Nikki didn't look up from the list, but she could feel Jess's relentless bouncing falter beside her.

"Um . . ."

Nikki didn't care if it made more sense to take some time and devise a strategy. She wasn't going to be forced to sit down next to so much plaid. Just the sight of it made her skin itch.

Her gaze went back to number seven. **The fallen king's head, once lifted and presiding over celebratory toasts. Now hidden away with the rest of the ghosts.** It had to be referring to the buck head that used to be mounted at the Staple. Her eyes narrowed.

Only the person who had stolen it would know where it was now. But who could that have been? And how was it fair that its thief was the only one able to take a picture of it? Nikki had thought it was good when the buck disappeared—if someone had dared chop off her head, then used it for decoration, she would've undoubtedly dedicated all of eternity to haunting them—but she didn't want whoever stole it to be rewarded for their crime with a leg up in the competition.

"What about number eighteen?" Jess said, quickly recovering from Nikki's rebuff. "**When science collides with a baby's bed and fruity cookies.** It makes no sense at all. It's like Jasper was watching *Inception* and got snacky."

"Newton's cradle," Nikki muttered without looking over. Jess claimed to work with words for a living. She must know she sounded stupid when she said things like *snacky*.

"He was watching Newton's cradle?"

Nikki sighed loudly. If Jasper weren't already dead, she would've seriously considered killing him for saddling her with this living cartoon.

"The answer to the clue," she said, her words clipped, "is *Newton's cradle*. That's what they call those hanging balls that men like to put on their desks. You know, where you swing one ball and it hits the others, making the one on the opposite end fly out."

"Hanging balls." Jess snorted childishly.

"You can cross that one off the list," Nikki said curtly. "I'll take care of it."

Kent had one in his office that he'd bring over if she asked. It was just a matter of if Nikki was willing to ask. They'd been dating for several months, and millions of dollars were at stake, so she knew she had every right to solicit his help. What bothered her was that she also knew he'd make the drive from Woodbridge without question. Was he a pushover?

There was nothing less sexy than a pushover.

That didn't feel like a fair description of Kent, though. He might have accepted her aversion to exclusivity, but he'd put a firm foot down the only time she'd stood him up. He'd been clear about the fact that he liked her, but she knew he'd be fine if his feelings weren't reciprocated. Kent had that unflappability that came from a lifetime of things working out his way. A perfect family, a good job, a handsome face—everything had come so easily to him. No wonder he was the nicest man Nikki had ever met. She'd be nice, too, if every day was her own personal Christmas.

Pulling out her phone, Nikki started to type her request instead of calling him. She preferred to keep direct contact with Kent at a minimum. He'd get sick of her eventually, or he'd figure out that she wasn't the kind of woman you picked to build a future with. The longer she kept him at a distance, the longer it would take for the whole relationship to come to its inevitable conclusion.

"Who are you texting?" Jess, ever oblivious to boundaries, peered over her arm.

"A guy." Nikki tilted her phone away from her. "Why are you so interested? Were you hoping to steal another one away from me?"

She felt Jess wilt beside her. *Good.* Jason had been a loser, but he'd been her loser. That had meant something back then, when there had been so little Nikki could claim as her own. Then she'd walked in on Jason kissing Jess, and she'd been forced to confront the realization that she truly had nothing.

"I didn't—"

"I don't care," Nikki said, cutting Jess off. "I didn't want to hear it then, and I certainly don't want to hear it after all this time. Just shut up for a minute and let me lock down number eighteen."

"Okay," Jess said, resigned.

Nikki sent the text and looked at the list again.

"Have you figured out number four yet?" she asked, sliding the phone back into her purse. "**Not at the edges. Not meant for one. Holder of horses turns setting of fun.**"

"Yep." Jess stayed silent long enough that Nikki was forced to look at her. When she did, Jess offered a hopeful smile. "The community center."

"Huh." Nikki should've figured that out herself.

"Do you think that's right?"

"I hate that they ever called that place Redford's community center," Nikki said, not wanting to give Jess the validation she was clearly seeking. "It was just an old barn that nobody wanted anymore."

"It wasn't just a barn. It was the place where everything fun happened. And Mr. Sanders didn't donate it to the town because he didn't want it anymore. He did it to be kind."

"Well, he wasn't kind enough to fix it after the storm hit it."

"He was on his deathbed, Nikki. He died like a month later."

Nikki threw her hands in the air. "I'm just saying that a month is plenty of time to write a check for repairs. You don't need to be on your feet to write a check, do you?"

"Let's just go there and get a picture," Jess said, picking up speed.

Nikki nodded and managed to refrain from pointing out that they already had prom pictures from there, and that Nikki had been forced to take hers with the last-minute date she'd found after she'd caught Jason cheating on her with Jess. But as fun as it was reminding Jess that she hadn't always been as saintly as everyone gave her credit for, Nikki didn't want it to look like she'd actually been hurt.

Allowing yourself to be hurt was for losers. And as her unwanted teammate would soon discover, Nikki always found a way to win.

Chapter 7

··········

JESS

Jess squinted at Nikki suspiciously. They'd already been running down clues for three hours, and the hunt had taken them all the way to the lake. Now, they were headed back to Main Street. While Jess's energy was notably lagging, Nikki's was somehow growing. Perhaps this was why Nikki never seemed to tire of torturing her: She was an actual Terminator, ungoverned by human needs such as rest or refueling.

"I could use a coffee," Jess said, testing her theory. "How about you?"

"Coffee is for old men in poorly fitted suits." Nikki didn't bother looking at her.

Jess tilted her head. "Is it?"

"Men with premature wrinkles," Nikki said decisively, "who work too many hours for too little pay."

"That's very specific."

Nikki ignored her and took another sip from the hot pink reusable water bottle she kept in her purse. It was probably a prop, tricking people into thinking she was drinking something normal instead of the WD-40 she consumed to keep her joints from squeaking when they bent.

"**The proper tool**," Nikki said, rereading the same clue from the list, "**to cut a lock that curls.**"

"What about one of those bike locks?" Jess said, pushing her sleeves up to her elbows. The sun still hadn't come out, but all of the running around made the chilly air feel good against her skin. "The stretchy ones that twist into a coil. That could be considered curly, right?"

"But is there a 'proper tool' to cut it? I mean, the word *proper* does insinuate that it's supposed to be cut, right? And the only reason you'd cut a bike lock is to steal something."

"True. But wouldn't that apply to all locks?"

They looked at each other, realization dawning for both of them simultaneously.

"Not a lock of hair," Nikki said, pride clearly seeping through the expression of mild disdain she'd maintained the entire morning.

Jess grinned, not caring in the slightest that Nikki had beaten her to the punch. It was the first time it had actually felt like they were working together since they'd left the square. Most of the morning, she'd just been following Nikki around like one of those toddlers on a backpack leash.

"So," Jess said, "we need a pair of shears."

Nikki nodded and began running toward Main Street, her heels clacking sharply against the cement. A flock of birds that hadn't yet accepted the coming winter exploded in a panic of wings, likely regretting their failure to migrate to safer terrain.

"What's the plan?" Jess called out as she raced behind

her, but naturally Nikki ignored her. So much for working together.

There were fewer people out in town than there were over the weekend, but Main Street wasn't empty. Pairs of people dotted the sidewalk, identifiable as teams by the colorful bands on their wrists. They looked up nervously at the gunfire sound of Nikki's heels. When they realized it was just her, no one showed signs of relief. Jess wasn't sure if they were more worried that her speed indicated she was further ahead in the competition or that she was going to run them over. Either fear seemed valid. From behind, Nikki looked surprisingly small. But when she was staring you down, she was a skyscraper. One with a façade lovely enough to distract your eye from the sniper rifles lining its roof.

Just as Jess was beginning to get a stitch in her side, Nikki veered left toward Cuts & Curls and flung open the door. A little bell above it jingled frantically in response.

"Hi, Annabelle," Nikki said, stopping just inside so that Jess crashed into her back.

Grunting, Jess slipped around her and waved awkwardly at Annabelle Stanton, arguably Redford's most stylish resident. Annabelle had graduated two years behind Jess and Nikki, moved to Atlanta, learned all she needed to know about hair in a single year, and returned to Redford with the sole mission of ensuring no one in town would ever be allowed to get a perm again.

When Annabelle had talked the owner of Cuts & Curls into hiring her on a thirty-day trial, there had been hesitation among the women of Redford to allow an inexperienced child near the hairstyles that had suited them just fine for the majority of their adult lives. But a year in the city had lent Annabelle an air of unmistakable glamour, and she'd been shrewd enough to use herself as advertisement, catwalking down Main Street with a new hairstyle every day until the requests began to roll in. *Do you think you could add highlights like those to my hair, Annabelle? Is my hair too short for a braid like that?*

Thanks to her inspiration, the ladies of Redford had now exited the age of the helmet hair modeled by *The Golden Girls* and entered an era of magenta streaks and whimsical styles. Today, Annabelle had added extensions that hung almost to her waist, twisting them into beachy waves that made her look like a mermaid.

"Nikki," Annabelle said, tucking her finger into the magazine she'd been flipping through. "I didn't expect to see you again until the end of the month. But, Jess." She shook her head like a middle school teacher who wasn't mad at her student's behavior, just disappointed. "You are long overdue for a trim."

Annabelle turned in her seat to survey the salon as if trying to find a spot to put the walk-ins. A Taylor Swift song was playing through the speakers, and the room was brightly lit and smelled of lemon cleaner. Framed photos of celebrities with famous haircuts dotted the walls. There were four cutting stations set up, a chair facing a mirror at each.

All of them were empty.

"Actually, I'm not here for highlights," Nikki said. "I need a favor."

"Oh." Annabelle straightened in her seat, her expression

turning remorseful. "This doesn't have anything to do with the scavenger hunt, does it?"

"Why?" Nikki tilted her head like a lion clocking its prey.

"Because I've had a couple of teams show up looking to take a picture with a pair of my shears."

"Who?" Nikki asked sharply.

Jess cleared her throat. Surely, it didn't matter who had beaten them here. Not unless Nikki was considering some kind of sabotage to slow them down.

"So, you do have a pair of shears," Jess said to Annabelle, hoping to keep them on track, "that you let them take a picture with."

"Not exactly," Annabelle said.

"Meaning?" Nikki asked.

"Nikki," Annabelle said placatingly, "you know I value you so much as a customer."

Nikki squinted, prematurely outraged. "*But?*"

"But I can't do anything that might help another team beat Bo in the scavenger hunt." Annabelle turned toward Jess, looking for understanding. "I couldn't compete because I had appointments with several women from Woodbridge this morning, but if he wins, he's going to get me the biggest engagement ring Redford's ever seen."

"Really?" Jess brightened. She must've spent more time behind her desk than she'd realized if she'd missed Bo Sutton finally winning Annabelle over. Since the moment Annabelle had strolled back into town, the handsome construction worker had been falling all over himself to impress her. Perhaps he'd finally found an excuse to work shirtless around her. Jess had caught sight of his abs once when he was fixing her dad's roof, and for a solid five minutes, she'd convinced herself it would be possible to fall in love with a man who'd once torn a page out of her well-worn copy of *The Secret History* to jot down a homework assignment. He hadn't done it to be mean, of course—Bo had always been a sweetheart. He just hadn't considered the fact that some people might want to keep all the pages in a book they'd already read.

"It's new," Annabelle said before Jess could ask. Her cheeks pinkened, giving her the glow that comes with falling in love. "We've only been together for a few weeks. But . . ."

"When you know, you know," Jess finished for her.

Annabelle beamed. "We do. We totally know."

Jess gave an excited clap of delight, and Nikki cleared her throat and shot her a look that clearly stated, *Pull it together, loser. We're not here to plan a bachelorette party.*

"Congratulations," Jess said weakly, her hands falling to her sides.

"Yes, congratulations." Nikki's smile looked surprisingly genuine. "But you've got it all wrong. We don't care about the scavenger hunt. We're actually just here as regular old customers."

Jess looked at her questioningly, but Nikki didn't bother meeting her eyes.

"Oh, fantastic." Annabelle pushed back the chair and stood up, waving them toward the empty stations. "What can I do for you?"

"Jess wants bangs."

"I do?" Jess honestly didn't know why those words left her mouth. Nor why they sounded like a question. She *didn't.* That was the clear and obvious response to such a statement. If she'd wanted bangs, she'd have them.

"You do." Nikki smiled sweetly. "And I'm going to make sure you get them."

"You're such a great friend," Jess said through clenched teeth. "But first, could you join me outside, please?"

"To take the 'before' picture?" Nikki clapped her hands in feigned delight. "That's such a great idea! Excuse us for a moment, please, Annabelle. And don't worry, we're totally going to tag you in the before-and-after post."

Jess smiled tightly and pushed the door open, the bell tinkling pleasantly this time. Apparently, it only jangled when attacked by Hurricane Nikki.

"What do you think you're doing?" she cried the moment the door closed behind them.

"Relax," Nikki said, rolling her eyes.

"I will not relax." Jess had made every effort to be a good partner, but it was time to draw the line. If nothing else, pride demanded she engage her spine. "You know who gets bangs? People who want to spend the next year and a half of their life growing bangs out."

"You're not getting bangs." Nikki sighed. "We're just going to put you in the chair long enough for her to raise the scissors up so we can snap a pic with both of us in it. Then you can jump out of the chair."

"Or I could not do any jumping with a sharp object near my face. Actually, I could *not* get in her chair in the first place. It's a pair of shears, not the Hope Diamond. Let's just go to my house. I've got a pair of scissors in my kitchen."

"You cut your hair in your kitchen?" Nikki looked unreasonably disgusted by this suggestion.

"I cut normal kitchen stuff," Jess said. "Have you ever tried to open a bag of frozen corn without scissors? It's impossible."

"The clue wasn't for frozen-corn scissors, Jessica. It was for a 'proper tool to cut a lock that curls.' Do you or do you not have hair-cutting shears?"

Jess sighed. She'd forgotten that Liz used special scissors to cut her hair. Those, like Liz, were no longer accessible. "I do not," she admitted. "Do you?"

"Do I *look* like I cut my own hair?"

This didn't feel like a trap so much as a warning, so Jess shook her head and attempted to distract Nikki from the unintended insult. "We can probably find a pair at Joe's market."

"Possible," Nikki said. "But if he does have any—and that's a big if—how many do you think he has in stock? One pair? *Maybe* two? And Annabelle said a couple of teams already showed up asking for them. Where do you think their next stop was?"

"Joe's," Jess admitted. "But it's not like they had any reason to buy them. I'm sure they just snapped a pic with them and moved on to the next item on the list."

"Oh, are you? Are you sure?" Nikki shook her head like she was dealing with the naivest child in all of Disneyland. "Because I'll tell you what I'd do. I'd take one look at a pair of five-dollar scissors and not think twice about buying up the stock so I'd have a better chance at millions of dollars."

"Yeah, but you're . . ." Jess trailed off, paralyzed by the glint of warning in Nikki's eyes.

"I'm?"

Diabolical. Ruthless. Evil.

"Let's go get me some bangs," Jess said, self-preservation kicking in.

Nikki grinned triumphantly and waved her toward the door. "Losers first."

Reluctantly, Jess led her inside. The Taylor Swift song had ended, replaced by something faster paced and irritating. She couldn't believe they were going to trick Annabelle into taking a picture with them. It was rude. And unnecessary. Surely it couldn't be that difficult to find a simple pair of hair-cutting scissors. They'd already managed to sneak onto Roger Young's leaky boat, after all, capturing a shot of **something that both floats and sinks**. If they could survive that without drowning or being shot for trespassing, how hard could it be to knock on a few doors asking about scissors? At the sight of them, Annabelle stepped behind one of the chairs and twirled it toward them.

"I swear, people have gotten so boring since the summer ended," she said. "I haven't done anything more interesting than a trim in days. It'll be so fun to give you a totally new look."

"Mhmm," Jess murmured in response, not wanting to contribute to Nikki's lie.

"Some light bangs will soften the lines of your face," Annabelle continued, ushering Jess into a chair. She tied a bib around her neck that smelled like a combination of the hundreds of flowery-perfume wearers that had sat in that chair before Jess. "Your hair has great depth of color, but it lacks shape."

"Mhmm," Jess murmured again, lower.

She didn't particularly like the idea that the lines of her face needed softening. Wasn't that how people recognized you? By your face looking a particular way? And her hair had plenty of shape, thank you very much. It was rectangular, starting at the top of her head and extending to mid-back. Rectangles were one of the strongest of all the shapes. A classic, right up there with the square and circle.

"I think you're being generous about the color," Nikki said to Annabelle, leaning in to peer at Jess's hair. She smelled like bubblegum and cotton candy, scents too sweet to suit her. Licorice would be better. And lighter fluid. "See that streak right there? That's straight-up orange."

"I don't think that's—" Annabelle got out before Nikki spoke over her.

"It's like a jack-o'-lantern vomited on your head," Nikki told Jess, her voice oozing with false sympathy.

"Autumn *is* my favorite season," Jess said.

"Is that why you always dress like Phoebe Buffay? Because you're so excited for Halloween?"

"Phoebe who?"

"You know." Nikki drew a finger through the air from Jess's orange sweater to the hunter green and orange-checked pants on her legs. "The blond one on *Friends*. The one who always looks like she's dressed to host story time for a bunch of toddlers."

"Yes," Jess said. "That's exactly the reason."

Jess was so focused on not letting Nikki get to her that

the spray of water came as a complete shock. She jerked back, feeling like a cat being punished for clawing at the couch.

"Sorry," Annabelle said, pulling a lock of hair over one of Jess's eyes without undoing her side part. She shot it with another spray of water as Nikki snorted with delight. "I thought you saw me."

It was a completely fair assumption on her part, since she was standing right in front of Jess holding a bottle in front of her face. Still, Jess had thought she and Nikki would be able to catch a picture with the scissors before her hair was actually altered, even if the only change was from dry to wet.

"If it's fine with you," Annabelle said, "I'd like to start with a bit of a side shag that will layer into your hair. Then, if you decide you want something bolder, we can straighten it out."

"Let's skip straight to bold," Nikki said, her eyes sparking with mischief.

"You're the professional," Jess said to Annabelle before shooting Nikki a look. "Let's start with the shag."

After a few more sprays and a comb through the wet part that pulled the hair over Jess's right eye, Annabelle finally picked up the scissors and lifted them in front of Jess's face. Nikki took a step closer to them and raised her phone toward the mirror, lining up the shot so that both of them were in it with the shears like the scavenger hunt instructions demanded. The scissors opened, the sound of metal sliding against metal louder than two small blades could possibly be. Jess widened her eyes at Nikki, but Nikki's eyes had widened as well. Nikki shook her head sharply, poking at the screen like it had frozen up or gone blank.

The back blade of the scissors skimmed close to Jess's forehead as Annabelle lined up the hair for the first snip. Jess cleared her throat loudly, but Nikki held up a finger in the universal sign of *wait* as she gave the phone a sharp shake like it merely needed to be wrangled into submission. Jess's heart rate picked up speed.

"Don't!" she cried finally, unable to take the charade any further. She pulled back, but it was too late.

Annabelle closed the scissors, and Jess heard metal slicing through hair.

"Got it!" Nikki ignored Annabelle's cry of understanding and shoved the picture in Jess's face.

In it, Jess was pulling back, her eyes wide with horror as a set of shears closed over a lock of hair that was meant to remain uncut. She squeezed her eyes shut, unable to believe that she'd fallen for it—that she'd allowed Nikki Loughton to destroy her hair. She *liked* her hair.

It would grow back, though. And there was no way she was going to allow Nikki to see that she'd gotten to her. If Jess did, Nikki would continue to pick away at her through the entire game. Pushing back the concern that Nikki was going to do that anyway, Jess forced her eyes to open and trained them on the snapshot Nikki was still waving in front of her face.

She hated the bangs already. The shortened clump of hair looked like it was trying to walk her eyebrow like a balance beam.

"Perfect shot," Jess said through clenched teeth. "You did a really fantastic job at holding the camera steady."

Chapter 8

. . . .

JESS

t's closed?" In her surprise, Nikki seemed to forget to look at Jess with antagonism or mockery. Instead, her eyes landed directly on Jess, searching for some confirmation that this couldn't be right. "The diner *and* the bar are closed?" Nikki's voice rose in outraged disbelief.

Jess nodded, her brain scrambling to think of any response that might convey that she was equally taken aback, to come up with some response that might further unite the two of them as partners. *That's unbelievable! How is it possible! I am* outraged *by the irresponsibility of some people!*

"I guess their employees are playing the game, too," she said instead, stupidly managing to both verbalize the obvious and align herself with the wrong side.

"Oh, is that what it is?" Nikki rolled her eyes. "And here I was assuming little green men had come down and ushered them all into a shiny silver ship with the promise of free pizza and a game of laser tag."

"Descriptive," Jess said, a smile tugging at her mouth. As disappointed as she was in her inability to stretch out the moment of partnership, she was growing numb to Nikki's hostility and might even have started to find it the teensiest bit entertaining. Not the loss of hair she'd suffered, obviously. She could overcome the change in appearance, knowing it would grow back, but that didn't make the unceasing tickle of it on her brow any less annoying. Still, she supposed she should just be grateful that Annabelle had agreed to finish them after she'd realized she'd been tricked. Luckily for Jess, Annabelle took enough pride in her work that she'd balked at the idea of a client leaving the salon looking anything less than fabulous.

"What are we supposed to do now?" Nikki slapped the curling "closed" sign that was dangling from the Staple's scarred wooden door.

It really was an unfortunate development. They were running out of places in town that were likely to have thirty forks they could take a picture with, but also, Jess's stomach was growling. She'd been hoping she could grab a sandwich for the road or at the very least a bag of chips.

"How many forks do you have at your house?" Jess asked. "My dad isn't one for hosting dinner parties, so I'm not exaggerating when I say he probably has four, maximum. But we could combine ours and his and then start knocking on neighbors' doors."

Nikki shook her head. "It'll take too long. We already lost too much time playing with your hair."

"Whose fault is that? Once you let her get the first cut in, I had no choice but to beg her to finish."

"As I was saying," Nikki continued sternly, but not before Jess saw the smile that flashed across her face at the reminder of what she'd done, "we already lost too much time playing with your hair. And, in case you haven't noticed, competition has clearly gotten the best of people. If we have to keep knocking on doors until we find enough people who don't have any motivation to prevent us from ticking another item off our list, we could be working on this clue until the sun drops."

"Do you have another suggestion, then? Because the market didn't have any, the Lakehouse wouldn't help us, and the bakery is closed. Unless you want to drive to another town, I think we're out of options."

Nikki's hands went to her hips, her brow furrowing. She clearly didn't want to admit that Jess was right, but unless she had a secret talent as a welder, she was going to have to.

"I could call . . ." Nikki trailed off.

"Who?" Jess asked once it was clear no name was forthcoming. "Cara? Lexi?"

Nikki looked at her like she was stupid but didn't offer an alternative. Instead, she shook her head as if she was knocking something ridiculous out of her brain, then tilted her chin up.

"We'll have to break in," she said decisively.

"What?" Jess must've misheard her. Maybe, if it were late at night and the bar abutted some seedy alley they could've snuck down to avoid being seen, this could be considered a case of desperate times calling for desperate measures. But it was the middle of the afternoon. And while the morning's clouds still hadn't burned off, it was daylight.

Never mind the fact that Main Street was called Main Street precisely because it was the most heavily trafficked street in town.

"We could break in," Nikki repeated, a little louder this time, like it was more reasonable for her to project her illegal intentions than it was for Jess to dare question them. "Like, enter on our own terms. Force our way inside. Do you really not understand the meaning of that phrase?"

"What I don't understand is how you propose doing that without getting caught. Should I hold up a sheet for you while you attempt to pick the lock? Or are we just going to smash a brick through the window and hope everyone has their noise-canceling Beats on?"

Nikki squinted at her like Jess was the one being ridiculous. "Old Man Burnham owns the clock shop next door. You really think he has Beats?"

"I wasn't saying . . ." Jess shook her head. "That really wasn't the point I was trying to make."

"Whatever." Nikki spun on her heel and started running, slowing only long enough to turn and shout, "Come on!"

Against her better judgment, Jess followed. They cut through the town square, tracing their way back up a parallel street. Jess wanted to shout, demand to know where they were going, but she suspected they were attracting enough attention without the added noise. If they managed to make it through this day without being arrested, she was going to insist that Nikki trade in her pointy-heeled boots for a pair of sneakers. She flinched as the vision of one of those heels lodged in her throat flashed through her mind. She reconsidered; Nikki was a grown woman. It was probably best to avoid weighing in on her fashion choices.

They slowed to a stop near a dumpster next to a discarded keg with an ashtray on top, likely left for both staff and patrons who needed a smoke. It had to be the back of the bar. It was darker here, more shaded. Even if a car did drive up the tiny street, the two of them would be mostly obscured from view by the dumpster.

"Pick the lock," Nikki said, pointing toward the door.

Jess squinted at her, then the door. There were two locks, actually. Luckily, the steel door on the outside wasn't fully closed, but the wooden one was. *Still.* "How am I supposed to do that? The closest I've ever come to crime is editing fictional stories about it."

Nikki looked at her in a way that said, *You certainly didn't have a problem stealing my boyfriend.*

Jess flinched, even though she knew she was interpreting Nikki's look through a prism of guilt—however unwarranted said guilt might be. In actuality, Nikki was probably just communicating her annoyance at Jess's lack of initiative. Or wondering how she'd gotten stuck with such a useless teammate. Regardless, Jess walked quietly to the door and twisted the handle. She certainly didn't expect it to turn. So she barely thought it through when her hand continued to rotate. She pushed the door open out of pure habit.

Her eyes widened when she realized what she'd done, and she turned to Nikki, who was attempting to hide her own surprise.

"Well," Nikki said, pushing past her, "I guess nobody

can accuse us of breaking and entering now. Not if all we do is enter."

"Wait." Jess was relieved when Nikki paused and turned to look at her. "This seems like a bad idea."

"What? Them leaving the door open?" Nikki smiled evilly. "I agree. We're going to rob them blind."

She disappeared down the dark hallway, leaving Jess to stare reluctantly after her. Jess's stomach lurched, twisting into a dense, lumpy pretzel. She should leave. She wanted to. But she knew she wouldn't.

She was built to be a part of a team. It was how she'd grown up. It had always been her and her dad, unbreakable partners. Then she'd joined forces with Liz, the two of them taking on adolescence together. Now, for better or worse—clearly, unquestionably worse—she'd agreed to a new partnership. At the very least, she needed to make sure the Staple was left exactly how Nikki found it. It was her job as a teammate.

She pulled out her phone and shot a quick text to Liz. I'm pretty sure Nikki is going to lead me into prison. If I end up doing hard time, you have my permission to anoint someone else Kai's godmother. She stared at the screen for a couple of moments, even though she knew it would be hours before she got a reply.

A few years ago, a message like this would've received an immediate response. Even when she and Liz had been at different colleges, it had sometimes felt like they were still able to spend every moment together. Not anymore, though. Not since Liz had braved motherhood and the effort to build a new life in a new town, all in the same few months.

For the moment, Liz's old life had rightfully been shifted to the back burner—Jess included. It had to happen, but the result had been difficult. As glad as Jess was that Liz's life had gotten so full, she couldn't help feeling the trade-off was that hers had gotten emptier.

With a sigh, Jess plunged through the door to find Nikki.

It was dim inside the Staple. The lights were off, but enough sunlight seeped through the closed blinds that Jess could see clearly. The bar looked bigger and felt colder without bodies hunched over tables and propped against the bar. Without the country music crooning through the speakers, the silence was eerie, punctuated by the little noises of old buildings.

Nikki had disappeared.

Jess crept forward, peeking into the back office that faced the bar. It was a tiny room with a cat calendar, three years out of date, on the wall. The desk was bare, save for a closed laptop and a pile of Girl Scout cookie boxes. If there was a safe inside, Nikki didn't appear to have found it. There was no way she could've broken into one that quickly, not if she didn't even know how to pick a door lock. With a sigh of relief, Jess continued past the service area at the end of the bar and pushed open the door to the kitchen. It smelled like bleach, and the lack of blinds made it brighter than the rest of the bar.

"See if there are more forks in the drying rack," Nikki said from the counter without looking up. She pulled another handful of forks from the drawer, dropping them onto the steel table with a clatter.

"Could you maybe keep it down?" Jess whispered but did

as Nikki said, going over to the drying rack and searching through the newly washed silverware.

"I probably *could*." Nikki reached for a large bag of chips, ripping it open and shoving a handful into her mouth. She crunched them loudly.

"A new bag?" Jess shook her head. There was an open bag of salt and vinegar chips that was already half empty right next to her. "Really, Nikki? They're going to notice that someone's been in here."

"Oh no. Think of the investigation that'll spark. Do you want me to burn off the tips of your fingers so you don't leave any prints behind?"

"Funny." Jess checked the pile to make sure she hadn't missed any of the forks. She'd only found seven. "How many do you have over there?"

"Chips? Sadly, not enough to share with you."

"Forks." Jess's stomach growled, and she sternly informed it that it would not be receiving any stolen chips. "Remember those? The reason we're here?"

"Shhh. I'm counting."

Jess looked around the room. It was more organized than she would've expected for a dive bar like the Staple. Loaves of bread were stacked neatly on a table next to hamburger buns. Her stomach growled, and she couldn't help herself; she set the forks on a countertop and slid over to the refrigerator.

The interior light felt like a spotlight when she opened the door, but her delight at the spoils inside overwhelmed the little voice inside her warning that breaking and entering was about to officially become theft. She was just so hungry, and there were stacks upon stacks of deli meat

inside, as well as multiple jellies to complement the enormous tubs of peanut butter on the counter. She could feed a
family of fifteen without putting a dent in the food.

With a hum of anticipation, she balanced the meats in
one hand, leaning the stack against her chest, and used her
free hand to grab one of the peanut butters. Staggering, she
pivoted quickly and let it all tumble onto the table in the
center of the room.

"What are you doing?" Nikki asked as Jess turned back,
catching the refrigerator door just before it swung closed.

"Looking for cheese," Jess mumbled as she scanned the
shelves. "They have to have cheese, right?"

"I have forty-one forks here."

"Great!" Jess attempted to direct her excitement toward
their goal, but it was clear she was more focused on the
drawer she'd just opened. Gleefully, she pulled out several
different kinds of cheese and tossed them onto the table
next to the meats before she began collecting condiments
and jellies.

"Is there anything left in that fridge, or have you emptied it entirely?" Nikki abandoned the forks and sidled over
to Jess, bringing the enormous bag of chips with her.

"If this isn't enough variety, open it up and search for
yourself." Jess's fear of Nikki seemed to have gone the way of
her fear of getting caught, thoroughly overshadowed by the
mound of food she'd collected. "I'm already struggling to
choose between these. Ham and pepper jack sounds good,
but turkey and swiss is a classic for a reason. And what about
peanut butter and jelly? You can never go wrong with a
PB&J."

What Jess really meant was that she wanted that strawberry jam filled with chunks of real fruit. She only had smooth gelatinous jelly in her fridge, because that's what her dad had always had in his. He claimed not to like the crunch of the seeds, but Jess suspected his aversion sprung more from the fact that Jess's mom had loved jam, the chunkier the better, and had been immortalized in one of the few pictures they had of her eating it directly from the jar as dessert.

So, the Reids were a jelly family. Not because her dad would've cared if Jess shared her mom's taste in preserves but because Jess didn't want to have anything in common with a woman who was capable of so easily abandoning the family who loved her. Jess didn't need those pretentious gobs of fruit when chunky peanut butter offered plenty of crunch on its own. Then again, if it just happened to be there, if she hadn't bought it herself . . . well, that was what was known as a *loophole*.

"Why choose?" Nikki grabbed a loaf of bread and pulled out a handful of slices, spreading them across the counter without bothering to put even a paper towel underneath. "Start stacking."

They made six sandwiches total. One peanut butter and jelly with grape jelly and another with strawberry jam. One ham and pepper jack, one turkey and swiss, one roast beef and cheddar, and one with all the meats, all the cheeses, and a handful of salt and vinegar chips crushed inside. Nikki grabbed a large knife, only swinging it in Jess's direction a couple of times before using it to cut all the sandwiches in half.

"Eat fast," Nikki ordered, grabbing the fattest sandwich with everything on it and taking a large bite. Through a full mouth, she added, "We still have seven pictures to get."

Despite the allure of the strawberry jelly, Jess started with the other half of Nikki's sandwich. She rarely kept fresh meats and cheeses in her fridge. They were too likely to go bad before she could eat them. She was always getting lost in one of her stories, hunched over her laptop until the growl of her stomach was so loud it seemed smarter to appease it with a Clif bar than take the time to assemble anything.

She also liked the idea that she and Nikki were sharing something. Not that she'd dare say that aloud. It just seemed nice, like the kind of thing they'd do if they'd chosen to be a team instead of being forced into it. As she chewed, she pulled the list out of her bag and set it between them. They still hadn't been able to figure number eleven out.

"**A blend of many colors**," she said, reading it aloud, "**all of which are brown**."

"It doesn't even make any sense," Nikki said. "How can it be many colors if it's just brown?"

"How can we be serving lunch," a male voice said from the doorway as the kitchen lights flared on, "if the bar is closed?"

Jess froze, a hunk of sandwich heavy on her tongue. Nikki, on the other hand, reached for the knife still lying beside her and whirled toward the door.

"Easy, girl." Bryce laughed, entering the kitchen with his hands held up. Carter followed him, looking significantly less amused by the sight of the two women. "Right now, you're just looking at a few years in jail for armed robbery, but if you kill us, the sentence is going to be a lot longer."

Jess inhaled sharply, and bits of sandwich slid down her throat. She began to cough, but three kinds of cheese and as many meats were blocking her breath. Her eyes bulged and her face caught fire as she attempted to hack it up. Panic infused her. This was instant karma. She'd been sentenced for their crime—it was going to be the death penalty for her. Nikki would merely end up in a cell, where she'd likely intimidate a guard into falling in love with her, and he'd inevitably slip her the keys so she could escape to a beach in a country with no extradition laws. Life was so unfair. She'd only wanted a sandwich, and she'd fully intended to sneak a twenty into Bryce's tip jar before they left.

Carter crossed the kitchen in long strides, swift but unpanicked, stepping in behind her and wrapping his arms around her chest. She leaned back, pressing into him. She'd noticed the sharp lines beneath his shirt the other day at the bar, but she hadn't expected him to feel so hard against her back. His fist went to the plate of bones between her breasts and stilled for a single moment before jerking inward. A whoosh of air rose from her chest, sending meat and cheese flying over the table to splat onto the middle with a disgusting sound.

Jess thought she might've preferred death. Unsurprisingly, Nikki burst into delighted laughter. A few flecks of food flew from her mouth as well, but unlike Jess, she didn't seem to feel any shame at the sight of them. Carter took a step back from them both.

"Thank you," Jess cried out, turning to him first and then continuing to pivot until she was facing Bryce. "And I'm so sorry. We just needed to take a picture of your forks."

"And you thought we might keep them submerged in peanut butter?" Bryce leaned against the metal counter and surveyed the mounds of food they hadn't yet bothered putting away.

Why hadn't they at least put the meat and cheese away as soon as they'd finished making the sandwiches? Jess was horrified that they'd been so careless with food that didn't even belong to them. Food meant to serve others. What if the turkey had begun to turn already? Or the cheese had gotten hard along the edges in the few minutes it had been out? And had they really needed to make *so many* sandwiches?

"No. We just . . ." As soon as the words were out, Jess gave up on the excuse, realizing there was no justification.

Nikki, naturally, was armed with a whole list of justifications. "We were hungry! And it's not like there's anywhere else in town to get food. Have you been by the diner yet? It's closed because everyone in Redford is more concerned with winning the prize money than doing their jobs!" Nikki threw her hands up in outrage. "And then you have the nerve to close this place, too? You're lucky people aren't knocking down the doors and taking the bar by storm simply to survive."

"I do feel lucky," Bryce said, nodding agreeably. "I mean, I stupidly assumed people might just go home to eat. Or even walk a few doors down to the market."

"I, for one," Carter said, "am impressed by your commitment to variety. No ingredient left behind."

Jess let out a little bark of laughter. They really had used everything in the kitchen that was small enough to fit on bread.

"It's too bad we were interrupted in the middle of enjoying the assortment," Nikki said sharply, causing Jess to laugh again.

Jess looked at Carter and Bryce and caught them snickering, too. It was just so very Nikki Loughton to act like they'd somehow inconvenienced her. Really, though. How dare Bryce show up at his own place of business when she was in the process of robbing him? And Carter, running around saving Jess from choking to death like some kind of hero? *Such* an annoyance.

"What've you got here anyway?" Bryce crossed the kitchen and grabbed a handful of chips as he surveyed the sandwiches.

"You can have half of a peanut butter one," Nikki offered magnanimously. "But only the one with the grape jelly."

Bryce nodded and used his free hand to snake one of the halves with ham. Carter squeezed in between him and Jess and plucked a half with roast beef and cheddar. His arm brushed against hers as he pulled it back, and her pulse picked up speed at the memory of how his arms had felt wrapped around her. His muscles had felt ropy, like he got them from scaling mountains or rowing boats instead of lifting weights at the gym.

But every time she'd seen him, including today, he was wearing a button-up shirt and a pair of dress slacks made from the types of materials that carried a sheen as testament to their quality. They were the kind of clothes that belonged behind a desk in an office with a good view and an assistant who guarded the door. Jess couldn't picture him sweating in the way muscles like those would indicate. He smelled too good. She inhaled covertly. Rich spices and the scent of leather filled her nose, tempered with the smell of the woods, like he'd been infused with the arriving fall season.

"You figured out question eight?" he asked, turning toward her.

"Eight?" Jess blinked at him, still caught up in trying to figure out exactly who he was. The need to define everyone like she would a character in a book was a flaw of hers. You couldn't monitor characters without bringing a little of that into the real world, though. Her friends always argued that people weren't so black and white, but in her experience, they did tend to follow a pattern. And she might not understand how all of Carter's pieces fit together, but she could still spot connecting lines between them: He was disciplined and driven. He wasn't a man who did things by halves.

"The forks." He tilted his chin toward the pile of forks Nikki had left on the counter behind them. "I'm assuming you didn't pull them out to eat sandwiches with."

"Oh." She shook her head, more to focus than to answer the question he hadn't really asked. "Yeah. We still have to take a picture with them. If Bryce will let us, that is."

"Why wouldn't Bryce let us?" Nikki demanded.

"Maybe because you've entered my place of business illegally?" Bryce grinned in that easy way that made it impossible to argue. "Or maybe because we're competing against you, and it would benefit us to slow you down?"

"But we've made lunch for you," Nikki said, neatly adjusting the facts to suit her purpose. "Think of the time we've saved you by doing that."

"Hmm," Bryce murmured, clearly unconvinced.

"If you think about it, you've already slowed us down," Nikki said. "So it would be unsporting and, frankly, pretty dick-ish for you to slow us down even more."

"Interesting strategy," Carter said, nodding thoughtfully. "It's never occurred to me to call someone a dick while asking them for a favor."

"First of all, I didn't *call* Bryce anything. I used an adjective to describe a behavior, as Mrs. Evanston taught us—"

"What if we helped each other out?" Jess spoke loudly, cutting Nikki off before she could dig them both deeper into her hole. "You let us take a picture with the forks, and we help you figure out one of the items you're struggling with."

"You mean figure out what it is, not help us get the picture?" Carter cocked an eyebrow when she nodded, his dark eyes flashing with amusement. "So, you just assume that you've been able to figure out something we haven't?"

Jess cocked an eyebrow back at him. "Are you really so arrogant that you can't fathom that people have different bases of knowledge?"

Jess struggled to hold in her grin as she waited for his return volley. The air between them felt like it had hummed to life. After hours of being the punching bag for her own teammate, it was fun to engage in some healthy competition with another team.

"It's not that." Carter smiled smugly. "It's just that we've already figured out all of the answers. Now all we have to do is get the rest of the pictures."

"Crap." The word slipped out before Jess could stop it. They'd figured out *all* the clues? She and Nikki still had at least three that were tripping them up.

Bryce laughed and shoved the rest of the sandwich into his mouth.

Nikki's gaze flicked back and forth between the two men, her eyes narrowing. "Nope," she declared after a moment of studying them. "The fancy one's lying. The bartender's never been any good at that, which is why he put enough food in his mouth to choke a hippo."

Bryce laughed. Or coughed. Or maybe he was choking. Whatever it was, it definitely resembled guilt.

"Really?" Jess turned to Carter.

"There's no such thing as lying when it comes to competition." Carter shrugged off her look of disapproval. "It's called bluffing."

Right. Jess's hands went to her hips. She'd been forgetting that friendly competition was unlikely when millions of dollars were at stake. She and Nikki could use Bryce and Carter, but they should never be foolish enough to trust them.

"All right." Jess nodded slowly. "So, tell us then. What don't you know?"

Carter's head tilted appraisingly. "I don't know why you didn't tell me that Mrs. Loveling would allow me to check in early."

Jess flushed with mortification. How had she thought he wouldn't figure it out? Mrs. Loveling had probably been waiting for him with a plate of homemade brownies, clearly desperate for him to arrive. Jess searched his face for annoyance, but his dark eyes gave nothing away. They just focused on her with an unwavering gaze that made her skin grow even hotter. Then, so quickly she almost missed it, one corner of his mouth flicked up.

He was messing with her.

She stifled the relieved laughter that tried to bubble out of her, and was almost able to keep her expression blank. Not as blank as his, of course—nobody was capable of that—but as expressionless as someone like her could be.

"Did you not enjoy your tour?" she asked, allowing a bit of feigned confusion to seep through.

"How could I not enjoy it?" The corner of Carter's mouth twitched again. "I got to learn about a pastry war and some fish guy's unrequited crush on the town librarian."

"The standard details included in any official tour of the town," Jess agreed. "I usually charge for my skills as a guide, you know. You're lucky I was volunteering for Redford's Welcome Wagon that day."

"Oh, trust me, I know. And that's exactly what I told Mrs. Loveling when I checked in," Carter said smoothly. "That I just got lucky with Jessica Reid."

Jess's mind translated the words, and her stomach somersaulted. The two of them. Getting . . . lucky. Images flashed through her mind, and her face grew warm, undoubtedly turning an unflattering shade of red.

"What?" Carter mimicked her feigned confusion from earlier so perfectly she could almost believe she was the only one with a dirty mind. "Did I say that wrong?"

"You're definitely focusing on the wrong thing," Nikki

said, squinting at them in confused annoyance as she grabbed another chip. "I don't know why you're talking about town tours and fish men when we're trying to figure out what clues you're still working on."

"What's a fish man?" Bryce asked through a full mouth.

Carter looked at Jess and lifted his eyebrows. She grinned at the silent prompt and resisted the urge to point out that he was the one who had come up with such a ridiculous description. They needed to focus.

"I think Carter was referring to Marty Beauford," she said. "Apparently, Carter thinks the technical term for owning a bait shop is *fish man*."

Nikki tilted her head thoughtfully. "Wouldn't that make him a worm man?"

"Moving on," Jess said firmly. "What clues are you guys still working on?"

Carter cleared his throat meaningfully.

"That equation," Bryce said, either not catching Carter's signal or choosing to ignore it. "The one that has equal signs next to the words. Do words have some secret numerical value?"

Jess knew immediately which one he was talking about.

War = _____
Freedom = _____
Ignorance = _____

Nikki knew, too. The two of them had already strategized over that one, which was why Nikki held up a hand to silence Jess.

"The thing is," Nikki said, "we've already figured out that we needed thirty forks, and we've already collected them, too. All we need is a quick picture with them. But you haven't figured out the answer *or* how to get the picture, so I'm not entirely convinced this is a fair trade."

"We'll get the picture on our own, though," Carter said. "It's an equal swap. A picture for an answer."

"You might think that, but you're wrong," Jess said, picking up on Nikki's implication. She and Nikki had already stopped by the library and discovered it closed like everything else in town.

War is peace. Freedom is slavery. Ignorance is strength. It was a quote from George Orwell's *1984*. And Jess just happened to have an old copy of the book at home.

"You won't be able to get the picture without us," Nikki said.

"Oh, you know that, do you?" Carter tilted his chin back, clearly unconvinced.

"What are you suggesting?" Bryce said.

"We give you the answer and a picture," Jess said. "And in return—"

"You give us the same," Nikki interrupted. "One answer and a picture."

"What about the fork picture?" Carter asked.

"It doesn't need to enter the negotiations," Nikki said. "We were always going to get that anyway."

"But Bryce—" Carter said.

"Was going to stop us?" Nikki said, cutting him off. She smiled sweetly at Bryce. "Let's see you try."

"Pass," Bryce said without hesitation. He reached for

another sandwich, ignoring Carter's grunt of protest. Bryce had never been the type to voluntarily engage in battle.

"Fine," Carter said with a sigh. "We'll help you, and you'll help us. Do we have a deal?"

Jess glanced at Nikki, who nodded.

"We have a deal," Jess agreed.

Bryce gave an approving whoop and stuck out his hand. "Shake on it?"

Jess thought about Carter's reminder that this was a competition.

"Nah." Jess did her best imitation of Nikki's terrifying smile. "There's no point in pretending to be allies when we fully intend to use you and lose you."

Bryce just shrugged, but Carter tilted his head and looked at her with interest.

His mouth curled in a half-smile as he said, "Noted."

Chapter 9

· · · · · · · · · ·

CARTER

Carter hesitated before taking the picture of the women with their thirty forks. It didn't seem like Nikki should be aiming one toward Jess's eye in such a threatening manner. Novak had been very clear about the fact that all rulings were solely at his discretion, and Carter wouldn't put it past him to render a submission invalid simply because he found it tasteless or even potentially criminal. On the other hand, this was a competition, so why should he bother worrying about another team? If he were really being smart, he'd "accidentally" cover the lens so the photo didn't count at all.

He couldn't do that, though. Everyone in town already thought he was a cheater. Proving them right was unlikely to help the situation.

"Got it," he said, despite the obvious sound of the button clicking. "Your turn."

Nikki jabbed the fork a little closer to Jess's face before finally tossing it into the open drawer. It was impressive that Jess managed not to flinch. Carter was beginning to believe she was the real poker player in the room. Bluffing on both sides. Pretending to be an enemy to his team and a confident member of her own. She made him nervous. Everyone knew the most dangerous competition was someone who thought differently than you. It made it impossible to predict their moves.

And what was with the change in hairstyle since this morning? It made no sense that Jess had taken time away from the game to get it cut. He could only assume the new sexy, shaggy style was a strategic move, designed to drive shallow men like him to distraction. Next thing he knew, she'd be trading in the fuzzy sweater for a low V-cut and rendering him a drooling idiot with her cleavage.

"Gentlemen first," Nikki said. She watched Jess cross the kitchen and rolled her eyes as Jess began to put their lunch ingredients back into the fridge. "We need the answer to number eleven."

Carter immediately knew which one that was because it was the very reason they'd come to the bar. Well, that, and to get the same picture with the forks the women had beaten them to. **A blend of many colors, all of which are brown.** If he gave them the answer now, there would be no incentive for the women to fulfill their end of the agreement. He looked to Bryce to see if he shared the same doubts, but the bartender's expression was as easygoing and devoid of suspicion as ever.

"Johnnie Walker," Bryce offered, without bothering to look at Carter. "Blended Scotch whisky. Red Label, Blue Label, Green Label, etc. We can get the picture here."

Well, that was settled. Now, they'd just have to rely on

the honor of two women who they'd just caught in the middle of a burglary. If Novak was giving bonus points for stupidity, Carter expected he and Bryce would receive several.

They all followed Bryce to the serving side of the bar, watching as he pulled out five bottles and lined them across the scarred wood.

"Ooh, gold," Jess said, eyeing the bottle on the end. "Is that the most expensive one?"

Nikki scoffed. "Gold is swill compared to blue."

It was a wild exaggeration but a sentiment Carter couldn't help appreciating. A shared love of scotch was not a reason to like someone. Especially not a hellion in heels like this woman. But facts were facts. Blue *was* far superior, and anyone who knew the difference deserved his respect.

"Gold is the most expensive one we have, though," Bryce said to Jess. "Blue is a little too rare to be found in these parts."

Carter averted his eyes as he thought of the bottle of blue he'd cracked open at his grandfather's house after the funeral. He'd only had one glass—it had been beyond depressing to sit there drinking alone—but it had tasted amazing. Like long chats with his grandfather on the phone and the satisfaction that came from settling on the next person they would secretly help.

When he'd taken the last sip, Carter had sat there for a while, the crystal glass dangling from his hand. Maybe he had chosen wrong in staying at the B&B. It was silly to pay to be annoyed by Mrs. Loveling when he could've had his grandfather's mansion to himself. But it had never been a place he wanted to visit, not once he'd found the pictures of it online. It was too much like the home Carter had grown up in, so large that he knew it would hold the winter chill, even deep into the heat of summer. Just as he'd suspected, it felt painfully still.

No. Not just still. *Lifeless.*

"Pour her a taste," Nikki said, widening her eyes and shaking her head like Bryce had failed some obvious standard of politeness.

"Oh!" Jess took a step back. "No, thank you. Whiskey isn't really my thing. That would just be wasted on me."

"She's clearly never had it." Smoothly, Nikki lifted four glasses off a stack and slid them to Bryce. "As a bartender, it's your duty to show her what she's been missing."

"And I need four glasses to do that?" Bryce pulled the bottle away from her.

"Well, as long as it's open, the rest of us might as well have a sip, too." Nikki held out her thumb and forefinger, squeezing them so close together they were almost touching. "A tiny sip, obviously."

"Obviously," Bryce said dryly.

Still, he pulled the glasses apart and lined them up on the bar.

"Really," Jess said, beginning to look a little anxious, "don't bother pouring one for me. I wouldn't know the difference between a good whiskey and a bad one."

"You heard her." Carter knew better than to pressure a woman to drink—there was still such a thing as chivalry, and he was certain this fell shamefully below the mark—but they weren't just talking about whiskey. It was scotch. And nobody should go their entire life without experiencing the difference. "An education is required. Let's start with red. We'll have to work our way up to gold."

Nikki gave a little whoop of approval, and Bryce laughed and grabbed the bottle. He poured a generous taste into each glass and gave them a serious look.

"Knock it back," he commanded. "We've got four more to try and a scavenger hunt to return to."

Carter nodded and lifted his glass into the air. "To joining teams."

"To winning!" Nikki slammed her glass into his before butting it against the others and tilting it to her mouth.

"To joining teams," Jess said, clinking her glass softly against his and Bryce's.

Carter smiled at the fact that she'd gone with his toast over Nikki's, and at the way her nose crinkled when she lifted the glass to it. He waited until she took a reluctant sip before drinking his.

It felt like he was tasting it for the first time.

········

THE WALK TO Jess's house wasn't far, but the two teams' progress was slowed by the effects of five glasses of scotch. Not that the liquor had affected Carter. He had only stumbled because of a crack in the sidewalk. He was used to drinking scotch. It was little more than water to him. Granted, he was more the type to sip at it than to pound the equivalent of five shots in fifteen minutes, but that was mere semantics. Scotch was his friend. He loved it. And it loved him back.

Really, though—was Redford always this pretty? It looked like it belonged in a commercial. For apples. Or bikes. Something wholesome like that. It was colorful in a way that Atlanta—despite its graffiti and neon lights—never managed to be. It was more than the changing trees and the painted houses, though. The sky felt larger here. And the sun had finally burned through the clouds, turning the day a brilliant blue. Carter wondered if he still had a pair of sunglasses in his car. He probably didn't need them, though. He could feel his eyelids drooping slightly, like shades being tilted.

In front of him, Nikki was riding on Bryce's back. Bryce had hoisted her up there after she'd started stopping at each mailbox they passed, wobbling in front of them as she riffled through their contents. Next to Carter, Jess was weaving her way down the sidewalk, focusing very intently on the ground. He was tempted to put his hand on her back, to make sure that she stayed upright. He couldn't do it, though. He already felt guilty for pushing for the taste test—although, in his defense, he certainly hadn't expected such generous pours from Bryce, nor for everyone to be quite so thorough (and enthusiastically *efficient*) about emptying their glasses—and he wouldn't risk doing anything that might feel like he was taking advantage of her inebriated state. Especially not after the way she'd blushed earlier when he'd mentioned getting lucky. He hadn't put any thought into the comment, but her response to it had caused him to think extensively about all the ways he could make her blush again. He snuck a look at her just as she began to clap her hands in delight.

"Elvis!" she cried. "Hi!"

Fantastic. He'd peer-pressured the woman into a state of hallucination. And now she thought it was 1957. In fairness, Redford did have a bit of a trapped-in-time quality.

Carter watched in dismay as Jess hit the ground, her legs crossing in front of her in a surprisingly graceful way. A dog bounded into her lap.

Oh.

"Elvis?" Carter reached down, petting the fox terrier. Its fur was a funny mixture of black, brown, and white, and coarse to the touch. The dog put paws on both Jess's shoulders like a clumsy dancer. A short, stocky woman, presumably the dog's owner, hurried toward them. Jess giggled as Elvis attempted to lick her face.

"Bad boy." The woman shook her head. "You leave that girl alone."

Her tone didn't match the words. Instead, it conveyed something more along the lines of, *You are the cutest dog in all of existence. Feel free to have that girl as a snack if it might make you happy.*

Jess pressed her forehead into the side of the dog's face, cooing unintelligibly, and Carter fought back the smile that tugged at his mouth. Her new bangs made more sense now; he and Bryce had only been allied with her for about half an hour, and he'd already found himself indulging in a five-part taste test, becoming uncharacteristically drunk, and was now stalled on the sidewalk while she settled into a cuddle-fest with someone else's dog. As far as race partners went, he seemed to have attached himself to the tortoise instead of the hare.

Funnily, hearing that story growing up, he'd never once pictured the tortoise as quite such a charming character.

"And you must be the grandson." The woman turned her attention to Carter, studying him curiously. Her cool demeanor didn't fit with the deep laugh lines grooved into her face.

Like the rest of the town, she must suspect he was a cheater.

It was fine. Carter knew he'd grown accustomed to an unnatural level of trust from near strangers because of his chosen career field. Clients couldn't let him handle their money without it. It was only natural that blatant distrust might leave him feeling a little . . . unsettled.

"Carter Barclay," he said, nodding politely.

"Sally Parker." Her nod was curt.

"The muffin maker!" His words came out embarrassingly enthusiastic, and he quickly adjusted his voice to a deeper tone. It was simply nice to recognize someone, even if he *had* never seen them before. Redford felt like a bedtime story told by his grandfather year after year, and now another of its characters had come to life.

He peered more closely at her, comparing her to the picture he'd formed from the stories. In appearance, she was as opposite from Luanne as a person could be. Her face shared none of Luanne's angles. Instead, it was round and bare, save for a smattering of freckles across the bridge of her nose. She wore sweats and a T-shirt, and where Luanne looked like she might bend in the wind, Sally's stocky, muscular build suggested that she wouldn't be moved unless she chose to be. Not that she looked rigid. Solid might be a more accurate description. Comfortable. Her hair was fluffy and tinted a light purple color.

"I've heard you're very talented," he said.

"Have you, now?" Sally looked pleased in spite of herself. "Well, you've heard correctly. I wonder if the same could be said of what I've heard about you."

That Novak was going to make sure he won the game? *No. Of course not.*

Except Carter couldn't say that. Not when he was ninety-five percent positive that what she'd heard was right and he was, in fact, being set up to win. Still, Jasper would want the other players to enjoy the game, and they couldn't do that if they knew they were going to lose. It was in everyone's best interest if he kept the truth to himself.

"If you're referring to the rumor that I roam the streets at night thwarting evildoers and rescuing innocents," Carter said, his buzz from the scotch tasting clearly impeding his ability to extricate himself from her unspoken accusation in a more normal manner, "then yes. It's accurate."

The smile lines in Sally's face finally deepened. "Well, I knew that. I was referring to the parrot you're rumored to have as a sidekick. How do you keep him quiet when you're staking out an evildoer's lair?"

"I give him bubblegum," Carter said. "He loves Bubblicious, but only the original. He won't tolerate any flavor other than pink."

"A purist." Sally gave a bark of laughter, causing Jess to look up. "I respect that."

"Are you doing the scavenger hunt?" Jess asked Sally.

Up ahead, Nikki arched away from Bryce's back so she

could slap his butt while she shouted, "Giddyup." Obediently, he began to trot down the sidewalk.

"Yep," Sally said with an amused shake of her head. Then her face tightened. "And I got paired with Luanne, of all people. She suggested I take Elvis out while she grabs something from Evangeline's. Like she couldn't possibly take me with her to her precious bakery. Like I'm going to steal one of her recipes for dried-out cake or flavorless icing."

"You can't pretend her cakes are anything other than delicious," Jess said. Her sternness was undermined by the way she pressed her cheek against Elvis's.

"Actually, I can. We both know Luanne is a master at icing, but just watch me claim it needs to be fluffier with a perfectly straight face. I'm excellent at lying."

Jess laughed and rubbed the dog's ears vigorously. "Can I stop by later, after we've both turned in all of our pictures to Novak? I ordered a Halloween costume for Elvis a couple of weeks ago, and it finally showed up."

"Is it a lion mane?" Sally's eyes lit up. "You know I love when people dress their dogs like lions."

"It's even funnier," Jess said.

"Not possible."

"We'll see. I'll text you when I'm walking back from the square."

"Actually," Sally said, "why don't you come over now? I have exclusive access to one of the items you need a picture of."

"Exclusive access?" Jess's eyes darted back and forth with thought. "Wait. Not number seven?"

Carter leaned forward, eager for any hint they might let slip. He knew number seven by heart because he and Bryce hadn't been able to figure it out, either. Unfortunately, Bryce did not seem to have much retention for the town's history.

The fallen king's head, once lifted and presiding over celebratory toasts. Now hidden away with the rest of the ghosts.

"You couldn't have," Jess decided. But her eager expression begged to be proven wrong.

"I could've," Sally said smugly. Her finger went to her lips in warning. "Not that I would ever admit it."

"Admit what?" Jess mimed zipping her lips and throwing away the key. Elvis barked and raced off to retrieve the invisible item.

"What are we talking about?" Carter asked.

"Nothing," Sally said quickly.

Apparently, his superhero claims hadn't won her over as much as he'd hoped.

"You can't tell me without telling him, too," Jess said. "Our teams have temporarily joined forces, and I owe him an answer."

Carter searched Jess's face. Was she so drunk that she'd forgotten they were supposed to be on their way to her father's house to take a picture of the answer she owed him? Her cheeks were flushed dark pink, and her eyes were unmistakably glassy. While he was inspecting them for answers, though, one of her eyelids dropped in an exaggerated wink. Jess grinned impishly, and he was so surprised that he almost laughed out loud.

"We have an alliance," Carter agreed, fighting to keep

the amusement out of his voice. "She can't hold out on me without breaking its terms."

"I don't know." Sally crossed her arms over her chest, looking back and forth between them before focusing on Jess. "If you win, I know you'd toss me a little bonus for helping you get there, but him? I wouldn't trust him not to run over me on his way out of town."

"I can hear you," Carter said.

"Shh." Sally waved him off. "The women are talking."

"'The fallen king's head' refers to a mounted buck head that used to be on the wall at the Staple," Jess said to Carter. "People used to toss their hats on it or balance unlit cigarettes in its mouth or pretend to feed it beer. Then one day it disappeared. In its place, there was a note on the wall saying it had gone to a place where it would be better respected."

Carter laughed.

"And it did," Sally said proudly. "After I washed all the stickiness out of its fur, I set it up in my basement, where it hasn't had a single dart thrown at it since."

"Nice," Carter said.

Sally must've heard the appreciation in his tone because she gave him an approving look. "Nobody else knows, so we'll be the only teams who get the picture. I assume I can count on you keeping my secret?"

"Of course," Carter said sincerely. "But why would you help us when your team could be the only one to get every single picture? Surely, that would guarantee that you win this round."

"This round, maybe," Sally said. "But Novak said there will be other rounds, and it's always possible—though, obviously, unlikely—that I won't come out on top every time. Like I said, if I help you out, I expect a little kickback if one of your teams wins."

"It's a reasonable enough strategy," Jess said, looking at her in a way Carter didn't understand. "I just wish that was really the reason you were doing it."

Sally grinned wickedly, and Carter was certain he was missing something.

"She likes you," Jess whispered a few minutes later when they'd caught up to Bryce and Nikki and all four of them were following Sally to her basement.

"She's tolerating me for your sake," Carter whispered back. Still, he felt pleased by Jess's take on the situation. It felt promising, like he had a chance of being something other than an outsider in this tight-knit little town.

"No, she definitely does," Jess said with a mischievous smirk. "And this morning you won over Luanne, so that makes two people in town who have decided to like you. It's just too bad Luanne is going to find out that Sally helped you complete the challenge."

"What?" Carter braced himself for an answer he knew couldn't be good. "Why is that too bad?"

"Think about it, Carter. Does it make any sense at all that Sally would give up a guaranteed lead? She's not doing it for practical reasons. She's doing it for emotional ones."

Carter felt like he should understand what she was alluding to, but he was drawing a blank. Was there an emotional element to a scavenger hunt?

"Such as?" he asked.

"Luanne hurt Sally's feelings when she wouldn't take her

to the bakery. But Sally would never admit that she cared enough to be upset, so she won't say anything. Instead, she's acting out, hurting Luanne's chance to win by helping us."

"Sally's trying to make her mad," Carter said, realization finally landing, "because she can't fight with Luanne about what she's really upset about without admitting that she cares."

"And it will work. Luanne is going to be furious." Jess grinned and slapped him on the back like an overenthusiastic football coach. "Congratulations, sport. You just became a player in one of Redford's biggest feuds."

Chapter 10

··········

NIKKI

Twenty minutes later, Carter, Bryce, Jess, and Nikki were all in Jess's childhood house searching for the book they'd promised to drop at Sally's as soon as they'd gotten a picture of it. The bedroom looked exactly how Nikki had imagined it would. *Cluttered* was one word for it—Nikki's question of why Jess hadn't taken her books to her new house no longer needed to be voiced. The answer was not only there in the overstuffed bookshelves but also piled into little stacks that were scattered across the floor. It was a mystery how a teenage Jess had found the time to read this many novels and still attend parties where she made out with other girls' boyfriends.

The bigger mystery, however, was how a bedspread could have that many colors in it yet still clash so terribly with her curtains. It was as if Jess wanted her room to be as absurd as possible. That shouldn't come as a surprise, though. She had always channeled a wildly ridiculous vibe. The oft-referenced tutu. The uneven haircuts Liz bragged about giving her. Blue eyeshadow—did Jess not *realize* her eyes were green?

Nikki had found her so fascinating when they were younger. The way Jess never seemed to notice when people were laughing at her. The way she seemed to live in some story that was playing out in her own mind, slightly removed from the angst of youth, like everything around her was taking place simply for her entertainment. Nikki had resented her a little for that, for reducing Nikki to a bit character in someone else's story. But she'd admired it, too.

It had certainly never been the reason she hated Jess. That came down to the Jason situation. Nobody liked seeing their first love kiss another girl. But Nikki's resentment toward Jess . . . well, *that* had festered long before any real hatred had developed. It had reared its ugly head the first time she'd watched Jess's dad pull her into a bear hug, and it had continued to grow with every subsequent interaction between them that Nikki had been forced to witness.

It sounded gross when she admitted it to herself. Just because Nikki's own father had left her didn't mean Jess shouldn't get to have one. Jess's mom had left her, after all. But that was the problem. Nikki and Jess should've been the same, both abandoned by one parent and left with the other. Only, they weren't. Because Jess's dad was great.

He was always volunteering to chaperone for school things. Then, rather than being embarrassed like a normal teenager should, Jess would flaunt their amazing friendship by spending the whole day cracking jokes with him instead of willing him to disappear. It was all, *Isn't he the greatest!* And Nikki couldn't help thinking that she should've ended up being best friends with her mom, just like Jess had with her dad. The left-behinds. But she couldn't, could she?

Because Nikki's mom didn't love her like Jess's dad loved Jess. Nikki's mom wasn't capable of it, not when all her adoration was reserved for vodka.

"Do you even know how to find the book we're looking for in all this crap?" Nikki put her hands on her hips and surveyed the teetering piles skeptically. They only had two more pictures to get after this, and now that Sally had gifted them number seven, she and Jess had a very good chance of winning the scavenger hunt.

Even if a few others beat them back to the town square, the four people in this room were the only ones who would've managed to check off every single item. Well, them and Sally and Luanne. But, given the way the competing bakers had started arguing when Luanne showed up, Nikki doubted they'd be getting back to the clues anytime soon. (Seriously, though, bless Sally Parker and the twisted joy she took in driving Luanne crazy. Nikki was going to insist Cara and Lexi buy muffins for a week as a show of gratitude, although she probably wouldn't tell them why; Cara had been unable to get off work to play the game, but Lexi was officially Nikki's competition.)

"I'm thinking we should check the spines," Jess said from beside the bookshelf.

It was a surprisingly sassy response, and Nikki had to bite her tongue to keep from grinning with approval. She jammed the toe of her bootie into one of the nearby stacks to warn against future displays of courage, toppling it loudly. To her gratification, Jess flinched at the sound.

"Why are all of these at your dad's house?" Bryce picked up a book from the desk beneath the curling *Juno* poster tacked on the wall. "Why haven't you moved them into yours?"

"I get lots of books, thanks to my job, so my shelves there are overflowing," Jess said, bending down to search the lower shelves. "And I'm here all the time to hang out with my dad. I can always pick one up if I want to reread it."

Must be nice, Nikki thought as she scanned the spines of the nearest stack. The last time Nikki had tried to hang out with her mom, she'd endured slurred insults until her mom had passed out.

She loved the woman, though. Often in spite of herself. And she was close to getting her back. When Nikki won Jasper's prize, she'd be able to force her mom into rehab. One of those horrifyingly expensive ones that pampered you with gourmet food and steam rooms so you were so eager to stay that you got sober in spite of yourself. *Still.* That time had not yet come. And Nikki didn't need to sit here listening to Jess gush about how her home life was so great that, at the age of twenty-six, she still hadn't managed to properly cut the cord.

"I'm going to get some water," Nikki said, kicking over another pile of books as she headed toward the door.

"Grab a beer for me," Bryce said. He'd set the book back down and was now flipping unhelpfully through a picture album.

"No beer for him," Carter said, looking up from his stack. "If he couldn't figure out that number seven was about the buck's head that spent years hanging in *the bar he works at*, we can't afford to have his mental capabilities dampened even more."

Nikki snorted in appreciation. The new guy wasn't bad. A little standoffish, maybe, but she liked that in a person. Not that she was into him. For all the effort she put into appearing polished, Nikki was attracted to a bit of roughness. Was there anything sexier than a man who worked with his hands? Someone whose scruff left memories of passion on your cheeks? If there was, she hadn't yet discovered it.

Not that it mattered anyway. Carter was always looking at Jess, his mouth fairly quivering with the effort not to smile. And Jess's cheeks flushed the color of her hair every time he spoke to her, which made her look like a gargantuan strawberry. Nikki didn't know what they found so enthralling about each other, but they'd be smart to knock it off. City Boy would be gone soon, and Jess would be left comparing the same handful of single men left in Redford to an ungettable ideal.

The rest of the house was less cluttered than Jess's room, although still severely lacking in color coordination. The walls were covered in mismatched picture frames, displaying so many pictures of Liz and Jess that Ross appeared to have two daughters instead of one. A wadded-up flannel blanket functioned as a throw pillow on the tattered couch, and a blue recliner clashed with the patterned green rug beneath the coffee table. The kitchen was no better. Nikki opened cabinets until she found a collection of mismatched glasses. At least they were clean. She was filling one of the glasses with tap water when she heard footsteps behind her.

When she turned, a wave of dizziness washed over her, and she nearly stumbled. Those drinks back at the Staple had hit her harder than she'd admitted to the rest of the group. She rarely drank more than a glass of wine. You couldn't grow up the way she had without becoming more than a little wary of alcohol. But she'd gone all in because Jess had seemed so repulsed by the scotch that it had been worth drinking it herself to force Jess to do the same.

"You all right there?" A strong hand cupped her elbow, its grip firm but gentle.

She blinked into gorgeous green eyes. *Ross Reid.* Her stomach flipped at the unexpected closeness of Jess's dad. She'd snapped at him the last time she'd seen him, in the gazebo, when he'd made those ridiculous claims about senility. He didn't seem to be carrying any animosity, though. Instead, he was looking at her with an expression of concern that made her heart thump painfully in her chest.

"I'm fine." Nikki couldn't make herself pull her arm away. "How are you, Ross? Still struggling with blindness?"

He grinned and her knees weakened. He was still as handsome as he'd ever been, only now she was old enough to match with him on a dating app. She'd done the math, and if Jess's mom really had gotten pregnant with her when she was sixteen, Jess's dad couldn't be more than forty-three. He wore every year of it well. Nikki had a flashback to bringing her car in to be repaired, him straightening up from where he'd been bent over an engine, rippling muscles streaked with grease. She'd never wanted to get dirtier in her life.

"It turned out I just had some dust in my eye," he said. "I tend to overreact."

Nikki heard herself giggle and was immediately mortified. Covertly, she pinched herself in warning. Hard.

"What are you doing here?" She was disappointed when her question made him let go of her arm.

"Actually," he said, moving to lean against the counter next to the sink, one ankle crossed casually across the other, "this is my house. So I show up here fairly often."

She waited for him to lob the question back at her, but he didn't. Instead, he gestured toward her glass of water.

"I think there's some juice in the fridge," he said, "if you'd prefer that."

"Are you referring to that red jug of 'fruit drink'?"

He grinned again. "I guess so."

"Tell me, Ross. What fruit do you think produced that particular shade of juice?"

"It's a special blend of fruits."

Nikki laughed. "It's a special blend of food dye and high-fructose corn syrup."

"That's a no, then?"

"That's a no." Their eyes locked, and Nikki felt her next words slip out like an escaping breeze. "But I appreciate the offer."

Ross nodded, unaware of how difficult it was for Nikki to acknowledge any kind of thoughtfulness directed her way.

"Are you and Jess on a break from the game?" he asked.

"We're actually here for number twelve," she said. "Have you gotten to that one yet?"

"No game playing for me. Bobby's doing it, so it's on me to keep the garage running."

"Seriously?" Nikki was outraged on his behalf. "That's not fair. You should just refuse to go back. We can tell you where all the pictures are. With your half of ten million, you can open your own repair shop and put him out of business."

"Is that what you're doing? Quitting your job in hopes that you'll win the money and start up your own company?"

"I kind of have my own company." Saying the words aloud sent a surge of pride through Nikki. She'd never expected posting on social media to become an actual career, but there had turned out to be an eager market for rural style. Lots of people didn't have access to high-quality brands, and Nikki was more than happy to give them tips on how to adorn both their homes and bodies without breaking the bank. "I don't make a lot, but it's enough to get by in Redford."

"So, you don't need the prize money," Bryce said, ambling into the kitchen.

Nikki glared at him, both for the uninvited entry and for eavesdropping, but mostly for ruining her chance to have Ross Reid to herself.

"And you do?" She rolled her eyes. "You get free beer and all the fried food you can eat at the Staple. What more does a guy like you need?"

"A boat," Bryce said simply.

"If I win the money, I'll buy you a boat," Nikki said. What would that cost? Twenty thousand? Fifty? Even a hundred grand would be chump change on a five-million-dollar prize. "Help us win and sabotage the competition, City Boy included, and I'll buy you any boat you want."

"City Boy objects," Carter said, strolling into the kitchen with Jess weaving drunkenly behind him.

"Nobody's talking to you." Nikki waved him off, more

interested in the slim paperback Jess held in her hand than defending her attempt to turn Bryce against his teammate. "You found the book?"

"I did." Jess held it up like a trophy.

"Take our picture, Ross." Nikki handed Jess's dad her phone without unlocking it. When he poked at the dark screen, she leaned into him, inhaling his intoxicatingly masculine scent before sliding her hand over his and pressing her fingertip to the sensor.

Flushed from the thrill of contact, Nikki practically skipped over to Jess. As she grabbed the book from Jess's hand to hold it up between them, she caught the scrunch of suspicion between Jess's eyebrows. Jess's eyes darted to her dad, then back to Nikki, causing Nikki's smile to widen.

Casually, Nikki leaned in and whispered into Jess's ear, "Thanks for bringing me over here. Your dad and I had some great quality time."

Nikki turned her smile toward the phone, hearing the little click of the camera over Jess's gasp of horror.

She had a feeling that picture was going to be frame-worthy.

Chapter 11

....

JESS

'm sorry you didn't get a picture with the buck," Jess said to Bobby Randall for what felt like the hundredth time, "but it shouldn't matter where I got it. The scavenger hunt is over." Hunger was making her irritable. It was dinnertime, and at least a hundred people were shivering in the yellow-lit square, waiting for Novak to announce which teams would be moving on to round two.

As she'd hoped, Sally hadn't shared her secret with any other teams, so only the six of them had been able to turn in all twenty pictures. Unfortunately, Bobby had somehow been made privy to this news.

He wasn't taking it well.

Her dad's boss was reacting as if they'd been given an unfair advantage that guaranteed a win, but even they didn't know if that was true. Seven teams had returned earlier than them, hoping speed might count for as many points as the pictures. And, for all Jess knew, they might be right. Only Novak understood how the results were being scored, and his lips seemed to be wrenching tighter together the louder the town's questions became. Didn't he realize that his opacity was suspicious? More important, couldn't he see that the sun had gone down and they wanted to leave?

Jess plunged her hands in her pants pockets, pressing chilled fingers against her thighs as Bobby continued his interrogation. She should've worn a coat.

"The buck's head belongs in the Staple," Bobby barked. "If you got a picture of it, you know where it is, which makes you an accomplice to its theft."

"Or she's the one who stole it in the first place," Nikki suggested.

Jess shot her a look.

"What?" Nikki's eyes widened innocently. "He said you might be an accomplice, and I'm defending you."

"By calling me a thief?"

"It's better than being an accomplice, isn't it?"

"*How?*" Jess exhaled with exasperation and felt an arm settle over her shoulders. She looked up to find Bryce leaning against her, an amiable smile on his face.

"You should just tell him the truth, Jess," Bryce said, his eyes springing from her to Bobby. "It's not like I knew someone had put it back on the wall when I let you into the bar."

Jess forced her expression to stay neutral, but she had no idea what he thought he was doing. Bobby spent most of his free time at the Staple. Obviously, he was going to notice that the buck head hadn't returned.

"It's back in the bar?" Bobby shook his head in disbelief.

"Presiding over the pool tables, just like it used to be.

Whoever took it must've known we'd all be hunting it down once the scavenger hunt clues came out. I guess they decided to return it before someone figured out they were the one who stole it."

"But . . ." Bobby trailed off, clearly still wanting to argue but at a loss as to what was left to be angry over.

"The buck's back?" Luanne inserted herself into the conversation, feigning disappointment. It seemed she'd forgiven them for their part in Sally's betrayal, at least for the moment. Small towns were funny like that. Offenses could be ranked, and Bobby Randall had racked up a significantly heftier pile of them with his bullying tendencies, lessening the rest of theirs by comparison.

"Last I checked." Bryce patted her arm. "But it's already run off once, so who's to say how long it'll stick around this time?"

"You know what they say," Carter added helpfully. "Once an animal gets a taste of freedom, it's hard to keep them locked up."

Jess bit back a laugh, suddenly grateful that she hadn't hesitated to let a competing team in on the picture with Sally's stolen buck. It might've cost them a clear win on this challenge, but she would've spent the next week trying to keep Sally's secret and stressing beneath the pressure. Obviously, she wanted to take home the prize money. Badly, actually. She could already imagine the books she could publish, the unearthed gems she might get to put her own tiny fingerprint on. It was so exciting she'd barely been able to sleep last night.

But Jasper had made this a game because he wanted them to have fun. And cold and hungry or not, today she'd had a great time.

········

JESS WAS WALKING up the steps to her dad's porch a little while later when her phone chimed with a text from Liz. It was a reply to the message she'd sent just before breaking into the Staple, and it read, **Be honest: If Nikki gets you thrown in prison, do you think she'd be willing to take your place as Kai's godmother?**

Jess laughed and typed out, **Whatever Kai's done to upset you, it couldn't possibly warrant such a terrible punishment.**

To her delight, answering blue dots began immediately. Leaning back against the railing, Jess waited to see what message they'd deliver.

You wouldn't say that if you'd seen what I just found in his diaper.

Jess chuckled again, even as her nose wrinkled at the visual. **I'll have to pass on the details this time. I'm heading into my dad's for dinner.**

Tell him I'm still mad that he didn't make it down for La-bor Day, Liz replied immediately.

I'll tell him you miss him, Jess tapped out, confident she'd correctly translated Liz's demand.

To her disappointment, no reply appeared. She'd no doubt lost Liz to yet another nuclear tantrum or cooking emer-gency. Still, Jess stayed on the porch for another moment, staring at the glow of her screen against the darkness of the night. A minute later, her patience was rewarded.

I do. But I miss you more. Talk soon?

Jess smiled and tapped out, Can't wait, then slid her phone into her back pocket. Reaching for the doorknob, she stalled. It had never once occurred to her to knock before entering the home she'd grown up in, but she'd also never considered the fact that an unannounced visit could lead to her interrupting something. Thanks to Nikki, she was certainly considering it now.

Her teammate had spent the second half of the day torturing Jess with visuals of her dad that no daughter should ever be subjected to. Jess knocked loudly before easing the door open. Ross wouldn't have a woman over—he never did. Still, Jess couldn't block out Nikki's insinuation that if Bryce hadn't walked in on her and Jess's dad, Nikki would've had her way with Ross right there on the kitchen table. The horrifying image made Jess gag loudly.

"You okay?" Her dad appeared in the hallway, scrubbing at the grease stains on his hands with a wet rag.

"You can't date Nikki." Jess blurted out the words and felt instantly foolish. She wasn't in charge of her father. She couldn't tell him who to date—even if the woman in question was a terrifying creature who probably unzipped her skin at night to let her poisonous tentacles out to breathe. Jess had only intended to introduce it casually into conversation over egg rolls, gently steering him to his own conclusion that giving in to Nikki's advances would be a terrible idea.

"I brought kung pao chicken," she added quickly, holding up the bags of frozen food she'd grabbed from the market on her way over. The diner had been so packed after being closed all day that it would've taken an hour to get a to-go order.

"Nice," her dad said, clearly choosing to ignore Jess's directive about his dating life.

She followed him toward the kitchen, wondering if his lack of response was indicative of something. *Please, no.* She'd spent one full day in Nikki's company and had gotten nauseatingly drunk, lost several inches of hair, and risked theft charges. If Nikki found a way to insert herself permanently in her life, she'd probably manage to end it early.

Her dad pulled out a pan before looking at the bags in her hands. "Are we baking or frying the egg rolls?"

"Let's fry them." Jess beamed. "We're celebrating."

"You made it to the next round?" He held up a hand.

"We're one of twenty teams remaining," she said, slapping his hand with hers before swooping a fist and snapping her fingers and double-slapping his hand again in one of their elaborate high fives.

"Top forty, huh? Did Novak tell you where you rank in that?" Ross started heating up the pans and ripped the bags open.

"Please. If half the town hadn't chanted 'Who won?' for three solid minutes, I don't know if he would've even told us what teams were still in the game. He doesn't seem to understand that people have to make plans to be out of work for an additional day. When it comes to giving out helpful information, the man makes Ebenezer Scrooge look generous.

Extraneous information, on the other hand, he pours out with abandon."

"But you're definitely in?"

She grinned. "I'm definitely in."

They continued chatting as the food heated up, taking turns stirring the chicken and frying the egg rolls as they moved around the kitchen, setting the table and getting drinks in a well-choreographed dance. They didn't eat together every night—if only because neither wanted the other to feel obligated—but truth be told, as much of an effort as they made to give each other space, they *did* end up eating a lot of meals together. Why eat alone when you didn't have to?

It wasn't until the mound of egg rolls had disappeared and Jess's plate was empty save for a few abandoned chunks of chicken drowning in sticky sauce that she decided to circle back to the Nikki situation. Her dad had never been the kind of parent who laid down the law. When she'd started hanging out with Ricky Hammermill, her dad had stayed silent, despite Ricky's ever-present eau de marijuana. He also hadn't said a word when she'd declared her love for Jamal Hill, even though Jamal considered himself too smart for school and could often be seen reading on town benches when he was supposed to be in class.

If Evan Saunders hadn't started coming around, her father probably would've never pulled out his underutilized dad card. But Ross had worked on Evan's car after Evan had gone after it with a baseball bat in a fit of rage. It turned out Jess's dad had a line, and violence—especially violence that had the potential to be directed toward his daughter—was on the wrong side of it.

It hadn't even occurred to Jess to ignore his worries. She'd cut ties with Evan, completely and unquestioningly, because she'd known there must be something very wrong with the situation for her dad to feel the need to insert himself into it. And now she understood where her dad had been coming from. If you see a tornado bearing down on someone you love, there is no choice but to shout out a warning.

"So . . ." Jess drew out the word before taking a sip of water.

"So?" Her dad cocked an eyebrow and shoved the last half of an egg roll into his mouth.

"Nikki really seemed to enjoy spending time with you today."

"Did she?" He seemed a little too baffled for someone who'd spent a lifetime being complimented on his looks. There was no way he hadn't noticed that he had an effect on people. Jess had been nearby too many times as women giggled inanely at everything he said, not to mention all the times she'd been forced to hear the term *hot dad*.

"What exactly happened between the two of you?"

"In the five minutes we were in the kitchen?" He shrugged. "I offered her juice."

"Are you sure you didn't offer her an engagement ring? Because she has started referring to herself as my future mommy."

Ross guffawed. "She has not."

"Oh, I assure you, she has." Jess feigned an imperial wave. "*Don't argue with future mommy. I'll be forced to send you to bed without supper.*"

Ross laughed again, but Jess could not join in. Her

reenactment had brought forth a fresh wave of horror at the memory. Nikki Loughton as a mother figure. An egg roll crept back up at the thought.

"She's just messing with you, J-bird," Ross said reassuringly.

"I know." And she did. Obviously, Nikki understood that no daughter would enjoy hearing that her father would be a shoo-in for the next *Magic Mike* movie because he looked like he'd "fill out a banana hammock well." Or that his mouth was uniquely "lickable." But that wasn't what had Jess so freaked out. It was the way Nikki's cheeks had flushed when she'd leaned in to unlock the phone for him in the kitchen. The way her voice went a little higher every time she'd brought him up afterward.

"She's single, though," Jess said after a moment. "And there aren't a lot of single men in this town. It would make sense for her to be interested in you."

"Maybe," he agreed. "If I was ten years younger."

"Right." Jess appreciated that they were both ignoring the fact that Bobby, who was less than a year younger than her dad, had recently taken up with Violet Mandle, an aggressively sexy girl who had graduated three years behind Jess and now spent all of her free time hanging out at the auto body garage like some kind of skimpily dressed mascot.

"And she's beautiful." Jess must still be drunk from the scotch tasting. "And funny. I mean, she's vicious and terrible, but you have to admit she's funny, too."

Her dad looked as confused as she felt. "She's a very attractive young lady. But you have nothing to worry about."

"It's just that I've known her for a long time. Nikki tends to get what she wants."

"How nice for her."

"And," Jess added, in spite of herself, "after today, I'm kind of worried that she wants you."

His confusion shifted visibly to exasperation, and Jess couldn't blame him for it. This wasn't the kind of thing they did, this form of circular conversation and questioning of intentions. If only she hadn't been there sophomore year when Nikki had convinced their biology teacher to skip the midterm and give them a participation grade instead. Or senior year, when Nikki bullied all the girls in their grade into wearing black to the prom so she'd stand out in her red dress. Or *just this morning*, when she'd managed to trick Jess into an unwanted haircut. Maybe then Jess wouldn't believe Nikki's powers of persuasion might be actual wizardry.

"It's not going to happen, Jessica," her dad said slowly and firmly. "For a variety of reasons."

"And those are?" She needed to hear them so she could run them through her mind tomorrow when Nikki would inevitably say something gross about his abs or their future family Christmases.

"Because you don't want me to, for starters." He shook his head like he was a little disappointed in her for not understanding that. "I'd never mess up this little family we have by bringing someone unwanted into it. But also, I have no interest in dating someone my daughter's age. I know men do it, and that's fine for them. But I can't look at someone I chaperoned on school field trips and find them attractive. It's just not going to happen."

"Hallelujah for that." A wave of relief washed over Jess.

"Also," he continued, "I saw her arguing with Bobby when she paid for her car last week, and I felt genuinely fearful for him. If we had a panic button in the garage, I would've been tempted to press it."

Jess laughed. "Right? Ever since I found out I got paired with her, I've started carrying around Mace. I mean, she's never actually been violent, but I just feel safer knowing it's there."

She stopped laughing when he opened his mouth and closed it again. His face looked normal, but there was something about the movement that unsettled her. It had been so intentional. Such obvious restraint. One of her favorite things about her dad was the ease with which he carried himself. He did not filter his words. He didn't hold back.

"What?" she asked nervously.

"What, what?"

"You were going to say something else. Another reason, I think?" She scrunched up her face. "If you've already hooked up with her mom, I am *not* going to be the one to break the news to Nikki. I have the Mace, but I'm afraid to use it. What if it gets in my face when I spray it?"

"I didn't hook up with her mom." His voice sounded odd, and Jess felt a flutter of panic across her chest.

"Dad?"

He closed his eyes, and the flutter turned into a tsunami.

She leaned forward anxiously. "What aren't you saying?"

"There's another reason I wouldn't date her," he said in a gruff voice. "Another reason I wouldn't date anyone."

She was silent, and she suddenly wanted him to stay

silent as well. They'd talked about this long enough. More than enough. It had been silly from the start. Her, worrying about her dad and Nikki Loughton dating? Ridiculous.

"I'm sick, J-bird."

His words hit her like shrapnel, not striking one part of her body but all of it in angry bursts. "No."

She couldn't pretend to believe he was referring to a cold, so her only option was to pretend he was wrong. He was young. Fit. Her *dad*. He couldn't be sick. Not like he thought he was, with that terrible finality in his voice.

Rather than argue, he stood up and rounded the table so he could wrap his arms around her. There, in the cocoon of his hug, the safest place she'd ever known, she felt it. The truth was in the tightness of his grip. His diminished strength. The coldness of his skin.

Desperately, she began to sob.

Chapter 12

··········

CARTER

In Atlanta, Carter's coworkers often referred to him as Rushmore. He hadn't asked for an explanation for that because to acknowledge it might imply he accepted the nickname—and, seeing as nicknames were meant for small children wearing slightly askew baseball caps rather than professionals who were at the top of their field, Carter *didn't* accept it. Nonetheless, Marissa Sumners had shown up in his office one day, eager to enlighten him.

Rushmore, it turned out, was short for Mount Rushmore. Marissa claimed part of the reason he'd been given the moniker was because his face looked like it had been chiseled from stone. Carter chalked this up to her tendency to flirt with him, despite the fact that he'd been very clear with her that he didn't date coworkers. But then she expanded on her theme, and he found himself listening with reluctant interest.

"You know how Mount Rushmore is so big, right?" she'd said, leaning against his doorway and crossing her arms over her chest. "The faces are, like, *right there*. But you can't actually touch them. And you know you can always count on them to be there and look over you, but you also know that they don't need anything from you. That's you, Carter. You're always here, but you're also . . . well, *not*."

Carter hadn't known if this was meant to be flattering or offensive, and he hadn't really cared. He liked that it portrayed him as present, at least. Sturdy and solid and dependable. And another thing about stone that Marissa had failed to mention? Stone was strong.

It was invulnerable.

You couldn't push a giant stone around. With this in mind, it was difficult to believe he'd been driven out of the room he was paying good money for by a tiny woman who smelled of brown sugar and butter. Yet, here he was.

Carter should, of course, have simply said no to joining Mrs. Loveling by the fire for a piece of cake. He'd spent the whole day running around doing Jasper's scavenger hunt, after all, and nine thirty at night was way too late for dessert. He'd panicked, though, and found himself slipping out the patio door instead.

It wasn't that he disliked the woman. It was just that Mrs. Loveling was like a drug dealer, pushing baked goods instead of narcotics. She dealt in excess, forcing him to eat three cookies instead of one, like his return could only be guaranteed if she got him well and truly hooked.

And the *questions*. There were always so many of them. About his family. About his work. About his love life. She wanted details that he had found difficult to share even with Jasper, and Carter worried that he was beginning to offend

her with his vague nonanswers and insistence on turning
the subject back to her.

Some space would be better for both of them, he'd ratio-
nalized as he'd eased the sliding door shut like a cat burglar
escaping with her jewels. And he was halfway around the
lake before he breathed out a sigh of relief, finally feeling
like he had an appropriate amount of space. Carter spotted
a bench down by the water and made his way toward it. One
side of it was lit by the moon and the other was darkened by
a thick patch of leaves above. The water lapped peacefully
against the shore, and a crisp breeze slipped through the
trees. He took a seat on the dark side of the bench and felt
the chill of the wooden slats seep through his slacks.

He pulled out his cell to check the emails from work
that were piling up. He'd made some headway on them before Mrs. Loveling had rapped on his door, but there was
still so much to do. It didn't matter that he was technically
on vacation. Once people had entrusted you with their
money, you became responsible for not only their financial
security but their emotional security as well. They could not
be ignored any more than their accounts could be.

A twig cracked behind him, and Carter whipped around,
surprised to discover someone coming his way. The person
gasped.

"I'm sorry." She froze in front of him like a nervous deer.
"I didn't see you there."

Her voice was so strange, so flat and wet, like a used
cloth left in a heap on a counter, that it took Carter a moment to realize the voice belonged to Jess. He resisted his

instinct to stand up, to make sure she was okay. She was out late at night, in the dark all alone; clearly, she was not okay. Being approached by a large man would likely only make her feel unsafe on top of whatever else she was dealing with.

"That was by design," Carter said, hoping she could see his smile in the dark. "As I confessed to Sally earlier, I'm here to thwart evildoers. We superheroes tend to hide in the shadows."

"You wanted to be alone," Jess said with a sigh.

"No." *Yes.* "I was told that this was where all the action in Redford happened. I'm glad you showed up, actually. I was starting to suspect I was being hazed."

Jess hesitated, and he imagined he'd be able to spot her skepticism if her face were more clearly lit. Then she closed the distance between them and slumped onto the bench next to him. She checked her phone, the brightness of the screen illuminating her face. Her eyes were lined with red, and her frown deepened at whatever she saw. Carter couldn't resist following her gaze. There were no new notifications.

"You were hoping to hear from someone?" he asked in spite of himself.

Jess nodded and let the screen go dark. "My friend Liz. I need to talk to her about something, but she hasn't replied to my texts. She's probably already gone to bed. She's living on a baby's schedule these days. You have to sleep when they sleep, right?"

"I guess." Carter pictured a tiny dictator with a rattle as its scepter.

Jess checked her phone again.

"You could talk to me," Carter said. "If you want to."

Jess shook her head. "I can't. It's someone else's secret. It's not mine to share."

"You were going to tell your friend."

"She wouldn't tell anyone."

"I'm not from here. Who would I tell?" Carter wondered what he was doing, trying to get this woman to open up to him. Like grief, Barclays didn't *do* emotion.

Jess studied him for a moment, and she looked so desperate there in the moonlight that he found himself needing to provide whatever it was she was looking for. He should say something. Offer her some secret of his own—a trade, sort of—to prove that he could be trusted with hers.

"I don't know anyone here," he added rashly, "because I never visited my grandfather. I just kept putting it off until it was too late."

The moment the words hit the air, he wished he could take them back. There were secrets, and then there were confessions, the latter being better left unsaid. Guilt had been gnawing for days, though, since the moment he'd passed the "Welcome to Redford" sign at the edge of town. It shouldn't have been the first time he'd seen its cheerful greeting. What kind of grandson never visited his grandfather?

"I told myself that I couldn't take the time off work," he admitted, because the words were out there now. Maybe their release meant they'd finally stop torturing him. "But that wasn't true. I could've easily come down for a weekend."

"So why didn't you?" There was no judgment in her question, just an effort to understand.

"I don't know." Carter had no reason to feel guilty about

holding back. Jess was little more than a stranger to him. "I just couldn't."

"I'm sure Jasper understood."

"He was good like that," Carter agreed gratefully. "He had a way of appreciating people for who they were without making them feel like they needed to be something more."

"You must miss him terribly."

"I do." It felt like an understatement, but it was all he could say. "So that's it. That's my big secret. You don't have to share yours, but you can if you want, confident in the fact that I'll keep my mouth shut. Otherwise, you now have proof that everyone is right about me. I don't deserve to be here, not when I spent years refusing to come."

"You deserve to be here, Carter." For the first time since she'd arrived, Jess's voice sounded like her own again. "Your granddad wanted you here. That's why he included you in the game."

"Maybe." Carter shrugged. "But you know there are people like Bobby who would use that information against me. So you can trust that I'd never say anything you didn't want me to repeat, because I'm trusting you to do the same."

Jess stared out at the lake, and when she finally spoke, her words were so quiet he could barely make them out. "I'm scared."

"To tell me?"

"No." She hesitated, unwilling to look at him. "I'm scared I'm going to lose my dad." She almost got through all the words before a rush of tears drowned them out.

Carter's stomach twisted with dismay. "What?"

"He's sick." She hiccupped, like her body was so repulsed

by the words that it was rejecting them. "He told me tonight. I guess he couldn't hide it from me any longer."

"Sick isn't the same as dying." Carter knew the moment
the words came out of his mouth that they weren't soft
enough. They were practical instead of consoling. Tactless.
He leaned toward her and wrapped his arm around her
trembling shoulders. "Your dad is young and strong, Jess,"
he said, trying again. "You can't give up on him already."

"The doctors have." She huddled into him, tears leaking
down her cheeks and settling into damp spots on his shirt.
"Whatever they told him made him think it's too late. He
doesn't believe they can save him."

Carter had questions. Lots of them. But he'd never really
been the shoulder someone had chosen to lean on. He didn't
know how it worked. Was he supposed to collect facts and
use them to build some kind of case that might prove comforting? Or did she expect him to offer baseless reassurances
instead, insisting her dad would be okay even though he had
no way of knowing if that was true? Silenced by uncertainty,
he stroked her hair instead. The scent of apricot drifted from
the silky strands. He was certain he wasn't supposed to be
noticing how good her body felt against his. Why was he so
bad at this?

"I gave up a job in New York for him," Jess whispered in
a confessional way. She looked up at him, squinting like she
worried he was going to judge her. Her face was so close to
his that he could feel her breath on his chin. "There were
other reasons, of course—other people, like Liz and my
neighbors—but my dad was who I was the most focused on.
I convinced myself it was this selfless decision, like I didn't

want to be another person who abandoned him, but it wasn't true. I did it for me. I wanted to choose family over my career, and I didn't care if that meant I lacked ambition. I knew that I'd be happier here, spending my days with the people I love. And I was right. I think about that job sometimes, and I do have regrets. But I never wish I was there instead of here."

Carter was surprised by the lump that lodged in his throat at her words. He understood what she was saying—her dad was her home, and she was terrified she was going to lose that—and his heart broke for her. But he was also overcome with something that felt, uncomfortably enough, a lot like longing.

Obviously, what Jess had with her father was the kind of relationship many sons and daughters dreamed of. But it was clear to Carter that they didn't just love each other. They liked each other, too. They were family but also friends. What would it have been like to grow up with someone who liked you as you were? Who wasn't always trying to mold you into something else?

How differently would Carter have turned out if his parents had liked him as he was?

Would he have turned out more like Jess? Probably not, but possibly. He liked the idea that he would. Jess was just so comfortable with herself. Carter was in awe of the fact that she could open up about all of this to him, a man she barely knew. The way she claimed her lack of ambition so truthfully, so entirely without shame.

He'd spent years trying to block out his parents' accusations when he'd turned his back on the family business.

Weak. Scared. Failure. He'd known that they'd been wrong, that he hadn't been running away from his responsibility. He'd been running *toward* something different. They'd gotten in his head, though. They'd made him feel ashamed of his choice. And shame had left him every bit as closed off as they were.

"I didn't choose ambition, either," he said, wanting to prove them wrong. "I chose freedom. And I didn't do it for family like you did—my parents would tell you I betrayed them—but that choice brought it to me anyway. It gave me the kind of family I'd always dreamed of."

"Jasper?" she whispered.

Carter nodded. "He and my mom were estranged. When I walked away from her, I reached out to him. It was the first time he and I had talked since I was three years old. And that's how I know you made the right choice when you chose to come home. One day, I would've ended up the head of a multibillion-dollar company. Instead, I got a grand-father. I got someone who made me feel like I was a part of an unbreakable bond."

A fresh wave of tears leaked down Jess's cheeks, and Carter's heart twisted in his chest.

"I lied to you before," he said. "I said I didn't know why I refused to visit my grandfather, but I do. I was scared. He seemed so different. He was honest and genuine, and he loved this whole town of people. But I grew up with two people who were masters of maintaining their perfect fa-çade. From the outside, they were the perfect parents, even though they only spoke to me when they were directing me on how to behave. They were the perfect members of their community, even though they looked down on everyone they knew and mocked their friends mercilessly behind their backs. I researched Jasper before I reached out to him. I saw his mansion online. And I was terrified that I'd walk inside it and discover my grandfather was no different than my mother. I was terrified I'd find out he was one person in public and a completely different one behind closed doors."

"He wasn't," Jess said, her voice soft but adamant. "Jasper Wilhelm didn't live behind closed doors. Redford used to have a community center. Actually, it was an old barn that someone let us use for community events, but we started calling it our community center. For years, it was the place where everyone threw parties or held dances. Then, one night, a big storm came through, and the barn got torn up. Jasper's response was to throw a party of his own. He called it the Storm Survival Celebration, and he invited everyone in town. Once we were all there, he announced that his house was our new community center. If anyone needed a place to gather, his doors would be open to us."

Carter nodded at this revelation, unable to speak. His eyes burned with unshed tears.

He'd been scared about nothing.

He should've come here a long time ago. He should've believed in his grandfather.

"Your dad is going to be okay," he said, no longer caring that he didn't know this to be true. This conversation felt like the most genuine interaction he'd ever experienced, and he didn't want to muddy it with false assertions, but he didn't think that was what he was doing.

He was just choosing to believe.

Jess didn't argue with him. She didn't claim to agree. She simply rested her head against his shoulder and whispered, "Thank you."

As tempted as Carter was to repeat the words back to her, he didn't. This moment wasn't about the comfort she'd given him. It was about her. So he pulled her closer and pressed his cheek into her hair. It didn't matter that Barclays kept their distance.

He'd already spent too many years forgetting that he was half Wilhelm.

Chapter 13

· · · · · · · · · ·

JESS

The next morning, the people of Redford walked toward the courthouse in a solid mass of bodies. Raucous music was playing from a portable speaker, though Jess couldn't determine who had thought to bring one along at eight a.m. The scene looked like a protest but felt more like a disorganized parade. The mood was festive, despite the grumbling from those who had unwittingly drunk one cup of coffee too many. The day's challenge would involve keeping one hand on the old stone building for as long as possible, and full bladders wouldn't be an advantage.

Luckily for Jess, she'd felt too sick to consume anything that morning, though the very thought seemed blasphemous. *She* wasn't the one who was sick. How dare she wallow in self-pity when her dad was dying of cancer? Except that he wasn't, because she was going to save him. Jasper's prize money would be more than enough to pay for her dad to get the best treatment possible, to pay doctors who hadn't already given up. With a surge of determination, she scanned the crowd, clocking her competition. Every one of them looked like children who had just been informed class was canceled and they'd be spending the day on the playground instead.

It no doubt felt like it. The day was beautiful and the task simple. Sally had already sent her niece to fill a basket of muffins to sell at a discounted "Courthouse Challenge" price. Spurred by the unspoken challenge, Luanne had searched the crowd for someone willing to do the same for her. She'd given her key to the Adams kid and kept turning back to peer down the street, clearly realizing he was much more likely to eat her cupcakes than make any effort to box them up and bring them back.

Half the people present weren't even participating in the game; they were folks who hadn't made it to round two or shift workers who didn't have work until later. Some were there to offer encouragement and support, others to heckle and mock. Most were there to do both, the lines drawn as thickly as ever; they cared almost as much about who they wanted to lose as who they needed to win.

Novak's rules were simple, though he had, of course, spoken on them long enough to make them sound complex. At least one hand must remain on the wall at all times. If you took both hands off the wall, you were eliminated. If you used your cell phone, you were eliminated. If either person on a team was eliminated, both team members were out. That was it.

Jess was holding on to a ridiculous hope that this event would be the final one, that the last team touching the wall would be declared the winners of the entire competition. It *was* possible, wasn't it? Novak had claimed the game could go longer than a week, but who knew how long today's challenge might last? For millions of dollars, people could hold on to a wall forever, couldn't they? Jess knew beyond a shadow of a doubt she could—she'd have her dad bring her an adult diaper, if that's all it took to win the money to save him. Spending days clutching a stone surface would be much better than facing unknown challenges. What if the next one was based on strength? Willpower and tenacity wouldn't be able to help her against the Bobbys and the Carters and the Bryces of the world.

She gave herself a shake, then forced a smile in response to Mrs. Monroe's concerned look. *Today.* Jess just had to focus on today. She'd started this morning by emailing the authors of all of her pending projects, providing new timelines for her feedback, pushing everything by a week. Now, the game could be her priority. Her job was to conquer this task and worry about the next when it came. No more sharing wins with attractive out-of-towners, though. Her eyes drifted to Carter, trailing silently alongside Bryce at the back of the herd. He didn't seem to be listening to whatever it was that Bryce and Luanne found so hilarious, and she shook off the temptation to fall back and pull him into the fun.

That was decidedly *not* her job. Despite what had happened last night by the lake, Carter wasn't her friend; he was the competition. She'd been foolish to sit down next to him, making herself vulnerable to someone who was only here for his own agenda. Carter had every intention of leaving Redford behind when he was done here. What was important now was that he didn't take the money that could be used to save Jess's dad with him.

Everyone was so convinced that he was being set up to

win, that he was the reason the scoring system was being kept secret. They kept saying he had some kind of deal with Novak, receiving extra points in exchange for a share of his inevitable winnings. And maybe they were right. But, unlike Jess, they didn't seem to understand that there was no point in being angry about that. There was nothing to be done about it.

They'd be better off focusing on themselves.

And that's what she needed to do. She couldn't help him win. She couldn't make mistakes like she'd made yesterday, vouching for him with Sally.

She'd been foolish, approaching this like a game, focusing on enjoying herself.

It wasn't a game. It was life or death.

Last night, she'd felt helpless. She hadn't yet realized how much she could do once she had Jasper's money.

Today was different. She'd be strong. Determined. Ruthless.

She couldn't be herself anymore. Today, she would need to be Nikki.

....

JESS'S PLAN WAS simple. She'd focus on winning, keeping her distance from anything—or, most important, anyone—that had the potential to distract her. With her head down, she beelined toward the sunny side of the courthouse wall, wishing she hadn't chosen to wear a wildly patterned, multicolored sweater. She was about as camouflaged as a peacock in the desert.

When Carter ended up right next to her, the sweater—kaleidoscope beacon of wool that it was—was what she blamed. Or, she theorized, maybe it wasn't her ridiculous sense of fashion's fault at all. Maybe Carter, too, had realized that their alliance yesterday had proven more fortuitous for him than it had for her. She searched him, hoping for a sign of cunning that would make it easier for her to push him away.

His jaw was clean shaven again, the chink in his armor the day she'd met him seemingly gone for good. He looked ready for a day at the office, his button-up and slacks so similar to yesterday's that she would've assumed he slept in them, unmoving and arms crossed stiffly over his chest like a vampire, if she hadn't ogled him enough yesterday to be able to spot that the gray in the pants was a shade darker and his shirt now had a tinge of blue in it. Were put together and undeniably handsome indications of deviousness? If CEOs in movies were correctly cast, the answer was yes.

"Good morning," she said in response to that one-sided lift of his lips that he probably thought was a smile.

"Good morning," he said in a quiet tone that made her feel like they were alone despite the throng of people around them. "Were you able to get any sleep last night?"

Her mind flashed back to the bench, his body warm against hers, his touch gentle.

Nope. She couldn't stay here all day. Not if she was going to stick to the plan. Was there a way to remove herself that wouldn't be rude? She wished she'd left sooner last night. She'd needed the comfort he'd offered. She couldn't deny that. But she should have left after that, sometime during the stretch of silence in which she'd huddled into his heat. Before she'd found herself babbling for an hour about nothing, in some ridiculous effort to hold on to the moment. She must've come across as so incredibly needy.

Tearing her eyes away from him, she spotted Nikki closing in on them.

"I slept fine," she said before waving wildly at Nikki. "Over here!"

She shouldn't have been surprised when Nikki sneered at the sight of her and turned deliberately toward the back wall, but she was. Carter laughed under his breath as she sighed. She'd just have to make up an excuse to leave. An urgent conversation she needed to have with someone farther down the wall. Not as far as the shade, though. Beneath her sunglasses, her eyes were red and puffy from a night of crying. The sunshine would be camouflage.

In a town like this, people noticed if you looked upset. And they didn't just notice and wonder what might be wrong. They *talked*. To their friends. To the mailman. To Madison, the sixteen-year-old girl who worked the checkout line at Joe's market and squinted at everyone like they were stupid for believing she might care.

Jess wouldn't mind if some whispered suggestion that she'd been fired from her job or turned down by a love interest spread across Redford. But what if someone dug deeper? What if someone had spotted her dad at the hospital or seen him picking up a prescription at the pharmacy? If people began to treat Ross Reid like he was sick, he'd be mortified.

"Well, hello there, neighbor." Elaine Rayburn, who had

lived next door to Liz's parents for as long as Jess could remember, turned to her with a bright smile. "It looks like we'll be spending the day together."

The woman pulled Jess into a hug, smelling of freshly dug earth and pungent flowers. Mrs. Rayburn spent so much time gardening that there was no knowing whether she'd already been out there this morning or if the scent had simply worked its way into her skin like a tan.

"How are the fall blooms coming along?" Jess asked when Mrs. Rayburn released her.

Mrs. Rayburn shook her head. "The crotons are showing off, but those celosias are making me work for it."

"Such divas," Jess commiserated as if she could pick out one from the other if her life depended on it. She rocked back on her heels, anxious to avoid getting stuck in a long conversation about flora or foliage or whatever the appropriate term was, but the screeching of a megaphone cut her off.

It was followed by the amplified and phlegmy sound of Novak clearing his throat. Jess turned to find him on their side of the building, his spectacles low on his nose.

"At the sound of the whistle," he called out in his nasally voice, "the clock will begin."

He lowered the hand with the megaphone and lifted his other hand, blowing into a whistle. It made a pathetic rattling sound. A few people in the crowd snickered, but the rest merely looked confused. Novak put the whistle in his mouth again, blowing harder this time. His cheeks ballooned comically, but the emitted sound was no more audible. His face reddened and the corners of his mouth sank. Next to him, the market owner, Joe, who had opted out of the game to keep his business running but had clearly decided it was worth opening it a couple of hours late to avoid missing today's drama, stuck two fingers in his mouth and sent an ear-piercing whistle ripping through the air.

Cheers broke out, applause from the bystanders but only whoops of approval from the participants, who now each had one hand determinedly pressed to stone. Even Jess let out a little yip of enthusiasm, mostly amused by the way Novak's cheeks kept expanding with his continued efforts to make his whistle work despite the game having already begun.

"Are you okay?" Carter's question came as a surprise, spoken in a low voice that slid under the cheers and into her ear.

"I'm fine," Jess said instinctively, turning to discover a surprising amount of concern in Carter's usually guarded gaze.

"I know you're not fine. You can't be. Not after what you told me last night. But is there something else going on? Did I do something wrong?"

She blinked in the face of his earnestness, her resolve wavering.

"Of course not." Jess wanted to tell him how much it meant that he'd sat there with her in the dark, patiently waiting for her to stop crying. She wanted to tell him how much his words had comforted her. But Nikki wouldn't do that, so neither could she. "I'm just trying to focus on the competition."

She gave in, offering Carter a reassuring smile to make up for the fact that she fully intended this to be their last

interaction of the day, then turned to make the ultimate sacrifice in the pursuit of victory.

"So, Mrs. Rayburn," Jess said, forcing the words out, "I've
always wondered how you keep so many types of plants alive
in one place. Don't some of them need different amounts of
water than others?"

As she'd anticipated, the question prompted a full twenty
minutes of tips that Jess, whose backyard stayed overgrown
and unusable most of the year, had absolutely no interest in.
If Liz were here, she would've been delighted to discover
Jess trapped again. When they were kids, the two of them
had made a game of sneaking through Mrs. Rayburn's garden, whistling and breaking the silence with random shrieks
to get the other caught so she'd have to endure a lengthy
lecture on the blooming habits of hydrangeas. Liz was not
here, though.

She'd finally called this morning, but not until Jess was
almost to the town square, surrounded by too many people
to start a conversation that would undoubtedly make her
start crying again. It felt weird, dealing with something of
this magnitude without Liz here to face it with her. It felt
even weirder that Jess had spilled the news to someone else
first. But what felt the absolute weirdest was that, in the
end, she hadn't needed Liz. Her conversation with Carter
had provided enough comfort to get her through the night.

A burning smell interrupted Mrs. Rayburn's rant about
tulips, causing her to sniff at the air with annoyance. Her
expression darkened, and she leaned forward, keeping one
hand on the wall as she peered past Jess down the line of
people.

"Put that cigar out right now," she snapped at someone toward the front of the building. "This is a public event."

"If the public doesn't like it," a man's voice called back, "they're welcome to let go of the wall and walk away."

"The sun's barely up," Mrs. Rayburn grumbled. She shook her head and leaned back against the wall, sighing with exasperation. "Can you believe Jasper paired me with such a disgusting creature? He lets his dog pee on my hydrangeas, you know. Bill, not Jasper. He's been doing it for years. I'd set up some kind of invisible electric fence if I knew where to get one—and if it was guaranteed to have a current strong enough to knock a grown man out."

Jess stifled a laugh.

"Have you considered using a liquid fence?" Carter asked from behind her, sabotaging Jess's effort to pretend he'd gone away.

"A what?" Mrs. Rayburn perked up.

"You spray it every four to five days around the area you want to protect, and it keeps dogs away."

"It's not poisonous to them, is it?" Mrs. Rayburn shook her head. "I couldn't hurt a dog, even if it does belong to a man intent on making the entire town reek of stale tobacco."

"It doesn't hurt them at all," Carter said. "It simply projects a subliminal message that encourages them to return home and pee on their owner's bed."

Jess's head whipped toward him, but Carter's expression was perfectly placid.

"Does it?" Mrs. Rayburn clapped her hands together, clearly delighted by the idea. "That's magnificent."

"I was joking," Carter said. "It has an odor that dogs find displeasing."

"How disappointing," Mrs. Rayburn said.

"As disappointing as the fact that you just took your hand off the wall?" Carter's clear lack of empathy made Jess cringe.

A sharp whistle punctuated Mrs. Rayburn's shock. Unfortunately for all of them, Novak seemed to have finally figured out how to operate the tricky device.

"Eliminated!" He shouted the word through his megaphone, despite being no more than three feet away from them.

Mrs. Rayburn blinked with surprise, looking around like the situation wasn't quite computing. In her defense, it was quite a thing to try to absorb. Five million dollars was a ridiculous amount of money to lose because of a two-second celebration over dog repellent.

"Oh, well," she said finally, throwing her hands in the air. "At least I don't have to spend the morning smelling the stench of that cigar."

With that, she marched away, leaving her unwanted partner gaping behind her.

"You just got her eliminated," Jess said, feeling as taken aback as Mrs. Rayburn had looked.

Carter leaned back against the wall, squinting at her. "You're welcome."

"What?" Jess blinked at him. "Are you seriously telling me you did that on purpose?"

Carter's expression lacked any sign of contrition. "You weren't the only person being forced to listen to her drone on about gardening."

Jess gaped at him, appalled. "So, you tricked her out of five million dollars as punishment?"

"Actually, I was trying to help. I thought the liquid fence was a pretty good suggestion."

"You told her Bill's dog would pee in his bed."

"That was a joke. But the chemical works. I bet she'll order a bottle."

"She *will not* order a bottle."

"Ten bucks says she will." Carter held out a hand as if offering to shake on it.

Jess eyed it distrustfully, then realization dawned. "Are you really trying to get me to let go of the wall to shake your hand?"

The grin that stretched across Carter's face was all the answer she needed.

"What is *wrong* with you?" she demanded. "I thought we were becoming friends."

He didn't respond, merely lifted an eyebrow instead.

It was enough. He'd noticed her effort to freeze him out. How could he not? She'd practically painted a "keep away" sign on her back before she'd turned it on him.

"Look," she said, feeling terrible. "I know I've been different today, and I'm sorry about that. But the truth is, I can't play the game how I did yesterday. I need to win that money. It's the only way . . ."

She trailed off, unable to say the words aloud.

"You think you can use it. To help." Carter left off the word *him*, but it hung in the air between them.

"Yes," she said, grateful he was sticking to his word, being careful with her secret.

He nodded thoughtfully. "And you can't do that if you're teaming up with other contenders like you did with Bryce and me yesterday."

"Exactly. I just think I have a better shot at the prize if I don't allow for any distractions."

"So, you're saying that you find me distracting." Carter's voice was so impassive that it took a moment for his words to sink in and her responding blush to bloom.

"I'm saying that it's best if I keep my distance from you while we're competing against each other. I can't stand here talking to you all day, putting myself at risk of losing focus. I need to go somewhere else. Away from you." She felt like she was being too harsh, but it had to be done.

Carter surveyed her for another moment before nodding decisively.

"Okay," he said before turning toward the wall and stepping back so his arm arced like a bridge.

"What are you doing?"

"Making a path," he said simply. "You can't take your hand off the wall, so you'll need to go under my arm if you want to get past me."

Just the thought of being between his hard chest and a wall brought to mind the rich, leathery smell of his cologne. She could actually smell it, like she was tucked against his shoulder again, resisting the urge to press her nose into the warm hollow of his neck. *No.*

"I'll go the other way," she said firmly.

But when she turned toward Mrs. Rayburn's abandoned spot on the wall, her nose filled with the stench of Bill's cigar. For some inexplicable reason, he was still standing there, puffing away like he hadn't been eliminated the moment his partner was.

"Why?" Jess groaned. "Hasn't anyone told him he can go home?"

"Maybe he doesn't want to." Carter shrugged. "Maybe he'd rather choke out everyone around him so they can experience the misery of losing the chance at a ten-million-dollar prize with him."

"See?" Jess grinned in spite of herself. "That's exactly why I can't be around you. Eventually, that evil mind of yours will turn on anyone close enough for it to destroy."

A responding grin flashed across Carter's face so quickly she wondered if she'd even seen it. "That's not fair. I don't want to destroy everyone. Just the top contenders for my money."

"Which will be me." Jess waved for him to move. "Stand back. I'm going around the front of you."

Obediently, Carter took a step back, pressing his body flush against the stone wall. Jess approached him determinedly, placing her left hand near his waist. With her right hand, she reached for the wall on the other side of him. It was farther than she'd expected, and her fingers scrambled for purchase as her chin pressed into his chest. Finally, she got her palm flat on the wall, but not until the entire length of her was pressed against the front of him.

Her breath hitched in her throat as she froze in the compromising position. This was not at all how she'd envisioned the transition going. In retrospect, Carter's original suggestion that she go under his arm had been a much better plan. She definitely should've done that.

Carter laughed as if he could read her thoughts. His breath smelled like chocolaty coffee, and his body was warm and hard. If the country song on the speaker weren't too twangy to project even an ounce of sexiness, Jess would probably be getting credit for performing her first lap dance. She felt her cheeks turn crimson.

"Just so I'm clear," Carter murmured, "this is what you meant when you talked about keeping your distance?"

"Not exactly." Jess grimaced and shifted her weight, pushing through to the other side. "I probably owe you an apology for the way that turned out."

"You probably owe me dinner," he said. "But I think the layer of clothes kept that from being considered third base, so I won't hold you to it."

"Someone needs to explain the bases to you."

"You're welcome to," he said, "but I do learn best by example."

The unexpected flirtation caused Jess's stomach to swoop in a slow, luxurious flip.

"I'm going now," she said, as much to herself as to him. With one final apologetic smile, she turned away and started down the wall.

A broad back blocked her path, and she paused for a moment before tapping on his shoulder. She would ask him to create a tunnel with his arm, like Carter had originally suggested. It had to be better than trying to navigate her way down the wall by straddling everyone she came in contact with. The man turned around, and Jess found herself staring into Bo Sutton's startlingly blue eyes. His flannel was unbuttoned, and the worn T-shirt underneath hugged the lines of his muscular physique. It was the first time she'd ever seen him without thick blond hair falling over his forehead. Instead, it was trimmed and artfully mussed in a way that said he'd spent the night with Annabelle.

"Bo!" She squealed the word. "Congratulations!"

"Uh, thanks." Bo tilted his head and smiled back at her questioningly. "We got all but one yesterday, and we were the first to turn our pictures in to Novak, so hopefully we're pretty high in the ranking. I heard you actually managed to get the buck, though, so you're probably ahead of us."

Jess laughed, although it *was* reassuring to hear that she and Nikki were being considered top contenders. "I meant your engagement with Annabelle. Or pre-engagement, or whatever. I saw her yesterday, and she seemed so happy."

Bo's smile widened into something worthy of a toothpaste commercial, and his face flushed adorably. "Did she?"

Jess nodded. "She was practically glowing."

"She said she's going to marry me." The pride in Bo's voice made Jess's heart melt.

"So I heard." Jess turned at the sound of footsteps and discovered Annabelle herself approaching them. Oddly, her expression lacked her usual warmth.

"Jessica," she said coolly in greeting. "I see the bangs are holding up well."

Oh. She must still be annoyed about yesterday.

"I love them," Jess said, feeling even guiltier because the bangs did frame her face in a surprisingly flattering way. She would've felt better if she'd hated them. At least then she would've been punished for deliberately tricking Annabelle into helping them get the photo. "You did an amazing job."

Annabelle smiled tightly, flicking a lock of freshly straightened hair over her shoulder. Since Jess had last seen her, she'd added a lovely soft pink streak.

Deliberately, Annabelle shifted her attention to Bo.

"I heard you'd be stuck here for hours, so I came to keep you company," she said in a high-pitched voice. "But I see you've already found someone to spend the day with."

OH.

Foolish, foolish Jess. It wasn't the picture Annabelle was reacting to but the idea of her new love hunkering down with another woman for what could amount to hours or even days.

"No," Jess said quickly. "I was just . . ."

She faltered. Something about Annabelle's response to seeing her fiancé talk to another woman gave Jess the impression it wasn't exactly the time to squeeze herself between Bo and the wall. And Jess didn't even want to think what would happen if she suggested the route she'd taken with Carter.

"Congratulating him," Jess said instead, taking a tiny step backward. "After all, he's one round closer to getting you that ring."

At the reminder, Annabelle's expression brightened, and she moved closer to Bo. Their eyes locked, and the air seemed to shift, warming like the chemistry between them was strong enough to change the physical properties of the world around them. Jess sighed at the sweetness of it. But then Annabelle took another step forward, and Bo's free hand snaked around her waist. The rhythm of their breaths changed into something dangerously close to panting.

"Oh." Jess eked out the word as their mouths met.

So much tongue.

Was Bo's extraordinarily long? And where had his hand gone? It seemed to be on a tour somewhere beneath Annabelle's skirt. Had they forgotten that they were surrounded by half the town? Annabelle let out a whimpering moan that sent Jess stumbling backward.

She crashed into a hard, warm body but managed to keep her hand on the wall.

"Sorry," she said, turning to face the man she couldn't seem to escape.

Carter looked down at her seriously. "I'd just like to congratulate you for doing such a great job with this distance plan of yours. You're really killing it."

She sighed. "I'm just going to sit here silently. Please pretend I'm invisible."

His eyes dropped down her body, scanning the boldly colored pattern for long enough that her cheeks grew warm at the attention.

Finally, he looked back up. "I think I've been blinded by your sweater. Does that help?"

Chapter 14

....

CARTER

T he early-evening air smelled of popcorn and muffins, and the crowd had grown larger, despite the fact that quite a few teams had already been disqualified. Normal business hours had ended, and watching people hold their hands to a wall appeared to be the best show on Redford's docket. A high school boy had brought out his guitar and was alternating between classic rock songs people could sing along with and some kind of punk or metal that elicited shouts of displeasure. The descending sun had tinged the sky with light streaks of orange.

Carter wondered if his partner was as hungry as he was. He hadn't seen Bryce all day, which felt stranger than it had any right to. He'd only known the guy for a few days, after all. But his fate *was* tied to his partner's, so it made sense that he would've preferred it if the two of them had ended up on the same side of the courthouse. Or, at the very least, in sight of each other. Bryce had probably charmed some bystander into making a food run for him and was halfway through a juicy burger right now. He'd better not be enjoying it too much to remember to keep a hand on the wall.

"I can't believe she wouldn't let me buy a sandwich," he grumbled. Carter had gone so far as to offer the woman twenty dollars for a turkey and swiss and had still been denied. Apparently, the sandwiches were only for sale for bystanders and the team the woman's sister was on. It was proof that his parents' life philosophy was flawed. Not everything had a price.

"Eat a muffin," Jess offered again as if he hadn't already explained to her that muffins didn't make a meal. She had bought one of each kind from Sally's basket and spent the last ten minutes happily comparing and contrasting them like she was at a uniquely buttery wine tasting.

Both of them were sitting on the ground with their legs stretched out in front of them, but only Jess's legs had five muffins balanced atop her ridged leggings. He tried not to smile at the sight of her, all giggly and hyper from the sugar rush. Her effort to be quiet had been a categorical failure. She'd barely made it ten minutes before she'd dragged him into a conversation that had spanned most of the day.

"Which one's the best?" he asked, giving in and eyeing the blackberry muffin with interest.

Jess studied them seriously, her gaze lingering on the one with white chocolate chips. She pulled her eyes away and hesitated. "The oatmeal raisin?"

Carter almost laughed. "Are you saying that because that's the one you least mind sharing?"

"Yes," she admitted with an apologetic grimace.

"I'd give you credit for your honesty, but I'm still not

over that lie you told about your most embarrassing moment." Superlatives had been a big topic of conversation. Favorites, as in movies, foods, colors, etc. (The fact that her favorite color was neon orange was another thing he'd prefer to assume was a lie.)

Firsts.

Bests and worsts.

Unsurprisingly, not one of their answers had matched.

"That *was* my most embarrassing moment." Jess's eyes turned serious, her chin jutting forward. "Do you not understand that I'd been abbreviating the word *tomorrow* to 'tomm.' for years? I was mortified when I finally realized there was no second *m* in the word."

"But you were thirteen." Carter shook his head. "Am I supposed to believe you were sending out memos to your staff? At risk of losing credibility in the newspaper industry? At worst, you were incorrectly shortening words in your diary or in love letters to some teenage boy who probably couldn't put down his video game controller long enough to read the entire thing. How embarrassing could it be?"

"You don't understand." For the first time since she'd given up her effort to be an island, Jess looked disappointed in him. It didn't feel good.

"Explain it to me." Carter's words came out softer than he'd intended.

"I love words," she said passionately.

"Okay."

"For as long as I can remember, I've loved them. I love them in books, and I love how you can put exactly the right combination of them together to make something sound better or worse, and I love the way the letters in them fit together so perfectly. So when I realized I'd been putting this terrible, wrong version of such a basic word—I mean, it was *tomorrow*, not *supercalifragilisticexpialidocious* or some kind of Latin-based medical term—out into the world, and in print, no less, I felt like I'd done something terrible. Like I couldn't have been reading all my books right if I'd failed to pick up such a basic word. And maybe, if I hadn't noticed that, I'd been missing the point of the stories, too."

"That's a lot to read into one misspelled word."

Jess's eyes narrowed as if in anticipation of a pun. When it didn't come, she let out a little sigh of relief.

She had nothing to worry about. Carter didn't do puns. On this, at least, they seemed to have finally found something in common.

"Yeah, well." Jess shrugged. "Like you said, I was only thirteen. My world was small and largely governed by hormones and a flair for the dramatic."

"Hence the tutu?"

Jess's mouth widened into a grin. "You think you're embarrassing me by continuing to bring that up, but I'll have you know I looked fantastic in that tutu."

"Oh, I'm sure you did," he said, trying not to reveal just how vividly he was imagining her bare legs stretched out beneath that tutu. She had great legs. He knew that for a fact, thanks to those leggings. He'd tried all day to focus on her eyes instead, but every time she looked away, some kind of gravitational force dragged his gaze south.

He smiled back at her for a moment before dropping his eyes to the muffin buffet. Without touching her, he plucked the oatmeal-raisin muffin from Jess's thigh. She might be terrible at keeping her distance, but he had a lifetime's worth of experience in the practice. If she needed space, he was fully capable of keeping his hands off her. He balanced the muffin on his lap so he could tear off a chunk without letting go of the wall.

"I feel that way about numbers," he admitted before taking a bite. It was dense but surprisingly tasty.

Jess leaned forward like he was a book whose page she couldn't wait to turn. "Do you?"

He nodded and swallowed. "They're kind of like the way you described words, where you can combine them together to get exactly the right thing. And I find it comforting that they have permanent and unchanging value. You can cross them from one account to another to elicit different totals, but you always know exactly what you're working with."

"I can see—" Jess's mouth clamped closed as something hit Carter's lip and bounced off.

"What was that?" He reached for his lip, swiping it to see if whatever had hit him had left residue behind. When he caught sight of Jess's reaction, he shook his head in feigned offense. "Are you seriously holding back laughter? I'm under attack over here."

She gave in, holding up her available hand in apology. "It looked like it was just popcorn."

He looked past her, and Jess turned to follow his gaze, but they were distracted by something bigger that was taking place.

"You bastard!" Annabelle screeched the words before

stomping off, leaving Bo holding the wall and shouting desperately after her.

It seemed impossible that the guy could've said something to offend her. From what Carter had seen, Bo's mouth had been too busy consuming Annabelle's face to form words. He'd clearly done something wrong, though. With a final shout, Bo abandoned the wall to run after Annabelle. The shriek of a whistle pierced the air, and Novak shouted "eliminated" into the megaphone. Nikki moved into the space Bo had just abandoned like some kind of well-groomed devil appearing from chaos, flinging popcorn instead of fiery embers. She tossed another kernel at Carter's face.

He batted it away with one hand.

"You were supposed to catch it in your mouth," Nikki said, feigning disappointment.

"My mistake," Carter said. But when she pulled another piece from her cross-body purse and cocked it for launch, he raised what remained of the oatmeal-raisin muffin and lifted his chin in a let's-do-this way. "You first."

They faced off like pistol-wielding cowboys in an old Western until Nikki shrugged and flung the piece of popcorn over her shoulder. It hit Bobby Randall's back, and he jerked around, slapping at the spot like he'd been bitten by a spider. Unfortunately, his other hand remained firmly on the courthouse wall. Carter popped the rest of the muffin into his mouth.

"I don't even know why you're still here," Nikki said, pointedly ignoring the drama taking place behind her. "Bryce got eliminated two hours ago."

Carter's breath caught in his throat, and his heart immediately began to pound with an intensity that didn't make sense, given the fact that he knew she was lying. She *was* lying. Obviously. Bryce would've found him immediately if he'd been eliminated. *Wouldn't he?*

"That's mean," Jess said, her tone so sharp even Nikki looked taken aback. "Don't say that to him."

"Even if it's—"

Jess cut her off. "It's not true. Tell him you're lying."

She looked so fierce in her certainty that Carter's breath eased out of his throat, leaving him only slightly light-headed with residual fear that he could've failed so soon at his grandfather's plan for him.

"Fine," Nikki said with a roll of her eyes. "It was just a joke. No reason to get bossy. You should be thanking me, you know."

"For?" Carter forced himself to lift a skeptical eyebrow instead of slumping over with relief like he wanted to.

"For doing my part to clear the wall. While the two of you have been sitting around all day like you're at some picnic in the park, I've been thinning the herd."

"Oh, Nikki." Jess leaned back as if distance could negate their partnership. "What have you done?"

"What you should've done eight hours ago," Nikki said unapologetically. "You think a woman marks her territory with her tongue like that if she's completely secure in the relationship? One teensy insinuation that I slept with Bo last weekend, and Annabelle ran off like he'd slapped her."

"You slept with Bo?" Jess slapped her free hand over her mouth when she realized she'd yelled the question loud enough to turn heads. It was cute but pointless. People had been staring at her and Carter all day, making no effort to pretend they weren't listening to every word of their conversation. If he'd been with anyone else, Carter would've clammed up just to avoid adding entries to Redford's gossip database. But he'd been enjoying learning more about her far too much to let his desire for privacy ruin the moment.

"Of course not." Nikki rolled her eyes. "A guy doesn't give up millions of dollars to run after a girl he's been cheating on. I said I *insinuated* that we'd slept together. In, like, a teensy way."

"But they were so happy." Jess gazed forlornly at Bo's abandoned spot on the wall like she was mentally willing them back.

"They were horny," Nikki clarified.

"And surprisingly flexible," Carter said.

"This isn't about their flexibility." Jess shot him a disappointed look. "It's about fixing what's been unfairly broken." She shifted her disapproval to Nikki. "Now, how are you going to make this better?"

"By sleeping with Bo for real?" Nikki offered. "After that thorough demonstration, I've realized that I haven't been giving our town heartthrob the attention he deserves."

Jess gaped at her, then looked more surprised than she should've been when Nikki took her open mouth as an invitation to throw popcorn into it. Jess wiped at the spot on her cheek where the kernel hit. "How would sleeping with him help in any possible way?"

"It would negate the lie," Carter offered helpfully.

"Exactly." Nikki tapped her nose and pointed at him. "If

my lie becomes the truth, then I didn't wrong either of them by saying it."

"Because it's never wrong to tell the truth," Carter said.

"But it *was* a lie." Jess threw up her hand with a disbelieving widening of her eyes, and Carter had to press his lips together to keep from laughing with Nikki. He'd begun to suspect that Jess wore so many bright hues because she felt things in color, and he wondered which particular shade equaled exasperation. "The lie caused the problem."

"If I tell Annabelle the truth tomorrow, will you stop waving your arm at me?" Nikki shot an admonishing look toward the bright pattern that stretched down Jess's sleeve. "A seizure seems imminent."

Jess dutifully let her arm drop to her side. "Will you really tell her?"

"I was going to anyway." Nikki flicked a kernel that hit Carter's forearm. "How else was I going to get the gratitude I deserve?"

"Gratitude?" Jess's tone was heavy with disbelief.

"Gratitude," Nikki confirmed. "Thanks to me, Annabelle now knows that Bo values her more than he does millions of dollars. There aren't a lot of people who get to enter into a lifelong commitment with that kind of reassurance. Honestly, I wouldn't be surprised if they're so grateful they end up making me maid of honor."

Carter would've laughed if he weren't so impressed with Nikki's contorted logic.

"So," he said instead, "who else have you managed to get rid of?"

Jess gasped and attempted to push him away with a futile shove at his chest. He caught her wrist lightly, despite his determination to avoid touching her. His lack of restraint was rewarded when he felt her pulse quicken beneath his fingers. At least he wasn't the only one struggling to retain control over his body.

"What?" He grinned, hoping it would be interpreted as taunting rather than pleasure in the fact that Jess hadn't pulled away. "I'm not offering to be the axe she chops the trees with," he said, letting go of her wrist, "but you can't expect me to pretend her actions don't benefit me."

Nikki nodded her approval and launched into the details on how she'd gotten rid of three teams, scowling as she described failing to get rid of Lexi and her partner, and Bobby and his. She was in the middle of brainstorming a new plan to lure them off the wall when Jess's dad appeared.

"I suppose I could tell him the garage is burning down," Ross offered, correctly interpreting that the Bobby they were referring to was his boss.

Of course, Carter realized, in a town this size, Bobby Randall might actually be the only Bobby in Redford.

"Would you?" Nikki batted her eyelashes in what Carter assumed was a shameless effort to flirt Ross into doing her bidding. It was impressive. Her eyes had actually gone all sparkly, like she was truly delighted to see him.

"Nope." Ross grinned and pulled his hands out from behind his back, presenting two plastic-wrapped squares. "But I *would* convince Karen I needed to buy two sandwiches for myself, then give them to my favorite team so they can stay strong and hold the wall longer than her sister."

"My hero," Nikki cooed. She reached for Ross's arm, but he shifted casually out of range without seeming to notice.

Carter looked to Jess to see if she was clocking Nikki's blatant attempt at flirting and was pained to discover her face had gone white and tight. It wasn't the look of someone who was merely annoyed or disapproving. It was the look of someone who had just remembered her heart was breaking.

She tried so hard to stay positive. It was as if she understood that her brightness lit up the world for everyone around her, and she was determined not to let them down. But she had her limitations, and she appeared to have reached them. He could see her struggle to hide her feelings—to be strong for her dad—but she hadn't been raised like Carter. She wasn't capable of putting on a mask.

"Did everyone know that Jess thinks *tomorrow* is spelled with two *m*'s?" he said quickly.

She blinked at him, her eyes going wide with betrayal. "I do not!"

"It's okay, Jess. There's no reason to be embarrassed. It's not like you spell words for a living." Carter lifted his finger to his chin. "Oh, wait."

"I know how to spell *tomorrow*," Jess argued, her previously ashen skin flooding red.

"I believe there are quite a few written notes that would suggest otherwise," Carter said tauntingly.

Nikki looked back and forth between them with disbelief. "Who cares about one stupid word?"

"Jess's clients?" Carter suggested. "I feel like they have a reasonable expectation that Jess can spell one of the most frequently used words in the English language."

"*I know how to spell* tomorrow*!*"

"*Tomorrow* can't be one of the most frequently used words in the English language," Nikki argued. "What about *the*? Or *and*?"

"*Be*," Ross suggested. "Or *to*."

"To be or not to be," Nikki quipped.

"I know how to spell *tomorrow*," Jess insisted.

She looked displeased when everyone ignored her. But at least she no longer looked heartbroken.

"*With*," Carter added, tamping down the smile of satisfaction that tugged at his mouth.

"*But*," Jess contributed after a defeated sigh.

"No need to get anatomical." Nikki looked at Ross with feigned disapproval. "Did you raise your daughter to have such a dirty mouth?"

"Nikki!" Jess flushed again, and Carter laughed.

Two hours later, their conversation was still going strong, bouncing around the little circle like kernels of Nikki's popcorn, until the shriek of Novak's whistle finally ended it.

"Half of the teams have now been eliminated," the lawyer announced into his megaphone. "Today's challenge is completed. The ten remaining teams will report to the square tomorrow at five p.m."

And then Novak kept them captive for another fifteen minutes, talking into the megaphone without ever really saying anything at all, but it didn't matter. Jess kept bouncing around like her muffins had been iced with cocaine, and

Nikki was waving her arms around in silent cheers of victory. Even Carter was shifting from foot to foot with repressed triumph until Bryce came bounding over and threw his arms around him, almost knocking him over. The resulting laughter turned giddy with excitement.

They'd made it to the next round.

Chapter 15

· · · · · · · · · · ·

JESS

'm late." Her dad shouted the words, probably stopping just inside the front door to shrug off his jacket and hang it on the hook. He could barely be heard over P!nk's "Raise Your Glass," which Jess had turned up so loud in her childhood bedroom it was a wonder she was working and not dancing.

She'd gone to his house to work, telling herself it was because she'd once done some of her best midterm cramming at this desk and not because she was worried her dad might die and was feeling morbidly desperate to hold on to the life they shared.

"Did you already leave?" Ross shouted as if it were possible P!nk was partying in his house alone.

"Yes," Jess shouted, embracing her regression to teendom. "You just missed me by five minutes. But if you hurry, you might be able to catch me on Main Street."

She turned down the music and flicked her cursor to the top corner of her laptop to check the time, shocked to discover it was already 4:42. She'd wanted to use her unexpected free day to call Liz back, to be able to pace from one end of her room to the other, stepping around piles of books as Liz comforted her, just like she'd done in high school when something terrible happened. Jess had only needed to tighten up a few chapters first. But, clearly, she should've set an alarm. She'd missed her chance now. Novak wanted everyone to be at the town square at five o'clock for his next challenge.

"Very funny." Ross appeared in her door, looking way too large and healthy to be taken down by something small enough to live inside him. "I would've been here sooner, but I couldn't, in good conscience, close the garage up until I got the engine running on Barker's old Pontiac, and that thing practically needed heart paddles to bring it back to life."

Jess blinked at him, surprised by the surge of resentment that hit her.

She didn't want to do this.

It was absurd that she was expected to pretend that everything was normal—like she hadn't spent half the day staving off the fear that this could all disappear at any moment. That the house could be sold, her stuff boxed up and moved to her own home, her dad's things donated to Goodwill for some stranger to use. That she could lose the home she'd grown up in and, much worse, the parent she'd grown up with.

In an alternate universe, she stood up, put her hands on her hips, and demanded answers to the questions that had been running through her mind since her dad had broken the news. *What are the odds that you'll beat this thing? What kind of treatment are they giving you?* And most important, *Why wasn't I there when you found out you were sick?*

They felt like fair questions to ask. Questions that should've been answered already.

She hadn't asked them, though. And she wasn't going to now. Not because she was scared to, or because her relationship with her dad was too restrictive or shallow. Not even because his response would be as hard for him to give as it would be for her to hear. Jess wouldn't ask because she didn't need to; she already knew the answers.

Her dad was a protector. He believed he had to be. It had always been just him looking out for her, trying to be two parents so she'd never feel the loss of one. If he thought he could beat this thing, he never would've suggested any other alternative. Whatever treatment he was receiving wasn't doing enough. Telling her that the doctors didn't expect him to survive meant he was certain the outcome was inevitable.

So in this universe, Jess didn't stand up. She didn't put her hands on her hips and give voice to the things that would make them both want to cry. Instead, she pretended to care about Phil Barker's stupid old Pontiac.

"I'm going to start calling it the Cat-mobile," she said, her voice only cracking slightly with suppressed emotion, "because it has nine lives."

"He's already got a name for it." Ross leaned against the doorframe. "Guess what it is."

"The Rust Bucket?" When he shook his head, Jess tried again. "The Pontiac Pirate?"

"Paul." Her dad laughed at her disbelieving expression. "He just calls it Paul, like the car is some guy from Woodbridge he hangs out with."

"Good on you for bringing out the heart paddles, then. It sounds like you might've just saved Phil Barker's best friend."

Ross tilted his chin toward the hallway. "You ready to go?"

"Not really," Jess said, getting up in spite of her assertion. "Doesn't it seem weird that Novak set today's challenge for so late in the afternoon? It's like he has something so embarrassing in store for us that he wanted to save it until after business hours so more people could witness it."

"Hmmm." Ross's murmur was vague, but the grin that appeared on his face spoke volumes.

"What?" Jess's eyes narrowed. "You know something."

"Not really." Ross's grin widened. "Just that I passed the town square on the way home, and there seems to be a stage set up."

Jess blinked. "A what?"

"A stage. Not a big one. It's only a couple of feet off the ground. But it's definitely a stage." Ross laughed. "And I'm guessing you're about to be on it."

....

GROANING, JESS SURVEYED the madness in front of her. Her dad hadn't been messing with her. A stage with two long tables stretched across it, both covered in red gingham tablecloths, was set up on the town square. Lights had been strung overhead, and folding chairs covered the lawn. Jess took zero comfort in the fact that only ten of the chairs had made their way onto the platform, because the piles of pie boxes on the table behind the stage suggested today's challenge was going to involve eating—and Nikki had made her thoughts on refined sugar clear last night when Jess had been foolish enough to offer her a piece of muffin.

If a member of their team was going to be shoving fork-fuls of baked goods into her face, it would be Jess. To her left, Bobby Randall was loudly informing a group of women that he'd once eaten thirteen hot dogs at a barbecue. It was amazing how many women actually found this buffoon attractive.

Jess and her dad rolled their eyes at each other simultaneously, even as she mentally began to reassure herself by running through every memory she had of inhaling a gallon of ice cream after a particularly bad day. Bobby and his pile of little wieners had nothing on Jess; this was the event she'd been training for.

Jess scanned the crowd as her dad led her deeper into it. She told herself she was looking for Nikki, even though Nikki didn't have dark, impeccably styled hair nor a uniform of button-up shirts and perfectly pressed slacks. As they neared the table of pies, Jess noticed that Sally and Novak appeared to be in an argument. At least, Sally was in an argument. Jess and her dad slowed at the sight of Sally jabbing an accusatory finger at the piles of pies.

"Those pies are from Woodbridge; I can tell from the boxes," Sally noted loudly.

Novak managed to tear his eyes away from his iPad while still appearing distracted. The device was constantly in his hands, a portable scoreboard only he was allowed to see. Given the luck he'd exhibited with microphones (and megaphones and whistles), Jess suspected the screen would freeze right before he determined the winner, losing all the data and necessitating they start the competition over from the beginning.

"Yes, I had them delivered from Woodbridge this afternoon." Novak's gaze returned to the iPad before he finished speaking.

"But we're in *Redford*," Sally said sharply. "We don't bring baked goods from Woodbridge into Redford. We have superior pies right here at Evangeline's."

"Hide me," a voice behind Jess whispered.

She spun around to find Luanne ducking behind her. Luanne had Carter with her, strangely enough, and she shoved him next to Jess to expand her cover.

"What's going on?" Jess asked Luanne, but her mind was fully focused on the way Carter's arm pressed against hers. Acting casual, she looked up and found him offering that half-smile of his in greeting.

She tried to shoot an equally unaffected smile back at him, but she could feel her mouth stretch to its fullest width, into what one of her authors would most likely describe as a beam. It was true. She was *beaming*. It wasn't her fault, though, that she was so utterly incapable of playing it cool. Warm was her go-to setting. And how could she be expected to stay away from a grown man who looked like he ran on espresso and dry toast but claimed S'mores Pop-Tarts were his favorite food? She couldn't. That was exactly the kind of information that made you beam when you saw someone.

"Why are you hiding?" Jess said, directing her grin toward Luanne. That's right, look at how delighted she was to see Luanne as well. She didn't just beam for handsome men.

"Sally is saying nice things about me." Luanne popped

her head between theirs as if to confirm it was true. With a satisfied nod, she ducked down again and added, "If she knew I could hear, she'd stop."

Jess laughed at the truth of the assertion as Novak waved Sally off.

"Luanne Walker owns Evangeline's," Novak said dismissively. "She can't make the pies for a game she's competing in. It's a conflict of interest."

"Are you questioning my friend's baking integrity?" Sally all but roared. "What are you suggesting she'd do? Hollow out her own pies? Fill the others with cement?"

"She called you her friend," Ross stage-whispered. He'd fallen in next to Jess, widening Luanne's cover to a three-person wall.

"And she said you have integrity," Jess said with a squeal.

"And she does not believe you would use cement as an ingredient while baking," Carter said.

"I can hear her," Luanne said, still ducking behind them. "They can hear her in Woodbridge."

"Because she's passionate," Ross noted with a satisfied nod. "About your *friendship*."

"And pie packaging," Carter added.

Jess pinched him deliberately on the top of his hand.

"What?" Carter looked at her with an expression so bewildered it could only be contrived.

Jess pulled him toward her by his neck and whispered into his ear, "We're trying to get their friendship back on track."

Carter looked at her as she pulled back, his hand copying hers and sliding against the back of her neck. He held her still for just a moment so that their gazes locked and the sliver of space between their faces heated deliciously, and then he pulled her forward like she'd done to him, and the warm whisper of his breath sent goose bumps scattering down her neck. "I know. And *I'm* trying to provide impartial commentary."

"That's not helpful," Jess murmured, too overcome by the increasingly familiar smell of him to infuse any reproach into the whisper. The heat of his fingers pulsed into her neck, and her cheek brushed against his as he shifted to respond.

"It wasn't intended to be." Carter caught her gaze again as he pulled back, his eyes smoldering as if he could see exactly how much he'd affected her.

And then his meaning hit her, and Jess gave a little snort of disapproval. At the sound, Carter unleashed the most unexpected, wide, and wicked grin Jess could imagine, causing tiny gymnasts to whirl into cartwheels of delight across her belly.

"She just likes to argue," Luanne continued, too focused to notice the whispered exchange happening above her. "I can tell you that confidently, from my years of experience on the receiving end."

"She does appear to be enjoying the yelling," Carter noted. His grin had disappeared as quickly as it appeared, the mask of detached carelessness back in place.

Jess knew now that it was under there, though, and she was delighted to have been the one to unearth it.

"See?" Luanne said to Carter, clearly pleased to have someone on her side. She gestured toward Ross and Jess. "They want Sally and me to be friends again, so they're making more of this than it is."

"Which is an odd strategy," Carter said casually. "If the two of you become friends again, your team is probably only going to be stronger competition."

"I suppose that's true." Luanne's eyes narrowed in thought. "So, wait. Are you saying you think—"

Carter held up a hand like a wall, effectively cutting her off. "I can assure you I've put absolutely no thought into your friendship, or non-friendship, beyond the ways in which it might affect me."

Jess swallowed back the giggle that burbled up through her throat. Reminding Luanne that she'd have a stronger chance at winning if she wasn't at odds with her teammate? The tiniest hint of derision Carter had placed on the word *non-friendship*, like the concept was so childish he could barely think of a word for it? It couldn't have been more perfect. Or inevitably effective.

As Sally stomped off, having failed in her effort to bring Novak to his knees in shame over his unpardonable sin of shopping outside of Redford, Jess could see the wheels in Luanne's head turning.

"If only one of us is going to be eating pies," Luanne said, proving Jess's hunch correct, "I should probably talk to Sally and figure out which one of us it will be."

"Smart," Jess said, but Luanne was already running off and didn't look back.

Ross had been waylaid by Brandy Hostetler, who was making her hundredth play to lure him into her bedroom with the offer of a home-cooked lasagna. So Jess had no other option than to drag Carter into her enthusiasm.

"You just did something really good." Her feet tapped

out a celebratory dance on the trampled grass. "They're totally going to become friends again."

"You're too invested in your neighbors' lives," Carter said. But the amusement in his expression took the sting out of his words.

"Not possible in a small town." Jess did a few jazz hands to top off her dance. "And what was I supposed to do—not notice how sad Elvis has been since Sally and Luanne stopped walking him together? His bark is like three octaves lower, and I haven't seen him sniff another dog's butt in weeks."

"Tell me something, Jessica." Carter leaned forward, gazing into her eyes intently like he was about to ask her something profoundly personal. "Are you the leader of a neighborhood watch? Does the town sheriff knock on your door, looking for leads when a newspaper gets stolen from someone's porch?"

"They should," Jess said pertly. "I've been watching Mr. Sanders sneak next door in his bathrobe every morning for the last two years. I would've shouted at him if I wasn't so scared of what I'd see if he turned my way."

"It's a small robe?"

"Narrow. It does its best, but its sides just can't meet in the middle."

"Well, hopefully the same won't be true of Sally and Luanne."

Jess clapped triumphantly at this proof that he cared, and Carter rewarded her with a quarter of a smile.

"What's your number?" Carter pulled out his phone.

"My phone number?" The thought of having access to

Carter with the press of a button rather than Novak's schedule dictating when she'd run into him was more thrilling than it should be.

"Yes, your phone number," Carter said, seemingly unfazed by the request for clarification. "Now that I realize how much of your time is devoted to monitoring the town's activities, I thought it would be easier if I texted you any changes in my normal routine."

"That's so thoughtful of you." Jess reached out a hand, and Carter touched enough buttons that the contact screen was all set up when he pressed his sleek black phone into her palm. Unsurprisingly, his phone didn't have a case on it. Jess could've guessed he was far too confident in his own grip to need a case.

Novak's whistle pierced the air just as Jess was hitting *save*, and his megaphone screeched and crackled before his voice filled the air. She passed the phone back to Carter and gave her attention to the stage.

"Tonight's challenge," Novak said, "will be a pie-eating contest."

The crowd applauded, and Novak held up a slender finger.

"When I say the word *now*," he continued, "a timer will begin, and each team will have five minutes to get one of its members on the stage. If neither member is prepared to participate, the team will be disqualified. If both members are on the stage, the team will be disqualified. In other words, if the team cannot agree on which person will compete within the five-minute time limit, they will both be disqualified. Once the decided-upon teammates are on the stage, I will explain how the competition will work."

Carter leaned in toward Jess. "And *that* was just the introduction-to-the-rules speech. Do lawyers typically get paid by the word? If so, there's probably not going to be any prize money left by the end of this."

Jess stifled a laugh and stretched up on her tiptoes to search the crowd, realizing that she'd forgotten to find her teammate. "Do you see Nikki?"

Carter tilted an eyebrow. "You think I'm going to help you find your teammate, knowing you could be eliminated if I don't?"

Jess's brow furrowed at him as she searched for outrage at his refusal to help. But she couldn't find any. So he wanted to win. She did, too. And she would.

With a perky smile, she slipped her arms around him for the briefest of hugs.

"Good luck," she said, laughing at the way he tensed in response before she pulled back. She held up crossed fingers on both hands as she backed away, calling out, "Hopefully, both our teams will make it to the next round."

She turned her focus to finding Nikki. Jess had been so close to the stage that her eyes had adapted to the brightness. But the sky had darkened, and the lights strung in crisscrosses over the audience put out a golden glow that, while atmospheric, didn't offer the same visibility. Jess's pulse began to race. She couldn't really lose like this, could she? She'd just have to go up on the stage herself. She knew Nikki was going to make her do it anyway.

But what if Nikki walked onto the stage from the other side at the exact same moment? It wouldn't just be a ten-million-dollar mistake; it could also be the death of Jess's dad. Jess's phone buzzed in her pocket, and she fumbled at it desperately, praying Nikki had gotten her number from someone. But it wasn't Nikki's name on the text. In fact, no one's name was on it.

The text was from a new number and read, **She's behind the stage, opposite side of where we were just standing.** Jess's stomach fizzed with pleasure at the realization that it had to be from Carter, and she quickly began threading her way through people to get to the stage. It wasn't until she was rounding the side of it, on her way to the back, that it occurred to her that Carter could've sent her in the wrong direction.

Her heart thumped deafeningly in her ears, raging at her stupidity. It was a brilliant strategy, so obvious Jess had been a fool not to suspect it. Hadn't he *just* told her to her face that he'd rather see her eliminated?

So sure was Jess of his betrayal, she didn't even see Nikki until the woman was right up on her.

"You're going to look so cute with a double chin," Nikki said in greeting.

Waves of relief crashed over Jess at the sight of her, and she didn't even flinch when Nikki pressed a manicured nail to her cheek, forcing Jess to shift her head so Nikki could study her profile.

"Oh, look at that," Nikki said brightly. "You already have one."

Chapter 16

....

JESS

Carter had helped her.

Jess sat on the stage, staring out at half the town singing along to "American Pie," mostly off-key, grinning at their enthusiasm, the fact that she lived on to compete in another challenge, and the surprising realization that Carter had helped her get here. Plus, she was about to eat a whole lot of pie. Who didn't love pie?

Sure, Jess's first choice wouldn't be to stuff it into her face while everyone she'd ever known—not to mention an intimidatingly attractive guy who had turned out to be a surprisingly good listener—looked on. And it might be nice if Novak had chosen something other than cherry. Something less colorful, like apple, that wasn't so likely to stain her face and clothes. But at least it was *pie*, not something healthy like collard greens or impossible like peanut butter.

While Novak continued to drone into his wireless mic about the rules of the challenge—a speech that could've easily been boiled down into *eat quickly*—Jess found herself searching the crowd for Carter. She finally spotted him all the way in the back and was amused to see that he was one of the only people not singing along. He *was* swaying to the beat, though. Not voluntarily. And not really swaying as much as being moved by the people on either side of him bumping into him as the crowd swayed. But he was definitely not managing to avoid participating entirely.

It would've been fun if he'd ended up onstage with her. She looked to Bryce on her right and mentally changed *fun* to *less intimidating*. Unlike Bobby, who was seated on her left, Bryce hadn't made any effort to trash-talk her, but she'd seen him go up against a half-pound burger at the bar more than once. He'd reminded her of a gator, jaw unhinged and inhaling rather than chewing. And he hadn't even been in a hurry. Just hungry.

"Tell me you ate a big dinner," Jess said to him hopefully.

"Seth wouldn't let me sneak anything out of the kitchen all day," Bryce said, referring to the Staple's main cook. "He's still sulking about getting eliminated when he took his hand off the wall to wave at Julia Foster."

"Poor guy," Jess said, sympathy momentarily overriding her disappointment at hearing Bryce's stomach was empty. "That crush has been nothing but ten years of heartbreak."

"It's on him now," Bryce said. "His dreams of cooking breakfast in her kitchen should've ended last year when she got married."

"I can't hear the rules over your gossiping over there," Bobby snapped, leaning close enough that Jess could smell the onions on his breath. At least she could be certain *his* stomach wasn't empty.

"Sorry," Jess said, attempting to appear somewhat

apologetic. It was a little rude of her to talk over Novak, even if his monologues did seem to be getting longer every day. Assuming everyone was smart enough to understand how an eating competition worked was foolish when she was in the presence of someone like Bobby.

"What are you doing up here anyway?" Bobby sneered as his gaze dropped the length of her body and back up again. "Aren't girls like you always on a diet?"

"Oh." Jess blinked at him. "Well, yes, obviously. But I traded in my body obsession card to the Female Inadequacy Council for a perpetual dissatisfaction with my nails. So now I can eat as much as I want, as long as I get regular manicures."

Bobby's face scrunched up with confusion before he finally grumbled, "Guys don't care about your nails."

"Don't they?" Jess smiled with feigned gratitude. "I'll have to report that to the council."

"Jess," Bryce said, squeezing her shoulder. He gestured to Novak, who was counting down, not from three but ten.

"Eight," Novak said, taking a long, slow breath before following it up with "seven."

Jess felt a surge of adrenaline as she moved her hand to hover over the fork. It built as Novak made his way painfully slowly down the ladder of numbers. Facing down the large crowd, and sandwiched between two beefy men, Jess suddenly felt very small. How could she do this? It typically took her the entire length of a sitcom to polish off a sandwich and a serving of chips. She was a chipmunk among gators.

"Two," Novak said, the breathiness of his voice suggesting he was losing steam.

Jess took a deep breath, reminding herself of what was at stake.

Her chest pounded as Novak followed up his "one" by putting a new yellow whistle into his mouth and blowing. The resulting silence was deafening. Not only did the whistle not make a noise but the crowd had seemed to inhale in unison, their breath now caught in the uncertainty of the moment. Had the contest begun? Jess looked from Novak to the other contestants uncertainly, but no one seemed to know what to do as Novak heaved breath into the unresponsive whistle again.

Beside her, Bobby hinged forward, plunging his face directly into the pie. The crowd roared with approval, and the stage exploded into activity. Jess grabbed for her fork and fumbled it, her trembling fingers unable to hold on. A second attempt secured it in her grip and sent it diving into the pie. Mentally, she cheered for herself and small victories.

Jess arced her fork through the lattice top, swooping it toward her mouth. The scent of sweet, tart cherries hit her nose just before the bite hit her tongue. Then her taste buds were reveling in the combination of buttery crust and gooey fruit. Her instinct was to savor it, but she pushed through, loading up her fork and beginning liftoff before swallowing the first bite.

In her peripheral vision, she could see Bryce shoveling it in with his hands. His pie pan was already a third empty, one of Novak's lackeys sliding another onto the table behind it, whereas hers was almost entirely full. So she dropped her fork and copied him, scooping gelatinous filling into her fingers. Cutting back on chewing went against every instinct

Jess had, but she managed it, swallowing big gulps of pie whole. And it paid off. Her internal cheerleader did the splits and shook her pompoms in the air at the sight of the restocker, appearing in front of Jess and sliding a new pie behind hers.

She was holding her own! The realization made her head buzz with excitement. Or maybe that was a high coming from the most intense sugar rush she'd ever experienced. Jess could feel laughter building in her chest at the hilarity of it all, and she swallowed it back down with a pile of pie big enough to choke a cobra. The filling had formed a layer over her fingers so thick they were no longer individual units.

It wasn't until the new song—ironically, "No Sugar Tonight" by the Guess Who—disappeared beneath the din of the crowd that Jess noticed the change in tone. The cheering had turned to shouts. She tried to tear her eyes away from her pie to see what was going on, but the pan was almost empty, and Bryce was already deep into his second. With a final frantic sweep, Jess finished hers off, using her free hand to shove the empty tin away and drag the new pie forward. Her stomach lurched at the sight of it, but somehow her brain registered that Bobby, too, had already made deep valleys into his second pie, so she dug in.

The triangle of crushed crust and filling wobbled as it approached her mouth, and she leaned forward to catch it. But then a hand slapped hers, and pie goo went flying across the table, landing in a splat against Bobby's forearm. Her eyes widened as she took in his snarl, and then her head snapped up as she registered the fact that Nikki had jumped onto the stage and was yanking her pie away.

"You can't eat it," Nikki cried, reaching toward Bryce's and swiping it off the table and onto the floor. "It's poisoned!"

Jess gagged, and her hands flew instinctively, frantically to her throat.

Chapter 17

....

NIKKI

Nikki doubled over, panting from the effort she'd exerted pushing her way through the crowd. At the end of the table, two men were lifting a swollen-faced DeMarco Davis from his chair as another woman pushed onto the stage. Ross had noticed the way DeMarco was clutching his throat before anyone else seemed to. He'd shouted, cutting off Nikki's attempt to flirt with him, and then he'd grabbed her forearm, the terror on his face evident as it occurred to him that his daughter was about to eat one of the pies that had made DeMarco sick.

Ross must have transmitted his fear to her through touch. That was the only explanation Nikki could come up with. He'd stumbled forward, but not before Nikki had felt his desperation and horror and compulsion to stop what could happen so viscerally that it had become her own. The next thing she knew, she was pushing people out of her way with a viciousness Ross wasn't capable of, and she made it to the stage in time to stop Jess from taking a bite from the contaminated second round.

And now, rather than falling to her knees with gratitude like she should've been, Jess was looking up at her like Nikki had shot her instead of saved her. Nikki would've laughed, but she actually liked DeMarco Davis—he'd dated Lexi for a while, and he'd treated her well, even ending the relationship kindly once he realized she hadn't been treating him nearly as well—and Nikki couldn't seem to shake the sight of him clutching his throat, his eyes bulging with fear. Her stomach twisted at the memory.

"You poisoned my pie?" Jess asked, her voice high with surprise.

"Yes," Nikki snapped, annoyed that she was being accused of attempting to end Jess's life after her Herculean effort to save it. "One bite and your insides would've melted like lava."

Nikki swiped other pie plates off the table and onto the floor as she spit out the words. It wasn't until after she was halfway through ridding the table of all of them that she realized the effort was unnecessary. She wasn't the only person who had made it onto the stage. DeMarco's mom had gotten to him and had plunged what Nikki assumed was an EpiPen into his outer thigh.

"What the hell is going on?" Bobby demanded, pushing up from his seat and towering over the table.

Bryce lifted his shirt, swiping it over his tongue, and Jess's eyes darted between her pie on the floor and Nikki's face like she was still trying to determine if Nikki had put something lethal in it. At the end of the table, the two men were attempting to pull DeMarco to his feet for the second time. To Nikki's relief, DeMarco stumbled between them, drunkenly but upright, his mom running over to say something to Novak before following after them.

"It looks like you're going to live to sweat through another sleeveless T-shirt," Nikki said, turning her attention toward Bobby just long enough to answer his question.

As Novak blew into his defunct whistle, Ross made it to the stage, less than a minute behind Nikki but what felt like an eternity. He leaned over the table, cupping Jess's pie-covered cheek with one hand and pressing the other against her forehead. Nikki wanted to find the gesture ridiculous but struggled to. The man's response to fear that his daughter had been poisoned was to check for a *fever*. It was perhaps the cutest thing she'd ever seen.

The whistle, finally choosing to participate in the night's events, blared shrilly, cutting through the square. The crowd quieted slightly.

"I ask you to be calm," Novak implored through the megaphone. "There's been an allergic reaction, but Mr. Davis is already on his way to the hospital."

"DeMarco?" Jess leaned back, scanning the chairs for him as if Novak hadn't just said he'd gone to the hospital. Her eyes returned to Nikki. "Is he okay?"

"I think he'll be fine." Jess's need for reassurance made it impossible for Nikki to point out the fact that she wasn't a doctor. "His mom had that EpiPen out so fast, I can only assume she already had it drawn and ready to launch at anyone who got too far ahead with the pies."

It made sense, really. No mother who had raised a child with a severe allergy would've felt comfortable watching him scarf down food at that speed. What didn't make sense was that DeMarco wouldn't share his mother's concern. He had lived his entire life with a deadly allergy. He couldn't have engaged in an eating competition without checking the ingredients first. Anyway, he'd been leading the pack, making a significant dent in the second pie before getting sick.

The first pie had been fine.

Nikki knew she wasn't the most trusting person in the world. You couldn't be abandoned and cheated on and learn as early as she had that nobody in the world had your back without developing a healthy sense of distrust. But she didn't think that contributed to the conclusion she'd reached. The first pie had to have been fine. It was the second pie that had made DeMarco sick. And the only way that was possible was if someone had added something to it. Intentionally.

And Nikki didn't seem to be the only one to have put two and two together and come up with sabotage. Around her, she could hear the whispered suspicions becoming hisses as conviction grew. Expressions of fear shifted to outrage.

"What did that partner of yours do?" Bobby turned to Bryce, barking the words so that half the crowd heard the accusation.

"Carter?" Bryce looked baffled, but Nikki spotted the steel beneath it. He might not be as direct as her, but he was smarter than he pretended to be. "He's never even met DeMarco."

"He doesn't need to have met him to realize he's competition." Bobby sneered and looked around, ensuring Bryce wasn't the only person listening to him. "Last I checked, Joe doesn't stock the market with poison. That's the kind of thing you have to go to the city for."

"Poison?" Bryce laughed, but Nikki missed what he said next because Bobby's absurd logic had caused her to realize something horrible.

She only knew DeMarco was allergic to peanuts because she'd been on double dates with him.

Nikki had been there to hear DeMarco double-check with the server that the fries weren't cooked in peanut oil. But, clearly, Bobby had never been out to eat with him. He wouldn't have known DeMarco had a deadly allergy. And Bobby probably wasn't the only one missing that information (although Nikki seriously hoped nobody else was stupid enough to suspect Atlanta of handing out poisonous powder to anyone flashing an Amex).

But Lexi had been the reason Nikki was out to dinner with DeMarco. She'd heard the question. *She* knew.

"Shut up, Bobby," Nikki barked as she spun around to find Lexi.

Her stomach sank when she spotted Lexi up on the stage, only about ten feet away, dipping one finger daintily into her partner's abandoned pie before lifting the jellied tip to her mouth. *She'd done it.* Fear slithered through Nikki, icy and sharp, but not because she was worried her best friend was an aspiring murderer.

Nikki knew with absolute certainty that Lexi was something far worse: terribly, ridiculously shortsighted. Lexi had never been capable of considering the consequences that might result from an action. Lexi's plan to sneak a look at their history final sophomore year so that she, Nikki, and

Cara would be guaranteed A's? That had somehow escalated from a quick search through Mrs. Ginneli's desk to a full-scale break-in in the middle of the night. The unfortunate janitor-slash-security-guard had lost his job and spent the next month collecting cans to recycle until Marty Beauford took pity and hired him to dig up worms for the Bait & Tackle.

And what about just last year, when Lexi had decided to make her ex jealous by luring some guy from Tinder into town? Nikki and Cara had warned her that he could be a serial killer, but Lexi invited the stranger into her house anyway, and then Nikki and Cara were the ones who had to try to drag him out of her pantry where he'd settled onto her floor, unwrapped all of her expensive carb-less meal-replacement bars, and was attempting to build a tiny cabin out of them.

Given Lexi's history, it wasn't at all difficult for Nikki to picture Lexi engaging in a bit of sabotage. Nikki herself had spent most of yesterday trying to trick people into letting go of the wall. And Lexi had been her right-hand woman for years, precisely because the two of them shared a similar sense of ruthlessness. The problem was, whereas Nikki would've realized that an allergic reaction could be deadly, Lexi would've stopped thinking past the fact that a swollen throat would prevent DeMarco from swallowing pie. It wouldn't have occurred to her that he could die, or that a medical emergency would stop the contest, or even that the discovery of her involvement would definitely lead to her elimination from the game.

It certainly wouldn't have occurred to her that being caught could get her arrested.

There was a part of Nikki that knew she should say something. For DeMarco's sake. For Carter's. For her own.

Nikki should accuse Lexi right now, loudly and while the town was still present and riled up with suspicion. Nikki could point out that Lexi was eating from the pies everyone else was irrationally scared of. Demand Lexi dump out her purse, hoping to discover an emptied pack of peanuts inside. At the very least, everyone would wonder enough to lessen the vitriol being directed toward Carter. And it would provide a bit of justice for DeMarco. Best of all, Nikki would have one less team to compete against once Lexi was kicked out of the competition.

Unfortunately, Nikki wasn't that kind of friend. She lived by a strange set of rules. The kind of rules that allowed her to secretly destroy a friend's relationship if she saw her being taken advantage of but prohibited her from ever hooking up with anyone her friend had shown interest in (even if there was no chance in hell of that interest being reciprocated). The kind that permitted her to veto a friend's unflattering outfit but forbade agreeing with them that their body was anything less than perfect. The kind that allowed her to ruin a friend's plans but never their reputation.

As frustrating as it might be, to Nikki, those rules were binding.

Nikki silently cursed her sense of integrity as Novak raised his megaphone and declared the competition canceled. She attempted to turn her frustration on Bobby, but Carter had finally joined Bryce and was taking all Bobby's attention, absorbing his accusations with an amused detachment that was clearly riling Bobby up even more. Damn it, if she didn't like him and his ridiculous standoffishness. He didn't deserve to take the blame for what Lexi had done.

Unfortunately, he would. That was how it worked when you were the outsider in a town this small. It was a harsh reality, but there were harsh realities to being an insider as well. Namely, that Nikki knew Lexi well enough to understand that her efforts at sabotage wouldn't end with one attempt.

Nikki had once believed you couldn't trust people, but she'd since grown up, and now she knew that wasn't true. She had no problem trusting that Lexi would come after her before the game was over. It wasn't nice, but at least she'd be prepared.

And there was always an upside to someone trying to take you down:

It gave you a great excuse to hit first.

Chapter 18

CARTER

C arter hadn't been raised to be relatable. His family was too rich for that, their circle too exclusive. Even after he'd turned his back on the wealth and the status that came with being the future head of Barclay Industries, he'd continued to hold his distance from the rest of the world. A psychiatrist probably would've claimed it was a way of protecting himself. Some subconscious reaction to a lifetime of being told he wasn't good enough as he was— that he had to stand taller, stand *above*.

Carter chose to see it as more of a conscious decision than that. If he were a bartender, he imagined he'd walk around with a big grin like Bryce. People wanted to see their bartender as a friend, someone they could laugh with and confess their secrets to. What they didn't want to do was hand over their life savings to a pal.

In a job like Carter's, it paid to be a blank slate (albeit a well-coiffed, professionally dressed one). People needed to be able to project whatever made them feel safest onto him to give themselves peace of mind when it came to handing over their money. It was a fact of his industry that Carter had never minded. It meant all those childhood years of being chastised for any show of emotion or neediness hadn't been as repressive as they'd felt but instead had been the training for his success outside of the path that he'd been groomed for. They hadn't been the cage they'd felt like; they'd been the keys to his freedom.

And if Carter had never quite learned to switch gears outside of the office—well, it was a small price to pay. At least he didn't have friends like the people his parents surrounded themselves with, there to toast his successes with four-hundred-dollar bottles of Miraval while predicting his failure in whispered tones the moment his back was turned. At least he was trustworthy.

Until now.

Carter sat on his stool at the Staple, wishing he hadn't listened when Bryce had convinced him going straight back to the Lakehouse would only make him look guiltier. He wanted to take a hot shower and escape into some mindless show, not drink alone in a loud, sticky bar full of people who believed he'd actually attempted to *kill* a man he'd never met. The whole situation was as absurd as it was, well, not hurtful. *Insulting.* That's what it was. Carter took a swig of his scotch, wincing at the terrible song playing over the speakers; the woman he was singing about clearly did not want to come back to the singer, so he should do all of them a favor and give her a little space.

At the reminder, Carter read his text again like it was a bruise he couldn't resist pressing. **How's your stomach doing?** He'd been aiming for considerate, but he must've veered into some territory Jess considered off-putting. Or maybe he'd broken an unspoken rule, like he was allowed to have her number but not use it. He'd requested it as a joke, after all, not so he could invade her life with personal questions.

The thought made him cringe. He didn't know how to do this. Not text a woman, obviously, although he wasn't much for communication beyond the exchange of the logistics involved in meeting up with someone. What Carter didn't know how to do was reach out to someone without purpose.

He wasn't trying to date Jess. All of Carter's past relationships, whether casual or long-term, had been the result of carefully determined compatibility, and he and Jess were not compatible. Facts that prevented the two of them from being a logical pairing:

- living in different places
- living very different lives in different places
- his suspicion that he'd been set up to win a prize that she badly wanted

All of these were reasons Carter shouldn't have sent the text that had turned out to be either too unexpected or unwanted or intrusive and made Jess ignore it. He wished he could just unsend it. How had someone invented the technology to communicate with anyone in the world with the touch of a button and not created an ability to retract said communication? They'd gotten cocky, that's how. They'd blown around the third lap but forgotten to cross the finish line.

"It's a good thing you're keeping that glass in your hand," a voice beside him said. It came from a man Carter had never seen before, wearing a trucker hat pulled low over bloodshot eyes and chubby cheeks. The man had the kind of face that could've belonged to someone in their twenties or in their fifties, depending on how often he double-fisted beers like he was doing now.

Carter nodded, and had he been in Atlanta, he would've left it at that. It might not have been friendly, but it wasn't technically rude, either. The man had made a statement of fact, not asked a question. Therefore, Carter didn't owe him any interaction. They weren't in Atlanta, though. They were in Redford, and Carter had been in this town long enough to have learned the rules were different here.

"Why is that?" Carter said conversationally, despite the fact that he suspected he wouldn't like the answer.

"Well," the man said, grinning in a way that would've been frightening if their conversation had been taking place in a dark alley, "if you put it down, I'd bet good odds on it being poisoned."

Carter's stomach sank. Hearing Jasper's stories, he'd always wished he could live in Redford. Carter had even looked up local real estate online last year. Places much smaller than his grandfather's mansion, but homes that had at least three bedrooms, because in a place like Redford, Carter could see himself as the kind of man who might turn out lucky enough to have a family.

He'd thought it was just his job that kept him from going for it, but, clearly, he just wasn't a match for this place. He was an outsider, as hated and distrusted as a snake that had slithered its way into someone's home. For a moment, folded in by Bryce and Jess and Sally and Luanne, Carter had felt what it would be like to be a part of this place. But it had just been a glimpse at a different life, like turning on the TV and finding yourself in an unrealistically well-lit police station or a hospital with models in colorful scrubs.

"I guess I'd better keep a tight grip on it," he said evenly to the man, tilting out his glass to clink it against one of the man's beer bottles.

"I guess you'd better." The man winked at him before pushing back from the bar and walking away, and it took everything in Carter's power not to turn around to protect his back.

Who knew a wink could be so . . . wrong? A wink was supposed to look cheeky or flirtatious, not like the precursor to a stabbing. Carter lifted his glass to his mouth and paused only for a moment before drinking it down. It felt contaminated now, like the man had managed to drop something in it through the power of suggestion. But Carter would be damned if he'd let himself be intimidated into wasting good scotch.

Someone slid into the spot the man had just been in, and Carter swore he could smell the scent of sunshine and apricots over the fryer and the pitchers and everything else in the bar, even before Jess's lilting voice said, "The stomach is all good, thanks for asking. I'm actually considering getting a basket of fried pickles."

"Really?" Carter focused all of his pleasure at her appearance into the word, hoping it sounded like surprise instead of an embarrassing amount of relief.

"No, not really." Jess's laughter reached her eyes, the green in them shining impossibly brighter. "I ate an entire pie tonight."

"I see that it's stained your face, too." Carter peered at her cheeks as if they were still covered in red goo like they had been a couple of hours ago. She looked so beautiful it made his breath catch in his throat. "It looks like you had dinner with Hannibal Lecter."

"What?" Jess's hands went to her face, rubbing the skin that actually had begun to turn cherry-pie red. "Really?"

"No, not really."

Jess laughed and pushed his chest. Carter resisted the urge to capture her hand beneath his and hold it there like he'd done at the wall. She'd said she needed space, and respecting her physical needs felt like the least he could do.

"You should probably sit somewhere else tonight," he said reluctantly. "I'm pretty sure everyone in here hates me, and I don't want you to catch any of the fire being aimed my way."

Jess looked around, nodding as if she could see the hate beams streaming toward them. Carter swallowed his disappointment. She *should* stay away from him. He would get to leave all of this behind the moment he'd collected his grandfather's money, but Jess could spend the rest of her life with these people. She didn't need them thinking she'd choose some saboteur poisoner over one of them.

"Let's get out of here, then," she said decisively.

Before Carter could answer, she was digging into a rainbow macramé bag and pulling a neon green change purse from it.

"How much do you owe?" she asked, popping it open to pull out two crumpled twenties.

It was the most unexpected, endearing display Carter had ever witnessed. "You're paying for my drinks?"

"I'm here to save you, aren't I?" She tugged him off his stool, her fingers still chilly from outside. "It wouldn't be a very good rescue effort if I didn't cover your bill."

"I think it still counts as an exceptional effort," he said, pulling out his own wallet. Unlike hers, its leather had been dyed a color so muted Carter wasn't sure it could be claimed as one at all. Gray, maybe. Or brown. Bray. He'd always liked that it matched anything he wore, but now he wondered if the blue might have been a better choice.

Carter tossed a couple of twenties on the bar and tried to catch Bryce's eye, but his teammate had been trapped in a one-sided conversation with a man who looked like Anderson Cooper's flannel-wearing doppelganger for the last fifteen minutes.

"But . . ." Jess looked at the twenties in her hand like she was trying to figure out how she'd missed her opportunity to use them.

Gently, Carter reached over and guided her hand toward the change purse.

"They go back in there," he explained, letting go and sliding his arms into his jacket. "You unzip that thing that can be seen from space and put them inside."

"Funny," she said, crushing them in her palm before stuffing them in.

"Should we stagger our exits?" he asked.

"Should we what?" Jess looked as baffled by his question as he felt by her strange aggression toward cash.

"I could go first, and you could wait five minutes so nobody knows we're leaving together."

Jess squinted at him. "So you'd just be standing outside in the cold?"

"It's better than you standing outside in the cold," Carter said. "Plus, nobody would get mad at you for leaving with me."

"What do you think this is? The country version of *West Side Story*?" Jess grinned and swirled her finger around. "People behave badly here because we're family, not because we're actually at war. Think of it like brothers. They love each other, but they pick on each other and wrestle and fight because they can, because they know they're stuck together for life. You know how it goes."

"Not really." Carter shrugged. "I'm an only child, and I think you've heard enough about my family to understand that they don't believe in overcoming grudges."

"How long has it been since you spoke to them?"

"Ten years." It was an easy number to remember. He'd been twenty-two, just out of college, when joining the family business had stopped being hypothetical and had become inevitable. Ten days behind a desk there, and he had a choice to make: his destiny or his soul.

It wasn't as if he'd expected Barclay Industries to be some happy commune where everyone was working together in perfect harmony. He knew the way his parents approached life, so it came as no surprise to discover they were equally ruthless in business. If he was being honest with himself, he'd even resigned himself to the idea that not everything he'd be expected to do would be aboveboard, legally speaking.

It wasn't until Carter took his position there, though, that his eyes were opened to just how corrupt the company was. How much happened under the table. How poorly the employees were treated. No matter how long he worked there, he'd never garner enough power to make any kind of substantial change. The darkness ran too deep.

"You haven't spoken to them at all in ten years?" Jess looked aghast. "Not even a hello at Jasper's funeral?"

He thought of the scathing look his mom had shot him from the other side of the aisle. "Not even a hello."

"That's sad," Jess said.

Carter shrugged. He was sure, to her, it was. She'd scored double with her dad, getting both a parent and a friend. It wasn't that different from what Carter had found in Jasper, only he'd gotten three: a grandfather, a friend, and a partner who brought him along on secret missions to improve lives. He didn't mention that, though, because he didn't want to remind her that people like that could be lost.

"So," he said instead, "you were saying that it's okay to leave together, even though I'm not . . . part of the Redford family?"

"I was saying that." She led him toward the door, ignoring the eyes that followed them, and continued to chirp brightly. "Except, I didn't say you weren't a part of the family. Maybe you're a crazy uncle who has shown up after a long trip hunting in the woods. And you're swinging your rifle around, so people are a little skittish and distrustful of your intentions, but that doesn't mean you don't belong."

"And to be clear," he said, pulling the door open and ushering her out into the glowing yellow lights lining Main Street, "in this scenario of yours, you and I are related?"

He loved how revolted she looked by the implication.

"It's a complicated family tree," Jess said, waving the idea away like a foul odor. "Lots of adoptions."

"Right." Carter fought off a smile. "Well, we escaped the reunion. Where to now?"

Jess tilted her head in thought. "Back to the lake?"

"Again?"

"It's our spot." She grinned. "Now we just have to make some happier memories there." She tugged at his arm, and Carter let her lead him down the street. Jess pointed at a building with an elaborately painted sign as they passed. It was lit up with twinkle lights. The sign above it read "The Growing Garden" in flowery script.

"They'd usually have decorated for Halloween by now," Jess said. "Every year, people argue that they should wait until October, but Sandra—she owns the place—can't resist lining the sidewalk in late September with pumpkins and stalks of corn and putting out a skeleton that's so old it looks like it's actually been dug up from the ground. I guess she got distracted by Jasper's game."

"It sounds like people will be happy about that," Carter said.

"Nah. People like to complain, but I think they secretly appreciate the premature kickoff to the season. Fall is fun around here. We've got the high school football games, of course. And there's hot apple cider everywhere. Every kid in town tries to sell cups of it for fifty cents, and there are hay-rides and bonfires and a costume competition that Sally is all but guaranteed to win. And two Saturdays before Hal-loween, everyone will get together in the town square to carve pumpkins, even though the jack-o'-lanterns will all be half rotten and ravaged by squirrels by the time the trick-or-treating commences."

Jess described it almost exactly as his grandfather had, and Carter wished he had come at least once to visit his grandfather in the fall.

"Do you know yet what you'll dress up as?" he asked.

"Guess." She looked up at him as she delivered the challenge.

He thought for a moment. "Well, you love books, so I'm assuming it will be a character you've always related to."

"Impressive. But what character will it be?"

"Joseph and his coat of many colors?" He felt a surge of pleasure when his answer made her laugh.

"Funny," she said, "but no."

He continued to guess as they made their way to the lake, and the more Jess laughed, the more outrageous his guesses became. By the time they'd reached they water, she'd somehow managed to assign Carter a costume of his own. In a different world, one where they celebrated holi-days together and both got to live in this ridiculous little town, she'd be Emily Elizabeth. And Carter, apparently, would be Clifford, her big red dog.

Chapter 19

··········

JESS

honestly think it's showing off for you," Jess said, peering up at the sky. Unlike the last time they'd been there, it had turned its stars up to full bright so their light shimmered off the water like the entire lake had been covered in glitter. The result was magical.

"It could've cut its effort in half," Carter said, tilting his head back to absorb it with her. They'd walked along the edge of the lake for a while, but an unspoken acknowledgment that a show like this deserved to be observed in stillness had stopped them at the end of a short wooden dock. Next to them, a rowboat bobbed in the water. "There's so much pollution in the city that my standards have plummeted dangerously low. Five stars and the headlights from a plane constitute a show."

"Are you from Atlanta originally?" Jess asked, eager to finally fill in the backstory of Carter's character.

"Just outside of it," Carter said.

Jess considered this. It was interesting that someone who hadn't spoken to their parents in ten years had chosen to settle so close to them. She hesitated before giving in and asking, "Do you think you stayed in the area because you hoped things would change with your parents?"

"No." He grimaced and shifted his gaze toward the lake.

She waited.

"Maybe," he admitted after a moment. "I mean, it's not like I didn't understand what I was doing when I quit working for the company. I knew they'd cut me off. But I guess I didn't realize that they'd cut me out entirely. I figured, at least, I'd still be invited to holidays, if only for the sake of appearances. But then Thanksgiving came around, and they still wouldn't take my calls. The same thing happened at Christmas and on New Year's. Eventually, I realized they weren't just mad. They were done with me."

Jess felt sad for him, and she wanted to acknowledge how poorly he'd been treated by his parents, but she had a feeling he'd only interpret it as pity.

"But by then," she said instead, "you were already settled in Atlanta."

"I already had a job there," he agreed.

"And you like your job?"

Carter shrugged. "It's work. It's not like when I was—"

He closed his mouth abruptly and cleared his throat before beginning to speak again. "I was doing something else. With a partner. It was kind of like philanthropic work. And I liked that. Loved it, even. But something went wrong, and my partner couldn't do it with me anymore. Only, now I think he wants me to start it up again without him."

"And you want to?"

"More than anything."

Jess had never seen Carter look so earnest before.

"You should," she said, eager to encourage anything that was capable of making him look like that.

"I will." Carter said the words so confidently she had no doubt he would. "I just have to prove myself first."

"Can I ask you something?"

His mouth tilted up into one of his half-grins. "Jess, you now officially know more about me than anyone else on the planet. Why start exercising restraint now?"

She grinned sheepishly, but that didn't stop her from saying, "I just want to understand. If you still ended up in a job you don't love, why not stick it out at the family business? Was it really that much worse?"

Carter nodded. "I guess you could say it was less straightforward. I work with numbers now, so I know exactly what I'm dealing with. I know when I get something wrong, and I know how to make it right. There, it wouldn't have been as clear cut. The company needed me to be weak—their personal monkey, willing to dance for them in exchange for a lifetime's supply of bananas—and I needed to be my own person. I would've had to sacrifice my values again and again, blurring lines until I inevitably lost sight of where they'd been."

"I like the person you are." Jess knew she probably sounded silly, but she didn't care. She was telling the truth. "And I admire the fact that you weren't willing to compromise."

"Thanks," Carter said. But he shifted away from her uncomfortably.

She felt the space between them change, and she suspected

he'd like to have one of those liquid fences on hand now. He'd undoubtedly spray it in a circle around himself, hoping its odor would be strong enough to keep even humans at bay.

"Let's go to the center of the water." Jess blurted the words out without thinking, but the moment she heard them aloud, she realized how brilliant they were. "It will feel like we're surrounded by stars."

Carter looked at her like she'd lost her mind, and maybe she had. She didn't care, though. She only cared that his choosing to open up to her resulted in something good, instead of regret or embarrassment.

"It's too far to swim," he said. "And it's definitely too cold."

"We'll take a boat, then." She looked down at the rickety rowboat tied to the dock. "That one."

"You want to steal a boat?"

Jess looked at it again, then nodded.

They locked eyes, and Jess wondered when the line of electricity between them had been turned to high, crackling like this at the slightest bit of eye contact.

"All right. Let's steal a boat."

He said it as casually as adding fries to a meal, but the words caused Jess to break into a bouncy dance of delight. Beneath her, the dock grumbled. It was a toss-up whether it was admonishing her for her jump kick or Carter for crossing to where the rowboat was tied up and tugging at the rope's knot.

"Hop in," Carter said when the rope came free.

Jess held on to the uneven edges of the planks as she

lowered herself into the shifting boat, where there was a disturbing layer of water about an inch deep. When she felt like she'd gotten her balance, she let go. Naturally, that was the moment the boat chose to dip to the left, sending her sliding toward the side. Her shriek hit the air before she could stop it, but, thankfully, she had more control of her limbs. Flinging one arm to the opposite edge of the boat, she was able to shift the balance long enough to park her butt on the board that functioned as a seat.

"Stealthy," Carter said, sliding into the boat behind her. "I'm pretty sure they heard you in Woodford."

"Woodbridge," she corrected him primly.

"If there's a Woodford anywhere in the United States, I stand by my statement."

Jess tried not to laugh. Instead, she picked up one paddle and gestured toward the other with her chin, making a determined effort not to acknowledge the icy water seeping into her shoes. "Ready when you are."

Carter lifted an eyebrow, giving her one last chance to turn back, but Jess didn't care that the wind felt colder this close to the water. She didn't even care that her paddle was so old it looked like it would disintegrate the moment it got wet. All she cared about was this feeling of wildness coursing through her blood and the fact that Carter's liquid fence wouldn't have a chance against all this water. Carefully, she shifted in her seat, lifting her legs over the board so she could turn to face the front. She plunged her paddle into the dark lake.

It made a delightful splashing noise, quickly echoed by Carter's paddle behind her. Within a couple of strokes, the sounds had synced up perfectly and the boat began to cut a straight line away from the dock.

"We're great at this," Jess called without turning around.

"We're amazing at it," Carter agreed. "If Novak's next challenge is crossing a lake in a boat carved from the wooden equivalent of Swiss cheese, our teams will be leading the pack."

"So you noticed the leak, too?"

"Hard to miss. My suede shoes are now the texture of moss."

Jess laughed. "That's what you get for wearing fancy shoes in Redford."

"I'll have you know these shoes have proven themselves an excellent icebreaker in more than one client meeting. Rich women love them."

"Trust me, it's not your shoes women are looking at." Jess felt a thrill at her blatant flirtation, despite his silence following it. He couldn't actually be appalled by a little banter, not after everything that had happened between them over the last couple of days.

"Did you . . ." Carter's voice trailed off, then reemerged full of suppressed laughter. "Did you just reference my penis?"

"What?" As Jess reran her words through her head, she heard the way they'd sounded and guffawed so loudly it bounced across the water like the sound of a cannon. "No! I was talking about your face. And your eyes. And, well, yes, your body. But the top half of it, mostly—"

"I'm going to cut you off now," Carter said, doing exactly

that, though Jess had no idea whether it was to stem his embarrassment or her own.

"Thank you," she said gratefully.

"You're welcome." He went silent, like he was going to leave it at that. And that would've been fine because Jess hadn't said anything that wasn't true. His shoes, no matter how fancy they might be, couldn't compete with his face. Or his eyes. Etc., etc. But then Carter said, "And, Jess?"

"Yes?" Her stomach fluttered at the softness of his tone.

"I like your face, too. And who you are as a person. And all the rest of it."

"I'm glad," she said, resisting the urge to turn around.

She wondered what might've happened between them if the circumstances had been different. If they weren't competing against each other. If Carter had come to Redford for some other reason, would he still have taken the time to get to know her? Would he have wanted to? Or, like her mother, would he have realized that she wasn't worth the effort?

"We made it," Carter said, and Jess shook herself out of her thoughts. The world around them had shifted.

They'd arrived at the middle of the lake, and it was every bit as spectacular as Jess had hoped it would be. Above them, the sky was vast and bursting with stars, a midnight disco ball that illuminated the water beneath them with its brilliance. Jess pulled in her oar and slid it onto the bottom of the boat before tilting her head back, her face up toward the sky. Sitting there, bobbing weightlessly in the water, felt like the closest she'd ever come to leaving Earth.

"It's beautiful." She sighed, turning around to face Carter, and the boat rocked with warning.

"This is the biggest the world has ever felt," he said, staring up at the sky for another moment before dropping his eyes to meet hers in a searching gaze. "Isn't that strange? How can the smallest town I've ever been to give me the largest glimpse of the world I've ever seen?"

Jess thought there were probably several obvious reasons for that—fewer buildings crowding the skyline, fewer people crowding the streets, the way the sky and the lake seemed to be blending together to create the illusion of infinity—but she answered the way that felt most genuine. "Redford can be magic like that."

Carter nodded gravely, like she'd said something profound.

"I was so excited to leave," Jess admitted, because it felt important that he understood she'd had choices. "One minute, a community college was out of my financial reach, and the next, somehow, this scholarship appeared, and all of a sudden, I was moving to the big city. It was unquestionably the most exciting thing that had ever happened to me. I couldn't wait to get out of here. And then I got away, and I just found myself missing this place terribly. There were so many things to love about New York, but it never felt like enough. It didn't have my dad or Liz or any of my neighbors. It didn't have enough trees, and the sky felt so small there. I hated that I passed so many people in the street that I'd never get a chance to meet. I meant it when I told you my dad was the reason I passed up that job. But without that job, I never would've considered staying in the city."

"You knew where you belonged," Carter said. "You're lucky. A lot of people don't."

"Do you belong in Atlanta?"

"I don't know. In another life, I like to imagine myself coaching Little League baseball. But not just a coach in name. I'm talking about one of those coaches out of a feel-good sports movie. The kind who encourages the uncoordinated kids to get off the bench, and infuses life lessons into their pep talks, and laughs when the kids dump Gatorade on his head."

"Why does that have to be in another life?"

"Aside from the obvious fact that I don't have a kid of my own, and people tend to object when childless men start hanging around school gyms asking young boys to call them coach?"

"Well, yes," Jess said. "Aside from that."

"I've never actually played baseball," Carter said dryly.

Jess couldn't help but laugh. "Really?"

"I went to a boarding school. We played polo and lacrosse." He laughed with her this time, and the sounds, one high and one low, bounced across the water like skipping stones.

Their eyes locked, and that electric line between them lit up again, pulsing in a way that couldn't be ignored. Carter's gaze went all smolder-y, and Jess's throat turned dry. He could kiss her here and it wouldn't be the terrible idea it was on land. If there was ever a loophole, leaving Earth to float in a sea of starlight had to be it.

She leaned forward, an unspoken invitation, and was thrilled when he matched the movement. His gaze dropped to her mouth, and her stomach flipped. The air around them seemed to thicken with intention. Her skin buzzed.

A noise cracked through the night, so loud and sharp she jerked back in surprise.

"What was that?" Carter looked around, his back stiffening with alert.

Jess heard a distant shout then. And even though it bounced around the water, she knew exactly where it had originated.

"Oh, that?" she said, disappointment crashing over her. She reached for the oars and passed one to him. "That was a gunshot. Time to get back."

To his credit, Carter didn't visibly panic. He didn't even suggest they *not* paddle toward an angry man firing shots. He merely gave a sharp nod and took the oar from her, plunging it into the lake with a synchronicity so perfect Jess couldn't even differentiate the sound of hers hitting the water from his.

She set the pace faster this time, and they cut across the lake with a speed the old rowboat probably hadn't experienced in years. Just as Jess had expected, its owner was standing at the end of the dock with jeans on and nothing else. No shirt, no shoes. Only a shotgun under one arm, pointing directly at them.

"You hunting fish, Billy?" she called out. "I've heard poles work better."

"Jessica Reid, is that you?" Billy shook his head and let the gun swing down to skim the side of his right leg. "I thought you were one of those delinquents taking poor old Bessy out for a joyride."

Jess grinned, knowing exactly how much he would've enjoyed the idea of attempting to scare some unlucky kid straight. "You can still pop a couple of shots into the water, if you'd like. Close enough to freak us out. We did steal your boat."

Carter cleared his throat, lifting an eyebrow when the sound got her attention.

"What?" she said. "We *did*."

He shook his head and turned to Billy. "Would you believe me if I said she stole your boat and dragged me along by force?"

"Without question," Billy said, holding out a hand to catch the rowboat's rope as Jess tossed it toward him. "You're clearly rich enough to buy a much better vessel than my Bessy, and Jess was tossing people around left and right at the self-defense lesson Sally taught in the square a few years ago. I'd have no problem believing she could swing you over her shoulder like a purse."

Carter looked down at his six-foot-two frame as if to double-check that he hadn't shrunk to tote size while he'd been paddling back to shore. "Thanks?"

"Sure thing," Billy said, pulling the gun up and swinging it like a goodbye wave. "Now, get the hell off my land."

Jess and Carter nodded quickly, in sync like they were still rowing ole Bessy, and Billy turned on his heel and started down the dock.

"Sorry, Billy," Jess called after him.

"Yes," Carter said. "We won't do it again."

"If you do," Billy said over his shoulder, "try not to shriek and giggle like you're at a slumber party. Crime is supposed to be serious business."

Jess began to giggle again, so Carter had to put on a serious face and say, "Roger that."

"We're like Bonnie and Clyde," she said through her laughter once Billy was almost back to his house. "Making outlaw life one big slumber party."

Carter smirked, and Jess's words played back in her head. But before she could explain that she hadn't meant they'd be spending the night together, Carter had moved on.

"Bonnie and Butch," he said.

Jess tilted her head. "Um, I'm pretty sure it's Bonnie and Clyde."

Carter nodded. "But they were a pair of outlaws, like Butch Cassidy and the Sundance Kid."

"And we didn't get paired up," Jess said, realization dawning.

Her stomach sank. He'd wanted to kiss her on the lake. She knew he had. But now that they were back on dry land, he'd come back to his senses. As he was reminding her, they weren't on the same team.

It was a fair point to make. Hadn't she made the very same one to him yesterday? Hadn't she told him that she needed to keep her distance from him?

"So, we can't be Bonnie and Clyde," Carter said, causing her heart to squeeze painfully in her chest.

"We can't," she repeated.

His eyes looked black and bottomless in the moonlight, and his teeth flashed white when he curled his lips into a conciliatory grin. "Bonnie and Butch has a nice ring to it, though."

The pressure on her heart eased, and warmth flooded back through her body. "It does, doesn't it?"

They weren't agreeing to anything meaningful. And Carter certainly wasn't still considering kissing her. But Jess felt better, somehow, hearing him link them together. Bonnie and Butch *did* have a nice ring to it.

You couldn't argue with alliteration.

Chapter 20

· · · · · · · · · ·

JESS

t was late when Jess got home. Almost midnight, which felt decadent for a work night. Everything about the evening had been decadent, though. Not the scary bit with DeMarco's allergic reaction, obviously. But the rest of it. You knew it had been a good time when you'd gotten to eat an entire pie and that didn't even register as the highlight of your day.

She hummed Pharrell Williams's "Happy" for a few lines before giving in to loud singing. That, of course, led to dancing, because you couldn't belt out lyrics like those without your feet wanting to get in on the action. Jess turned on lights as she moved from room to room, even firing up a couple of candles to combat the lingering smell of microwave popcorn that had been last night's midnight snack. It wasn't until she'd sunk into the couch, kicking her mismatched-socked feet up on the bright yellow coffee table, that she looked at her phone.

Unsurprisingly, given Jess's last message to her, there were several texts and a missed call from Liz. There was also a missed call from Jess's dad, which was strange, given he was the kind of person texting had been created for. He'd once messaged **stove caught fire** as if this were the kind of news that didn't require a more in-depth conversation. Tonight, unbelievably enough, he'd actually left a voicemail.

Clicking *play*, Jess waited to hear a reminder that she'd left her laptop in her old bedroom or a suggestion that she pick it up early enough to have pancakes with him before he left for work. Instead, she was shocked to hear Nikki's voice. She sat up straight, pulling the phone away from her ear and looking at the voicemail. It still said *Dad*.

Tentatively, Jess slid the voice bar back to the beginning and put the phone to her ear.

"I called your dad's house because, apparently, you weren't capable of entering your own cell number on Novak's form," Nikki's voice said. Despite the accusation in her words, the tone lacked the gleeful antagonism it usually carried. It was uncharacteristically soft sounding. Worried, even. And it made Jess's heart race so frantically that it was hard to hear Nikki's message over the pounding.

"When Ross answered, he sounded weird, so I came over," Nikki's voice continued. "And . . . well . . . I think you might want to be here, too."

Before the sentence was over, Jess was up and racing around. She remembered to put on shoes but didn't think to grab a jacket. She managed to blow out candles but forgot to flip off the lights. And then she was running out the door and down the street, having remembered to close the door but not to lock it.

Memory must have led her to her childhood home,

because Jess wasn't conscious of the road or any of the houses as she passed them. All of her attention was directed inward at the terrible scenes her brain had painted for her in vivid detail. Her dad paralyzed by a stroke. Her dad covered in burns from another stove fire. Her dad dead of cancer.

Cancer. The word pinged around her brain like a shot designed to cause the most damage possible. She'd spent the last two days trying to wrap her mind around its horrifying appearance, but she hadn't managed it. Not like now, when she could feel the spiky panic at the idea that he could already be gone, that her world had just bottomed out and she was no longer standing but plummeting into a terrifying free fall.

The door was unlocked when she arrived, and she flung it open and barreled down the hall toward her dad's bedroom without thinking to close it behind her. Her feet jerked to a stop a few paces past the living room. Slowly, she backed up, already rubbing her eyes in response to the hallucination her brain had fabricated. But no. They were still there. Her dad and Nikki, cozily laughing at the TV together. The room was warmly lit with lamps instead of the harsh overhead light her dad usually flipped on, and it smelled, oddly enough, of freshly baked brownies. Her dad didn't have the patience for brownies. He always ate them directly from the pan, burning the top of his mouth so badly that he'd complain about it for days afterward. For both of their sakes, he'd given up making them.

What the hell is going on? Jess's eyes closed and her hands went to her knees as she panted for breath, heaving and sweaty and overwhelmed with relief.

"Jess!" Her dad's obvious surprise pulled her eyes open and up from the ground. "What are you doing here?"

"And did you even close the door behind you?" Nikki shivered dramatically and pulled Jess's favorite blanket up over her shoulders.

"Are you okay?" Jess said to her dad, ignoring Nikki.

"Of course," he said, his smile dropping into a frown of concern. "Why wouldn't I be?"

Jess had heard the difference in his voice when he first called her name, but now, without the whoosh of her panting filling her ears, the painful-sounding raspy quality to it was obvious. Something had happened. And her dad didn't want her to know about it.

The realization hurt. They'd always been so close because they'd chosen to share the details of their lives with each other, both the good and the ugly, the proud and the shameful. Difficult conversations had never been something they avoided, and hard truths had always been faced head-on, together.

Until, apparently, now.

In this life-threatening situation, Ross seemed to have found the line between being her friend and her dad. And he'd chosen dad over friend—protection over partnership. Jess was certain it was his way of loving her, but that didn't make her resent it any less. It felt unfair that they could have lived her whole life facing the world together, and now, when he needed someone by his side more than ever, he'd benched her on the sidelines.

But if that's what he needed, she had no other choice. As

her dad, he deserved her respect. And, as her friend, he'd earned it.

"I was just worried," Jess said, injecting all the lightness she could muster into her tone, even managing a feigned smile, "because Nikki called me from your phone. Naturally, I assumed she was holding you hostage until I found a way to win Jasper's prize for her."

"Worse," he said, his expression relaxing into one of amusement. "She's forcing me to watch *Lust Island*."

"*Love Island*," Nikki corrected him sternly. "It's basically a documentary on the coming together of soul mates, and you should be embarrassed you hadn't watched it before tonight."

"Embarrassment *is* one of the things I feel while watching it," he said agreeably.

"Don't act like you're not already obsessed with the future of Jake and Maura's relationship." Nikki rolled her eyes. "You light up every time they're onscreen."

"I light up?"

"Like an adorable little firefly."

Ross shook his head. "Please refrain from comparing me to anything adorable, little, or insect-like in my own home."

"Finish your fake juice," Nikki said.

Obediently, Ross finished the glass.

Jess watched this exchange with her mouth slightly agape. Nothing about it computed. Her dad didn't watch reality television. Not only had he refused to watch *The Bachelor* with her but he'd demanded she go home and watch it on her own TV so as not to contaminate his with its mushiness. Then again, Jess supposed she lacked some of the persuasiveness Nikki was capable of.

Jess's face tightened at the thought. How persuasive, exactly, was Nikki capable of being? The fact that Ross was on his usual chair instead of sharing the couch with her was reassuring, but that relief was tempered by the fact that the two were hanging out at all. Her dad needed real friends around him now, not terrifying women willing to use his vulnerable state to weasel their way into his pants. The thought made Jess wince.

"You all right, hon?" Her dad leaned forward in his chair as if to get up and rescue her.

"Fine," Jess said quickly, waving him back down. "It turns out eating an entire pie by yourself isn't the greatest idea. Seven hours later, and it's still trying to make its way back up."

"Gross," Nikki said, scrunching her face in disgust.

"I think I need some water," Jess said. "Can I get either of you anything?"

"I'll come with you," Nikki said, surprising her. She slipped out from the blanket and stood up, revealing a skirt the size of a Band-Aid over bare legs so golden they had to have been covered in self-tanner. She'd paired it with a silky top, loose enough to appear classy despite the significant display of cleavage, and a delicate gold necklace. The overall effect was stunning—and informative.

It certainly wasn't the kind of outfit a person wore to watch TV on a friend's couch. Either Nikki had ditched a date to hang out with Jess's dad or she'd come to his house looking to find one. Neither option offered Jess much comfort.

"No more," Ross said as Nikki swept his glass out of his hand as she passed.

"You'll thank me later," Nikki said without looking back. "High-fructose corn syrup is the top recommendation for a sore throat."

Ross widened his eyes at Jess in a silent plea, but she just widened hers back, unable to get him out of something when she couldn't figure out how he'd gotten himself into it. Turning, she followed Nikki down the hall toward the kitchen, despite feeling certain she was meant to be leading the way. Before this week, Nikki had never stepped foot into this house. When, exactly, had she become the boss of it?

All the lights were on in the kitchen, and a pan of brownies sat on the counter. Surprisingly, there were no dirty mixing bowls in the sink. And the pan was half empty.

"Did he eat all of these?" Jess leaned toward the pan, inhaling the rich, chocolaty smell.

"We shared them," Nikki said, wrinkling her nose.

"You ate a quarter-pan of brownies?" Just the thought of it made Jess laugh.

"You ate an entire pie," Nikki said defensively. "And you would've eaten more than that if I hadn't slapped the second one out of your hand."

"I wasn't giving you a hard time, Nikki. You just made it pretty clear the other day that you find sugar disgusting. Remember? I dared to offer you a piece of my muffin, and you looked at it like it was rat droppings?"

"Why are you always so gross?" Nikki looked at Jess like *she* was rat droppings.

"Was it because my dad offered you brownies?" Jess said, ignoring her question. "You're capable of eating sugar if it's an excuse to hang out with him?"

Jess didn't intend to sound as accusatory as she did, but she was upset, and it was late, and she didn't understand why Nikki was here at all, much less why Nikki seemed to have become a part of something that Jess's dad was keeping from her.

"For your information, I offered *him* the brownies," Nikki snapped, taking a step back and leaning against the counter so her long, bare legs stretched tauntingly between them. "I thought he needed something in his stomach, but he wouldn't let me make them for him, so I told him I wanted to make them for myself. And then I had to keep eating them so he'd keep eating them, which is probably going to make me break out like a preteen after a soda binge, so I think the words you're looking for are 'Thank you, Nikki, for sacrificing your figure and your face for my father and my ungrateful, suspicious self.'"

Jess blinked, taken aback by this uncharacteristically emotional and verbose speech from a woman she'd never considered capable of caring what Jess thought.

"I'm sorry for offending you," Jess said after a moment of consideration. "Maybe it would help if you could just fill me in on how you ended up here."

"Fine." Nikki lifted her eyes to the ceiling and sighed as if this basic catch-up on extraordinary events was the most exhausting, irrational thing that had ever been asked of her. "So because the pie-eating challenge ended so abruptly, Novak had to call all the teams that are still in to tell us that tomorrow's challenge will begin at ten in the square. But he'd already called you, and some guy named Barry answered and said he'd never heard of you, so Novak told me

I was responsible for getting you there on time or we'd both be disqualified. But I don't have your number because, you know, I don't like you and we're not friends, so I looked up your dad's landline and called him to get your cell number. But he sounded really weird when I answered, so I came here to see if he was okay."

Jess's stomach sank. "And he wasn't?"

"He wasn't." Nikki's expression shifted from feigned annoyance to genuine concern. "He was throwing up. A *lot*. He said he was trying a new medication and he thought he was just having a bad reaction to it, but I panicked because there was so much coming out that I was worried he wasn't able to get enough oxygen back in, and that's when I called you and told you to come over here. But then he eventually stopped throwing up, and I tried to get him to eat something, but the only thing that seemed to appeal to him was a box of brownie mix. And that's how we ended up in here with you simultaneously accusing me of binging your dad's brownies and wanting to lick the batter off his abs."

Jess laughed in spite of her horror. "In my defense, you've spent a considerable amount of time trolling me with references to yourself as my stepmother."

"I wasn't trolling you," Nikki said. "I mean, obviously, it was fun to make stepmother jokes, but I do actually want to get in your dad's pants. Because he's hot. Not just because it would have the added benefit of making you unhappy."

"Okay?" Jess grimaced as she attempted to push the image of Nikki getting *in her dad's pants* out of her mind. "Well, thanks, I guess? It was nice of you to take care of him, even if it was only because you wanted to . . ." *Nope.*

She couldn't say it. "Because you're interested in him romantically."

"That's not why I stayed." Nikki mumbled the words before turning around and opening the cabinet with the plates in it. Not seeming to find what she'd been looking for, she flicked it shut and opened another.

"I don't understand," Jess said, watching as she continued searching for something. "You just said—"

"I said I wanted to get into his pants." Nikki turned around with a plastic container in her hand. "And I'm sure you'll be thrilled to hear that he has no intention of letting me near them."

Jess was, in fact, thrilled to hear this.

"He wasn't exactly gentle about it, either." Nikki grabbed the used brownie knife on the counter and jabbed it aggressively into a gooey piece before using it to transfer the rest of them into the container. "Maybe he'd vomited up all his tact, but there's a way of saying no without making it sound like 'No way. Not in a million years. I'd rather be covered in vipers than feel even the slightest touch of your skin against mine.'"

This time, Jess was able to hold her laugh in, if only barely.

"I'm sorry," Jess said, wanting to mean it. And she actually did, in a way. Everyone should get the chance to have someone like Ross Reid in their lives. "It's not you. It's him."

"But not just because he's sick?" Nikki said it like she knew the answer, but Jess saw the flash of hope in her eyes.

"Not just because he's sick," Jess confirmed.

Nikki nodded, her hope fading. "He is sick, though."

"I just found out." Jess felt her eyes fill with tears, and

she blinked them back, knowing it didn't matter how nice Nikki was being—she was not the kind of person you turned to for comfort.

Nikki spotted the tears and reached out a hand like she might offer a hug or some other gesture of support, but the knife was still in her grip. Tilting her head, she patted the flat side of it on Jess's shoulder as if she was knighting her, likely staining Jess's shirt with chocolate in the process.

"Is it bad?" Nikki asked, dropping the knife on the counter.

"He won't tell me too much, but yeah. I think it's bad." A few tears broke free, sliding resignedly down Jess's cheek. "I'm hoping I can get him in front of some specialists if we win Jasper's money. It doesn't sound like his doctors are giving him much hope, but five million dollars should open a lot of doors. If I can win it, that is."

"We will," Nikki said. "There was never any question about that."

Jess laughed wetly at her confidence, unable to resist believing her. Nikki wasn't nice, but she was unfailingly honest. She always had been.

"Can I ask you a question?"

"You might as well," Nikki said with a grin. "I don't intend to ever talk like this with you again."

"Of course," Jess said. "If you believed my dad when he said nothing would ever happen between you, why did you stick around, making him brownies and forcing him to drink juice?"

"Besides the fact that I like bossing people around?"

"Assuming there is a reason other than that."

"Honestly?" Nikki waited for her nod, then grabbed Ross's juice glass and filled it up, giving Jess the impression she was stalling. But, finally, she said, "Because he's nice, and he makes me laugh, but also because I knew, if the situation were reversed, that's what he'd do for me. And that sounds crazy because I barely know the man and he has no reason to even like me. But he would. I just know it."

"He would," Jess agreed, her tears spilling over in earnest now.

"I should go," Nikki said, shifting Ross's juice into her other hand. "And you should stop doing that. Your face is going to look like a marshmallow tomorrow."

"Right." Jess grinned soppily. She wiped her eyes and busied herself getting a glass of water instead of following Nikki down the hall, hoping a few minutes would be enough for the evidence of her tears to fade.

"I'm logging out of my account so you're not tempted to keep watching without me," she heard Nikki say from the living room. "We'll pick this up later."

"How about the last Tuesday of 2045?" Ross said. "Then we can look them up on social media and see who's still together."

"If that's your clever way of trying to ensure I'm still in your life twenty years from now, I'm flattered." Nikki was in the hallway now, calling back to him over her shoulder as she made her way toward the door. "But you lost that guarantee when you shoved me into the friend zone, so you're just going to have to settle for tomorrow."

And then she was gone, slamming the door behind her and taking the last word with her.

"Jessica!" her dad hollered, but his throat gave up on him halfway through the word, sending Jess scurrying into the living room. He gulped from the glass Nikki had brought him before continuing. "I want to make it very clear that I blame you for bringing her into this house. I don't know if we'll ever get rid of her."

His brow was furrowed in exaggerated annoyance, but there was an unmistakable brightness in his eyes that didn't match Jess's image of a man who had spent a considerable portion of the evening vomiting. Even if Jess hadn't caught his laughter when she'd arrived, she knew him well enough to spot the playfulness in his mood. As inconceivable as it might be, he'd enjoyed watching *Love Island* with a dictator pushing brownies and juice.

"At least she doesn't hate you," Jess said, settling onto the couch and curling her legs under the blanket Nikki had been using. "Imagine what it's been like for me."

Jess ran her hands through her bangs as if to remind herself just how awful it had been, but another scene sprang to mind, replaying itself for the first time since it happened, shifting with context. Nikki, knocking a pie out of her hand, not because she'd poisoned it but because she'd been worried someone else had. She'd been looking out for Jess, just like she'd looked out for Ross.

Huh.

Nikki might not want to be her friend, but if she wasn't careful, Jess was going to be forced to start thinking of her as one anyway.

Chapter 21

....

JESS

J ess's dad was gone by the time she woke up. She'd likely find a note on the kitchen table when she went to make coffee, but she could feel his departure in the absence of creaks in the house, the stillness of the air. She had crashed in her old room so she'd hear him if he started throwing up again, but she hadn't heard him leave, so the effort felt like a failed one. She should've woken the moment his alarm went off instead of almost sleeping through her own.

She should've reminded him that sick people need sleep.

Propping her head up on the pillow so she could stare out the open blinds at the dreary, rain-soaked sky, Jess indulged her guilt for a moment, pretending she'd pulled a Nikki and demanded he stay in bed—as if his sickness were something she felt she was allowed to address. She should be more attentive. More insistent. More of a friend than a daughter. She was an adult, after all, not a child. Then the snooze alarm on her phone went off, and the moment was over. There was no more time for wallowing. She had a game to win. Prize money to earn. She had to do something to help this situation that felt terrifyingly out of control.

She forced herself out of bed, then stood in the middle of her room for a moment, staring at her phone. Her dad wasn't the only one Jess had failed. There were six texts from Liz, her tone growing more frantic with each one that went unanswered. It was a natural reaction. Jess's message the other night had simply read, please call, but that was the equivalent of launching a fistful of emergency flares over Redford. Those two words combined said, *I need you. I can't handle this alone. Texting is not going to cut it.* And what had Jess done after sending out her digital S.O.S.? She'd gone dark.

Sure, she'd been busy with the game. And magical late-night boat rides. And horrible middle-of-the-night emergency calls. And fitting work into every moment in between. But she'd had an entire free day before the pie-eating contest, and she hadn't taken even five minutes to call her friend, who she was desperate to talk to. And now it was too late. Jess needed to leave soon, and she couldn't start a conversation that was guaranteed to render her a sobbing mess. *Why hadn't she called Liz yesterday?*

As frustrated as Jess was with herself, she found her inability to answer her question strangely comforting. She hadn't neglected to call Liz because she didn't love her or didn't want to talk to her. She did love Liz, and she didn't just want to talk to her, she *needed* to. But Jess's life had been upended over the last few days. Her schedule had ceased to be her own, and she'd lost control of her routines.

This must be exactly what it was like for Liz.

Jess felt a pang of sympathy for her friend who was not only taking on this new challenge of motherhood but also attempting to do it while creating a new home in a new town. Liz probably needed Jess just as much as Jess needed her. If she wasn't as accessible as she used to be, it certainly wasn't because she didn't want to be.

Sorry to have worried you, Jess typed out quickly. **I'm feeling better now. I ate an entire pie.**

There. Not one lie told. But as soon as she could, Jess would call her, and they would confront this situation together. Not just so Jess could take comfort from Liz but because Liz would need her as well. Liz had grown up with Ross. He was as much her dad as he was Jess's.

Jess's heart wrenched at the thought of all the other people who would be devastated to hear her dad was sick, but she tried to shake it off. It would be too easy to let the weight of everything drag her back into bed. Instead, she yanked off her T-shirt and flung it across the room like the world's problems resided within the fabric of it.

She searched her old closet for something to wear, pausing at the tutu Carter took such enjoyment in teasing her about. It wasn't an option, obviously. She was too old for tutus, and the weather was all wrong for tulle. She was almost certain, however, that the sight of her in it would elicit one of Carter's rare laughs.

Just the thought of it made her grin. A pair of leggings, after all, would make a tutu warm enough for fall. With a chortle of anticipation, Jess tossed it on the bed and ran to the shower.

· · · · · · · ·

EVERYTHING OUTSIDE HAD been darkened by rain. The dirt was black instead of brown, the streets a deep gray. Even the sky itself was dark, as if the day was ready to end, despite the fact that it was not yet ten o'clock in the morning. The air was warmer than it had been all week, so thickened by the humidity that it clung like a hug. It smelled fresh, like pine and newly raked earth.

Jess inhaled deeply as she hurried to the town square, swinging her closed umbrella like an ineffective cane. A drop of water from the edge of an awning plopped onto her forehead. To her surprise, the crowd at the square was considerably larger than the ten teams still remaining. She'd expected the dreary weather to keep spectators away.

"Beautiful day, isn't it?" Oscar called out to her. He'd dragged his stool over from his usual corner and placed it on the corner in front of the square. It was strange seeing him perched somewhere new.

"Couldn't get any better, Oscar," Jess sang in response.

"No." He nodded cheerfully. "It certainly could not."

Jess joined the crowd and ran into Nikki almost immediately. Unsurprisingly, Nikki's prediction about the effect of chocolate on her complexion had been wrong. There was no sign of the brownies or even the late night. With her blond curls scooped into a ponytail and her navy pants tucked into boots, she looked fresh out of the pages of a polo magazine, ready to sling herself elegantly astride a horse and mow them all down.

Nikki arched an eyebrow at the sight of Jess, her gaze dropping to her feet and traveling slowly back up.

"Nope," she said firmly. "I don't care how much you were paid to make balloon animals at a kid's birthday party. You're staying right here until we've won whatever challenge Novak has in store for us today."

"I have no other plans," Jess said, thoroughly unfazed. She hadn't, after all, dressed for Nikki's enjoyment. She'd done it for hers, to brighten this bleak morning, and to make Carter laugh.

Nikki shook her head at this assertion but didn't bother replying. Instead, she studied the crowd with Jess.

"He's up there," she said, tilting her chin to the left. "At the front, up by Novak."

Jess followed her gaze to Carter and blushed.

"I wasn't . . ." Jess trailed off and offered an abashed grin. "Thanks."

Even through the throng of people, there was enough space around Carter that she could see his collared shirt, black today, with buttons dark enough that they blended into the material. She could see this, likely, because people were keeping him at arm's length. She wondered if he even realized that, or if he was so accustomed to holding them at arm's length himself that their distance didn't even register. Jess hoped, for his sake, it was the latter.

"Ummm." Nikki drew out the word, dragging Jess's attention off Carter and back to her. She moved her head back and forth before turning around in a complete circle. "Who *are* these people?"

"What?" Jess followed her eyes as they swung around the crowd, quickly realizing that she'd been so focused on Carter that she'd blown right past everyone else. At least half of the sixty or so people in the courtyard were new faces to her. She looked behind her and spotted at least twenty more who had shown up in the last few minutes.

Her eyes widened. "I have no idea."

Nikki grabbed the arm of a poor unsuspecting woman unfortunate enough to be walking by them.

"Who are you?" Nikki demanded as the woman squeaked in surprise.

"Muriel," the lady said, freezing like a startled animal and visibly shrinking into herself. At Nikki's clearly dissatisfied expression, she added, "Muriel Bryson from Woodbridge. I'm married to Byron Bryson."

"Byron Bryson," Jess said. "Let's all try saying that ten times fast."

Nikki shot her a look. "And what brought you here today, Muriel Bryson from Woodbridge?"

Muriel looked to Jess, who nodded in a way she hoped looked reassuring.

"I came to watch the challenge?" Muriel said, her eyes dropping nervously to Nikki's grip on her arm. "A lot of us did. Jen Adams and Jilly Ray delivered pies here yesterday, so they stayed to watch the competition. It sounded so exciting that we all wanted to see what happened next."

"You mean, you wanted to see if someone actually died this time?" Nikki dropped her arm with a sneer of disgust.

"No." Muriel cringed. "I . . . I don't know." She ducked

her head and whispered, "I'm going to go," before scurrying away.

"If Luanne ever offers you a spot with the Redford Welcome Wagon," Jess said to Nikki, "you should just say no."

"If anyone offers you a job at the circus," Nikki said, "you should put that outfit back on and head straight to the clown tent."

"I can't believe she described DeMarco's near-death experience as 'exciting,'" Jess said.

"Right?" Nikki shook her head before pointing at Novak, who had climbed onto last night's stage and was trying unsuccessfully to blow his whistle. "It's about to start."

Jess nodded and was surprised when Nikki leaned closer and whispered into her ear.

"After I left," she said, "everything stayed fine?"

"It did." Jess wanted to hug her—for asking, for caring, for, as strange as it was, being in this with her and her dad—but she didn't dare. "And I think I forgot to say it last night, but thank you for showing up."

Novak's whistle shrieked, and Nikki looked relieved when the crowd silenced in response. She simply shrugged like her concern had meant nothing, which was fine. It didn't change the fact that, to Jess, it had meant everything.

"Good morning, everyone," Novak said into the megaphone. In a happy twist, it didn't unleash its usual screech. "The morning's rain has complicated today's challenge, as you'll no doubt discover. I'd like to warn everyone in advance that this is a physical challenge that should not be attempted by anyone who feels they might be susceptible to

injury. I'd also like to remind you that each person participating has signed a release absolving all organizing parties
and myself of responsibility for any harm that might come
to you during any portion of Mr. Wilhelm's game. If you
feel unsafe at any point today, it will be your responsibility
to remove yourself from the event."

A laugh burbled out of Jess before she could stop it. Novak's speech was just so *ominous*. It sounded like they were
about to swim with sharks or juggle balls of fire.

"For those of you," Novak continued, "who are here as
spectators, I ask that you remain in the square while our ten
remaining teams follow Mr. Beauford. Competitors, please
find Mr. Beauford on the corner of Main and Second Street."

"Excuse us, please," Jess said as she turned to make her
way back through the crowd, but the strangers were already
looking at Nikki and backing away to make a path, as if her
reputation had spread all the way to Woodbridge. Perhaps it
had, or maybe, when you had the face of an angel, people
always responded reverentially.

They were the first team to the corner, and Nikki looked
for Novak as if to ensure he was giving them a point for
this on his secret scoring list, but he was still on the stage
fiddling with his whistle. It didn't matter anyway because
the rest of the teams trailed right behind them. Jess was
happy to see that DeMarco was among them, looking well-
rested and perfectly healthy. But it was Carter who sent her
pulse racing. He looked intimidatingly sharp, and it delighted her to remember that, just last night, those fancy
shoes of his had been wet from an adventure the two of
them had shared.

He stood back as everyone greeted one another, but she caught the moment his eyes landed on her. Jess had expected him to laugh at the sight of her tutu, but he didn't. Instead, his mouth widened into a slow smile that looked so delighted, so unquestionably admiring, that Jess felt her blood turn to sparkles. It might have been the most beautiful she'd ever felt, though not necessarily in a pretty way. It was more like having a spotlight turned on you and discovering you're a born star.

The feeling was so overwhelming that she spun away, turning her attention to Marty Beauford like a properly focused competitor.

"Morning, Marty," she said, then stopped and looked at him curiously. He'd opted out of the game from the beginning, unwilling to close the Bait & Tackle for even a day. "How did you get roped into this?"

A sturdy, ruddy-faced man who preferred nature over people, Marty tended to skip any community event that didn't offer food. From his love of potlucks, Jess had discovered he was a vegetarian, a conviction Jess found charmingly incongruous for a man who sold fishing bait and hunting gear for a living.

"Money," he grunted with an unselfconscious shrug that shifted the massive backpack on his shoulders. "That lawyer of Jasper's came in for boots. You know that flashy pair Luanne talked me into ordering that nobody in town has ever even tried on?"

Jess nodded. On a shelf filled with earth tones, the green boots had been hard to miss. They were so bright, they had a noxious quality, like they'd been dipped in one of those glowing barrels of acid from a Batman cartoon.

"I sold him those," Marty said, "plus my services for a day."

"I didn't realize you were for sale," Nikki said, leaning over Jess's shoulder. "Do you do gutters?"

"You couldn't afford me." Marty's eyes swung over the group. All twenty people were spread around the corner, ten teams in total. "DeMarco, you hydrated?"

"Excuse me?" DeMarco looked down at his body as if to double-check that it was still the finely sculpted masterpiece he'd spent years cultivating in the gym.

"Have you hydrated after last night?" Marty enunciated the words, clearly already regretting his agreement to spend the day with people. "I can't have you getting sick again halfway up the mountain."

"I didn't fail to drink the recommended eight glasses of water for the day, Marty." DeMarco had to speak loudly over the murmured response from the group at Marty's reference to a mountain. "I had an allergic reaction."

"What are you talking about, halfway up a mountain?" Bobby Randall demanded loudly.

"If you went to the hospital," Marty said to DeMarco, ignoring Bobby, "you got sick."

"Well, unless you're planning to throw peanut dust at me, you have nothing to worry about."

"What mountain?" Bobby shouted, echoing the thoughts of everyone present, if significantly more aggressively.

"We're hiking, son." Marty slapped one hand against the shoulder strap of his backpack. "Got everything you need in here."

"Hiking?" Lexi's hand went to her hip as she kicked out

her stockinged leg, highlighting the three-inch heel of the stiletto she'd paired with her sweater dress. "How am I supposed to hike in these?"

"Pretend they're crampons," Marty said. "As muddy as the trail is likely to be, you might be the only person here who doesn't get halfway up and end up sliding right back down."

With this encouraging prediction, he turned on his heel and started toward the lake. After a moment of hesitation, the entire group followed him. Apparently, they had hiking to do.

Chapter 22

· · · · · · · · · · ·

CARTER

Carter's shoes had not been crafted for traction. Their soles were smooth, the designer logo etched so delicately into them that the lines of it did nothing to provide grip. Every step he took along the trail caked them more heavily with mud, sending him sliding back and forth like a cross-country skier who'd had two hot toddies too many before venturing out of the cabin.

Despite the sharp burn in his thighs and the restrictive pace, he found himself enjoying the hike. The trail zigzagged across the mountain rather than forcing them straight up, and the canopy of trees was brilliantly colored. Up close, the reds were redder, the golds appearing lit from within. It was the orange leaves that stole the show, though, that burnt color so exclusive to autumn.

He wondered what it would be like to live so near to a place like this, so close it could almost be considered his backyard. You didn't have to go far to find hiking trails in Atlanta, but it had been at least a year since he'd made his way to one, and he didn't remember them feeling quite so magnificent. This place smelled different. Rich and earthy and pure. And it was comfortingly quiet. Not actually quiet, obviously—with a group of twenty-one people, someone was always involved in conversation—but their words drifted off the mountain, absorbed by the trees and the trill of birds and the rustle of leaves rather than bouncing off buildings until they were amplified into a never-ending roar.

"My shoe is stuck again," Lexi whined loudly from behind him.

Carter stopped to look at her before scraping his own shoes on a conveniently squared rock. Lexi was, indeed, stuck. It was obvious by the way her toes were pointing up and her heel was almost entirely flush with the ground. Forcing his gaze forward, Carter spotted her partner, Melvin Martin, up ahead. Melvin had slunk away after Lexi had slapped off his previous attempts to help with no effort to hide her disgust. Even five million dollars, it seemed, wasn't enough incentive for him to risk further humiliation. Lexi was on her own.

Bobby certainly wasn't going to help, not after she'd shrieked in response to his offer to rip the heels off the last time she'd gotten stuck. And Marty, still trailing along behind the group, had made it clear he was only here to monitor their progress. According to him, it didn't matter if they made it up or even off the mountain. As long as he made note of where he left them, he'd still get paid.

With a sigh, Carter pivoted back toward Lexi, even as he reminded himself she wasn't on his team. He simply couldn't shake the feeling that his grandfather wouldn't want one of his neighbors to be stuck in mud. Sliding his feet carefully forward, he backtracked past Bryce and Nikki.

"How is eating a Hershey's Kiss with a red Skittle any

different than eating a chocolate-covered strawberry?" Bryce was asking Nikki, in their ongoing argument about mixing chocolate with fruit-flavored candies.

"For starters," Nikki said, "the red Skittles are cherry flavored, not strawberry."

Carter considered pointing out that they didn't have to agree—it seemed unlikely the two of them would ever be in a position to buy candy together or share it for any reason—but at least they'd moved on from arguing about yoga. (He now knew that Bryce didn't practice it but was in favor of any exercise that included napping on a mat. Nikki was against it because she claimed flexibility was for people who'd given up on standing their ground.)

When Carter reached Lexi, he nudged a couple of rocks against the mountain side of the path before finding one that felt stable enough to press his weight against.

"Put your hand on my shoulder," he directed her as he leaned down and reached for her shoe. Her perfume hit his nose like a punch, overwhelmingly floral and sweet.

"My knight in shining armor," she cooed, letting her thumb slide against the bare skin of his neck before settling on his shoulder.

His urge to recoil was so intense that it almost made him lose his balance. There was something about Lexi that he found repulsive. Even thinking such a strong word made him feel guilty enough to take care as he grabbed the back of her shoe and pulled, but the guilt didn't make it any less true. He wasn't sure what it was. The obvious reason was that he'd seen her intentionally spill a drink on Jess's laptop, but it couldn't be just that. He'd seen Nikki go after Jess as well, but she didn't provoke him like Lexi did. There was something steely about Nikki, tempered. Like she was prodding without shoving, knocking people off-balance but not toppling them. Lexi gave the impression she'd swing a hammer with the same lack of restraint as a Wiffle bat.

"You might want to take Bobby up on breaking the heels off," he said as the suction broke and the spike glopped out of the ground.

"Or you could just walk with me," she suggested, her eyes batting like a bug had flown into one of them, "and save me again the next time one of them gets stuck."

Carter lifted half his mouth into a tight smile and started back up the trail again. This time, he moved faster, digging his heels in at the completion of each step. He hadn't spoken to Jess yet today, not because he didn't want to but because of how badly he did. Last night, taking that rowboat into the middle of the lake had been one of the most pleasurable, freeing, visceral things he'd experienced in years. Then she'd shown up this morning looking so ridiculous and beautiful, like starlight personified, and he'd felt it—that falling feeling he'd heard other people talk about. Like he'd wandered up to a roof intending to catch a pleasant view and found himself plummeting over the edge instead.

In that moment, he'd wanted to run. Barclays weren't built for out-of-control sensations like falling. Fleeing, however, wasn't an option. Not if he wanted to win his grandfather's money and continue the work they'd been doing together. So Carter had forced himself to shift focus. He'd reminded himself yet again that Jess was his competition. He reminded himself how hurt she'd be when he won. He reminded himself what it would feel like to get in his car at the end of all this and leave her behind.

It was a simple recalibration, a rerunning of the numbers. And it had worked. Mostly. He'd managed to keep his distance for almost an hour. The day's challenge had made it easy, forming the contestants into a line so narrow only two people could comfortably walk side by side. All he'd had to do was stand back while she started the hike with Sally and wait until the gap had filled in between them.

Only, now, Carter's excuses were failing him. True as they were, they'd led him in a direction that felt wrong. Why *wasn't* he with Jess? Because it would end badly? Because he wouldn't get to be with her long enough? That was asinine. You didn't refuse a glass of 15-year Macallan Double Cask because it would be gone after you drank it. You just enjoyed the burn of it as it slipped down your throat.

Carter could be someone who enjoyed something without worrying about the consequences. Sure, he'd never done it before. But he'd also never tried. He would aspire to recklessness. Children were reckless with no effort at all. Surely, he could manage it at least once.

As he slid around people to make his way up the trail, Carter wasn't certain what, exactly, he was hyping himself up for. It wasn't as if Jess had propositioned him and he was on his way to take her up on something. That didn't feel like the point, though. He was attracted to her, and he'd gotten the impression she found him attractive as well, but it was more than that. He wasn't hurrying to get something from her.

He was hurrying so he didn't miss any more time with her.

Chapter 23

···········

JESS

Jess squatted down, balancing her umbrella against her side as she pretended to tie her shoe. She'd seen Carter passing the people behind them and wanted him to catch up to her. She waved Sally forward, hoping to talk to him alone. This would feel less pathetic if she actually had something to talk to Carter about, but she didn't. Even scrolling conversation topics in her brain, she couldn't come up with a single thing she could pretend needed discussing. Her thoughts felt a little blurry since she'd hit the ground, actually, but her desire to have Carter to herself was crystal clear.

She stood up and tried to be cool and continue onward but turned eagerly instead, lighting up when she discovered him directly behind her. He'd undone one more button than normal, and his sleeves were rolled up almost to his elbows. The sight felt like turning around to discover him naked.

"Hi," she said in an embarrassingly breathy way. It was how she imagined she'd sound if she came face-to-face with Judy Blume, starstruck and awed.

"Your tutu." He frowned forlornly as he took in her mud-covered outfit. With a glance behind him to confirm that Bobby was catching up to them, he started to walk, urging Jess forward by placing his hand on her back.

"I fell." Jess was disappointed by how quickly he removed his hand once she slid into step beside him. "Well, I ran into a tree branch, and then I fell."

Her balance had already been precarious, despite the umbrella she was using as a walking stick, so she should've been focusing on the path instead of trying to make Sally laugh with her impression of Elvis hunting the neighborhood's stray cat. If she'd been paying more attention to hiking, Jess would've taken the single step to the left needed to miss the spindly branch. At the very least, she could've swatted it out of her way. It had broken easily when her forehead attacked it, after all. But when the branch against her forehead caused her to rear back in surprise, the slippery mud had kept Jess's bottom half moving forward. Her feet found air while her head met the ground, a gymnastic feat Bobby had loudly rated only a four out of ten once he realized it hadn't rattled her enough to make her withdraw from the challenge.

"Are you hurt?" Carter's brow furrowed as he searched hers for signs of bruising. He looked so concerned that she opted not to tell him that it was the back of her head that developed a painful lump, not the front.

"Winners don't feel pain." Jess tried to keep her expression serious but could feel a cheeky smile tugging at her mouth.

"Right." Unlike Jess, Carter was able to project perfect seriousness.

He looked at her so gravely, in fact, that Jess felt a twinge of anxiousness. Maybe referring to herself as a winner had sounded too much like she was trash-talking him. Maybe the last thing they needed was a reminder that they were in a competition.

"Pain is just weakness leaving the body," Carter added soberly, the corner of his mouth turning up for a blink-and-you'd-miss-it moment.

Jess almost laughed but reined it in just in time.

"Just do it," she said sternly, adding a swoop of her finger meant to illustrate the Nike symbol.

"Tiger blood."

The deadpan reference to one of the most infamous "winning" rants of all time broke her restraint, and she let loose a snort of laughter. Carter looked pleased with himself.

"Did you see the 'provisions' Marty brought for the hike?" he asked.

Jess shook her head. She'd been eager to be the first person on the trail. Hiking was no fun when someone was in front of you, blocking your view. The whole point was to feel like an explorer, not a newly enlisted soldier at basic training.

"We do have water," Carter said, "but all he brought for snacks was trail mix . . . with peanuts."

Jess gasped. "Are you serious? After what happened last night?"

Carter nodded. "Even Bobby said he wouldn't eat it."

"Well, of course we can't eat it," Jess agreed. "Even if DeMarco says the peanut dust isn't an issue outdoors, it's a matter of solidarity."

"That's pretty much what Bobby seemed to be trying to say, except he got distracted by the idea of building squirrel traps and a fire to cook over, and then Marty said that he was going to tell Novak to dock points for anyone who couldn't manage to hike for two hours without eating, so Bobby got mad and started pushing his way around people to get up the trail."

"Are you talking about me?" Bobby called out from behind them. "I heard my name."

"We're talking about Bobbi Brown lipstick," Jess said over her shoulder. She slipped as she turned, and Carter reached out a hand to steady her. "I would've worn their Force of Nature shade if I'd realized we were going to be hiking."

"Don't care about that." Bobby slowed and waved them forward as if distance was required to ensure he didn't get dragged into a conversation about makeup.

Jess grinned impishly at Carter as she jammed her umbrella in the mud to regain her footing. "My dad always forgets to turn the volume up on his phone when he's at work, so I stop by the garage sometimes if I need to tell him something. That's how I discovered the quickest way to get Bobby to leave you alone is to start a conversation about literally anything other than football or beer."

"So the next time he's accusing me of poisoning someone in town," Carter said, "I should start talking to him about nail polish?"

"Yep, that's guaranteed to send him running." Jess hesitated before plowing on. "You know, Carter, last night at the bar, I said this town fights because it's like family. And I did mean that. But I also wanted to say that I'm sorry you've had such an unwelcoming experience. I swear, we're normally a lot friendlier. It seems competition has brought out the worst in us."

Carter shrugged. "*You've* been welcoming."

"Yeah, well, I figured out that you were okay that first day when you pretended we were in a conversation to get Nikki and her minions to leave me alone." Jess smiled at the memory. "Everyone else is still getting to know you."

"So you're saying you already know me?"

Jess couldn't tell if the curve of his lip was indicative of his pleasure at the idea or amusement at it. She *did* know him, at least as well as someone could possibly know a person they'd met just last week. Because of the hours they'd spent holding the courthouse wall, she knew Carter had never had a pet but had always wanted one, and that he'd come close to adopting a puppy named Drago but had been too worried his long hours at work would make the dog unhappy.

She knew that he was exceedingly skilled at masking any expression, except when his grandfather was mentioned, and then little lines around his eyes would appear, like a smile that had been banned from his mouth but couldn't be stifled entirely. She knew he valued pragmatism but didn't always let it win out over kindness.

"Are you saying I don't?" She tilted her head back in challenge. "All right, then. Tell me something new about you. Something nobody knows."

"That nobody knows?" He swiped at a speck of mud on his slacks that was invisible compared to the layer of mud covering her leggings. "What if I've already told everything about me to someone?"

"You haven't," Jess said confidently. "I'd bet every cent in my bank account that you can think of at least ten things off the top of your head that you've never shared with anyone."

"As a finance man, I'd advise against wagers of that magnitude."

"Am I right, though?"

Carter's answering smile was wider than the half-grin he usually offered. It almost reached two-thirds. "Have I mentioned my brother, Augustus?"

Jess felt a strange pang of hurt. "You told me you were an only child."

"I was," Carter said, "until Augustus came along. I suppose, technically, he was my imaginary friend, but I thought of him as a brother. He was always covered in dirt and smelled like hot dogs roasted over a fire, but he was wickedly funny. While I'd be parroting whatever well-behaved response my parents had taught me, he'd be whispering something wildly inappropriate into my ear."

Jess felt an immediate and irrational desire to meet this precocious little imaginary boy. "But you never repeated anything he said aloud?"

"I didn't have to. Just hearing him whisper it was as satisfying as saying it myself," Carter said. "I did laugh out loud the first few times he weighed in, though, and I quickly learned that parents do not appreciate their child responding to a rhetorical question like, 'Is there a reason you didn't get one hundred percent on your math quiz?' with hysterical giggles."

"You don't strike me as ever having been a giggler."

"It was an abbreviated phase."

"I think I would've liked Augustus," she said. "How long did he stick around?"

"Until boarding school. He didn't like having a room-mate, and he'd always had a fascination with train-hopping, so he ran off to do that."

"Sad," Jess said. "And what about you? Do you have a thing for train-hopping?"

Carter looked at her sternly. "Train-hopping is incredibly dangerous, Jessica. Only imaginary people can do it safely."

Jess laughed, and a drop of rain plopped onto her fore-arm beneath her pushed-up sweater and began a slow slide toward her wrist. It felt warmer than she would've expected for September rain, but that might just have been because hiking had made her hot.

"I do have a bit of a thing for trains, though," he said. "Especially in Europe. Some of the best views I've ever seen have been from the window of a train."

"I've never ridden on a train." Thanks to him, she now badly wanted to ride one. She wanted to go to Europe, too, but focusing on the train felt like a more reasonable goal.

"What about the subway? Did you ride that when you lived in New York?"

"I did." Jess brightened. "That counts?"

"It's on a rail. I don't see how it couldn't."

She clapped her hands together in triumph, and the end

of her umbrella scraped against the bark of a tree. Carter put a hand on her shoulder, correctly presuming a celebratory jig in the mud was imminent.

"If you wait until we're back at the bottom of the mountain," he suggested, swiping a drop of rain from his still perfectly styled hair, "you can celebrate both your mastery of train life and the completion of another of Novak's challenges."

"You're worried I'm going to fall," Jess said, too pleased by the fact that he cared to be offended at his lack of trust in her balance.

"No." He let his gaze drift pointedly over her muddied clothes. "Why would I be worried about that?"

A drop of rain splatted against her cheek, and she gave him a warning look. "Sarcasm isn't going to earn you a spot under my umbrella when those single raindrops start to procreate."

Carter laughed. It was a short, startled burst of laughter, but it was an actual laugh.

"Great," he said, pulling himself together, "now I'm going to think of storms as the result of frenzied raindrop mating."

"And just think how badly you're going to want to be under my umbrella then."

He gave her umbrella a look that was strangely judgmental. "Why is it black?"

"Why is every umbrella you've ever owned black?" Jess retorted. Technically, she was guessing, but she was certain she was right. No matter how unlikely it might seem after such a short time, whether Carter wanted to believe it or not, she *did* know him. And given the choice of a hundred umbrellas, Jess was confident he'd choose a black one every time.

"Because black umbrellas are practical," Carter said, proving her right. "They don't get dirty and they don't stand out."

"Then, that's why I have a black umbrella."

He looked at her with suspicion. After a moment, his expression shifted with understanding and his mouth widened into a devilish grin. "Jessica Reid, did you steal that umbrella from someone?"

"What?" She hid it behind her back. "No!"

"You didn't go out and buy a black umbrella," he insisted.

"I did. I went to Joe's market and asked for the most understated, practical umbrella he had. 'Price is no object,' I told him, 'as long as it's guaranteed to never get dirty.'"

Carter laughed again, and Jess couldn't believe this was the way she'd broken him. A simple black umbrella. Who knew?

Unfortunately, that was the moment it began to rain in earnest, big, fat, pelting drops.

"It's really helping with the mud," she said, gesturing at the umbrella when Carter looked at her expectantly. She jabbed it into the trail to make her point, but Carter's suspicious expression had returned.

"And the rain feels kind of nice after all this exertion, right?" she added.

"Tutu," he said sweetly, "can I please walk under your umbrella with you?"

"I . . ." She trailed off, thoroughly unable to resist his

imploring look. It was like gazing into swirling pools of melted chocolate.

With a sigh of defeat, Jess pushed her umbrella open and lifted it over his head. The blue sky dotted with fluffy clouds that covered its underside was so bright that it elicited another laugh from him, the most prolonged yet. She chose to focus on that victory, even if it had come at the expense of him being proven right that she'd never in a million years choose a boring, basic umbrella, no matter how practical.

Carter's fingers grazed against hers as he took over the handle and moved the umbrella so it was covering her completely, even though the adjustment left his right side to be pounded by rain. Jess's skin warmed at the contact. She looked up to meet his eyes questioningly as she moved into him so they could both stay dry. If she saw even a hint of discomfort, she'd pull back. She wouldn't even be offended. He was so clearly the type of person who walked alone that Jess felt silly at her unspoken insistence that they could climb a mountain pressed into each other's sides like two people in a three-legged race.

She couldn't help offering, though. Generosity was the Southern way, ingrained in her from years of living in a small town. Her offer had nothing to do with the thrilling way her skin sparked every time Carter touched her. If he pulled back, she'd insist he use the umbrella himself. A cold shower, she realized, would likely do her good.

Jess was so focused on what her reaction would be when Carter rebuffed her offer that it took her a moment to realize he hadn't.

"Your turn," he said, settling into her and shifting the

umbrella so it covered both of them completely. "Tell me something about yourself that nobody knows."

He gave no indication that he'd noticed the intimacy of the moment. He just bent his head over hers awaiting her answer. So Jess did as he asked. She told him about the mouse that had lived in her house when she first moved in, and how she'd tried to catch it at first but had ended up making friends with it instead. She even admitted how sad she'd felt when the single cube of cheese she'd begun to leave out daily had gone unclaimed for the first time.

It was an embarrassing story, but it was the only thing Jess could think of that nobody else knew about her. She hadn't told her dad or Liz at first because she'd known they wouldn't see the mouse as a fluffy little creature with adorably trembling whiskers but as a living transmitter of bacteria and disease. Once the problem was gone, Jess had continued to keep the story to herself, not because she secretly hoped the mouse might return but because she knew it wouldn't.

She had bored it with her constant offerings of cheese. A wild creature like that had probably needed variety. A scoop of peanut butter every now and then, left in another room to provide more of a challenge. Whatever she'd done wrong, the fact remained: Jess hadn't even managed to keep a rodent from abandoning her. Jess liked to imagine that now it spent its days feasting on Roquefort and Camembert, or some other variety Joe had deemed too exotic to stock in his market.

"Good riddance," Carter said in response to the news of the mouse's abandonment.

"Right." Jess sighed and gave in to reality. "Mice are

disgusting. They are carriers of bacteria and disease and should be lured into traps and deposited outside where they belong."

"Not because of that." His shoulder pressed against hers, solid and warm. "Because that particular mouse was stupid to leave a loving home that served up cheese daily. You deserve a better mouse than that, even if it is just another disgusting little intruder carrying bacteria and disease."

It was, strangely enough, one of the nicest things anyone had ever said to her. Jess laughed and pivoted to famous mice in history—if you considered the immense popularity of Mickey, it was mind-boggling that mice hadn't replaced cats and dogs as the pet of choice years ago—but the warmth from Carter's conviction that she deserved more continued to glow within her. It combined with the heat of his arm, still pressed against hers, filling their tiny little circle of refuge from the rain. She'd known when she'd bought this umbrella that it would be fun to look up at dry sky when everyone else saw a storm.

She hadn't realized having someone else under here with her would feel like walking in actual sunshine.

Chapter 24

··········

CARTER

They'd been halfway down the other side of the mountain when he'd spotted the crowd. Until that moment, he'd believed they were in the homestretch. They'd been hiking for hours, his shoes were covered in a layer of mud so thick he was probably obligated to donate them to a gym for leg weights instead of tossing them in the trash, and he wanted lunch. Suffice it to say, Carter was not pleased at the indication that today's challenge wasn't merely the hike itself.

When he'd pointed out the throng of people to Jess, she'd adorably assumed it was a show of support. *They'll want to make sure we all made it back*, she'd told him assuredly. *They'll want to celebrate that we all made it to the next round*. But Carter didn't think so.

Maybe, in the Redford Jess was accustomed to, people showed up for no other reason than to celebrate their neighbors' triumphs. This town had ceased to be the normal Redford, though. The competition had divided its residents. It had become overrun with outsiders. There was only one reason a group like this would enter the damp woods, willing to stand around for an indeterminate amount of time while the branches above them shed leftover raindrops on them every time the wind blew.

They'd been promised a spectacle.

Carter kept this certainty to himself, though, peering instead down the mountain every time the cover of trees thinned. Given the poor visibility, it took a while for him to determine what he was seeing. At first, he'd thought people had simply divided themselves, settling into camps on the opposite sides of two fissures in the mountain. He was only now realizing the lines were high, rather than low, built deliberately out of something that looked like . . . stacks of hay?

It resembled the end of a marathon site, only wider, and Carter grimaced at the implication. It looked to him like exactly the amount of space required for twenty people to line up side by side with a couple of feet between them. The hike wouldn't end with them snaking down the mountain in a group. It would end with a race.

He supposed he understood the need for one. No one had tapped out of the hike, so Novak would require some other way to cull the herd. What didn't make sense was the jumble of unnaturally bright colors at the top of the hill. Carter peered at them again, his eyes struggling to turn the shapes into something recognizable. It wasn't until Marty shouted that the hike had ended and they slowed to a stop that Carter finally began to understand what he was looking at.

"Are those . . ." He shook his head, not wanting to say it.

Not really even knowing how. They looked like Easter eggs on wheels.

Jess leaned into him, following his gaze. Then, she gasped.

"Barbie Jeeps!" She clenched his arm like her glee was so great she needed the weight of his trepidation to keep her on the ground.

"I don't understand." Carter shook his head again like this was the kind of thing he could rationalize away. "Even if you ignore the fact that dolls can't drive, how could Barbies require a vehicle that size? Aren't those dolls the length of your forearm? How would one reach the steering wheel on something that big? You'd have to have ten of them sitting on each other's shoulders for one of them to see through the windshield."

He was certain he was making valid points, but Jess just laughed like he was joking and lifted both hands in the air to wave at the applauding crowd. The group they'd left in the square that morning had doubled, if not tripled, in the couple of hours the teams had been on the mountain. Carter was under no illusion he'd been in town long enough to recognize every Redfordonian, but most of the faces at the pie-eating contest had begun to feel familiar. Many of these were not.

"This should be fun," Bryce said, catching up to Carter and Jess. His voice was cheerfully devoid of sarcasm, perhaps because he already looked like he'd rolled down a mountain in a vehicle built for little girls.

"Did you fall, too?" Carter asked, taking in the sight of his mud-splattered flannel.

Bryce's hand went to his hair, half brown now instead of

blond, and worked at a lock stiffened with mud. "Nah. Nikki and I got into a mud fight."

Carter's gaze moved from Bryce to Nikki, who, with the exclusion of her boots, was spotless.

"She won," Bryce added helpfully.

"I can see that," Carter said.

"You asked for it," Nikki said to Bryce, holding her hands up as if officially cleared of all guilt in the matter. "You should know better than to talk about a woman's weight."

"Bryce!" Jess's eyes widened with a look of such shocked disapproval that Carter felt grateful it was his teammate and not him on the receiving end of it.

"I didn't." The denial was stated with all the adamancy Bryce's laid-back drawl was capable of. "I just said Sally and Luanne are probably our biggest competition for the prize money."

"Nikki!" Jess's disapproval shifted with impressive decisiveness. "You had to know Bryce wasn't referring to size. Bobby is at least six-four and makes Godzilla look cuddly."

"Well," Nikki said, her jaw jutting out unapologetically, "it was still rude of Bryce to say they're the biggest competition when it's so obvious that we are."

"I don't know," Sally said, leaning into their little circle. "I think Bryce had it right the first time."

"Godzilla has T. rex arms," Bobby said, speaking over her.

"Hence the comparison," Nikki responded with an evil smile.

"I'm pretty sure she meant to compare me to King Kong." Bobby glared at Nikki before jabbing his chin toward Jess. "Didn't you, Jess?"

"If you think anyone is going to call you king anything," Nikki said, "you need to look into the ventilation at the garage. Clearly, you've been sniffing too much gasoline."

"Did you hear that we're the contenders to beat, Luanne?" Sally called out to Luanne as if the conversation weren't chaotic enough.

"I don't know why everyone insists on underestimating me," Lexi muttered loudly, "but I swear you're going to regret it."

Carter looked over at Novak and was equal parts grateful and uneasy to discover he was already engaged in the process of getting his megaphone to function. The lawyer held his mouth to it again before pulling it away and looking at it reproachfully. He slapped it on the side a couple of times, returned it to his mouth, and managed to produce a staticky shriek. A man next to him curled his fingers to his mouth and sent a piercing whistle through the air, effectively quieting the crowd.

"If I may have your attention," Novak said into the megaphone as if unaware that the eyes of every person on the mountain were already on him, "we're ready to begin the second portion of today's challenge. Because all ten of our teams successfully completed the hike, we'll be sending them the rest of the way down the mountain in two different groups. The rules are simple: Every contestant must ride in one of the vehicles we have provided. They must ride it from the starting line to the finish line. Their feet may hang over the sides of the vehicle to aid in steering, but their bodies must remain inside the vehicle. If a vehicle crashes or topples over, its driver may remain in the race as long as they are able to resume their ride where it stopped and complete the entire path."

As Novak continued to drone on, Carter studied the path that had been lined with hay. It was steep but not terrifyingly so. The bigger concern was how uneven it was. Whoever had set this up seemed to have cleared the ground of large rocks, but they wouldn't have been able to reshape the earth itself. Simple gravity dictated that a mountain would create runoff. Carter would have to look out for rivulets, which was guaranteed to be difficult barreling down a hill on child-sized wheels, if not impossible under so much mud.

At least it was no longer raining. Carter had no doubt Jasper had chortled at the vision of a bunch of adults careening down a mountain on plastic Barbie Jeeps, but he was surprised Novak, as a lawyer, had signed off on it. Surely, this was a lawsuit waiting to happen. Then again, Novak had already made a point to remind them that they'd put their signatures under those many paragraphs of fine print. Undoubtedly, their signatures would be used as proof that breaking a leg beneath a hot pink kid-mobile was all in good fun.

"Please confer with your teams," Novak continued, "and send one person to choose a vehicle."

Carter turned to Jess instead of Bryce. Would it be a bad thing to ask her to wait until the second group? Would she find it possessive or infantilizing if she knew he wanted to go down first to ensure it was safe? He worried that might imply he thought he could do something she couldn't, when, really, he had no idea if he could do it himself. All he knew was if someone was going to get hurt, he would unquestionably prefer it be him, not her.

"You have to go in the second group," Jess said, thwarting his intention. Her eyes sparkled. "I can't even pretend that I don't want to be at the bottom so I can see your face when you're barreling down a mountain on a Barbie Jeep."

"I can assure you," Carter said, "my face will not be providing you with any amusement. You're far more likely to find my expression demoralizing, due to my supreme confidence that I'll be first to cross the finish line."

"Fine." Jess shrugged, her sparkle undiminished. "Then I'll just enjoy the illusion of Business-Casual Ken doll having expanded to human proportions."

Carter looked down to see what he was wearing. The genius of buying everything in compatible color palettes was that you never had to think about what matched. It was a strategy that had worked perfectly for the office. But he had, strangely enough, been unprepared for his grandfather to start dictating his days from the grave.

"Mattel prefers Career-Driven Ken," he chided dryly. "Have a little respect for the brand, Jessica."

"So I'm going first, then?" Bryce interjected, surprising Carter once again with the reminder that, despite Jess's ability to fill his vision completely, they were not alone.

"If that's fine with you?" Carter had a general policy of making statements rather than asking questions, but it occurred to him that he'd spent the day acting as if he was paired up with Jess rather than Bryce. And, despite the lack of sarcasm in Bryce's question, surely even he was capable of annoyance if pushed hard enough.

"Sure." Bryce shrugged. "Watch my technique. If it goes badly, you should probably try something different once it's your turn."

"Will do." Carter stifled a laugh and slapped him on the back. "Good luck."

"And what about me?" Jess called as Nikki shoved her toward the plastic Jeeps. "Don't you want to wish me good luck?"

"Eat dirt, Bonnie." Carter was shocked to find himself winking, as if his body was incapable of pretending he didn't want her to progress to the next round almost as badly as he wanted to win the whole thing himself. If she got eliminated, he'd no longer have an excuse to hang out with her.

"Choke on my dust, Butch," she sang back sassily.

Less than five minutes later, the first group was lined up, Jeeps in front and riders holding on to them from behind. Despite the width of the track, there were too many vehicles to offer more than a couple feet of space between each one. This must be why Novak had split them up. It was reassuring to discover he'd at least given that much regard to their safety.

Novak had also provided helmets. Every person had one strapped to their head, though Jess's looked too large. Carter suspected she'd chosen it because the bright teal color matched her Jeep. Another bolt of worry flashed through his stomach.

It would be fine, he reminded himself. Funny, even. The mud might make the slope slicker, but it would also make for a softer landing. He focused on Jess's smile as she hammed it up for the crowd, waving and giving little jump kicks so that her tutu bounced ridiculously over her leggings.

"On your mark," Novak said in a formal tone into the megaphone.

One of the guys who had been divvying out bike helmets grabbed the megaphone from his hand and took over.

"Get set," the guy roared with all the energy of a monster truck rally announcer.

The crowd went wild.

"GO!"

Carter tried to whoop with everyone else, but his heart filled his throat as he watched Jess jump into the seat, a leg over each side so her feet could shove at the ground to get momentum. Only, once she started moving, she didn't leave her feet hovering like everyone else but instead lifted them into the air so she was flying rudderless. Irrationally worried as he might be, Carter couldn't help but laugh at the sight of it. Her utter abandon was awe-inspiring.

The Jeeps weren't moving as quickly as he'd feared, but neither were they going straight. Instead, they immediately began to veer drunkenly. Bobby's started off fastest, likely because of his size, but the same factor caused the Jeep to tip over, dropping him over on his side like a beached whale. Cheers turned to hysterics as he kicked angrily at the hot pink plastic. Sally crashed into DeMarco, stopping her progress and accelerating his. Lexi's partner, Melvin, made it farther downhill than anyone before his Jeep crashed into one of the hay barriers on the side. Jess continued to weave wildly down the track, making slow but sure progress. Only

Bryce was riding his Jeep like a wave, looking so relaxed atop the colorful plastic that it was unsurprising it seemed to have responded in kind and was rolling him cheerfully forward, moving him into the lead.

Laughter ripped from Carter's throat as the madness of the race overcame his worry. Sally was pushing her car back into motion, running behind it just long enough to achieve speed before thrusting her body forward and landing heavily inside the little seat. Bobby was back in motion, too, using his heels to propel his Jeep forward. His legs were like tree trunks, holding the path in line, giving him an unmistakable advantage. Sure enough, he passed Jess, and Carter heard himself cheering loudly for her to catch up.

Maybe she heard him, or maybe she'd just remembered this wasn't only a game but a competition. Whatever the reason, Jess finally lowered her feet to the ground and scooted herself forward, picking up speed. She didn't have the strength to keep her path as straight as Bobby's or the momentum that had sent Sally careening into the lead, but her lightness worked in her favor, sending her skimming over the mud instead of getting bogged down in it.

Carter's adrenaline raced as Jess passed Bobby and caught up to Sally. Neck and neck, the two women zoomed toward the end of the track, fighting for first place as Bryce's leisurely ride took an unfortunate turn toward the meandering. Jess threw her head back with clear exhilaration as they hit the last moment for peak speed before they'd have to dig their feet into the ground to slow themselves after the finish line. Carter was shouting for Bryce to reclaim his lead when disaster struck Jess's ride in the form of a root or a rock.

Whatever it was jerked her Jeep to the left and lifted it off the ground like it had sprouted wings. Unfortunately, the Barbie Jeep wasn't built to fly. It soared for only a moment before hitting the ground with a sickening crunch, rolling twice to take it over the finish line but trapping Jess underneath. The crowd gasped, and Carter's insides clenched as he watched several men run toward the overturned vehicle.

He stopped breathing when he saw Jess's teal helmet on the ground several feet north of her head. One of the men tossed her Jeep to the side, and it skidded sadly across the ground. Another's broad back blocked Jess from sight. Then the man stepped back, and Jess was visible again, rising to her feet without assistance and enabling Carter to breathe again. Still, he didn't know for sure she was okay until she leapt in the air, throwing her arms into the air in a triumphant V.

The crowd went wild.

Chapter 25

· · · · · · · · · · ·

JESS

Jess giggled at the sight of Nikki and Carter fighting their way down the mountain. They looked like posh jockeys whose steeds had been replaced at the last moment with Barbie Jeeps. She bounced with excitement. Any anxiety she'd had about the competition had been swept away by the euphoria of discovering her flight at the end of the last race had rocketed her into first. She'd just never realized how similar euphoria felt to dizziness.

Her head swam as she cheered her teammate on. Not that Nikki needed it. Predictably, she was riding her Jeep like some poor pony she'd trained with a whip. Every time it tried to veer off course, Nikki jabbed a boot heel into the ground and jerked it back to the straight and narrow with a screech of disapproval so loud it could be heard over the crowd's cheers. From her spot behind the finish line, Jess could practically see her grinding her jaw.

Carter, on the other hand, had the focused expression of a man studying a column of numbers. His progress down the mountain had been remarkably smooth, save for the moment Lexi had swung left and clipped the front of his Jeep. With all the vehicles sliding left and right, Jess's belief Lexi had done it intentionally felt unfair, but she couldn't help noticing that Lexi's stilettos—as detrimental as they might've been on the hike—had proven remarkably advantageous in the Jeep. All she had to do was jab one into the mud and her vehicle swung obediently in that direction.

Intentional or not, Carter hadn't allowed Lexi to throw him off course. He'd responded to the resulting skid like he was driving in snow, refusing to fight it until he was sure a correction wouldn't cause him to flip over. Once he'd gotten back on track, he'd sped himself up by sweeping his feet against the ground repeatedly, but the damage had been done. Lexi had gotten ahead, and he'd be lucky now to come in fourth, a dangerously low placement when combined with Bryce's fifth-place finish. Jess had only a moment to feel disappointed before Luanne inched past Nikki, hitting the finish line first. Jess erupted into cheers with the rest of the crowd, as excited for Luanne as she was for Nikki, who barreled across the line only a moment behind her.

They'd done it.

They'd tied with Sally and Luanne for first place. Unless this was the last challenge, she and Nikki would be progressing to the next round. They had to be. She leapt into the air with excitement, continuing to cheer, even as she watched Lexi take third and Charity, DeMarco's partner, take fourth. It wasn't until Bobby's partner crossed the line fifth that her elation began to fade. With a final push, Carter slid past the person in front of him and managed to take sixth.

Jess's stomach sank. This was more than a disappointing

showing for Carter and Bryce. It was very possible their team wouldn't make it to the next round. The thought hit heavy and hard. If the game ended for Carter, it didn't just mean Jess would miss out on seeing him during the challenges. He'd leave Redford altogether.

"I *had* it." Nikki tugged Jess back into the present with her furious words.

For a moment, Jess thought Nikki had found a way to blame coming in second on Jess. Nikki's eyes burned furiously as they lifted to meet hers, and it wasn't until Jess caught the regret in them that she realized Nikki's anger wasn't directed at her but at Nikki herself.

"You did so well," Jess said. Her hand lifted like it had forgotten to consult with her head and was determined to offer a sympathetic pat on Nikki's arm. Then it seemed to remember that Nikki didn't like Jess, so it froze in the air, conspicuously still amid the frenzy of the crowd.

"I lost." Nikki looked at her searchingly as if trying to determine if Jess was actually too stupid to understand how races worked.

"Um?" Jess wondered if perhaps she *was* more dull-witted than she'd realized. Her head had been throbbing ever since it hit the ground, so intensely that it was becoming difficult to think. "You came in second? You beat everyone except Luanne."

"Second place isn't going to get my mom—" Nikki's mouth snapped shut, and she glared at Jess as if Jess had tried to trick her into revealing something.

With a sharp inhale, Nikki restarted her sentence.

"Treatments can't be paid for with money you *almost* won, Jessica."

Jess took a step back, feeling like she'd been hit. "I know that."

"We have to beat everyone," Nikki reminded her, as if Jess weren't taking her dad's situation seriously—as if the threat of his death weren't the biggest, most terrible thing that could ever happen.

"I *know* that." Any remaining joy at their showing in the race seeped out of Jess like a deflating balloon. "But we can only do our best."

"Are you saying that I'm not capable of winning?" Nikki's eyes narrowed at her.

"Of course not!"

"Then, I didn't do my best." Nikki spit out the words as Bryce sidled up and slung an arm around her.

"You're not doing a particularly great job at celebrating, either." Bryce's brow lifted when Nikki snarled at him. "What? It's not my fault you came to the bar after you got the sponsorship offer from that Kumbaya brand. If you hadn't, I wouldn't know for a fact that your best celebrating involves a lot of dancing."

"It's Cuyana, you idiot," Nikki said, but her words lacked their usual venom, and she slid an arm around his waist in a gesture of friendliness that made Jess wonder if she, too, had considered the fact that he was unlikely to make it to the next round.

Around them, the crowd was growing restless. Some people were inching over the lined bales of hay as if tempted to grab a Jeep and ride it down the mountain themselves. Others had rushed the finish line to pull the rider they'd come to cheer for up from the ground or out of the tiny seat in which they'd been wedged. During the race, the mood had focused on the moment, but now it was shifting toward the future. Through all the laughter and race retellings that could be heard, one question kept popping up across both competitors and spectators alike: Which teams would be moving on to the next round?

Finally, the screech of the megaphone suggested an end to their wait.

"I'd like to congratulate our contenders on successfully completing the race," Novak said from up on the mountain where the Jeeps had launched. "However, as you all know, it was only one challenge in a series of them. We have combined the efforts of each team across the two races and will now announce which five teams will be moving on to the next round."

A murmur of disapproval permeated the audience. Five teams meant half the group would be eliminated. Could ten million dollars really hang on one's ability to navigate a child's toy down a mountain? It didn't demonstrate determination like holding the courthouse wall had, or even an understanding of the town, like the scavenger hunt had required. It was sheer luck, too random to be a legitimate disqualifier.

Jess allowed herself to indulge these same thoughts, even though she knew without question that Jasper wouldn't have felt obliged to follow any rules of legitimacy when formulating the challenges. It was his game, and he would've been focused on fun rather than merit. It didn't seem fair, though. Not if it meant that one stroke of bad luck would end Carter and Bryce's ability to continue to play. Especially not if it meant Carter would return to Atlanta.

She looked up at him sympathetically, but his expression showed none of the worry she was feeling. If she hadn't watched him cross the finish line with her own eyes, she would've assumed he'd finished first rather than sixth. Then again, maybe he had. The entire race had taken on a dreamy quality, and Jess wouldn't have been surprised at all to learn that she'd been mistaken. The thought made her heart beat faster. Maybe she'd been wrong to assume she and Nikki were a lock to move on to the next challenge.

"In no particular order," Novak said, infuriatingly relentless in his pursuit of opacity regarding the competition's scoring, "the five teams moving on to the next round of Mr. Wilhelm's game are DeMarco Davis and Charity Meyers."

Novak was forced to pause when the crowd responded to his words with cheering. From the bottom of the mountain and through her slightly hazy vision, Jess could only see his pale, rigid frame, but she was confident he was radiating disapproval at the interruption.

"Alexis Farley and Melvin Martin." His words were followed by another round of cheering, though Jess wondered if this one was slightly more muted, likely because she wasn't the only one who had noticed Lexi's antics during the race.

"Nikki Loughton and Jessica Reid."

It took a moment for Jess to process her own name. The whoop of joy ripped out of her mouth before her brain fully realized what was happening. She swung her arms around

Nikki, and Nikki jumped with her, cheering wildly, for a full three seconds before remembering her feelings toward her teammate and spinning out of Jess's embrace.

"Robert Randall and Edwin Matthews," Novak announced.

"Oh." Jess stopped jumping. "Oh no."

The words slipped out in spite of herself as she searched Carter's face for any sign of understanding. Bobby's team had been the fourth one called. It was over. Luanne and Sally would be the last ones called. They'd been the only ones besides Jess and Nikki whose advancement to the next round seemed guaranteed.

"Aw, hell," Bryce said, clearly coming to the same conclusion. He gave Carter a we-tried shrug, but Carter wasn't looking at him. He wasn't looking at Jess, either. He was firmly focused on Novak, looking as confident as if he'd already seen the list Novak was reading from.

"And the final team continuing on," Novak said, "will be Bryce Howard and Carter Barclay."

Jess gasped, and the sound was amplified by the echoing gasps of the crowd around her. *What?* The word bounced through the air, exhaled by so many people that it seemed to take on a life form of its own. The argument was so obvious that it took people a moment to begin to verbalize the details. Once they did, the gasping quickly escalated to shouting. *First* was one of the most predominantly used words, although *cheating* was a very close second.

For a moment, an actual expression broke through Carter's mask of impenetrability, and Jess tried to determine what it indicated. Guilt? Gratitude? Relief? But it was gone as quickly as it appeared, leaving behind only the perfect features of a man in a cologne commercial. For the first time, she felt a surge of resentment toward this outsider. As badly as she wanted him to stay, it wasn't right for him to steal Luanne and Sally's place.

Up at the launch site, Novak was waving off the shouts being directed toward him. He pulled out a handkerchief and dabbed at his forehead, turning away from the grumbling. It seemed to get to him, though, and he lifted the megaphone back to his mouth.

"I am under no obligation to disclose how points are awarded in the game," he reminded them in his squeaky, amplified voice. "However, I will remind you that the rules of this race specifically addressed the requirement that every competitor ride their Jeep all the way down the slope. When Sally Parker ran part of the way behind her vehicle, she failed to adhere to the standards of the race and was disqualified. That is all I have to say on the situation. Today's challenge is over. Tomorrow's will begin at ten a.m. in the town square. I will see the remaining teams there."

With that, Novak lowered his megaphone to his side and refused to acknowledge any demands for further explanation. The truth was, he didn't have to say more. He didn't owe any of them anything. The ten million dollars would be awarded at his discretion, and the only person whose opinion mattered had already been buried.

Jess turned to look for Sally and Luanne, but they'd been swallowed up by a group of townspeople doling out consolation hugs. Suddenly, it all felt like too much. The roller coaster of emotions. The noise. The suspicion that

Sally and Luanne had been cheated, that Carter actually was in on it with Novak. The insistent, unceasing throbbing in her head.

"I have to go." Jess didn't know who she was saying the words to. Her teammate, who she'd just made it another step closer to ten million dollars with. Carter, whose jaw twitched at her proclamation as if he suspected, possibly correctly, that she was running away from him. Bryce, so visibly uncomfortable with the way things had played out that Jess felt a strange urge to console him.

Turning on her heel, she tried to slip through the crowd that seemed to be shifting so quickly it blurred in her vision.

"Wait," Nikki said, grabbing her arm. "I saw your dad over there. He'll want to celebrate with you."

Jess shook her head, feeling guilty when she saw the confusion on Nikki's face. "You celebrate with him," she said, already feeling horrible before her words hit the air. Her dad wasn't some chore to pass off, but she couldn't help herself. She needed to go home, now. She needed to lie down.

It wasn't until she'd left everyone behind, taking the shortcut down by the lake instead of walking the road with the crowd, that Jess realized the wind wasn't strong enough to make the trees sway like they were. She looked up at them suspiciously, stumbling at the sudden change in focus. The tallest one called her name, its tone surprisingly deep and masculine. With its sultry red leaves, she would've predicted it to have the raspy purr of a female jazz singer.

"Jess." An arm slid around her waist and intense dark eyes peered down at her from Carter's face. "Are you okay?"

"My head hurts," she said, blinking rapidly. "Every time it pounds, the earth moves."

"That must make it very difficult to walk," he said in a light tone that belied the concern in his gaze.

"It really does." She sighed and nestled into the warmth of his side.

"Let's get you out of here."

It didn't sound like a question, so Jess didn't answer. She just matched her steps to his and allowed him to lead her out of the woods.

Chapter 26

JESS

thought you were a tree," Jess said a couple of hours later.

Carter had wanted to take her to the hospital, but she'd insisted he bring her home. Her insurance would probably cover about twelve cents of a doctor's bill, and she hadn't won Jasper's prize money yet. If she did have a concussion, as Carter feared, watching movies had taught her that doctors would only insist she stay awake and give her something for her headache. She could do both of those things from the comfort of her own couch.

"That's not reassuring," Carter said, unsuccessfully hiding the amusement that curled at the corners of his mouth. He was sitting next to her on the bright fuchsia sectional, looking surprisingly relaxed amid the clutter of her living room. Though, she reminded herself, his refusal to use her favorite sequin-covered blanket *had* felt unnecessarily adamant.

"What if you have a brain injury?" he said.

"The entire point of a helmet is to prevent such injury."

"Your helmet came off," he reminded her. "And we're

not sure if you're feeling the effects of the Jeep wreck or from falling on the trail."

"You're making me sound clumsy." The complaint didn't come out as genuinely as Jess intended because she had snagged on his use of the word *we*. She liked the way it sounded, herself and this self-contained man grouped as a unit. *Bonnie and Butch*. She liked everything about this moment, actually. The Excedrin Carter had found in her bathroom might've been expired, but it was also extra strength, resulting in a disappearance of her headache and a caffeine high that made her leg bounce excitedly beneath the rejected sequins. Combined with the wooziness she still felt and the warmth of her home after a day spent trekking through a damp forest, the overall effect was like dancing through a dreamworld.

"Please accept my apologies for failing to contort the truth to more flattering proportions," he said formally.

Jess laughed in spite of herself. "You're terrible at apologizing."

"Yes, well, I was raised to be exceedingly polite." He grinned, then wrangled it back under control. "So apologizing isn't something I've needed to do with the frequency required to properly excel at it."

"For future reference, the classic 'I'm sorry' usually works best. That's what I'd use the next time I saw Sally and Luanne if I were you." Jess heard the words slip out and wondered distantly if it was considered passive aggression or actual aggression if the truth just happened to sound accusatory.

She'd been so dazed when Carter had found her in the woods that it had been easy to leave the Barbie Jeep race behind like it had happened in some other world, one where trees didn't talk and she could've walked a straight line if required to pass a sobriety test. Then they'd gotten to her house, and Carter had been so caring and attentive that she'd been unable to resist burying herself in the moment.

She'd sipped at the rooibos tea he'd made for her, savoring both the spiced vanilla flavor and the feeling of being taken care of. She'd answered the questions he asked as he wandered around the room, picking up books from her shelf and studying her knickknacks. She'd felt like she was seeing her life through new eyes—his eyes—and it had all felt special again, like it had when she was collecting each of these trinkets that made her feel most like herself.

It had all been so nice that she hadn't wanted to ruin the moment by asking if he was in cahoots with Novak—or worse, having to wonder if he was lying to her if he denied it. But, apparently, she hadn't needed to ask the question to get an answer.

"You think I had a hand in their elimination," Carter said, realizing the same thing. He appeared surprisingly unoffended by the suggestion.

"Did you?"

"No," he said simply.

And, strangely, it was enough. It wasn't okay, of course. The scoring should have been more transparent, and one mistake shouldn't have been enough to knock the leading contenders out of the game entirely. But the truth was, it didn't matter if everyone else was right. It didn't even matter if Novak was stacking the deck in Carter's favor.

The shock of seeing Sally and Luanne eliminated had

forced Jess to acknowledge exactly how out of control this whole situation was. As badly as she wanted the money, there was no magic button she could press to secure the win. All she could do was play Jasper's game to the best of her ability and attempt to enjoy the experience in the way she was certain he'd intended. The fact that the stakes were high for her didn't mean things would go her way. The other contenders had their own motivations, and she couldn't count out the possibility that Novak did as well. She couldn't worry about them any more than she could expect them to worry about her. They all just wanted to win.

"Okay," she said, just as simply as Carter had. Then she leaned forward and pressed her lips to his.

She didn't intend to do it. If she'd had time to think it through, she would've tested the waters with a light touch on his arm, a slow lean, anything that would've provided Carter an opportunity to pull back. She didn't think it through, though. If she had, she would've been forced to acknowledge not only the fact that Carter might not want her to kiss him but also the many reasons it was a bad idea to do so. She would've considered the fact that he would be leaving soon. She would've remembered how long it took for her dad to recover after her mom left.

Her brain wasn't working like that, though. It was stuck in happy, dreamy mode. In fact, it seemed to be more of a distracted spectator to the show than the thing supposedly running it. Her body had taken the reins, and it was drawn to his.

His lips were surprisingly warm, but they were completely still for a moment that stretched on in her mind long enough for embarrassment to come crashing through. Then they came to life, covering her mouth as one of his hands slid around her waist, tugging her toward him, and the other slipped up her back. Jess didn't know what she'd expected, but this was even better, her skin burning deliciously every place he touched.

His teeth nipped at her lower lip, sending a shudder through her body, and she wound her fingers through his hair, pulling him even closer. His hair was softer than she'd imagined, silky against her cheek when his mouth dropped to the tender skin of her neck before traveling north again to reclaim her lips. He tasted like cinnamon and spiced bourbon—not the drink itself, which she didn't actually like, but something complex and intoxicating. She wanted to inhale him whole.

Which was why it felt like being doused in cold water when he pulled back. Jess breathed heavily under his intense gaze, preparing herself for him to say something that would put her safely back at arm's distance. *What was that?* she anticipated him saying. Or, *Well, that was unexpected.*

"I've been wanting to do that since you talked me into stealing that leaky boat," he said instead, shocking her with a smile so full it lit up his gorgeous face.

"Then why did you stop?" Her voice was husky with lust as she unsuccessfully attempted to tug him back toward her.

"Because it's probably a bad idea, for several reasons. But also because you might be concussed," he said gently, his fingers still caressing the nape of her neck. "And I can't be sure that you're thinking clearly."

"Would it help if I said the alphabet backward?" Jess wasn't actually confident she could.

"It might," he said with another smile that lit up the room, "if I thought you were drunk."

"Maybe we should get drunk," she said, wondering if champagne bubbles, which typically felt like the ultimate in celebratory decadence, could hold a candle to the feeling of Carter's skin against hers.

"Maybe we should talk," he proposed instead.

She pulled back, wondering if this was the moment where he reminded her that his presence in Redford was temporary. If this were one of her romance novels, that's what he would do. He'd use the complication to push her away. But Carter shifted with her instead, settling back into the couch and folding her into his chest.

"Tell me about the book you're editing," he suggested.

So Jess did. She told the whole story and was pleasantly surprised when he asked enough questions that she found herself solving the plot hole that had been tripping her up since last Friday. They talked until the sun dropped, filling her living room with a dusty rose-colored light, then they ordered pizza and argued about *Killing Eve* until it arrived. Over greasy slices of pepperoni and mushroom, they fired up an episode from season two, each attempting to use it to prove their point—Carter's being that Eve was more out of control versus Jess's belief that, as an actual assassin, Villanelle clearly displayed the most worrying behavior.

Eventually, the show sucked both of them in, and they stopped evaluating and simply enjoyed it. When Jess's cheek was pressed against Carter's chest, and the rhythm of his heartbeat was lulling her to sleep, she felt him clear his throat.

"Jessica?" he said over the ominous music playing on the screen. "Is your head feeling better now?"

She stiffened at the tone of his voice. It held no flirtation, no indication he was finally ready to kiss her back. Instead, it warned that she wouldn't like whatever it was he intended to say. For one cowardly moment, Jess considered pretending she still felt woozy. She just needed things to remain this way for a little while longer, his fingers playing with the ends of her hair, his heat surrounding her.

"It's firing on all cylinders," she admitted. Reluctantly, she pulled herself away, sitting upright to face him.

"I have to tell you something." His jaw tightened like it was tempted to stop him.

"I'm listening."

"They're right about me. They're right to be suspicious." Carter frowned and looked away, then returned his eyes to hers, meeting her gaze determinedly. "I don't have a secret deal with Novak, but I think Jasper did."

Jess shook her head, hoping she was misinterpreting his words. "What are you saying?"

"I'm saying I think the game is rigged in my favor." Carter's voice was clear. Unwavering. "I think I'm going to win the prize money."

Chapter 27

··········

CARTER

Carter flinched at the look that crossed Jess's face as his words sunk in. He hadn't wanted to tell her, but it hadn't felt fair not to. She deserved to know. Maybe if she had, she wouldn't have kissed him. Maybe if she'd known, he wouldn't have had to stop kissing her.

"Jasper wouldn't do that," Jess said, shaking her head.

"Wouldn't do what? Incentivize people to play a game? Trick them, even, if that's what it took to ensure his death would result in something fun?"

"He wouldn't rob us of the chance to win." She tossed the words out with a confidence that made no sense. Did she really think he'd be bringing it up if it weren't true?

"He would," Carter said. "If he was certain I'd spend the money the way he wanted, he'd do exactly that. And he wouldn't even feel guilty about it."

"So what? Are you saying he asked you to do something in particular with the money?" She looked curious instead of angry, and Carter began to wonder if her head injury was still affecting her more than she wanted to admit.

"In a way," he said. "It was more of an unspoken agreement."

"Then why didn't Jasper just leave an inheritance for you in his will?" Jess asked the question with a gentleness that didn't fit the moment.

"*Because*—" Carter heard the edge in his voice and cut himself short. It wasn't her fault she wasn't listening. She was exhausted, and she'd hit her head twice today. He'd just say what he needed to say. And tomorrow, if Jess still hadn't properly processed his confession, he'd have to tell her again.

"Because," he repeated more evenly, "people wouldn't have played his game if there wasn't a prize to win. But they don't really have a chance at winning it."

"Because you're going to," she said, every bit as evenly.

"Right."

"Because you know Jasper wants you to do something with his money."

"Right."

"And what does he want you to do with it?"

Carter tensed. He'd been waiting for this, and he suspected it might be the very worst part of the conversation. If it had been up to him, he'd happily tell Jess everything. She'd love that he and Jasper had done nice things for her friends and neighbors. She might even be pleased to discover her scholarship had come from them. Unfortunately, Carter had made a promise to Jasper. He'd made many promises to Jasper on the topic, actually, assuring his grandfather repeatedly that he'd never tell a soul what they'd done. Secrecy was part of the mission. It was what made it so special. Jasper had let him in, and Carter would never allow himself to betray that trust.

"I can't tell you." He could feel himself leaning away, bracing for her hurt or outrage or insistence. "It's Jasper's secret, and I have to keep it."

He told himself he'd said enough, but there was something about the way Jess was looking at him, a softness to her expression that made him think he wasn't getting through to her.

"You're going to lose, Jess." Carter grimaced at the harshness of his words but didn't stop speaking. "I'm not going to drop out of the game, even though I know it's not fair that I keep playing. I'm going to win, and I'm going to get the prize money. And I can't care that I'm cheating everyone else out of it. I have to do what I know Jasper wanted."

Jess nodded, studying him for a moment as if to make sure he was really done speaking this time.

Finally, she lifted one shoulder in an easy shrug. "Okay."

Carter froze. Not once in his entire life had he been so brutally honest. Not once had he opened himself up so completely, refusing to present things in the smoothest light, simply laying them bare. And he'd fully expected it to go badly, but he'd done it anyway because he'd wanted Jess to understand what was happening. He'd needed to warn her. But he'd done it for nothing, because she wasn't even listening to him.

"We should talk about this tomorrow," he said, trying to hide his disappointment. "You're probably still feeling woozy."

"I feel perfectly fine." Jess put a hand on his thigh and leaned forward, looking at him intently. "I understand what you're saying, Carter. You believe you're being set up to win, and you feel guilty about that but not guilty enough to quit."

He couldn't understand why she didn't look angrier. Or, at the very least, disappointed. "So? Don't you want to throw me out?"

"You mean, turn my back on you like your parents did?" Jess got that sympathetic look in her eyes again. "Why would I do that? Maybe you *are* getting set up to win. Or maybe you just need to believe that because you lost your last bit of family and that prize money is all that's left of him. But here's the thing, Carter: I believe I'm going to win the game, too. I believe that I'm going to get that money, and I'm going to use it to save my dad. And if I found out Novak planned to declare me the winner, fair or not, I wouldn't consider quitting for even a moment. I'd celebrate. So I hear your confession, Butch, but you're not going to get any judgment from me for being human."

There had been several ways Carter imagined this conversation going, but not one of them had involved a response like this. If Carter had been standing, he probably would've rocked back on his heels. Since he was sitting, he tilted forward instead. It was as if he'd been thrown off-balance, the world upended.

He told himself he should say something, anything that might convey how her words had affected him. Instead, he kissed her. She was just so beautiful there, wearing her ridiculous T-shirt and those fuzzy socks and looking at him like his mind was a book she was enjoying reading.

He captured her mouth with his, savoring the feel of it, the softness of her lips and the way they melted against his. His hand plunged into her hair, his touch turning gentle when he felt the lump on the back of her head. The scent of apricots filled his nose. She tilted her head to deepen the kiss, and he wrapped his other hand around her waist, pressing her back against the couch. Beneath him, she gave a little moan of pleasure that destroyed any sliver of self-control he'd managed to maintain. The last shred of his restraint snapped, and he picked her up, carrying her into the bedroom.

Chapter 28

....

NIKKI

Sally and Luanne's elimination had freaked her out. That was the only explanation Nikki could come up with for her ill-advised visit to her mom's house at a time of day that fell clearly after happy hour. She'd seen the top contenders lose their shot at the prize money, and she'd realized the same thing could've just as easily happened to her. Anyone would have found it unsettling. And it wasn't as if she'd gone running to her mom's looking for some kind of comfort or reassurance or anything else a cookie-baking sitcom mother might offer. She'd merely wanted . . . Well, she had no idea what it was she'd wanted. Just something to shift the weight off her shoulders for a single moment. The smallest sign that her mother was capable of getting sober on her own, even if Nikki was unable to win Jasper's money and send her to rehab.

"Well, if it isn't Miss Barbie Jeep Racer." Her mom swayed in the doorframe, squinting at Nikki like she hadn't decided yet if she was pleased to see her.

So. She was just drunk then, not wasted. There were

other signs, of course—the slight overpronunciation of her words to prevent slurring and the glassy eyes, rimmed with liner applied a little too heavily—but there was no more accurate measure of her inebriation than her attitude toward Nikki. When Nikki was younger, the pendulum of her mom's moods had swung wider. Exaggeratedly cheerful and loving when sober, a range of playful to indifferent when drunk, raging hostility not exploding until she was truly wasted. Now, it had pared down to two modes: mostly defensive when sober or drunk, enraged when wasted.

Nikki smiled tightly. She wondered if other people had to knock on the door of their childhood home, or if they just let themselves in and called out a cheerful hello without having to worry about what they'd find inside. She bet they didn't find themselves standing outside, stopped at the threshold like a courier trying to serve unwanted papers.

"I heard you made it to the next round in Jasper's game," her mom added, like her ability to hear anything outside of the clinking of ice cubes was something to be proud of.

"You weren't there?" Nikki despised passive aggression—such a weak, sniveling option when actual aggression was so much more straightforward—but the words slipped out, like the mere act of returning to this house reverted her to a powerless child. "I just assumed you were in the crowd somewhere, cheering your only daughter on."

"Karen called and told me. She wants you to buy her a Corvette if you win."

"Does she?" Nikki didn't even like Karen. In fact, she suspected she might actually hate her. Once, when Nikki was nine years old, Karen had left her mom to "sleep it off" in her basement for three days. By the time she finally thought to call her friend's daughter, Nikki had been so certain it was the police that she'd been unable to answer. She hadn't wanted to hear that her mom was dead.

"Are you going to invite me in, Mom?" Nikki made a show of pulling her camel-colored wool coat closed. The temperature had dropped with the sun, and it actually was getting chilly outside, but she wasn't cold; the little ball of rage glowing inside her provided a surprising amount of heat.

"Of course." Her mom stumbled the slightest bit as she flung the door open. Her feet were bare beneath oversized flannel pants, collarbones too sharp above the curved neckband of her sweatshirt. The darkened roots of her hair suggested it hadn't been washed today.

Nikki patted at her own hair, tucking one side neatly behind her ear. She'd washed and blown it out before she'd come over. She'd also put on her softest sweater, the one that clung to her figure, and paired it with buttery leather pants. It was a defensive move, designed to prevent her mom from taking shots at her appearance, but it had the bonus effect of making Nikki feel the tiniest bit in control. She took a small step forward.

"You can't stay long, though. I have plans soon." Her mom's eyes drifted toward the half-empty glass on the coffee table.

She meant she'd need a refill. They both knew it, but Nikki supposed she could choose to take some comfort in her mom's attempt at subtlety. The effort implied her mom remembered her promises to quit drinking, even if she hadn't yet gotten to the place where she could follow through on them.

"You probably want to shower, then." Nikki said the words gently, offering them as an excuse, a way for both of them to avoid twenty minutes of awkward conversation in which she was wishing her mom was someone else while her mom was undoubtedly wishing Nikki was anywhere else.

"What, I'm not presentable enough for you?" Her mom grabbed the glass and chugged it defiantly. "I don't fit into the perfect little pictures you put on your Instagram page?"

"Trust me," Nikki said, taking a cowardly step back without meaning to, "I didn't come over here looking for content."

"Why did you come over here?" Her mom shook her now-empty glass at her. "To catch me? Well, there you go. You did it. I hope you're happy."

Oh, definitely. Nikki was *so* happy. What could be more delightful than this?

"I didn't come over to catch you," she said. "I just wanted to . . ." Nikki trailed off, still not able to determine what she'd been hoping for. Whatever it was, it seemed clear she wasn't going to get it. "I just wanted to tell you that I'm still in the game," she said finally. "But Karen already told you, so I guess that's it. I don't want to make you late for your plans."

She didn't put any emphasis on the word *plans*, but it somehow came out sounding like she had. Her mother must have heard it, too, because she didn't try to convince Nikki to stay, instead following her to the door in a way that didn't necessarily imply she was kicking her out but very clearly conveyed that she expected Nikki to leave. It was almost worse than an explosive argument or being given the boot. She was just left feeling so terribly . . . unwanted.

The ball of heat in her belly turned to ash, and Nikki shivered as she stepped back into the night. She tried to summon the anger back, reminding herself of all the empty promises her mom had made about getting sober, but she couldn't reignite it. Had her mom ever had any intention of following through, or had she just wanted to shut Nikki up, willing to say anything if it would make her daughter leave her alone?

"Good luck with the game," her mom said, offering an olive branch. Or maybe she just wanted to ensure her daughter would think of her if she suddenly found herself the winner of a ten-million-dollar prize. It didn't really matter.

Nikki tried to return the gesture, but she didn't know what to say. *Good luck with your drinking*?

"Enjoy your plans," she said finally. This time, she managed to keep the emphasis off the word *plans*, and her mother softened.

"It's just one night, Nikki," she said quietly before easing the door closed. "Tomorrow is always a new day. I'm still trying. I really am."

So Nikki nodded and left, also trying—trying to believe her mom meant what she said, even though Nikki swore she could hear the soft glug of a bottle being poured into the empty glass as she headed to the street. She strode purposefully down the sidewalk, despite having no idea where she was going, letting the porch lights lead her. The town hadn't had enough money to extend Main Street's lampposts to the residential streets, so everyone did their part, leaving their outdoor lighting on throughout the night. The road was still dim, but Nikki could see well enough, considering she wasn't trying to get anywhere in particular.

All she knew was that she couldn't go home. She didn't have a roommate, and she didn't want to be alone. She couldn't call Cara, either, because Cara and Lexi were at the Staple, and Nikki didn't trust Lexi as long as Lexi was her competition—or, more important, as long as Lexi considered Nikki her competition.

A Honda Accord drove by, offering a cordial little honk in greeting as it passed, but Nikki couldn't make out the face behind the wheel. She wondered if it was a sign. Kent drove an Accord. He'd offered to take her out tonight to celebrate, too. She'd told herself she'd said no because it was important to play hard to get, but the truth was she hadn't wanted to see him when she was feeling unsettled. She could barely face him when she was settled. He was too in control of himself. Too successful. He made her feel like a mess in comparison.

In fact, the only flaw Nikki had been able to find in him was how much he seemed to like her. It was unnerving. If her mother had taught her anything, it was that Nikki was guaranteed to disappoint. So Nikki was careful to keep her distance. She saw Kent when she was at her best. When she was at her worst, she spent her time with other men, the kind who were only good for a meaningless fling. Sometimes it was better to not get what you wanted than to be found wanting.

She could only imagine what Kent might think if he

could see her now. He'd probably hide his disgust under a layer of pity. He'd feel bad that she was all alone, because he was much too nice to point out that it was her fault for being so mean to everyone. And he was *way* too nice to suggest that it might have been Nikki's fault that her mom started drinking so heavily in the first place. She'd done everything she could, but it had never been enough. She wasn't as good as liquor. It was stronger than her—it had more of a bite.

Unbidden tears came to her eyes, and she blinked them back. She would not wander the streets with black streaks down her face. She would go home and get her car. Drive somewhere else. Maybe she'd go all the way to Atlanta, have a drink with a handsome stranger, then be back in time for tomorrow's challenge.

She didn't turn around, though. Her feet led her forward, like they'd shifted to autopilot, and she continued to blink back tears. It wasn't until the door appeared in front of her that she realized where she'd ended up. She knocked without deciding to, feeling just as shocked as Ross Reid appeared when he opened the door.

He looked different, now that she knew he was sick. Not diminished in any way, certainly not less attractive or manly. Just different. More real, somehow. Like he wasn't just Jess's dad or the sexy mechanic who thought he was too old for Nikki but an actual, complex person, one who had chosen not to allow his own difficulties to prevent him from showing kindness to others.

"I can't help her." Nikki exhaled the words wetly, like she'd been holding them in the entire walk here without realizing it. "I can win the money, I know I can, but I still can't help her. I can help you, though."

Ross's face softened in an expression so sympathetic it made Nikki run her words back through her brain, checking to make sure she hadn't switched them around. That she hadn't shown up on this man's doorstep asking *him* to help *her*. The words jumbled as she replayed them, though, leaving her embarrassed and confused.

"You're late," Ross said, swinging the door open to the warm glow of his home. "I started episode four of *Love Island* without you."

Before Nikki could argue—that she wasn't late, that they hadn't had plans, that continuing a series without waiting for the person you'd started it with was the most serious act of betrayal of her generation—he was walking down the hallway, leaving her to make herself at home.

So she did.

Chapter 29

· · · · · · · · · · ·

CARTER

You got in late last night," Mrs. Loveling said, a twinkle in her eye as she caught Carter coming down the stairs in search of coffee. "Or should I say early this morning?"

Carter shot the woman a cool look intended to remind her that his personal life was none of her business. He could tell the message hadn't landed, though, when she merely laughed knowingly in response.

"You missed all the new arrivals," Mrs. Loveling added, clearly aware enough to realize her subtle prod for details wasn't going to be answered. "Don't worry, though. I've saved you a seat at breakfast."

"You rented out one of the other rooms?" Obviously, Carter had known another guest might show up at some point, but he'd had his run of the place for so long he couldn't help thinking of any newcomer as an intruder. He hoped they planned to sleep in. Carter liked his solitary morning runs by the lake. Although, he supposed, the fact that Mrs. Loveling could now coax other people into happy hours and late-night desserts meant he wouldn't have to sneak out at night anymore.

"I rented out *all* of the rooms." Mrs. Loveling's pleasure in this fact was palpable. "Apparently, someone's camera footage of that ridiculous Barbie race went viral, and now reporters have shown up to film whatever fresh nonsense Jasper has in store for you kids today."

"Perfect," Carter said with a sigh. If Carter's boss caught sight of that video, he'd be horrified. How were potential clients supposed to trust millions of dollars to a man-child in a Barbie Jeep?

"Now, go grab yourself a big helping of homemade biscuits and gravy before those reporters snatch them all up," Mrs. Loveling said cheerfully. "They're friendly as can be, but they emptied out my cookie basket like vultures."

"We're out of coffee in here, Mrs. L.," a man said, popping out of the dining room and tilting an empty cup at Mrs. Loveling. When he spotted Carter, he offered a too-wide smile and joined them.

"Hey there," he said, proffering a hand. "Baxter Butler, *Steerburn Weekly*."

"Carter Barclay," Carter said, taking the man's cup instead of his hand. "Brewer of coffee."

He started toward the kitchen as if it were his own, Mrs. Loveling following happily behind him.

⋯⋯⋯

THE BRIGHT SUNSHINE and crisp breeze blowing off the lake gave the air of Redford an energetic buzz, but it wasn't just the weather making the town feel different. The sidewalks were teeming with people, and signs had been placed outside of the businesses, welcoming people inside. A few Halloween decorations had gone up overnight.

"And what's that?" The journalist with the dark hair and nose ring pointed at Evangeline's.

"A napkin shop." Carter experienced a niggling of guilt at robbing the reporter of the tour Jess had given him of the town, opting for fibs instead of insights and charming details. In his defense, however, Jess had offered him a tour, while he'd done no such thing. The reporters had followed him from the Lakehouse, entirely uninvited, crowding the sidewalk around him and pointing at various places and people with loud questions, like they were visiting a movie set instead of a real place where real people lived.

He didn't like them.

There were four of them in total—two men, two women, each with different attitudes and styles and personalities. Carter found all of them off-putting. It was the look in their eyes that made him uneasy. That shared sharpness as they peered around the town, like they were attempting to ferret out secrets, and the way their eyebrows rose every time he answered a question. He felt like he could actually see their brains breaking down his words, restructuring them to shift his meaning into something better suited to a story.

"A napkin shop?" The woman wrinkled her nose, and the diamond stud flashed in the sunlight.

"Yes," Carter said flatly. "They don't just sell paper or cloth napkins. They also have an entire wall of napkins made from repurposed plastic bottles."

"That sounds—" She wrinkled her nose again.

"Eco-friendly?" Carter spoke over her, pretending he didn't hear her say *painful*. "It is. The people of Redford have great passion for the environment."

"Do they," said the man who appeared to be in his late twenties (but was inexplicably wearing a newsboy cap, like he didn't write the news but rode a bike around suburban neighborhoods, throwing it at doorsteps). He tilted his head in exaggerated thought.

"They do," Carter answered sharply, despite the fact that the way he'd said it hadn't sounded much like a question. He crossed the street toward the throng of people in the square, and one of the reporters stepped on his heel in their effort to keep up. His poor shoes. The water marks from the boat excursion had been covered with mud from the hike, so the exterior was beyond ruined. But did the soles really deserve to be sacrificed to some vulture in a stupid hat?

"Then let's just hope today's challenge won't involve tearing up the side of a mountain with SUV wheels," Baxter Butler of *Steerburn Weekly* said.

Carter heard the insinuation in his words and responded with the dismissive side eye it deserved. "You mean tiny doll wheels?"

"Sure." Baxter smiled in a way that made Carter want to shove him into his trunk and leave him just outside of the "Welcome to Redford" sign. "That's what I meant."

If Carter had gotten to spend the entire night in Jess's bed last night, he might've had more patience for this situation. If he hadn't had to tear himself away from her at four a.m. to get a couple of hours of work in, maybe he would've been more inclined to guide the reporters' attention to positive things instead of defensively batting them back.

As it was, his head felt all over the place. So did his feelings. One moment, he'd be thinking of Jess and he couldn't stop grinning. The next, a reporter would open their mouth and he'd become aggressively defensive. Where had this protectiveness over Redford come from? Only a week ago, he'd been a detached spectator, and now he was morphing into some kind of snarling guard dog for the town. The change felt embarrassingly undignified.

"You can't forget that all of this is just a game the people of Redford were invited to play," Carter said, attempting to recalibrate. "They didn't get to choose the challenges."

"It was Mr. Wilhelm who did that," the man in the newsboy cap said.

"Right," Carter said.

"He must have been quite the character." The blonde with long bangs and freckled cheeks smiled encouragingly. "Making a game out of giving away his money. It's such a fun idea."

"Especially fun for the person who wins it," Newsboy said.

Oscar was on his stool in front of the square again, and he called out, "Beautiful day, isn't it?" as they approached.

"Couldn't get any better, Oscar," Carter said without thinking.

He'd resisted the expected answer again yesterday, opting instead to point out that it was dark and gray outside, but now he was distracted by the sight of Jess. She was with the other competitors up by Novak, her red hair shimmering in the sunlight like a lick of fire.

"No," Oscar said happily, "it certainly could not."

Carter barely heard him. There had to be a hundred people between him and Jess, but she turned as if she could feel his eyes on her, a brilliant smile stretching across her face when her eyes found his. He felt himself beaming in response and couldn't be bothered to tamp the smile down. His skin buzzed like it was already anticipating the moment it would make contact with hers again, like they were alone instead of surrounded by people who had come to see a show.

For a moment this morning, after he'd finally gotten back to his room, Carter had almost convinced himself that nothing had changed. Sure, he'd slept with Jess. But he'd slept with plenty of women without getting emotionally attached. He was leaving. Long-distance relationships never worked, but maybe they could remain friends. He suspected Jess could easily become the best friend he'd never had.

Then he'd realized he was fooling himself. For the first time in his life, Carter had stumbled. It was entirely his fault for walking so close to the edge, but here he was, his footing well and truly lost. Jasper would've absolutely loved it. How many times had Carter insisted they think more strategically, not giving out money just because it might feel good but because it would be best utilized? Where had that pragmatism been when he was opening himself up to a woman who lived in a different town than him, one that was full of people who hated him?

Carter cut through the crowd like a man in a trance, not

breaking eye contact with Jess until she was right there in front of him, a vision in— *How many colors are in those checkered pants? Six? Eight? Hadn't the designer ever heard of the concept "less is more"?*

"Hi," she said in a husky voice, and Carter came to the immediate and resolute conclusion that he'd been foolish to ever buy into the idea less could be enough; more was clearly so much better.

"Good morning, Jessica. How is your head today?" He searched her eyes for any signs of the blurriness they'd held after the race, but it hadn't returned. She didn't even look tired. If he hadn't spent most of the night in her bed, he would've assumed she'd gotten a full night's sleep.

"It's good, thank you," Jess said with exaggerated formality, then laughed and reached for his hand, sliding her fingers through his with such easy familiarity Carter couldn't resist lifting her hand to his mouth and pressing a kiss against it.

"Um, what's this?" Nikki slapped at their joined hands.

"Team bonding," he said in answer.

He should've been mortified. Public displays of affection had always seemed insincere to him, like the way his dad would reach for his mother in front of their friends, despite never touching her behind closed doors. Surprisingly, though, Carter discovered he didn't feel even a flicker of embarrassment. He just felt lucky, like he'd been unexpectedly called up to the sixteenth floor and informed that he was being promoted.

"You're not on the same team," Nikki said, poking her

nail in between their palms since the slapping hadn't separated them.

"Hence the need to bond," Carter said without loosening his grip. "If we were on the same team, the bond would already be set."

"*We're* not bonded," Nikki said, side-eyeing Jess.

"Of course we are," Jess said cheerfully. "I think of you as a sister now."

Jess's eyes widened when her words hit the air, and she covered her mouth like she could sweep them back inside. She took a step back and wrinkled her nose.

"What?" Nikki snapped. "Why are you looking at me like I'm pointing a gun at you?"

"I'm bracing myself for some disgusting comment about incest."

Nikki looked baffled for a moment, and then she laughed. "Are you talking about your dad? Please. There's no way I'm going to be your stepmother now. Not when you look like you're about to get pregnant just standing next to City Boy. Becoming a grandmother this young would be terrible for my brand."

"You're going to be a grandmother?" Bryce asked, inserting himself into the conversation. He rocked back on his heels, his hands pressing into his pockets, when Nikki whirled on him in warning.

"If that rumor starts going around," she said evenly, "I will *burn down your bar*. Do you understand me?"

"Not a lot of room for misinterpretation," Bryce said.

"With all due respect to the grandmother," Bobby said

loudly, "could you all please shut the hell up? Some of us want to find out what today's challenge is."

Nikki hissed at him, and Bobby attempted to cover up his flinch by pretending a bee landed on his shoulder. The crowd hushed as Novak announced that they were about to begin their last challenge. True to form, the lawyer used the most words possible. When he finally stopped talking, not a single person cheered—not even, as was typically the case, to signify their enthusiasm that he'd finished speaking. Carter didn't know if they were too disappointed at learning the game would soon be over or, like him, merely too confused.

Their final challenge would be rebuilding Redford's community center.

"I don't get it," Bryce said, putting voice to the thing they were all thinking. "How do you compete at rebuilding an old barn?"

"Screw competing," Nikki said. "How do you *win* at rebuilding an old barn?"

You couldn't.

Realization dawned, and Carter's stomach sank. Finally, Jess would have to believe he'd been telling her the truth about Jasper's plans. It was so obvious. If the final challenge had been a straightforward race, there would be no way to guarantee his victory. But this? There was no set point value to putting up a roof or painting the walls of some old barn the town used to hold community events in. The scoring would be entirely up to Novak's discretion.

It was Jasper's final encouragement from the grave.

This was how Jasper had ensured his fortune would wind up in Carter's hands.

Carter turned anxiously to Jess, but she was looking at Nikki, earnestly considering Nikki's question as if Carter hadn't already given her the answer. *There was no way for them to win. They were going to lose to him.*

"How do we not win," Jess said, "if we end up with a new barn?"

Nikki's eyes narrowed as she absorbed Jess's words. Almost immediately, her head began to shake back and forth. "Nope. We're not doing that. We're not getting all *Ted Lasso* right now. Not with ten million dollars on the line."

"Five," Jess reminded her. A smile so confident stretched across her face that Carter felt his first real flicker of doubt. "You're only going to win five million dollars. The other five are going to me."

Chapter 30

··········

JESS

Entering the old barn had felt like stepping directly into a time capsule. The last time Jess had been inside, it had been to play bingo. Tables had been lined up in rows, overflowing with players, and the air had been full of the sweet, buttery smells of the baked goods people were passing around. Sally had stood on a little wooden stage in front, calling out numbers from a punch bowl full of folded slips of paper in front of her. And Luanne had screeched with disapproval every time one wasn't on her card, like Sally was rigging the game against her. It should've gotten old after a while, but it hadn't. The other players had erupted into laughter every single time.

Jess had attended other events here—parties and weddings and dances—but the bingo game was the one she remembered best. Only a few weeks later, the storm hit and a tree had crashed into the roof. The town had planned to fix it, but there was always a more pressing use for the funds. By the time they'd realized the hole in the roof and the water it had let in caused the structure to decay rapidly, the damage had been done. Instead of a simple patch-up job, the building would require major reconstruction. The town budget simply couldn't accommodate something like that.

Now, thanks to Jasper, the reconstruction would finally begin. Unfortunately, it would be done by a group of people who were realizing they were distressingly unqualified to attempt such a task.

"I can paint walls," Jess said, knowing this would only be helpful if even one person had claimed to actually know how to erect walls.

They were going around the circle, each contender sharing their experience with construction, so they'd understand who would be taking care of what. It had sounded like a good idea until they'd begun to realize that none of them had any experience to speak of. They were, it seemed, not a group accustomed to working with their hands. Bobby was the notable exception, but he'd responded defensively to DeMarco's suggestion that his skills as a mechanic might translate into some use.

"Are you kidding me?" Nikki's hands went to her hips as her eyes swung around the circle. "Ten people, and not one of you knows anything about construction?"

A few mouths twitched, but nobody dared point out Nikki's offering of "flawless décor" would be useless if she couldn't come up with a way to fix the hole in the roof. Jess studied the place anew, trying to figure out if there was anything else she could claim to be good for. If they could come up with a saw, she could help cut away the branches that were still dangling through the hole. The rest was a disaster she didn't know what to do about, though.

The floor where Jess had learned to square dance was discolored from water damage. The walls were beyond weakened, some of the boards so bowed beneath the weight of the tree's trunk that beams of light shone through, slicing the room with sunlight. It smelled damp and earthy inside, which meant mold would most likely have to be dealt with. Maybe she could figure out how to take care of that.

"There aren't just ten of us, though, if you think about it." Lexi waved a hand at the onlookers who had followed them from the town square, grouping together along the two walls that looked the least compromised. The crowd had diminished by more than half once everyone realized the only humiliation the contenders would experience would be the result of their own incompetence, but there were still plenty of people who'd chosen the opportunity to heckle over returning to the drudgery of a normal workday.

"Bo has been doing construction for years," Lexi continued, wiggling freshly manicured fingernails at him coquettishly.

Bo's eyebrows went up at the flirtation, and he looked to Annabelle as if to prove he only had eyes for her. It appeared to be an unnecessary effort. Whatever issue had been causing Annabelle's jealousy before seemed to be entirely behind them. She wore the smug grin of someone whose almost-fiancé had given up the chance at millions just to be with her.

Jess stifled a laugh. She knew Nikki in no way deserved credit, and requiring great sacrifice as proof of devotion didn't strike Jess as the healthiest for a relationship, but she couldn't argue that it seemed to have worked out.

"*Bo* would be happy to help," Bo called out once he realized he was in no danger from Annabelle. He crossed his arms over his well-defined chest. "If Bo could be guaranteed a small percentage of the prize money."

"Really?" Jess gasped, perking up. She couldn't imagine that any of them would have a problem with sharing a portion of their hypothetical winnings, not if it meant getting professional help, and especially not if it meant they'd all end up with a functional facility at which to hold town events again.

"Sure." Bo shrugged. "If I got a big enough team together, we could get this place back into shape in a matter of days. It's not a total rebuild, you know. It just needs a little reinforcement and a lot of cosmetic work."

"That doesn't sound so hard," Bobby said. "I don't see why we should start giving away our prize money when we could just do it ourselves."

"Oh, *now* you can do it yourself?" Nikki scoffed.

"We'd be willing to guarantee some of the prize money in exchange for help," DeMarco interjected, having just exchanged silent nods with his partner. "But it would have to be a flat fee, negotiated up front. A 'percentage' sounds excessive."

"Any amount will be some percentage," Carter said, and Jess found herself smiling at this unhelpful assertion. "And it feels only fair that participation in the win earns him a percentage of the prize."

"This is just one of multiple challenges, though," DeMarco said. "We're the only ones who have done them all."

"Well, you didn't really *do* them all, did you?" Lexi smiled sharply. "I seem to remember one where you choked."

"Are you kidding me?" DeMarco's expression turned incredulous. "Someone tampered with my pie and triggered my peanut allergy. I didn't choke, Lexi. I literally stopped breathing."

"All I know is that it was an eating competition," Lexi said, "and it ended with everyone but you still eating."

"Paying for outside assistance is prohibited," Novak said into the megaphone. It wasn't turned on, but his words managed to break through DeMarco and Lexi's argument anyway. Still, Novak took a moment to turn it on and click his tongue into the mouthpiece before continuing. "According to the rules of the challenge, outside help may only be accepted if it's offered freely."

"Would you be willing to round up some of your buddies and help us for free, Bo?" Lexi asked, losing interest in DeMarco almost as quickly as she had after they'd broken up.

"As fun as that sounds," Bo said, "watching you try to patch this place up with duct tape and paint sounds like a much more entertaining use of my time."

"Raze it to the ground," a man Jess had never seen before shouted. At least, Jess thought he was a man. The newsboy cap he was wearing was too big for his head, giving him the appearance of an overgrown child.

"The reporters seem to be getting restless." Carter leaned over to whisper the words in her ear, and she caught a whiff of his cologne. Images from last night flashed through her mind, his hands exploring her body and his mouth on hers. She'd known he'd be confident in bed—Carter was always confident. And he was the kind of man who would be good at anything he put his mind to, so his skill hadn't come as a surprise. But she hadn't expected him to be so wild.

Beneath his perfectly buttoned shirts, Carter had become an insatiable beast who had ravaged her until she was left whimpering with satisfaction. Jess's cheeks burned at the memory, and her mouth curled up in a smile. She liked that he camouflaged himself behind a layer of crisp professionalism. Everyone else saw Bruce Wayne, and only she got to know that he had the Batmobile hidden downstairs.

"I don't think hanging out in an old building is the clickbait they showed up for," he continued, and Jess blinked, trying to focus.

"There are reporters here?" Jess knew, of course, that yesterday's race had gone viral—she'd woken to countless texts linking to the picture of her victorious leap at the finish line, her mud-covered rainbow tutu flying wildly over her leggings and the overturned Barbie Jeep at her feet—but she hadn't realized the interest would lead people to Redford.

"At least four," he said. "They're all staying at the Lakehouse."

"Good," she said, brightening. "If they get bored with us, maybe they'll go in search of a slice of cake or grab lunch at the diner. Or maybe one of them will decide it's the perfect time to change their hairstyle. Any of our businesses getting mentioned in an article would be great publicity for them and for the town."

Carter grimaced in a way that looked a lot like guilt.

"What?" she said.

"Nothing." He grimaced again. "It's just that I might

have inadvertently given them a little tour this morning. And I also might have been so focused on getting them to leave that it didn't occur to me to share all the great reasons to stay."

"Carter." Jess exhaled his name, adding a little *tsk* on the end. In a small town, you didn't have to like one another—you didn't even have to get along—but you always looked out for one another.

"Right." The corner of his mouth flickered up like her kindergarten teacher voice had amused him. "What if I stop by the bakery later and order a bunch of cookies to leave out at the Lakehouse? Do you think that might get Luanne some free advertising?"

"If you include several of the white chocolate and toffee, I don't see how it couldn't." Jess beamed.

She knew his mention of the great reasons to stay in Redford hadn't necessarily meant anything, but the idea sent little bubbles of delight rushing through her anyway. If Liz were here, she could've been counted on to point out that Jess was letting her sense of romance get away from her, but Liz, of course, wasn't here. So Jess let her imagination go wild, allowing herself to picture leisurely mornings with Carter, the two of them chatting over coffee, and passionate nights with all of his buttons undone. It was an embarrassingly fanciful response to what amounted to little more than a one-night stand, but she didn't care. If someone presented you with a fat, juicy burger, you wouldn't refuse to eat it just because once you'd finished it would be gone forever, would you? She certainly wouldn't.

She'd dive right in and savor every delicious bite.

....

JESS LIFTED HER arms over her head, looking around the old barn as she stretched out the aching muscles in her back. It defied reason that they'd done so much work yet accomplished so little. Or maybe the actual defying of reason had occurred when they'd chosen to believe emptying the place out and cleaning it up would change the fact that the structure itself was crumbling. She doubted any construction crew worth its salt had ever prioritized tidiness over structural stability.

"I'm starving." Bryce had been unflaggingly cheerful during the many hours of work they'd put in, but now his voice carried an unmistakable whine.

It wasn't unwarranted. Jess checked her phone to discover it was almost five. Her dad had stopped by during his lunch break, bringing sandwiches for her and Nikki, but several of the contenders hadn't eaten since this morning. They'd attempted to order food but had been told by both the diner and the pizza place that business was too busy for deliveries. And maybe it was; boredom had long since caused the spectators to abandon the barn, and they had to have gone somewhere. But the resulting argument among the teams over whether it was true or whether they were being punished for the wealth one of them would soon have had raged on for long enough that Novak had looked up from the card table he'd set up in the corner.

Everyone had stilled when he began to poke deliberately at the screen like he was taking detailed notes of their childish behavior. Then, they'd sprung back to work almost in unison, and a group meal had never been procured. Instead, those of them with loved ones generous enough to bring food had been forced to eat guiltily in front of those who were less fortunate.

"Don't act like I didn't offer you half of my sandwich," Nikki said, waving a broom at Bryce. Clumps of dirt fell from it, and a spiderweb trailed out, glittering in the fading light.

"Ross brought that for you," he said sulkily.

"That didn't stop Carter from eating half of Jess's."

"I doubt Jess tried to make him agree to a future favor—Wait, what was your exact wording? A favor to be paid back however and whenever you wanted, regardless of any moral objections I might have?"

Nikki rolled her eyes. "Jess didn't have to make him agree to that because they both already knew he was going to pay her back with sexual favors."

Jess froze in her stretch, her eyes shifting toward Novak, who, thankfully, had gone back to dozing upright in his chair. Then she realized the arc of her back was pressing her breasts into the air like she really was some kind of seductress. Quickly, she lowered her arms to cross her chest, but the barn had already filled with laughter. The contestants all seemed to have reached a point where the fruitlessness of their efforts had become a source of giddy hilarity rather than dejection. When Melvin pointed out Bobby's attempt to staple torn tarp over the cracks in the wall like it was as simple as patching a pair of jeans, several people had laughed so hard their cheeks had sparkled with tears.

"It was turkey with cranberry spread," Carter said,

pausing in his effort to patch a hole in the floor long enough to shoot Nikki a withering look. "You think she'd trade that away for something as easy to get as sex? I had to offer her something much more valuable than that."

Nikki's eyes lit up with intrigue. "What?"

"Your Instagram password." Carter flashed her a wicked smile before returning to his task. "She couldn't post those pictures of you shoveling feces out of the corner without it."

"That wasn't feces," Nikki said, her face twisting with horror. "It was mud!"

"Was it?" Jess stifled a laugh as she watched Nikki whip her phone out and jab at it frantically. "My mistake. It seems pointless to change my caption now, though. It's already gotten two thousand likes."

The barn filled with laughter again as Nikki searched her page with wide eyes. When she realized they'd been bluffing and began lecturing them on the importance of image to her career, their roaring only got louder.

"I'll bring my ring light tomorrow," Lexi said, feigning helpfulness.

"Seriously, though," Jess said when the hysterics ebbed, "we are actually going to need lamps or some source of light if we want to get this done anytime soon. Otherwise, we'll only be able to work during the day."

The mood visibly dipped at the reminder, like she'd opened a door to reality, allowing a gust of cold wind to sweep inside. They'd done everything they could today, but they all knew it wasn't even close to enough. The necessary renovations could take weeks for people with their lack of experience—months, even—and none of them had time for that. They'd been away from their responsibilities for long enough as it was. It was ridiculous to imagine they could not only learn to construct a building but accomplish it in any reasonable amount of time.

"I have extension cords," Edwin said with a self-conscious shrug. "Connected, I have enough that they'd stretch a couple hundred feet."

"Um," Charity said, "why?"

Edwin's face flushed a lovely shade of pink, despite the fact that her question sounded more curious than mean. "I'm kind of into electronics."

"What does that even mean?" Lexi asked. "Like, do you have a bunch of toasters?"

"At times," Edwin admitted. "I use the parts to make other things."

"If you tell me you make robots," Bobby said to his teammate, "I'm really going to regret all those times I shoved you in a locker back in high school."

Edwin smiled in a way that said, *Feel the regret, my intellectual inferior,* and Bobby's eyes widened, indicating he was smart enough to, at least, interpret that.

"So, Edwin will bring the extension cords," Jess said. "Who's got a spare lamp?"

A few people volunteered lights, and others offered to bring tools, though no one knew how, exactly, they'd be used. The group broke for the day with the pride of people who were confident they'd done all they could, rather than worrying over the fact that they'd be expected to do more than they were capable of tomorrow. Novak lifted his head long enough to remind them that he'd be back at eight in the morning, and anything done before then would not count toward his scoring, whatever that might consist of.

"We should all watch home improvement YouTube videos," Jess called out as they abandoned the sad old barn. She should probably do so at her dad's, since her headache had caused her to miss checking in on him last night.

She wondered if Carter would think it was weird if she invited him to hang out with her and her dad. Obviously, it *was*. You couldn't spend a night of passion with someone and then invite them to get to know your father better, not without giving the appearance that you're dreaming of said father dragging them down the aisle. Still, she thought she might do it anyway.

"I was going to head to the diner for dinner," Carter said before she could ask. "Care to join me?"

Jess grinned. She could text her dad to make sure he was all right and swing by his house afterward. "Are you trying to make up for eating half my lunch?"

"No," Carter said matter-of-factly. "I'm trying to ask you on a date."

"Oh." She felt her grin widen. "A date, huh? That sounds weirdly formal for something that can never be more than a fling."

"You think we'll only be a fling?" Carter looked at her curiously.

"Well, I figured, you know, you'll be leaving soon," Jess said.

Carter flashed a rare full smile, and it was so gorgeous it made her chest ache.

"Did you not see how little progress we made on the barn today?" he asked, cocking an eyebrow. "If I can't leave until we finish that, you and I have all the time in the world."

Chapter 31

·············

CARTER

think Jet Skis sound fun," Jess was saying to a married couple whose clothes seemed to have been color-coordinated like fraternal twins dressed up by their mom. These two were just the latest in a long line of people who had stopped by his and Jess's booth over the course of their dinner. "And if Joe is worried they'll keep him up, just tell him you won't use them while he's sleeping. It's not like you're going to hit the lake at six a.m. or ride them late at night. He can text you if he lays down for a nap."

Carter had to tamp down his smile at the way Jess dove as passionately into this conversation as she had the one about Mrs. Yang's cat and that surly man's rant about his malfunctioning Wi-Fi router. It was no wonder the two of them had only been able to get a few bites into the slice of carrot cake they were sharing. He would've imagined constant interruptions to their meal would be annoying, but he'd been pleasantly surprised to discover it was entertaining. Nobody stayed too long, and Jess had a way of folding him into the conversations that felt inclusive, rather than making him feel like he'd been put on the spot.

"What do you think, Carter?" Jess said, doing it once again. "Should they get matching Jet Skis or do you think they'll be too loud?"

Carter thought Jet Skis were the mechanical equivalent of a buzzing swarm of mosquitos.

"Have you tried paddleboarding?" he said instead. "They're fun to use and don't make any noise at all."

"But why paddle when you could ride?" Jess's smile arched challengingly. It had become something of an unspoken game for them to approach the conversations from different sides. "Why go slow when you could go fast?"

"They're looking for something to do together," Carter said. "Have you ever been on a Jet Ski? Once you're on it, the noise drowns out the rest of the world. But if they're on paddleboards, they can still chat and enjoy the view. It might not provide the same adrenaline rush as a Jet Ski, but it would still be fun."

Plus, he restrained himself from saying, their neighbors wouldn't be tempted to murder them.

"I like that," the woman said decisively. "And paddleboards are so cute. Maybe we could get the same pattern on them, but in two different colors. Or the same colors on both but inverted!"

"But, remember how cute you thought the Jet Skis were." Her husband sent Carter a pleading look, either because his power toy was quickly turning into a waterlogged balance beam or because he'd just realized he was going to be having conversations on the water instead of flying across it. "Don't you think those would look better by the dock than a couple of paddleboards, Carter?"

"Oh, aesthetically speaking?" Carter said, choosing to take pity on the man. "Paddleboards are the worst. Their color fades quickly, and they're left looking like discarded trash cluttering up your yard."

"Oh no." The woman shuddered at the thought. "I guess we're going to have to get Jet Skis after all."

The husband nodded silently but gave Carter a grateful slap on the back. And when the conversation wrapped up and the wife gave the cursory promise to have both of them over to dinner soon, the husband held out his hand, adding that he'd expect Carter to hit the water with him once they got those Jet Skis.

Carter shook on it.

Jess turned to Carter once they were gone, her eyes shining with unconcealed amusement. "Look at you, making friends."

"I hate Jet Skis," he said dispassionately.

"Well, get your water spurs on, cowboy, because you're about to be riding one." She scooped up a heaping bite of carrot cake with her fork and shoved it into her mouth with a satisfied smile.

Carter allowed himself to imagine it for a moment, picturing endless meals in this very diner, hoping this booth, *their booth*, would be empty whenever they arrived. They'd hike on Saturday mornings, cooling off in the lake afterward. Then they'd go home and barely make it through the door before he'd grab her in his arms, too riled up from seeing her splash around in a bathing suit to care that their muscles were already aching from the climb up the mountain.

Carter had never had a partner in life, but it was far too easy for him to picture Jess in that role. The thought of nights together made him grin. He'd read whatever book she was working on, offering one helpful suggestion for every ten she'd already considered, while she danced around in mismatched socks, making it impossible to concentrate. She'd said she didn't enjoy cooking, so he'd take care of that and leave her to cajole dessert out of Luanne.

"We should finish this," Jess said, plunging her fork back into the cake, "before someone else interrupts us."

He did as she said and carved off a bite of his own, suspecting she was right. The diner had been full since they arrived, but they'd been there long enough that tables had turned over, wiped off and quickly reseated. A whole new set of people to chat with had come in, although Jess had pointed out the strangers she hadn't seen before, clearly pleased at the idea that Jasper's game was bringing in tourists.

For the first time, it occurred to Carter that maybe this was Jasper's intention all along. Carter had been so quick to assume his grandfather was just trying to provide a bit of fun because Jasper had loved a good time. But Jasper had also loved Redford. Maybe he'd realized a spectacle was bound to bring attention to the town. Maybe he'd also known it would bring visitors, people who could fall in love with this place and return again and again, putting money into the hands of the local business owners.

It was brilliant, Carter realized, taking another bite of

cake. The taste of thick cream-cheese icing hit his taste buds, and he almost groaned with satisfaction. As unfortunate as it was that Luanne had been eliminated from the game, he was confident she'd be fine. Anyone who could make cakes like this would always have people lining up to buy them. He was so caught up in the perfection of the moment that he didn't hear the sharp clicking of heels until the sound stopped at the edge of their table. Before he could react, Lexi had slid into the booth next to him, filling his nose with floral perfume.

"I want in." She made this statement with a matter-of-factness that didn't match its opacity.

"Okay, but you'll have to get your own fork." Jess shrugged, taking the strangeness of the situation so in stride that Carter almost laughed.

"Don't mess with me," Lexi hissed. "Either you let me in on the plan, or I will take you down."

"Ooh," Jess said with delight. She looked to Carter. "The second option sounds fun. Can we choose that?"

"I don't see how we could resist," he said, not wanting to spoil her fun. But he did wonder if Jess had forgotten how ruthlessly Lexi had gone after her laptop, not caring if it had hours' or even weeks' worth of unsaved work on it. It didn't seem wise to provoke someone like her.

"We choose option B," he said in spite of his misgivings. If Jess wanted to taunt the tiger, that's exactly what they would do. "Please commence with the taking us down."

Lexi's eyes narrowed, flicking back and forth between the two of them.

"I'm serious," she warned.

"I can see that." Jess pointed enthusiastically at the divot between her eyebrows. "Look, Carter! Lexi's first wrinkle is going to be because of us."

Carter couldn't decide if he admired Jess's recklessness or if he was scared for her. He settled on feeling both.

"Fine," Lexi snapped, her finger rubbing at the space between her eyebrows like she could erase the offending line. "It's not like it wasn't going to come out anyway."

She pulled out her phone and brought up a page before pushing it into Jess's hand. Before Jess could even look at it, Lexi made a spectacle of slamming her fist on the table and raising her voice.

"I can't believe you were a part of this!" Her cry, as intended, sliced through the diner, turning everyone's attention toward them. "It's no surprise to learn that Carter was trying to cheat us out of the prize money, but *you*? I expected better of you, Jessica Reid."

"What are you talking about?" Jess was still smiling at the absurdity, but her grin had tightened like it had just discovered it had shown up to a party in costume where everyone else was wearing frowns.

"It's right there. Or you can google 'something stinks in Redford' if you want to read it on your own phone." Lexi said the last part in a slow, deliberate voice, more instruction for the listeners than actually conversing with Jess. Then her voice flared dramatically. "I can't believe you tried to fool all of us into believing you just met Carter, getting half the town to root for this ridiculous love story of yours like it was some fairy tale instead of a scam, but you had to, didn't you? If we knew about your history—that Carter had already *given you half of Jasper's fortune*—we would've realized you were working together to cheat the whole town out of the rest of it."

"What?" Jess laughed weakly, looking to Carter, searching for proof that her laughter was warranted.

His stomach plummeted at the realization he couldn't give it to her. He reached for the phone instead, feeling sick at the sight of the article on the screen. Lexi hadn't exaggerated. It really was titled "Something Stinks in Redford," and he could only imagine the exaggerations it likely contained.

"I didn't . . ." Jess attempted to defend herself but trailed off, not understanding what she was being accused of. "He didn't . . ."

"What?" Lexi threw her hands up like she was exhausted by the charade. "What lie are you going to tell now? That you paid for college with your happy-go-lucky nature and a smile?"

"I got a scholarship," Jess said, her words too wobbly to be convincing.

"For what? Most accommodating between the sheets?"

Carter's head jerked back, snapping him out of his shock, but before he could say anything, a man appeared at the edge of their booth.

"That's enough, Lexi," the man said sharply. "I won't have that kind of talk in my diner."

"What kind of talk? The truth?" Lexi looked around and tried to suppress her smile at the results of her accusation; she'd gotten everyone's attention, and those whose heads weren't bent over their phones, undoubtedly reading the same article Carter was looking at, were staring at Carter and Jess with varying expressions of hurt and suspicion. "Read it for yourself, Hank. It's all right there. These two have known each other for years. Carter stole money from Jasper to pay for Jess's college."

"He did not!" For the first time since Lexi shoved her phone in her hand, Jess's words were clear. Adamant. "I know you want to believe whatever lies this website thinks they dug up, but there's no world in which Carter would steal from his grandfather. He just wouldn't do that. He loved Jasper. Tell her, Carter."

Jess was so sure of him that he found himself nodding in agreement. He wanted so badly to be worthy of her trust. He wanted nothing more in the world than for her to be right.

"I didn't steal anything." He felt a weight lifted off his shoulders at the way her smile stretched gratefully at his words. "And it wasn't half of Jasper's fortune. It was only two hundred thousand dollars."

He understood immediately that it had been the wrong thing to say.

Chapter 32

· · · · · · · · · · ·

JESS

When the clock hit six the next morning, Jess groaned, gave up on her effort to get back to sleep, and covered her face with her pillow. She wondered if five million dollars was worth getting out of bed. If she had five million dollars, she'd pay at least a million of it to avoid facing reality. So taking that into consideration, the real question was whether four million dollars was worth getting out of bed.

No.

The answer popped into her head, loud and resolute. She didn't know how to build a barn, and she didn't want to attempt do so with a bunch of people who didn't know any more than she did about construction. She certainly didn't want to attempt it with a bunch of people who thought she was a sneaky cheater, conspiring with another sneaky cheater to swindle them out of a fair chance at the prize money. Most of all, she didn't want to face Carter, who she'd abandoned at the diner, running off like a petulant child the moment he'd admitted to using Jasper's money for her "scholarship."

Jess would happily give up the remaining four million to avoid all of those things. Unfortunately, the money wasn't for her. It was for her dad. And how much of her dad's health would she sacrifice to continue burying her head under a pillow? Not a single cent. With a sigh, Jess knocked the pillow off her face and reached for her phone.

Its screen was still desolately, heart-wrenchingly empty. Neither Sally nor Luanne had returned any of her messages since they'd been eliminated from the game. Liz hadn't called her back, and Carter hadn't sent anything since the series of texts in which he'd attempted to explain himself. Jess wished she'd stayed at her dad's last night so she wouldn't feel so alone, but it had been unsettling when she'd arrived to discover Nikki already there. Granted, her dad had been in his chair and Nikki had been at the far end of the couch, but they'd been giggling at their show like their brownies were more pot than chocolate. Pretending to be equally high had been more than Jess could manage.

"Okay," she said aloud, kicking off the covers. She'd edited enough books to know that there was always a point in the story where the protagonist feels like she's lost everything. This was hers. All she had to do was put on the right music and keep herself moving forward, and eventually this would all be edited down into a montage that would set her on the path to being a stronger person.

Jess played the most encouraging music she could think of—"Don't Stop Believin'" while she was in the shower, "Fight Song" and "Walking on Sunshine" as she tried to pick an outfit cheerful enough to bolster her mood but that also said, *Trust me, I'm not trying to cheat*—but nothing seemed to work. She felt sad. Sad that the relationships she'd spent a lifetime cultivating might forever be tainted with distrust. Sad that she'd willfully translated Carter's standoffishness into something sexy instead of the secrecy it was.

She was sipping coffee, staring blankly into the open fridge, when her phone trilled. She jumped and coffee splashed onto her hand, the liquid so hot that she let go of the cup without meaning to. It hit the floor and exploded, spattering her pants and socks. Shoving the burned hand into her mouth, she grabbed her phone off the counter with the other. Her stomach swooped as she looked at the screen, then soared. She swiped to answer.

"You're calling me," Jess said with a grateful sigh.

"Of course I'm calling you," Liz said. "You left a five-minute voicemail about how everyone hates you and the guy you like lied to you. What did you think I was going to do? Text you a gif of The Rock flexing his biceps and tell you to stay strong?"

She sounded so close. When Jess closed her eyes, it was almost like she was there.

"It's so good to talk to you," Jess said.

"I'm sorry I couldn't call earlier. I didn't get your message until I woke up, and then Kai completely refused to eat. I mean, if I offered to put you on my lap and pour food into your mouth, wouldn't you just say thank you and tilt your head back? I certainly would. But you and I have had to brave grocery stores on Sunday mornings and deal with the drudgery that is meal planning, so we understand what a gift a meal that doesn't involve cooking is. This little guy doesn't know enough to be appropriately appreciative."

Jess's eyes filled with tears. It was exactly how it had been when she and Liz had gotten home from college—like their conversation had simply hit *pause* and was ready to play again the moment they reconnected. She laughed wetly.

"Hey," Liz said, her voice going soft. "Is it really that bad?"

Jess began to sob in earnest, because it was. It was terrible. Truly, the worst thing she ever could've imagined. And, as much as she didn't want to make it real by telling her best friend, she knew it was time.

"My dad is sick, Liz," she choked out. "He's really, really sick."

．．．．．．．．

"HE DID NOT," Jess said twenty minutes later. Somehow, she was actually giggling.

That was the magic of Liz. Her friend had cried with her, shared in her grief, then shifted their conversation from sorrow to reminiscing with a deftness only she was capable of.

Jess shook her head at Liz's assertion that Jess's dad had thrown away the recorder Jess had spent a month learning to play when she was fifteen. "He wouldn't."

"I caught him red-handed," Liz insisted. "He tossed it in the trash and dumped a pot of old spaghetti on top of it. And he wasn't even embarrassed when I told him I saw."

"He must've been." Her dad had been so lovely and encouraging when she practiced. He was always cheering her on. "What did he say? Do you remember?"

"Oh, I remember verbatim. I said, 'Mr. Ross, how could you do that? Jess plays that thing every day.'"

"And he said?"

"'You're welcome.'" Liz guffawed. "That's it. *You're welcome.* And you know what? I mean, Jess. You did play that thing all the time. And you were *so bad* at it. It was like being forced to listen to cats fight."

"It was not." Jess could barely get the words out through her laughter. It *was.* She'd even known it back then. Playing an instrument had not turned out to be a skill she'd been capable of picking up. As much as she'd loved the idea of herself prancing through the streets, delighting everyone with a whimsical musical treat, she'd been unable to produce a single song that didn't sound like a dying animal. Taking her show on the road would've been an assault on the community.

A loud banging on the door jerked her out of the memory.

"What was that?" Liz asked, hearing the sound through the phone.

Jess cupped her hand over the phone and whispered, "Someone's here."

"A SWAT team?"

Jess's hand went to her hair, running anxiously through the still-damp strands. It couldn't be Carter. She couldn't picture him showing up at her house uninvited, not if he thought she was upset with him. He wasn't the type of man to put his needs above hers. At least, she hadn't thought he was. But who else could it be? A strange mixture of disappointment and excitement swirled through her stomach.

"Hold on," she said to Liz. "I'll check."

Jess looked down at herself before easing the door open, discovering she'd thrown on her raglan shirt that read "daytime pajamas" with a pair of joggers. It wasn't the most flattering thing she owned, but it was, she supposed, accurate. Small victories.

She peered through the crack in the door and was surprised to find not Carter but Nikki, wearing leggings with pockets, an oversized sweatshirt that bared a single delicate shoulder, and a scowl.

"You're *laughing*," Nikki said in an accusing tone.

"You're here," Jess said, unable to mask her confusion.

"I thought you'd be upset." Nikki's face scrunched up at the admission, and she shook her head, already holding up a hand to stave off the smile curling across Jess's face. "Clearly, I was wrong. I certainly didn't expect you to be cackling so loudly I could hear you through the door."

Jess blinked at her, trying to figure out why Nikki Loughton would show up at her house—anyone's house, really—this early in the morning. The conclusion she came to made her mouth fall open.

"You were worried about me," Jess exhaled, awed.

"Who is that?" Liz asked in her ear.

"My teammate," Jess said into the phone, grinning with delight. "She came to check on me."

Nikki shifted with discomfort and leaned toward the

phone, calling out, "I came to make sure she wasn't screwing me out of the prize money."

"She loves me," Jess said to Liz, cupping the phone to her chin. "She wanted to make sure I was all right."

"I don't like this," Liz said, laughing in a way that suggested she did, in fact, like it very much. There was not much Liz enjoyed more than the unexpected, and hearing her friend tease the girl who had mocked them mercilessly all through high school was nothing short of astonishing. "Is she trying to replace me as your best friend?"

"Nikki," Jess said, "are you trying to replace Liz as my best friend?"

"I have plenty of friends," Nikki said with a grimace. "I don't need any more."

"She said yes," Jess told Liz. Her voice took on an apologetic tone. "I'd better go. My new best friend deserves my full attention."

"Stop it," Nikki ordered sharply.

Jess responded by pulling her inside.

As Jess ended her call, Nikki looked around the cluttered little house without leaving the safety of the door, despite Jess having closed it deliberately behind her.

"Your décor is pure pandemonium," she said. Her tone didn't sound entirely critical.

"Is it?" Jess followed her gaze, taking in the open floor plan. While there was no real color scheme to speak of, there was some sense of cohesion in the fact that the furniture was all old and previously used. "I followed all the guidelines from the 'cheerful thrift store' style manual."

Nikki coughed to cover her laugh. "So," she said once she'd regained control, "I guess you're not as upset over the article as I thought you'd be?"

Jess began to take slow steps toward the couch, hoping Nikki might follow her. She thought of dropping a trail of bread crumbs like for a skittish squirrel, but she suspected carbs might be more of a deterrent than an incentive.

"Nope," she admitted as she eased herself into the worn cushions, bouncing a little to make them appear more enticing. "I'm pretty broken up about it. It's a terrible feeling knowing everyone thinks you're trying to cheat them."

"Are you?" Nikki continued to stand at the door, and a flicker of something that looked a lot like hurt flashed across her face. "Are you trying to cheat me?"

Realization crashed over Jess like a tidal wave as it occurred to her for the first time how all of this might look to her teammate. Nikki knew, after all, that Jess had been the one who had insisted on bringing Carter and Bryce along to get the picture of the buck. If Nikki believed that Carter and Jess were in it together, she'd also believe Jess was working against her own teammate to help Carter win. It was a wonder that she'd knocked on Jess's door at all, instead of storming in with guns blazing.

"No," Jess said, horrified that Nikki might think she would betray her like that. "You have to believe me. That article totally misconstrued the situation. I had never met Carter before he came to town for the funeral, and I am in no way working with him to manipulate the outcome of the game."

"So you've never talked about sharing the prize money?"

Jess tensed at the question, the specificity of it making her realize something terrible. She and Carter hadn't, of course, colluded in the way they'd been accused of. They had, however, talked about the money. They'd been in bed, naked and exhausted when he'd whispered the words, *I know you want the prize money for your dad. If I win it, you can have anything you need to help him.*

It had been a kind offer but one she'd barely bothered turning down. Surely, Carter understood that Ross Reid would never allow himself to become someone's charity case. Jess would have a hard enough time convincing him to take the money from her.

"He offered to pay for my dad's treatment if he won," she admitted.

Nikki nodded curtly, and Jess felt a flame of fear lick through her.

To her shock, Nikki didn't respond to her confession with outrage or more accusations. Instead, she crossed the room and settled reluctantly on the other side of the couch.

Meeting Jess's eyes, she simply said, "Good."

It was so unexpected, so full of unearned trust, that Jess gaped at her for a moment, then blurted out, "And I never kissed Jason. I know you don't want to hear it, but I need you to know. I would never kiss someone else's boyfriend. He just grabbed me in the middle of the party and spun me around and shoved his mouth on mine before I knew what was happening. And he didn't even want to do it. He told me after he'd only done it to win a bet."

The truth poured out of her like a waterfall, all the things she'd tried to tell Nikki after she'd walked in on them. Nikki let Jess finish, watching her coolly as she mounted her defense.

When Jess got it all out, Nikki shocked her again by shrugging and saying, "I believe you."

"You do?" Could years of hostility and animosity so easily be wrapped up? It didn't seem possible.

"I do," Nikki said. "It never seemed right that you would've kissed him. I always knew you were way too good for him."

It was like she was speaking another language. If Jess was interpreting it correctly, there was a definite compliment in there. Maybe even something akin to an apology, albeit a very distant relative of one.

"You—" Jess started to say, but Nikki waved her off.

"I was too good for him, too," Nikki said. "I know. I knew it back then."

It felt like Jess should drop it, not rock the boat, but she couldn't help saying, "Then why were you with him?"

"I don't know." Nikki shrugged again. "Sometimes you just want the wrong thing. And, I guess, sometimes you're not really sure you deserve anything better than that."

It took a moment for Jess to digest this, to fully understand that Nikki was admitting that she wasn't always confident of her worth. By the time she had, Nikki had already blown past it, expertly turning the spotlight back on Jess like she could distract her into forgetting the uncharacteristic moment of vulnerability. Jess wouldn't, though—she'd forever look at Nikki a little differently after this. It wasn't the unfeeling who needed armor, Jess realized; it was the ones who had experienced pain.

Chapter 33

JESS

G et over it," Nikki said as they left Jess's house for the barn.

"Carter and I had an entire conversation about my scholarship," Jess reminded her. She balanced her hammer with the hot pink handle and a flashlight with a yellow yarn pom-pom under one arm as she locked the door. She might be unwanted at the barn, but at least she'd be contributing to the tool pile. Nikki clearly hadn't been inspired to do the same. "It was the perfect opportunity for him to let me in on the secret, but he said nothing. How am I supposed to trust him after that?" Jess continued as she followed Nikki down the porch.

The sun had burned off the dreary clouds she'd woken to, turning the sky a brilliant shade of blue. She suspected Nikki had given it a talking-to before she'd arrived, warning it that she intended to post about today's efforts at the barn and wouldn't tolerate anything less than flawless lighting for her photos.

"You mean, how are you supposed to trust him after that

display of loyalty to Jasper?" Nikki rolled her eyes. "Try to make sense, Jessica."

It might have been a mistake letting Nikki read Carter's texts. Nikki had clearly switched to Carter's side after reading that he'd promised to protect Jasper's anonymity.

"I can't," Jess admitted. "It's not about sense. It's about how I feel."

"So, explain it to me, then." Surprisingly, Nikki looked genuinely curious. "How do you feel?"

Jess sighed. She didn't want to admit that she didn't actually know. She was embarrassed to find out that she hadn't earned a scholarship on her own merit but was still grateful that she'd gotten it, and even more so that she'd been able to accept it; it certainly would've been harder to take Jasper's money had she realized it wasn't an anonymous scholarship. She also felt angry that the article had made her out to be a cheater, and she felt nervous to face the town. She felt a million different things, but she realized that wasn't what Nikki was really asking. Nikki wanted to know how Jess felt about Carter. And though it might be easy to tangentially tie each of these things to him, none of them really had anything to do with him.

When it came to Carter, what Jess really felt was scared.

"I feel like maybe I was wrong," Jess said, dropping her eyes to the sidewalk as they walked. Fading grass poked its way through the cracks. "Even though I haven't known him long, for some reason it just felt like I knew him really well. And this whole thing was like a glass of water to the face, like a wake-up call that I don't actually know him at all, I only know who he is here. Outside of Redford, he lives in a world that I know nothing about, and he's going to leave soon. He's going to go back to his real life, and I won't be able to pretend that I'm a part of it anymore."

"So, it's all about you." Nikki waved off the way Jess's eyes widened with hurt in response. "I'm not judging you," Nikki added. "I love making things all about myself. I'm just pointing out that it's not actually about Carter at all. He got roped into all of this, just like you did. But you're freaking out that you're probably going to lose him, so you're pushing him away."

"I don't think I'm . . ." Jess floundered. Was Nikki right? The suggestion that Jess was pushing Carter away implied she'd applied some kind of force to him, when really, she'd run in the opposite direction. But if both actions resulted in distance between them, was there really any difference?

The Farthingtons came toward them on the sidewalk, and Jess slid behind Nikki to let them pass. They averted their eyes, making a point to ignore Jess's wave.

Jess exhaled her frustration. "Can you believe them? Maybe I want to blame Carter for this disaster because if I don't, I have to accept that it doesn't matter that I gave up two hours of a perfectly good Saturday afternoon to attend a backyard funeral for the Farthingtons' *cat*. I have to admit that the people in this town aren't really my family. They're just homeowners who happen to share a zip code with me."

"Families fight," Nikki said in singsong voice, parroting the excuse the residents of Redford had hidden behind far too many times.

But Jess was sick of hearing that. She was sick of *saying* it. Families were supposed to stand by one another. She'd stood by Redford. So, why couldn't she count on Redford to stand by her?

Jess kicked a stick like a toddler, sending it skittering down the sidewalk. She wanted to be angry with the couple who had just slighted her, but all she felt was disappointed. She'd spent years carving out her place in this town, and with one online article, she'd been knocked out of it. She wished she could go back home and hide. She didn't want to run into anyone else on the street. She didn't want to face the people in the barn.

Actually, that wasn't true. She wanted to see one of the people in the barn.

She wanted to see Carter.

Carter could be counted on. Hadn't he just proven it by being so loyal to Jasper?

She shook her head, realizing Nikki had been right. Jess hadn't been looking at the situation clearly. She'd been too focused on herself to consider what Carter had been dealing with. Jasper had taken his secrets to the grave. How could Carter have shared one?

It wasn't about her. And even if it had been, Jess had edited enough romances that she should've recognized this for what it was: the obstacle. Romances always started promisingly, but they never continued smoothly. There would always be some difficulty that felt insurmountable. Only, with her and Carter, it wouldn't be just this one. If they overcame this, he'd inevitably win the prize money that she was counting on to save her dad. And, even if Carter was wrong, and he wasn't guaranteed to win the prize, Jess would still have to watch him leave after the game ended.

They were destined to fail; it was just a matter of whether it would be sooner or later. The realization gave her every excuse she needed to walk away. If she did, at least she might be able to salvage her relationship with the town. *Or* she could stay and face the obstacles. She could run straight toward them and hurl herself into the air, knowing she might land badly but savoring that rush as her feet left the ground.

"I think I'll get over it," Jess said, breaking the companionable silence they'd fallen into. She hopped over one of the cracks in the sidewalk.

"The Farthingtons or the situation with Carter?"

It was a good question.

"Both," Jess said decisively.

"Hmm," Nikki murmured.

"What?" For the first time since Lexi had ambushed her and Carter with that article, Jess was feeling hopeful about things again.

"Nothing," Nikki said. "I just wanted to turn *getting over it* into a sexual joke about being on top, but you kind of ruined it by including the Farthingtons in the equation."

Jess half choked and half laughed. Just as she was about to regain control of her breathing and thank Nikki for the lovely imagery, Annabelle Stanton flung open the door of Cuts & Curls and blocked their path.

"Is it true?" Annabelle's hair was blue today, with a shimmering silver tint that made her blue eyes stand out. They practically shined with Jess's betrayal. "Have you really been working with him this whole time?"

Jess shook her head, her inhale of surprise at Annabelle's

sudden appearance thwarting her attempts to clear her throat.

"Jess is *my* teammate," Nikki said, answering for her. "How could she be working with him when she's working with me?"

"Maybe you're in on it, too," Annabelle said. But she didn't sound like she wanted to believe it. And, Jess realized, she probably didn't. Not only was Nikki one of her most consistent customers, but Nikki also had a nice local following of people who wanted to have their hair cut and styled exactly like hers.

"You think I'd be fine with sharing my winnings three ways?" Nikki scoffed. "Please. You've known me too long for that."

"You did say you'd give Bo the money for a ring if you won." Annabelle brightened, but her eyes flicked from left to right as if trying to determine if this proved or disproved Nikki's point.

"Because you're a friend," Nikki said, and Jess was tempted to laugh at the way she made it sound almost like a warning. "And I wanted to acknowledge that my actions at the courthouse could be interpreted as a bit ruthless. But I in no way intend to share my winnings with Bo. I only wanted to reward him for loving you enough to run after you. He deserves the ring, and I hope Jess and I win so he can get it."

"I hope you do, too." Annabelle's eyes turned dreamy, and she smiled as she looked down at her bare ring finger.

Jess peered at Nikki, looking for something—a dangling earring, swirling pupils—that might explain how she'd just hypnotized the hairdresser.

"We should go," Nikki said, "but I really am loving the blue hair on you. And that sweater is to die for."

"Isn't it?" Annabelle looked pleased with herself. "I ordered it from Cuyana with your promo code, and the colors turned out to be even prettier in person than they were online."

"I wish I'd seen it first," Nikki cooed. "But I never could've done it justice. It's like it was made for you."

"That's exactly how I feel about your Steph jumpsuit," Annabelle gushed. "Every time you wear it, I find myself thinking I can pull off strapless, despite all the castoffs in my closet reminding me otherwise."

Jess watched this exchange in amazement, marveling at the quickness at which a showdown had turned into a volleying of compliments. It was surreal. But the icing on the cake didn't come until the end of their conversation, when Nikki slid her arm through Jess's and led her jauntily down Main Street.

Sure, they passed people who didn't wave.

But not a single one of them dared to get in their way.

Chapter 34

....

JESS

Jess's stomach turned at the sight of Bobby and Lexi, despite the reassuring presence of her teammate by her side. They were standing outside the barn, waiting for her, one massive, the other poisonous. It was the least welcoming sight Jess had ever seen.

Sure enough, they struck the moment she was in range. Ignoring Nikki, they lobbed their accusations directly at Jess. She pushed past them, realizing how pointless it would be to defend herself. They had no reason to believe her.

Other contestants were already inside, and Jess wondered if she should be grateful that they hadn't joined Bobby and Lexi or hurt that they all averted their eyes at the sight of her. Novak was sitting at the card table he had set up right inside the door. She supposed that was why Bobby and Lexi hadn't dared block her from entering.

"You should be eliminated," Lexi shouted again before turning to Novak, her tone shifting to a whine. "She should be eliminated."

"No," Novak said without bothering to look up from his iPad.

No?

Just, *no?* Jess widened her eyes at Nikki, and Nikki rolled hers in response. How easy would it be for the man to acknowledge the fact that he'd never spoken to Jess before arriving in Redford? Especially considering they still hadn't spoken, not unless his instruction to sign her name on the waiver counted as interpersonal communication. It wouldn't just be helpful to her; it would be helpful to him as well. Any accusation of collusion tainted Novak in the process. After all, Novak held all the cards.

The lawyer said nothing, though. He merely poked at a game of Minecraft on his screen. In all fairness, nobody was working, so there wasn't exactly any activity to score yet. Those who weren't watching Bobby and Lexi yell at Jess pointedly looked anywhere else. And Carter was nowhere to be seen.

Jess's breath caught at the realization. Where was he? He had to be here. She scanned the barn again, her eyes skipping over the new piles of extension cords and the motley collection of tools and focusing instead on the contenders. She began to feel sick as she moved past them and searched the spectators lounging against the wall.

He wouldn't have just left, would he? Could he have been so desperate to prove his innocence that he'd decided to abandon the game? She grabbed for her phone, trying not to panic. Bobby's and Lexi's accusations faded to a dull roar in her head as she checked the time. It was only 8:03. Carter was just a few minutes late. She tried to ignore the fact that he was never late.

It didn't work. He wasn't coming. Misery settled over

her, heavy and thick. She'd messed up by ignoring his texts. She'd made him think she was mad instead of explaining that she was confused. She'd lost him, just like she'd lost her place in Redford. Just like she was going to lose her dad.

She'd lost everything.

"We have muffins," Luanne called out, appearing in the doorway with a cheerful smile that seemed to laugh at the maudlin turn Jess's thoughts had so quickly taken. Sally was next to her, an identical basket dangling from her arm.

"And pumpkin bread," Sally added brightly.

The sight of them shot a sliver of light through the gloom that had descended on Jess. It glowed a little brighter when Sally crossed the barn and pulled Jess into a one-armed hug.

"Hi," Jess said, as Luanne air-kissed her on one cheek, then the other. The two bakers sandwiched her like she was the marshmallow-fluff filling of a whoopie pie.

"Hi, yourself," Luanne said, laughing at the clear uncertainty in Jess's tone. "We thought you might need some backup today."

"In our experience," Sally added, "people have a hard time staying angry once their stomachs are full of sugar."

The weight of their words hit Jess, and warmth bloomed in her chest. "You mean, you came because of me?"

"Of course we did, sweet pea." Sally looked a little put out by Jess's disbelief. "We couldn't just leave you to deal with the fallout of that article by yourself."

"But I haven't heard back from either of you since the Barbie Jeep race." Jess regretted the words as soon as they hit the air. There was a proper response to such a generous show of support, and it required little more than the words *thank* and *you.*

"Sorry, hon," Luanne said. "We just needed a minute to lick our wounds. You know how it is. Then Sally decided to teach me how to bake muffins, and she's like Novak with a megaphone once she gets going."

"It's not my fault you have the attention span of a toddler," Sally argued happily.

"The two of you baked together?" Jess couldn't believe it. It was like discovering The Rock and Vin Diesel had decided to bury the hatchet and make another car movie together.

"We had to," Sally said with a sly grin. "You can't go into business together if you don't know how you'll work together in a kitchen."

"What?" Jess squealed and bounced on her heels. "You're going to run the bakery together?"

"With a little help from your friend Carter," Luanne said. "We ran into him on the way here, and he said he'd help us work out a plan to merge our finances."

Jess's heart began to race. Carter was still in Redford. They'd just run into him on the way here.

"He's a good egg, that one," Sally said. "And if I might say so, the new look suits him."

"The new look?" Jess wanted to see the new look. She wanted to see *him*. Her legs ached with the desire to run out and find him, to make sure he didn't leave, but she knew she couldn't. Not when Sally and Luanne had shown up for her like this. And especially not when her dad's chance at getting the best doctors money could buy was on the line.

"That *new look* clearly doesn't include a watch," Bobby said, not bothering to pretend he hadn't been listening to them. He spoke even louder when he added, "I hope it's being noted that it's now 8:07, and everyone is here except for Carter and Bryce."

"I'm not sure that means much when nobody is actually working," Luanne said sharply.

"Have a muffin, Bobby," Sally said, tossing one at his chest dismissively as she pushed past him.

It shut him up, but it didn't stop the murmurs that flared up around the room. *Would Carter lose points for being late?* people wondered aloud. *He doesn't care,* someone whispered, *because he already knows he's going to win the money.* Jess could feel the eyes on her, full of suspicion, and she wondered if the contestants really believed she was in some kind of cahoots with him or if it simply benefited them to believe it at the moment. Would people return to normal after this was all over, or would Redford never be the same for her?

She looked around the barn. What she saw made her wince. In the bright light of day, the progress they'd made last night had disappeared. The place looked just as dilapidated as it had when they'd first seen it, only now it was cluttered with tools that looked more suited to gardening than construction work and cords that hadn't been put to use. Jess was ready and willing to get her hands dirty, but she had no idea where to begin.

A low whistle of surprise rang from the door, causing her to whirl around. Bo was standing there, looking around disapprovingly.

"I see you decided to leave the place as you found it," he

said, shaking his head and whistling again. "Bring it in, team."

Jess thought for a moment he was referring to the contenders, and she scampered toward him. But then other people appeared in the doorway, carrying ladders and saws and all sorts of things that made the group's tools look like toys in comparison. She wanted to ask what was happening, but she didn't dare. She was just too grateful that someone had arrived with a plan, and that the plan appeared to involve actual construction work.

Bobby, however, didn't share her restraint.

"What the hell is going on?" he bellowed.

"Shh," Lexi hissed. She turned to Bo and thrust out her chest. "If you're here to help, you have our undying gratitude. Luanne! Give him a muffin."

"What's in the other basket?" Bo asked before taking one of each. Then he refocused. "We're here to help, but not because we think any of you are particularly worthy of winning ten million dollars."

"Well—" Lexi said.

Bo cut her off.

"None of you," he reiterated firmly. "But especially not you, Lexi. I'll have you know that I was trying to have a nice dinner with my soon-to-be fiancée at the diner last night when you started shouting about articles. Just so you know, Annabelle did not appreciate the interruption. But what *I* didn't appreciate were all the things I heard after Jess ran out of the diner. Now, nobody can accuse me of being here because I want her team to win—not after her partner was the one who got me eliminated."

Bo paused long enough to glare at Nikki.

"I'm here," he continued once Nikki's expression turned appropriately sheepish, "because Jess has lived her whole life in this town, volunteering at every ridiculous event, doing whatever she can to support the rest of us. Ever since my grandmother got her hip replaced, there hasn't been a week that's gone by without Jess stopping in to drop off a few books for her. And that might not mean anything to all of you, but it sure means something to me. It means something to my team, too. We don't want to be a part of a town that would turn its back on one of its own like that. So here we are. Showing up for our neighbor. Mr. Novak said outside help could be used if it was offered freely. Well, we're offering. Tell us what you need, Jess."

Jess blinked in response to this unexpected backing. She'd always liked Bo, but as far as she knew, she'd barely registered on his radar. It was overwhelming to hear him refer to her as one of his own. To belong was all she'd ever really wanted. Not even to fit in or be liked, just to be connected to a group of people who were willing to live their lives with her.

And now that need had been wonderfully, astoundingly met.

"Thank you." Tears leaked down her cheeks in big, embarrassing rivulets, but she couldn't help herself. Between Sally and Luanne showing up, and now him, Jess's heart was overflowing.

Bo shifted with discomfort. "Um, maybe I'll just take over. Okay?"

Jess laughed soppily and nodded. Then her eyes went to the door, and she saw him. Carter was hovering just outside, looking at her. When their eyes met, he held out the plastic cup he was holding and shook it. She nodded at Bryce as he slipped by, but her eyes snapped right back to Carter. So, *this* was the new look Sally had referred to.

Carter clearly hadn't shaved, and the resulting stubble was incredibly sexy. Not only that, but he'd finally shed his business-casual wear. The Henley he was wearing clung the slightest bit to the muscles underneath in a way his button-ups had been too starched to do. Where the stiffness of his collared shirts had conveyed a clear hands-off message, the softness of this one offered to wrap its arms around you and pull you closer. Jess suddenly felt exceedingly grateful that she'd worked out her feelings toward him before she saw him; it would be foolish to allow her emotions to be dictated by something as shallow as physical appearance, but she seriously doubted her ability to resist.

"I brought a peace offering," Carter said when she followed him outside.

"I see that." Jess noticed that his eyes were tinged with red and couldn't help wondering if he'd slept as poorly as she had. "Did you bring me a daiquiri for breakfast?"

"I wanted Bryce to make it with coffee instead of alcohol, but he said there was no way to make coffee colorful." Carter's sheepish flash of a smile looked brighter against the dark stubble. "So it's basically just ice and sugar."

"It's perfect." And it was. It looked like the tropics in a cup. There was even a chunk of pineapple speared through the straw. Jess took it from him and their fingers touched, sending sparks through her hand.

"I should've told you," he said seriously.

"Should you?" She shrugged and took a sip of the daiquiri. Sweet, fruity goodness exploded against her taste buds. "Or were you being honest in your text when you said Jasper asked you not to?"

"I was being honest," he admitted.

"Then you did the right thing."

Carter looked unconvinced.

"You have so little left of Jasper, Carter. I can't be mad at you for wanting to hold on to his secrets."

"It can't be that easy." Carter ran his hand through his hair, too distressed to remember that it was perfectly styled. The gesture left it deliciously mussed. "You were upset."

"I was," she agreed. "It was crappy that it was interpreted how it was and even crappier being blindsided by it. And I felt embarrassed for thinking I'd earned that scholarship, only to find out that it was nothing more than charity."

"It wasn't—" He stopped abruptly when she held up her hand.

"And I hated that you knew something about me and didn't tell me," she continued. "And all of those responses are real and valid, but they're about me. Not you. You helped send me to college, and you kept a promise to your grandfather. Those are good things. How can I possibly be mad about them?"

"Because I should have told you," he insisted.

"Tell me next time." At his surprised look, Jess smiled. "I'm not naïve, Carter. I know you're going to leave. But I can't help feeling like there's something real here, something bigger than distance or competition or whatever other obstacles we might face. So even if I'm wrong—even if

Jasper's game is all we get, I don't want to focus on the past. I want to focus on the future. And if something comes up in the future, you can tell me."

"I will." Carter said the words as seriously as an oath, then slid his arm around her waist and stepped into her. His chest felt warm and hard against hers, and her stomach gave a long, slow somersault at the intensity in his gaze. For a breathless moment, she was certain he was going to kiss her.

"I'm ready to tell you another one of my secrets," he whispered instead.

"Yes?" she asked, her eyelids growing heavy.

"I've never bought a purple shirt before."

Jess laughed and looked down at the deep hue, more mulberry than purple. It suited his skin tone, warming it in a way that the cool whites and blue-grays he typically favored didn't.

"Did you buy it at the Bait & Tackle?" It was the only place she could think of open so early in the morning. "I'm surprised Marty didn't stock it in black."

"Oh, he did. Gray, too. But I couldn't stop thinking what color you would've chosen if you'd been there with me."

Jess's smile widened. "So you went with purple?"

He grinned back at her. "It was the brightest color they had."

"That was a very good secret," she said approvingly.

"Give me a second chance at dinner tonight," he said, "and I'll tell you about the first time I bought a pair of jeans from a shelf next to a fish tank full of worms."

"Was it this morning?"

"Shh," he said. "No spoilers."

Chapter 35

· · · · · · · · · · ·

NIKKI

Nikki wasn't built for manual labor. She'd been sore before—Pilates could make you feel like you'd pulled muscles you didn't know you had—but she'd *never* had chipped nails. She scowled down at them as she shifted on the recliner, her thighs groaning in protest at the effort. They'd been working on the barn for four days. It felt like ninety.

On Ross's TV, one of the *Love Island* couples was arguing about a tweet. They were wasting everyone's time. It was so obvious that they were going to break up.

Nikki looked at Carter and Jess, wondering if the same fate was in store for them. They certainly didn't act like it. They were cuddled up on the couch—which, by the way, was where *she* usually sat—fingers intertwined like a couple of teenagers. She could practically smell the pheromones bouncing between them. It was disgusting.

"We need to get Lexi eliminated from the game," she said loudly.

"Shhh." Ross looked over with an expression so chastising

she had to tamp down a smile. He'd gotten way too obsessed with this stupid show. Each episode was almost an hour long, and they'd been watching several per night.

Nikki reached for the remote and hit *pause*. "As I was saying, Lexi has got to go."

"I thought you were friends with Lexi," Carter said. One of his arms was around Jess, his thumb stroking her shoulder, and the other was on her lap so they could hold hands.

"And I thought you were going back to Atlanta after this," Nikki said. "But that seems unlikely now that you've surgically attached yourself to Jess."

"Leave them alone, Nikki," Ross said, motioning for her to throw him the remote. "They're in love."

"Dad!" Jess's face turned scarlet.

Nikki grinned with satisfaction but didn't let go of the remote.

"All right," Ross said, shifting in his chair to give Nikki the attention she needed. "Why do you want to go after Lexi?"

"Um, maybe because she tried to get my teammate kicked out of the game, which also would've disqualified me?" Nikki didn't think this should require an explanation, but she continued anyway. "And she clearly ran into Carter's Barbie Jeep on purpose—which, I'll admit, I didn't mind at the time because I was also racing against him. But she also could've killed DeMarco when she put peanut dust on his pie."

Jess and Carter sat upright, like two puppets whose strings had gotten tangled together.

Nikki cringed.

That last bit had slipped out.

"Are you serious?" Jess's eyes had gone wide. "Did Lexi really put the peanut dust on DeMarco's pie?"

"I don't know." Nikki shrugged dismissively. "Probably not. But wouldn't it be fun to blame her?"

She felt a little better when her words made Ross laugh.

"Nikki!" Jess shook her head and settled back into the couch. "You can't just go around making accusations like that."

"Sitting in your dad's poorly lit living room hardly constitutes going around," Nikki argued half-heartedly. "Anyway, the rest of it was true. And would it kill you to invest in a few lamps, Ross?"

"Don't worry about Lexi," Ross said, leaning back in his chair and kicking his feet up onto the coffee table. "If what you say is true, she's going to get what's coming to her."

Nikki perked up. "How do you know?"

"Because Bobby told me they started hooking up a couple of days ago. Trust me, I've seen enough of Bobby's girlfriends at the garage over the years. If you were hoping to make Lexi miserable, a few weeks with him will do all your work for you."

"Huh." Nikki considered it, her nose wrinkling with distaste. *Yes.* Being forced to see Bobby naked was a harsher punishment than any jury would've sentenced Lexi to. And if, in a few weeks, Nikki needed to worsen their fate by provoking a fight between the couple, she was more than capable of doing that.

"Well, that's settled, then," she declared. "Lexi's been taken care of."

"On that note," Jess said, "Carter and I are going to call it a night."

The two of them stood in unison and said their goodbyes before heading out.

Nikki smiled evilly at Ross. "They're totally leaving to have sex."

Ross groaned. "You're the worst. Don't you understand how terrible that is to say to a father?"

"I understand completely. That's why I said it."

"Get out of my house." Ross made the demand in a resigned tone that suggested he had no hope she'd heed his directive.

She wouldn't. She liked being here, eating junk food and watching junk TV. It felt like the home she'd always wanted. Anyway, Ross needed her. His voice was almost back to normal after last night's vomiting spell, but if it weren't for her, he'd drink that terrible juice instead of the Gatorade she'd switched it out with. He wouldn't be replenishing his electrolytes at all.

"That's exactly what you should've said to Jess and Carter," she said. "Don't you think they're ruining *Love Island* with all of their cuddling and whispering? That show is meant to inspire mockery, not provide the soundtrack to their real-life romance."

"I'll give them a written warning," he said dryly.

"It's not enough. They're killing the vibe. They need to be banned."

Ross coughed to cover his laugh, and Nikki glared at him. He should know better than to fake a cough. His throat was undoubtedly still tender.

"I'm not banning my daughter from my house," he said sternly.

"But the *vibe*," Nikki whined.

"Maybe they're not the problem," he said. "Maybe it's us. We're not providing enough mockery to set the tone. We need to beef up our numbers."

"Are you suggesting we invite other people?" Nikki's aversion to this terrible idea was so intense that she almost couldn't get the words out. Who did he want to replace her with? Someone nicer? Someone less disappointing?

"I'd love to meet Kent," Ross said. "And he must miss you. You're at the barn all day and here every night. How long has it been since you've seen him?"

Too long.

Nikki knew this for a fact because he'd said exactly that in his last text. It had been too long since he'd seen her, too long since she'd taken one of his calls. He hadn't made it sound like a warning, but she'd read between the lines. He was going to break up with her soon. Sooner than later, if she didn't start making time for him. The problem was, she missed him, too. Usually, the longer she stayed away from someone, the more in control of her feelings she felt.

This time, that hadn't been the case.

"I'm not inviting Kent," she said sharply. "I don't want him to know I spend my night hanging out with some weird family, watching trashy reality shows."

Ross looked at her for a moment, and her stomach churned. Surely he knew she didn't mean that. He and Jess weren't a weird family. They were a wonderful family. Anyone on earth would've been lucky to end up in a family like theirs.

His expression grew serious, and he pointed at her. "I was told that *Love Island* was a documentary."

Nikki choked down a startled laugh of surprise, then felt inexplicably teary.

"I can't invite Kent," she confessed.

"Why not?"

She hit the *play* button on the remote, and the show started back up. The arguing couple was too close to the pool, and they shrieked as one of the guys in the villa cannon-balled into the water, spraying them with water.

"I like him too much," she said over the shouting on the TV.

She half expected Ross to snap at her for talking over the drama. Maybe she'd even done it with the intention of annoying him. She'd spent half her life being told she was a nuisance. Might as well perform as expected.

Ross nodded, shifting his gaze from the TV to her. "And you don't think he likes you enough?"

"I'm the worst." Nikki forced a grin. "You just said it yourself."

"Maybe," Ross said. "But you're also pretty incredible. You're loyal and creative and you're one of the funniest people I've ever met."

She scoffed but didn't respond. She wasn't sure that she was capable of speaking.

"I'm not sure any of that matters, though," Ross added.

She lifted her eyebrows in a silent question.

"You're not a tilting scale, Nikki." He sounded so confident of this strange proclamation that she found herself sitting straighter as if she could physically absorb his words.

"You're not sliding back and forth between too much or too little. You're *you*. The perfect amount. And the people who are meant to be in your life will appreciate that, and they'll hold on to you. I know I, for one, intend to. And I doubt you'll be escaping Jess in this lifetime, either."

The tears finally breached Nikki's eyes, and she blinked them back, annoyed at the way they stung.

"You sound like such a *dad*," she said, looking away so he wouldn't spot the trickle of wetness that slid down her cheek.

"Don't mock me," Ross said with a stifled laugh. "I do have a shotgun, you know. I'm not above meeting Kent at the front door and demanding to know what his intentions are."

Nikki cringed at the thought. "Well, now I'm definitely not inviting him over."

"Sure you are," Ross said confidently. "You can't wait to take that couch over from Jess and Carter."

At the reminder, Nikki abandoned the chair for the couch, kicking her feet up on the cushions and making a show of taking up as much space as she could. She returned her attention to the TV, trying to focus on the show instead of the things Ross had just said.

Finally, she gave up and pulled out her phone. It's not like she could be expected to invite Kent over *tonight*. He'd be going to bed soon. She'd just throw it out there, suggest that he might want to join them sometime. If he didn't, no big deal.

As Ross had said, she liked having the couch to herself.

Chapter 36

. . . .

CARTER

Stop," Carter said, reaching for the sander Bryce was using with a heavy touch more appropriate for a sledgehammer. "Please, just go help Nikki and Melvin stain the walls."

Bo, noting the takeover, shot Carter an approving look that made him feel prouder than he cared to admit. Carter had enjoyed learning from him over the past several days. He'd never worked with his hands before, not in any substantial way, and there was something satisfying about knowing he could patch a hole in a roof or, if the need ever arose, erect an actual wall. His entire body ached, and his muscles were shredded from so many days in a row of manual labor, but it felt good knowing he had it in him. He'd grown up in a house where people were hired to do that kind of thing. In his home, things would be different.

At the thought of his home, his eyes went to Jess. She was laughing about something with DeMarco as they repainted the barn door red. Carter felt a smile tug at his mouth as if he'd heard the joke and was in on it with them, even though so many people were talking that it was impossible to make out their words. The barn was never empty anymore. People were always stopping by to bring food, offer encouragement, or even lend a helping hand. Every now and then an audience would form, but the teams took great joy in mocking their laziness, so the spectators would inevitably give in and grab a broom or find a way to jump in on the work.

Even Oscar had moved his stool just outside the door so he could greet people as they entered and exited. He answered questions, too, when he wasn't declaring the day beautiful. It turned out he was an electrical engineer before he retired and took up reading and greeting. When Bo ran into any difficulties on the project, Oscar was the first person he turned to.

They'd all become a sort of giant, interchangeable team. There were still arguments, of course. The remaining contenders worked too hard for emotions not to fray, and they could never entirely forget the ten-million-dollar carrot dangling above—nor the fact that only two of them would reach it. The barn had changed them, though. Six days of working on it had sucked them in like a week at camp, turning it into not just a structure they felt unbelievably proud of but also a little world of their own. Unlikely friendships had formed, delighting Jess to no end.

She loved to tell Carter the backstories of the people they'd worked with that day. She'd give him the details at night, when the two of them were curled up on the couch or lying naked and entwined under the sheets, her voice drowsy and content as she explained why it had meant so much when Bobby complimented Edwin on his electrical skills.

She'd even managed to do the unthinkable and humanize Bobby by telling Carter how Bobby had inherited the garage when his father had died. It had been, she claimed, a flailing business before Bobby had gotten his hands on it. Then, he'd instituted a policy of honesty and transparency that had earned him so many devoted customers that more than one car with failing brakes or a smoking engine had been driven in from another town out of loyalty to his garage. The blatant disregard for road safety didn't impress Carter, but he supposed some credit was due for the integrity that inspired it.

"Come on, man," Bobby said with a groan as if he'd picked up on Carter's thoughts. It wasn't Carter he was looking at, though. He was looking past him toward the barn door. "Don't you understand that I'm your boss? When you come here, I know you're not at the garage."

Carter turned to follow Bobby's gaze and spotted Jess's dad. His stomach growled in a Pavlovian response, but, sadly, Ross's hands were empty of the sandwiches he usually brought. He'd taken to bringing one for Carter, too, so Jess wouldn't share hers. But now Jess just gave half to Bryce instead.

"I'm only taking a quick break, boss," Ross said with a cheerful salute. "Things are looking good here."

"No thanks to Charity," Lexi said snidely.

Charity's head jerked up from the part of the floor she was working on. "Excuse me?"

Her surprise was warranted. Granted, if Carter's attention wasn't on the work at hand, it was usually on Jess, but even he had noticed nobody contributed less to the group's efforts than Lexi. Where everyone else was covered in a layer of sweat and grime (or, in Jess's case, red paint), Lexi still looked as fresh and inappropriately dressed as when she'd arrived that morning.

"I'm just saying," Lexi said, "you've been working on that floor for at least an hour."

"Which is an hour longer than you've been working on anything," Charity said sharply.

"If it weren't for me, that door would've been crimson instead of classic red. Who puts crimson on a *barn*?"

"If you don't have a paintbrush in your hand, I don't want to hear you taking credit for anything that's happening with this door," DeMarco said. "And what my teammate is doing is none of your concern."

Carter looked to Jess, remembering what she'd told him about DeMarco and Charity's falling-out in the past. Jess would appreciate that DeMarco was sticking up for Charity now and referring to her as his teammate. Only, to Carter's surprise, Jess wasn't looking at him in silent conversation like she usually did. Instead, she continued painting the door as if she couldn't hear the argument at all.

"It is my concern, actually," Lexi said. "In case you haven't noticed, we've almost completed this challenge. So I think we should all be concerned with who did what to make that happen. But, since your *teammate* has done nothing to put you in the lead, I don't find it surprising at all that you'd rather we not pay attention to her."

If Lexi had stomped one of her stilettos into a beehive, it couldn't have stirred up a bigger swarm of chaos. Carter took an involuntary step back. While a couple of people chose to defend Charity, Lexi's reminder that their efforts were all being measured caused most of the contenders to begin pre-emptively defending themselves. The air filled with a cacophony of shouted lists of tasks accomplished, verbal résumés for a ten-million-dollar job. Then, just as quickly, focus shifted from themselves to one another. Instead of insisting on what they'd added to the renovations, they took the Lexi route, pointing out how little others had done.

Carter wondered if this was what whiplash felt like, not only watching everyone spiral into arguments but witnessing the quickness with which they'd gone from working together to turning on one another. It felt wrong. Weren't they past all of this? He still wanted to win—he'd had a dream about Novak pronouncing him the victor just last night—and he didn't expect the rest of them to want it any less, but they couldn't tear one another down to get it. Surely, they understood that.

"Stop it!" Jess demanded finally, with a ferocity Carter had never once seen her exhibit. "You're ruining it!"

She stood, one fist at her side, the other strangling the paintbrush, and Carter felt a surge of admiration at the respect she commanded.

"We built this place!" she cried, stamping a foot. "We built it together, as a team. It doesn't matter how much or how little any one person did. What matters is that we accomplished something incredible. We took something broken and we made it new. And yes, we did it as part of a game. But that's going to end, and this community center will still be here. For our town. For *us*. This is the place where we'll dance together and watch our neighbors get married. It's the place we'll have fun together and where we'll celebrate holidays. So show it a little respect and stop arguing in it, because this is where we'll be when we're experiencing the best of our town. The best of each other. This is where we'll remember how lucky we are to live here, to be able to call Redford our home."

"Testing." The word crackled through the air, and it took everyone a moment to realize where it came from. "Testing," Novak said again into the megaphone. He was sitting upright at his card table, looking the most alert he'd been in days. "Jessica Reid has just triggered the 'Impassioned Speech on Behalf of the Town' clause. According to Mr. Wilhelm's instructions, this makes her team the official winners of the game."

Shocked silence met his announcement.

"Excuse me?" Lexi said finally.

Novak patted his iPad against the table like it was a stack of papers he was jostling into shape. Shifting his spectacles higher on his nose, he peered at it. "As I explained before, Mr. Wilhelm loved this town. He wanted to use his money to help it, but he felt like the one thing it needed most was harmony. So he devised a way to pair enemies together, hoping that a common goal would cause them to overcome their past issues. The prize money is real, but it couldn't be awarded to just anyone. Mr. Wilhelm wanted it to end up with someone who wouldn't merely use it for themselves but who loved Redford so much they might choose to pour some of it back into the town. He believed this person could be revealed in a variety of ways, one of which inspired the 'Impassioned Speech on Behalf of the Town' clause. If that clause hadn't been triggered, the winner would've been determined by one of the many others, such as 'A Sacrificial Act for the Betterment of the Town' or 'A Gesture of Extreme Generosity Toward a Resident of the Town.' All were listed in the fine print on the forms you signed. Printed copies are available if you'd like to read them again."

"So . . ." Jess trailed off, looking dazed.

"So she won?" Carter said, confirming it for her. "Jess gets the money?"

"And Nikki," Nikki called out. "Jess and Nikki."

"That is correct," Novak said dispassionately. "Ms. Reid and Ms. Loughton have won the game."

Shock rocked through Carter. He braced himself for the crushing weight of disappointment, but it didn't land as heavy as he expected. Instead, he found himself running across the barn, sweeping Jess up into his arms. He *was* disappointed. Later, he'd undoubtedly be devastated—not only because he'd lost but because he'd been wrong in assuming Jasper had wanted him to win; clearly, Carter had failed to convince his grandfather he was worthy to continue their mission. For now, though, he couldn't help being thrilled for Jess. Nobody deserved the win more than her. And he must not have been the only one who felt that way because the two women were quickly crushed into a group hug.

"Boundaries," Nikki cried in a muffled voice, likely being suffocated by enthusiasm. "Back off."

Jess waved her hand in the air as people began to fall away, and she bounced excitedly on her heels, even as she gasped for breath.

"I just want to say one thing," she said, as soon as she had enough air to speak. "If Jasper wanted the money to go back into the town, that's where my half will go. I need some of it for a particular Redfordonian, but I'm happy to pour the rest into the community."

A cheer went up at her words. And then every head in the barn swiveled in unison toward Nikki.

"Oh," Nikki said, waving them off. "My half is going to be poured directly into shoes and skin care."

Uncertain laughter followed her words, but she merely smiled unapologetically.

"What about the barn?" Bo asked. "If the challenge is over, is anyone staying to finish it?"

"I am," Carter said without thinking. It belatedly occurred to him then that he had less reason than any of them to stay and work on it. It wasn't just the challenge that had ended but also his excuse to be here. The game was over.

The realization made him feel sick. He had a life to get back to. Maybe not the fullest life, but it did include a job—albeit one with an exceedingly displeased boss who had begun to leave Carter daily voicemail reminders that he was expected back in the office, not today but *yesterday*.

As people around him began to chime in that they, too, would stay, Carter continued to stand frozen, his mind scrambled by the reality that this was really it. The end. It felt ludicrous. How could he go? How could he leave all of this behind? How could he return to Atlanta without

Jasper's projects to give his life some sense of meaning? How was he supposed to walk away from someone he loved?

The thought stunned him.

He couldn't really *love* Jess, could he? Was it even possible to fall in love with someone in such a short period of time? Carter didn't know the rules. He hadn't grown up in a house where love was discussed, had never heard his parents say it to each other, much less offer those words to him. He'd often wondered if love was even a real thing, or if it was a fabrication of fairy tales, like the concept of happily ever after.

But did it matter?

It was just a word. Why did he need to understand it when he could feel so clearly that he wanted to be with Jess for as long as he possibly could? There was something to be said for pragmatism, but Carter had followed his gut when he'd walked away from his parents' fortune. Surely, he was capable of following his heart.

He'd been expected to stay at the family business, but he'd left. Now, he was supposed to leave Redford. *But he could stay.*

His relief at the realization caught him by surprise. He couldn't imagine leaving this town, couldn't imagine never seeing Bryce or Sally or Luanne or even Nikki again. He couldn't imagine walking down the sidewalks of Atlanta day after day and never having Oscar there to point out what a beautiful day it was. He loved this strange little place with its feuds and friendships.

And he loved Jess. Maybe it wasn't something he could rationalize, but it was unquestionably true.

He turned toward her and met her eyes. They were shimmering with unshed tears.

"You did it," he said softly.

"I did it," she repeated sadly. "I just wish both of us could've won."

"Me, too," he admitted. "Luckily, though, the cost of living in Redford is rumored to be a lot lower than it is in Atlanta. What do you think? Have my new skills impressed Bo enough that he might consider taking me on?"

Her eyes widened, so spectacularly green that they made her T-shirt look muted in contrast.

"Wait," she said, her smile blooming with hope. "Are you . . . Are you thinking about staying?"

"Well, I can't leave," he said pragmatically. "You're here. And I think we both know Sally and Luanne will kill each other if I don't stick around long enough to mediate their efforts to join forces."

Jess threw her arms around him, and Carter pulled her in tight. He'd never get over how perfectly she fit against him—then again, maybe now he'd never have to. Without the slightest consideration of the crowd around them, he lowered his mouth to meet hers. Cheers and whistles erupted around them, but Carter barely noticed the noise. Considering the enthusiasm Jess put into the kiss, he thought she didn't, either. But then she broke it off, pulling away and looking up at him anxiously.

"Really?" she asked. "You're really not going to leave?"

"Not unless you want me to." He swept her bangs to the side with his forefinger, the memory of seeing them for the first time making him smile. She'd been in the kitchen of the Staple, feasting happily on stolen sandwiches with her brand-new haircut like she was the only person in town who hadn't spent the day in a race against time. He'd known then he needed to watch out for her. He just hadn't realized yet how impossible it would be to look away.

"Never," she said.

"You don't know that." Carter ran his hand down her back. "Maybe you'll want me to go with you somewhere. Do a little train-hopping together."

"Maybe." She smiled contentedly, her gaze drifting over her friends and neighbors before returning to him. "I'm kind of partial to rowboats, though."

Carter remembered how badly he'd wanted to kiss her that night on the lake and decided he needed to take her back. Maybe this time they'd manage to steal a rowboat that wouldn't leak at all.

"Pardon me," a voice behind Carter said, following up the words with a discreet cough. "Mr. Barclay?"

Carter grimaced, unwilling to loosen his grip on Jess. Was it too much to ask for a moment alone with the woman he loved, in a barn crowded with everyone they knew? Slowly, he turned to find Novak standing behind him. The lawyer was holding a crisp white envelope with both hands like it carried something impossibly heavy.

"Yes?"

"I have a letter for you from Mr. Wilhelm." Novak held it out. "I'd advise that you read it alone."

Carter's heart began to race. His grandfather. He'd been so certain he'd never hear from him again. For a moment, Carter had the absurd thought that Jasper, clever force of nature that he'd been, had found a way to transcend the grave. That their conversations wouldn't have to end after all, but could just be slipped back and forth on paper through Novak.

There was so much Carter wanted to tell his grandfather. How ridiculous his game had been. How it had turned out to be the best thing that had ever happened to Carter. How much he'd miss being Jasper's right-hand man. How certain he was that the right winner had been declared, and that their baton had been passed to the best possible person.

Jess might never seek out Carter's help distributing the money like his grandfather had, but Carter hoped he'd be allowed to become her partner in other ways. In *life*. And he wanted—no, *needed*—to thank Jasper for bringing her to him.

But it was just a wishful thought. Death didn't work like that. Novak was a one-way delivery system, so Carter simply took the letter and nodded his thanks.

"Do you think we can sneak outside for a minute?" he said, turning to Jess. "I don't think I can wait to read this."

"Of course." She looked uncertainly at Novak. "But don't you want to go by yourself? He said you were supposed to read it alone."

Carter's impatience disappeared, and he reached for her, dropping a light kiss on her temple as he wrapped his arm around her waist and turned her toward the door. Finally, the crowd seemed to fade away.

"Come on, Bonnie," he said as they began to walk, their steps syncing into a perfect rhythm, "didn't we already come to an agreement about this? I don't keep secrets from you."

FROM THE DESK OF JASPER P. WILHELM

To my favorite grandson:

I hope the game made up for the dreariness of my funeral. You enjoyed it, didn't you? Every time I think of you riding down a mountain on a Barbie Jeep, I chortle. I'd bet my fortune on the fact that you were wearing slacks and a pair of leather loafers when you climbed that mountain. I'd apologize for ruining them, but let's be honest, I'm not sorry at all.

I am sorry that you thought you had a chance to win the game. You didn't, of course. The prize money was always going to go to a Redfordonian. I paired you with Bryce, though. I thought you'd have the most fun with him. If you end up staying, which I suspect you will, the two of you will likely become close friends.

Speaking of staying, has Redford gotten into your blood? I hope so. We have work to do, after all. You didn't really believe it was over, did you? A mission doesn't end just because the team gets smaller. You know the people now. You'll remember their faces, even if you do decide to return to Atlanta and continue our efforts from afar.

I hope you won't, though. I love my daughter, but I'm perfectly aware she didn't provide the warmest of families for you. You deserve to feel like you belong somewhere, and I'm confident that Redford can be that place. It feels imperious to insinuate I can give you a town, but humor an old man, won't you? Let me give you Redford.

And the trust I set up for you before leaving the remaining ten million to the town, of course. I believe you'll have about forty-three million to work with. Novak will give you the details. Make sure you insist on speaking with him in person, though. The man will talk your ear off, but it's better than trusting him to use any kind of device. He's terrible at operating them.

With all my love and the utmost respect,
Jasper P. Wilhelm

Epilogue

. . . .

ROSS

The barn is sweltering when he arrives, despite its doors being propped open like big red shutters on a window. It always is in the summer, though, even when there's not a mass of people line dancing in the middle of the room. People joke about the fact that it was built by a group of amateurs who didn't know how to add air-conditioning, but they don't complain. They're too grateful to have a place to celebrate.

No one is more grateful than Ross, though. He stands just outside the doors, looking at the way the twinkle lights turn orange in the setting sun and thinking about how this was the place that saved his life. Without it, he wouldn't have seen his daughter get married. He wouldn't have gotten Carter as a son-in-law. He would never have met his granddaughter.

The thought chokes him up a little, and, of course, that's the moment Nikki appears in the doorway and yells at him for being late. She'll have someone lined up to dance with him already. It's been this way since she declared herself in charge of his social life. He's tried objecting, but the truth is, he's always found her bossiness amusing. Still, he holds up a finger, silently telling her to wait. As Nikki's boyfriend, Kent, always reminds him, if you give her an inch, she'll take a mile.

Ross supposes, though, it wouldn't be the worst thing in the world for him to hang out with some people his own age. It's probably weird that his closest friends are his daughter and her husband, and his daughter's . . . Well, he's not sure Nikki and Jess have ever really become friends in the normal, uncomplicated sense of the word. It's more like they never stopped being teammates. The money connects them, even though Nikki insists on pretending to everyone else that she kept her half for herself. Together, they decide how to invest it into the town, bickering like sisters over every choice they make.

It's an entirely different effort than the way Jess and Carter dole out Carter's share of Jasper's fortune. That's more personal and covert, provided to people in a way that they never quite realize exactly how or why the trajectory of their life just changed. Ross loves nothing more than when his daughter and son-in-law show up with dinner, brimming over with details to share with him. As the first recipient of their generosity, it's like finding out his club has gained yet another new member.

"Dad?" Jess joins Nikki in the doorway. "Mia is looking for you. She says you promised to dance with her."

Ross smiles at the thought of Mia's adorable little face. She got her dad's serious eyes, but her smile is all Jess's.

"Coming," he says, taking one last look at the sun

setting over Redford, coloring the town with its red and orange streaks.

"Oh, for me, you're busy," Nikki grumbles, "but for that
kid, you're ready to dance."

Ross laughs and wonders how his life got so full. There
was a time, when Jess's mother left him, that he wondered
how he could ever be enough for his little girl. But he'd soon
discovered he didn't need to be; the town was there for her.
What he hadn't realized was that it would always be there for
him, too. He'd never known there were so many types of casseroles until they started showing up at his door in piles after
word got around his treatment had taken a turn for the worse.
And the casseroles were nothing compared to the pies.

Thank goodness Liz had moved back to Redford to help
him eat it all. The moment she'd heard Jess was pregnant,
she'd begun making plans to return. It had been inconceivable to her that Kai and Mia wouldn't grow up as best
friends, just like their moms had. Of course, Ross knew Liz
had also used his health to convince her husband she was
needed back home, but Ross was over that now. It might've
been pity that brought their family to Redford, but it was
friendship and freezers full of Luanne's chocolate pecan pie
that made them stay. Liz had gotten her wish: Kai and Mia
adore each other.

Ross trades greetings with people as he enters the barn,
but he doesn't stop until he has Mia in his arms. She's only
three, but she started playing T-ball this year and is surprisingly not the worst player on the team, despite being a year
younger than the rest of the kids. Even Nikki has shown up
for a couple of her games. She pretends she's there to make

fun of Carter, so serious in his role of coach for a group of little girls who spend most of the game whispering with their friends or wandering into the middle of the field in pursuit of a butterfly. But Ross has seen the way she cheers when Mia hits a ball. The pride on her face is nothing less than that of a second mother.

Out on the dance floor, Ross bounces Mia to the music. He watches Carter twirl Jess around and dip her low. He grins when he spots Nikki and Kent, who are, as usual, both attempting to lead. He feels the energy of the other dancers, and Mia's giggles reach his ears. Ross dips her to make her laugh harder, and he thinks life doesn't get any better than this.

A hot barn with a roof that still leaks in one corner, filled with all of his favorite people. He'd call it heaven, but that's a destination he's managed to put off for a while longer. It's just Redford, a little town full of big personalities. And there's nowhere else he'd rather be.

Acknowledgments

I cannot believe I got to put out another book with the incredibly talented team at Putnam! Thank you to all of the people who have done their part to put this story out into the world: my amazing editor, Kate Dresser, who went into full manic mode with me to get this thing out on time; her fantastic assistant, Tarini Sipahimalani, who held my hand while Kate was away; the amazing Shina Patel in marketing; and the brilliant Elora Weil in publicity. I am so grateful to be in such good hands.

To Claire Friedman, agent extraordinaire, I am endlessly thankful to have you in my corner. Your guidance in both my career and my writing has been a godsend. Cheers to outlines, despite how truly terrible they might be!

When I wrote this book, I wanted to tell a story about the joy that comes from putting down roots. It's ironic that I wrote it as I was making a cross-country move, during which I would end up spending three and a half months living out of a roller bag. Still, I believe that I've planted my roots in the friends I've made along the way. (Forgive me if that sounds dirty. It wasn't intended to be.) A big fat "thank you for being in my life" goes to:

My DC family, most notably Autumn Christensen and Christina Babcock, who understand the importance of a coozie. Thank you for braving the world of video messaging so we can stay up to date on the least important parts of our days.

My Nashvillians, including all the ex-Jazzercisers and McGavockers and friends and neighbors who have been there to help me celebrate my books. It's been years since I've lived there, but you keep that town feeling like home.

My new buddies in LA. I never imagined that I'd meet so many cool people here, and certainly not so quickly. But I feel like there was an actual welcome wagon waiting for me when I arrived. Thank you to our Monday Writers' Group for making writing less lonely; to Markus Redmond for teaching me to write screenplays and making me feel like I'm super funny; to everyone at The Ripped Bodice for acting like it's normal that I try to hang out with y'all every week; and to the Placard Table for allowing me in.

But if we're really talking about roots, mine are most firmly planted in you, Isaac Waldon. (And if that sounds dirty, I'm fine with it.) Thank you for agreeing to spend the rest of your life with me. It doesn't matter where we are or where we aspire to go—as long as I'm with you, I know I'll always be home.

Discussion Guide

1. Jasper curated the challenges for his beloved people of Redford with seemingly a specific intention in mind. What about his Redford experience do you think led him to orchestrate such a challenge? If you were a participant, how would you have reacted to Novak's announcement? How did your initial impression of the game's purpose evolve over the course of the story?

2. Jess finds comfort in words: "how you can put exactly the right combination of them together to make something sound better or worse . . . the way the letters in them fit together so perfectly" (pages 168–169). How does Jess's role as a book editor influence her approach to life?

3. Jess is a small-town girl, and Carter is a big-shot city boy. The worlds they've each known for so long are literally miles apart. Similarly, Jess's best friend and sole confidante lives far from her. Using a challenge as an example, discuss how proximity can either foster or hinder a sense of intimacy.

4. Out of all the challenges, choose one and discuss the tactic you'd use to win. Now, pair up and reenact that challenge.

5. Like Jasper, author Lacie Waldon deftly depicts the nature of opposites, from insider versus outsider roles to the Sally-versus-Luanne muffin rivalry. Discuss which pair of thematic opposites spoke to you best and how the tension between the two made for interesting reading.

6. For a narrative with such a colorful cast of characters, there must be a villain. Who in the narrative would you say is a "bad guy"? In what ways does this person emanate a sense of villainy?

7. Jess and Carter naturally grow closer throughout the course of the competition. What was your favorite moment between them, and why?

8. Carter, like Jess, has dealt with many forms of familial loss. What are the similarities and differences between Jess's and Carter's respective relationships with their parents? How do these show themselves in Jess and Carter's day-to-day dynamic?

9. Novak is a quiet but almost omnipresent character in this story. Apart from carrying out the instructions in Jasper's will, what would you say is Novak's purpose?

10. For one ambitious game, there are a series of many wacky challenges. Discuss the implications of the title *The Only Game in Town*, and answer what you believe to be the one and only true game.

11. *The Only Game in Town* pays homage to many kinds of love. Recall an incident in the book that you deemed an act of love among two or more Redford residents, and explain why that moment spoke to you.

Photograph of the author by Amanda Lomax

About the Author

Lacie Waldon is a writer with her head in the clouds—literally. A flight attendant based in Los Angeles, Waldon spends her days writing from the jump seat and searching the world for new stories. She is the author of *The Layover*, *From the Jump*, and *The Only Game in Town*.

VISIT LACIE WALDON ONLINE

laciewaldon.com

[Instagram] AllAboutThat_Lace